LAST OF HER KIND

LAST OF HER KIND

By Ann Frailey

A. K. Frailey Books
110 Possum Lane
Fillmore, IL 62032

Cover and Interior: Trese Gloriod • DESIGNproChristus.com

ISBN: 978-0-9970675-6-9

PROLOGUE

In serene, black-enshrouded silence, Earth turned on its axis, a sharp contrast to the bustling reality on the surface. The gaze of a hidden mind slipped past the blue and white sphere, shifting between burning stars and vast planetary systems, all of which moved according to their own placid, pre-determined paths. His interest focused on one planet, Lux, a world of light beings, luminous in the reflection of their own glory.

On the balcony of the Capitol building, as the sun nestled itself over the horizon, two figures faced each other. Roux, a Luxonian guardian, glowed as a golden brown, humanoid figure, while Sterling, draped in his Supreme Judge robes, shimmered yellow-white, faintly defined by his elderly human outline.

Sterling, somber and erect, turned his back on Roux and faced the Luxonian world gloriously set before him. The sky burst with brilliant colors, while shreds of gray clouds drifted aside and revealed three distinct moons. His voice rumbled.

"You understand your role when you return?"

Roux grinned, a mischievous sparkle in his luminous eyes. "I'm your inside man, a guardian and—a spy."

Sterling pulled his mesmerized gaze from the scene and faced his companion. "You use such colorful phrases, Roux. All I ask is that you stay alert. Watch for an opportunity."

"For what, exactly?"

"I'm not sure. Humanity won't survive the coming crisis. But Earth will remain."

The sparkle faded and Roux's features hardened, defining his human figure in greater detail. His curly, black hair, sharp chin, and muscled arms clarified his youth but little else. His eyebrows rose. "You're going to harvest an abandoned planet?"

"Whatever is left. Perhaps more. Maybe the remnant. We need help, too. You do realize that?"

Roux sighed, his broad shoulders slumping. As he strode across the room, his figure gained definition. He snatched up a stack of clothes with a pair of shoes perched on top.

"It's them or us?"

Spreading his shimmering arms wide, Sterling returned to the setting sun. "Let's just say that their loss may be our gain."

In a few steps, Roux retreated behind a partitioned wall. A zipping sound punctuated his grunted words, and shoe thumps pounded against the hard ground. "And Cerulean? You know—how he—feels—about humanity."

Sterling stepped to the very edge of the balcony, his eyes following the sinking glow. "I'm afraid I do. So like his father. But not like his son. I've sent Viridian over, just in case."

Roux reentered the room dressed in jeans, a sweater, and a pair of tan loafers on the wrong feet. He frowned at Sterling. "To take his place?"

Sterling shrugged, stared at the shoes, and then returned his gaze to the horizon line. "We'll see. Time is running out. Do your job, and we might just survive."

April
THEIR PLACE IN THE UNIVERSE

Bright sunlight flooded the bedroom, casting a glow around Anne, the center of Cerulean's universe. Unaware of being observed, Anne stared at the white rectangular stick in her right hand. Her left hand moved to her middle as her eyes widened. Her lips trembled. "Damn!" Taking one last look at the stick, she blinked back tears.

Her disappointment surprised Cerulean; she had never given any indication that she wanted children. The last time he had visited, she had made it quite clear that she never wanted children. She had been seventeen then; she was twenty-seven now. Things had obviously changed.

Dropping the testing stick into the trashcan, Anne flushed the toilet, her face pale and pinched. She stepped into her bedroom.

Peering through the open doorway, Cerulean contemplated the wedding photo on the dresser. Had her husband wanted children? Ten years ago, Anne had wanted nothing more than to concentrate on a career and travel. Framed teacher certificates, graduation photos, and vacation pictures now lined the walls. Cerulean had no doubt in his mind; Anne may be established, but she was not happy.

"Stupid!" Anne pulled on her blouse and adjusted her skirt, "Dang it, why doesn't this skirt ever hang right?" Tugging at the waistband, she adjusted her clothes and then glared at the mirror. She turned sideways, smoothed her hand down her slim figure, eyed her 5' 6" frame, and then patted a few stray hairs back into place. Her weight was good; her brown eyes were steady, her skin clear and tanned. Wiping away the last vestige of a tear, she pinched her cheeks to add color. Her chestnut hair hung down her back in a thick braid.

Cerulean evaluated the grown woman before him. There was nothing extraordinary about her, but then there was nothing to object to either. To his surprise, Cerulean felt a sensation run through his being, a sensation he thought had died with his wife. When Anne's brows furrowed as she silently surveyed the room, Cerulean dimmed his exuberance. Could she feel his presence?

Anne looked at the closed door and then the window. The view went on for miles with no interruption in sight. Only the birds flying by could see anything. If they tried. Which they wouldn't. "Stupid birds!" Anne hurried into her stockings and bundled her nightclothes onto the bed. "Later."

Cerulean's gaze shifted as Anne's husband, Philip, walked into the room. The lawyer tapped his expensive watch. "Do you know what time it is? You'll be late."

With an exaggerated sigh, Anne scowled. "Don't remind me, Philip. I'm never late, and I don't want to start a rumor that I've died or something." Anne wiggled her foot into her shoe and shook her head. "Fifth grade is precarious enough without giving them that anxiety."

Slender with sandy blond hair and deep blue eyes, Philip moved across the room in fluid, confident steps. "Anything wrong? You seem a little tense. I could—" His hands opened in a beckoning motion.

Anne stared, daring him to say one more word.

Philip's hands dropped to his side as he shut his mouth.

Anne waved her finger. "You better stop. I'm in no mood. Now grab me that sweater, and I'll be out of here."

Surveying the assortment of skirts, sweaters, and various apparel draped across a chair, Philip gestured. "Which one, the black or the blue?"

"Give me the black one. I feel like I've been to a funeral."

After handing her the sweater, Philip ignored the earlier warning and reached out, putting his hands on her shoulders and gently massaging them. "You going to be okay?"

Anne stiffened as she blinked back new tears. "No, but that doesn't matter. I'm an idiot. I should have my head examined. Or my heart." With an unrelenting shrug, Anne moved past her husband. "Sorry, but I've got to go." She rushed through the door.

Philip shook his head as he watched her disappear, her shoes clicking down the steps. A moment later the front door slammed. Walking over to the dresser, Philip swiped up his car keys. He started to whistle and then stopped. The sound of water running caught his ear. Stepping into the bathroom, his gaze fell on the towels lying askew. He frowned.

After jiggling the toilet handle, he snatched up a piece of paper from the floor and bent over to throw it in the garbage. The testing kit caught his eye. He lifted it, examined its single pink line and, with another shake of his head, dropped it into the trashcan. While examining his reflection in the mirror, Philip adjusted his tie with a slight nod of approval to his well-tailored suit. Running his fingers through his hair, he appraised his chin where he had nicked himself earlier. After a final adjustment of his suit coat, he left the room. His footfalls made hollow thumps as he sped down the steps. In a moment, the front door slammed a second time.

———

A brief flash of light illuminated the bedroom as Cerulean appeared with his son at his side. Dressed in jeans and a brown leather jacket, Cerulean had assumed the look of a muscular, middle-aged man. A few streaks of gray in his dark hair and a couple days' growth of beard gave him a casual but dignified look. His somber, brown eyes bore testimony to a spirit, which had experienced more than words could say.

His gaze rolled over his son. "Observe, Viridian: humans have the capacity to lie, even to themselves. We are not allowed that luxury."

A flash of anxiety filled the youth's eyes. His bulky figure with brown hair, brown eyes, and tan skin stood hunched in dejection.

Flicking a lock of his son's hair back into place and examining his human form, Cerulean changed the subject. "I like it. The look suits you. It took me a long time to get used to a human body, but now the transition is easy. I like the sensation: limiting yet strangely safe. I understand them better this way."

The lock of hair slid back into Viridian's eyes. "I hate it. Humans don't admire fat boys. I'm as ordinary as a rock."

Cerulean nodded. "Exactly. You're an uninteresting, teenage boy, a boy who will excite no comment and attract no attention. Besides, I like your coloring: variations on a simple theme, so different from our natural state. Light captures every color, but humans, they make do with less. They can find great beauty in mere shades. And you're not unattractive—plump maybe, but not overweight. In any case, *I* know what you really look like. Humans would be overwhelmed. As it is now, you won't excite much interest."

"Interest? I'm repulsive." Viridian paced across the room. "Humans will avoid me like one of their plagues! And besides that, I can hardly move. How do they see anything? It's like being underwater. Everything is so distorted and blurred."

"You'll get used to it. True observation is more than seeing with the eyes. Besides, if we are to observe, we must be able to interact, at least sometimes. And we can't interact well if we don't at least appear human. Though there are guardians who like to take animal or plant form." An image of a rodent-guardian he once knew came to mind. Cerulean stifled a shiver. "I don't enjoy that so much."

Hunching his shoulders, Viridian stuffed his hands in his pockets. "But what if something happens—something unexpected? What if someone attacks us? Or there's a storm and the house falls on us, or one of their insane vehicles crash into us? What then?"

"We get out of the way if possible, but if necessary, we die and come back later."

"Humans will want to know who we are, who our bodies are anyway."

"Humans face conundrums all the time. Eventually, they just close the file." Cerulean's brows furrowed. "If I didn't know better, I'd say you were frightened."

"I am not frightened!" Viridian scowled. "I just don't like it here. Sorry if this offends you, but humans are pitiful. They're not like us at all."

Taking a few steps away, Cerulean folded his arms over his chest. "You're not here to do a comparative study, just learn your place. You'll be a guardian when your time comes, and you must be willing to see everything but not judge. Judging is for others."

Cerulean gazed out the window. His son would have to learn, as he had learned after long years of service. How long ago? It had been centuries. He had followed in his father's footsteps, as he did his, a long tradition that wound back seven thousand years, for as long as Luxonians had been observing this race. Before that time.... Well, there hadn't been much to see.

Viridian surveyed the silent room. "So why here? Why this one? What's so special about her?"

With a deep sigh, Cerulean marched into the bathroom. "It's an odd thing about humans. They're surprising. I once heard a well-known, human author declare that no one cares about the man on the bus or the woman in the grocery store. But he was wrong. That's where I first noticed Anne—in the grocery store. She was with her mother, and though she was only seven, she actually helped. Unlike most children, she knew how to keep to the designated list. Her mother was ill, a frightened woman, terribly frightened. Margaret—that was her name—she saw danger everywhere. She once told Anne that when they drove up a hill, the other side might not be there. Anne learned to cope with fear early on. I could see her strength—even then."

Stepping over to the trashcan, Viridian pointed inside. "She was afraid today. She was afraid when she thought that she might be pregnant."

"No, that's where you're wrong. You must be more careful. Don't leap to conclusions too quickly. You must not only look at the actions but the motivations." Cerulean's eyes darted to the wedding picture on the wall as he moved back into the bedroom. "Why did Anne act as she did? She was not frightened that she might be pregnant; she was frightened when she realized that she *wanted* to be pregnant. And well she might be."

Viridian sneered, one eyebrow rising. "Why?"

Pursing his lips, Cerulean strode to the window. A sharp pang of disappointment disturbed his usual equilibrium. With forced detachment, he pointed at the sky. "We can come and go. We know there are more worlds than our own. We've been observing various races from time out of mind. But she," Cerulean turned back to the picture of Anne and Philip on the dresser, "she knows nothing about us, or our kind, or that the human race is not alone. She both fears and craves intimacy, the kind of intimacy motherhood would demand. Humans are often blinded by fear. I have observed for a full year every decade. This is the third time I've met Anne, but I never know when it will be the last."

Viridian bit his lip.

Cerulean patted his son on the shoulder as a brief flicker of hope welled up inside. "It's time to go. Anne will be at school, and our job is to observe. Let's see what she's up to now." He started forward, but his son stood silent, unmoving. Cerulean heaved a heavy sigh and stopped. "What?"

"How long will we watch them? I mean; will I have to do this my whole life?"

Cerulean tried not to let the question hurt too much. "I don't know. The human race won't last forever."

Gazing up at the sky, Viridian stepped to the window. "Is it a punishment? Their not lasting very long?"

A cloud covered the sun, plunging the room into shadows. "Remember, we don't judge. We observe. Funny, though. Humans believe their end will come with fire and storm, war and pestilence. But not necessarily. Their end might come slowly, quietly, like a sunset with no sunrise."

Viridian sucked in his breath and glared at his father. "Should we warn them? What's the point of observing them if they're just going to die anyway?"

"That's not for us to decide. We observe to learn. Eventually, humans will understand their place in the universe, and we'll watch until they do."

With one last look around the silent room, Cerulean raised his hand in command. "Let's go." He stepped forward.

Viridian hesitated for an instant.

With a brief flicker of intense light, they both disappeared.

May
DR. MITCHELL

When he heard the familiar heavy tread of his colleague striding into the laboratory, anxiety crept along Dr. Mitchell's spine. Unable to resist, he glanced up.

As usual, Dr. Peterson appeared perfect. A master could have chiseled his face in stone, while his neat, brown beard glistened in the light. His immaculate lab coat accented his professional attire: dark pants with a blue dress shirt, everything pressed with that just-from-the-cleaners look. Walking directly to a wire cage, Dr. Peterson peered inside, frowned, and then rattled the cage. Scratching his jaw, he murmured. "Mitchell, come here a minute, would you?"

Thirty years old, slightly overweight with dark skin, Dr. Mitchell felt his annoyance mount even as he tried to keep his reactions professional. He turned away from his work, mumbled, "*Dr.* Mitchell," and slowly rose from his stool. Walking over to where the senior doctor stood staring, he peered into the cage, adjusted his glasses, and looked again.

The dead rat lay forever immobile before the two doctors' gaze. Nodding, Dr. Peterson assented to Dr. Mitchell's low grunt. "Yeah, that's what I thought. Strange, eh? It shouldn't be, but it is."

Opening the cage door, Dr. Mitchell pulled the stiff body out by its tail. "It's been dead some time. Didn't anyone check the cages this morning?"

Glancing around, Dr. Peterson bellowed, "Sarah? Sarah, where the hell are you?"

With a cringe, Dr. Mitchell sighed. He knew Sarah's precarious situation at the hospital, and remembering his own early travails, his jaw clenched. "I wish you wouldn't."

Swiveling back toward the man at his side, Dr. Peterson snapped. "What? What the hell am I doing now? You always get so—so damn defensive. I can't figure you out."

Sarah bustled into the room, her face as tight as the blond bun wrapped on the top of her head. Her slight figure appeared swallowed up by her long white lab coat. She held up her gloved, sterile hands. "Yes, doctor? I was just finishing up—"

"I don't care what you were finishing up. Come here and explain this." His blue eyes frosty, Dr. Peterson watched as she stepped closer.

Sarah's eyes widened in alarm as she peered at the dead rat and blinked. "He was fine when I last checked him."

"And when, exactly, was that?"

Panic flooded Sarah's eyes. She shot a pleading glance towards Dr. Mitchell. "I thought I checked this morning…I mean I was almost sure I checked…." With a sudden intake of breath, Sarah gazed back at Dr. Peterson. "Oh, my gosh! I'm sorry, sir. I really am. I was running late. There was an accident on 15th, and I had to go around; it took me a whole thirty minutes longer with all the traffic and I must—I must have gone right to the—"

"You're fired."

The morning's French-Vanilla coffee churned in Dr. Mitchell's stomach.

Sarah's eyes grew even wider as her mouth dropped open. Reaching for the edge of the table to steady herself, her voice rose. "But sir, you can't mean that. I'm not usually late, and I've never forgotten my duties before. I need this, I mean, if you fire me, I won't be able to keep my position with—"

Staring down at the young woman, Dr. Peterson's form remained as immovable as his judgment. "It's not my concern. You had a job, and you didn't do it. Now, don't start whining, telling me how you've always done your best. You've been late three times this month, and this isn't the first animal to die under suspicious circumstances."

Dr. Mitchell's jaw clenched tighter as tears slipped down the young woman's cheeks. His eyes darted back to the remorseless stare of the senior doctor.

Struggling for control of the situation, Dr. Peterson growled, "Damn it, Sarah! Don't cry. I mean it, really, don't cry. I hate that."

The room fell deathly silent. Deciding that diversion was sometimes the best mode of preservation, Dr. Mitchell turned away from the scene and refocused his attention.

A slight smell of decay wafted up to his nose. With a furrowed brow, he studied the dead rat. "Dr. Peterson, could you take a moment to look more carefully here? As I said earlier, this rat has been dead for some time. Sarah didn't kill it. There's still food and water in its dish, see?" Dr. Mitchell pointed with his index finger. "No, something else killed this fellow. You know, I'm beginning to think that when we cloned that last batch, we made a mistake. Every one of them has died. And Sarah had nothing to do with it." He glanced at Sarah and offered a conspiratorial wink.

Dr. Peterson exhaled loudly as he returned his gaze to the woman in front of him. "Oh, all right, I guess that lets you off the hook. Though, one more slip up, Sarah, and I *will* fire you, so help me. I know you can't really understand it, but the work we're doing here is of life and death importance. There're whole cultures facing extinction. But if cloning works, well, there's hope for us all."

Wiping her eyes with the back of her wrist, Sarah mumbled, "Yes, sir, thank you." Still attempting to keep her hands sterile, she retreated into the back room.

In silence, Dr. Mitchell laid the dead rat on a metal tray. He arranged an assortment of dissecting knives on the rolling table nearby. With his back to Dr. Peterson, he spoke in a near whisper. "You act like such a bigot sometimes."

"Excuse me?" Dr. Peterson approached and stood next to his colleague, his hands on his hips. "I've never treated you with anything but the highest regard. I never even think about the fact that you're African American."

Dr. Mitchell laughed as he shook his head. "That's probably because I'm not. My mother was Haitian, and my father's Puerto Rican." He straightened and looked Dr. Peterson in the eye. "No, I mean the way you treat that young girl and everyone else around here. You call people without using their proper titles; you say things like, 'I don't expect you to understand,' as if we're all too stupid to comprehend your noble ideals, and you threaten people constantly. Remember that orderly the other day?"

With a snort, Dr. Peterson stepped back to his desk. "That boy dropped a whole tray of sterile equipment for God's sake! What was I supposed to do? Reward him? Pat him on the back and tell him he was a poor, misunderstood boy from the hood, and I understood what he meant to do even when he ruined—"

"There you go again. Just because someone doesn't have lily white skin, you assume—"

"Not true! That boy *is* from the hood! I happen to know because I hired him myself. His name is James, he's twenty-three years old, and had been in prison on a minor drug charge. But when Tom over in Admissions told me that he knew the family and that they were good people, I believed him. He just wanted me to give the boy a chance. I told James right from the start that he had to live up to my standards; I wasn't going to coddle him like some token minority, so I could feel good about myself. I was hiring him to do a job because I believed he could do it and unless he proved me wrong, he could rise to whatever position he could handle. It was all up to him." Dr. Peterson breathed heavily. "You just don't like the fact that I swear and I get riled when people act stupid. I'm not a sensitive person, Mitchell. Deal with it!

But I am good at what I do and anyone who works with me, or for me, had better be good at what they do, or they're outta here!"

Dr. Mitchell picked up a thin scalpel and bent down to begin the dissection. "I guess this little guy failed you then." He shrugged. "Well, at least I know you have a heart, even if you don't use it much."

Blowing air between his lips, his hands up, Dr. Peterson surrendered. "Alright, alright, you win. I'll try to clean up my act. Everyone is so damn finicky. You know, Margaret told me the other day that if I have a heart attack, it'll be my own damn...I mean...my own fault."

Without breaking his concentration, Dr. Mitchell made the first incision. "Margaret? I don't remember a Margaret."

"Tina wanted more than I could give."

"Oh, yeah...Tina."

Dr. Peterson shifted papers around on his desk. "When was the last time you checked statistics?"

"I gave that job to Sarah. She's supposed to have a full report by the end of the week."

"Oh." Dr. Peterson rubbed his hands together. "Glad I didn't fire her then." Chuckling as he pulled his laptop forward, he pressed the on button.

Dr. Mitchell frowned as he dug further into the rat. Nothing he saw made any sense. And that was a problem. A big problem.

June
PLANS

The scene, miles above the Earth, left Anne breathless. The rainbow spread so far and wide across the open field that she had to crane her neck back to see it. The reds, pinks, oranges, blues, and purples blending into a visual symphony; it was spectacular. A shiver of joy rippled over her skin. Anne wanted so much to respond with her own joy, but then the thought of what lay ahead came to mind, and her nervousness returned.

I'm not sure I can do this. She hunched her shoulders, the former weight of doubt pressing her mood back toward an unrelenting Earth. Her gaze blurred over the wet gravel.

On a sudden impulse, almost against her will, she looked up once more. The rainbow had not faded but grown in size and majesty. She gasped. The sight of the glorious, colored spectrum against the rain-washed sky and the lush, green, wooded hills lifted her spirits once again.

There was no turning back. She had to face herself and her life honestly, or she'd never really live. Rainbows were only for the brave.

The glow of the setting sun softened the rustic kitchen in a golden bath. Butter yellow walls decorated with grapevine wreaths, rural pictures, and a solid wooden table depicted a scene that might be found in any *Country Living* magazine. Anne had prepared a perfect dinner of fried chicken, mashed potatoes, and green beans, with a hearty glass of Philip's favorite white wine. She planned to execute the I-Want-a-Baby pitch near the end of the meal, in the hope that Philip would be in a receptive mood. But somehow she found herself blundering forward like a beached whale trying to get back to the ocean. While Philip munched contentedly, she stirred her food with her fork. Darting a cautious glance his way, she launched into space.

"Philip, I want a baby—soon! I can't wait any longer, and neither of us is getting any younger. I've got needs too, you know." Graceful, she was not. When his jaw clenched, her hopes disintegrated.

Wiping his lips with great care, he glared at her. "Say that again. You want what?" Without waiting for a response, Philip took a last sip of wine and then leaned back in his chair, clasping his hands behind his head. "So, you want to tell me the whole truth or just march forward, leaving me behind—as usual."

Anne put her fork down and wiped her trembling hands on a paper napkin. "That's not fair. I tell you everything. It's just that this is a personal matter, and I—I had to think it through before I told you."

With a shake of his head, Philip dropped his hands onto his lap. "You honestly think that having a baby is your personal matter? Like it doesn't affect *me* in a personal way? I'm assuming *I* would be the father."

Anne stood, her face burning. "That was cruel! Of course, you'd be the father."

"It was a low blow," Philip admitted as he got to his feet, "but you have no idea, really, no idea what you've put me through."

Anne's gaze dropped to the floor even as she stiffened, listening intently to Philip's every word.

"You know, when we first got married, I had visions of having two or three kids, a boy and maybe a girl or two. I loved that dream. But then you announced that you'd never have children. And whenever I tried to bring it up, you told me it was your choice. Not much I could do about that. Just about every woman in America would agree with you. But it hurt; it was a painful dream to let die. And now, after several blissful but childless years together, you announce, just as unceremoniously, that you want a baby!"

Philip picked up his dinner dishes and carried them to the sink, side stepping Anne's immovable form. "Well, now I'm not so sure I want to go along for the ride. What if you change your mind again and want to abort it? Where does that leave me?" He slapped on the hot water, tossed the chicken bones aside, and threw his dishes into the sink with a sickening crash. "No, I'm not sure I could handle that."

Anne stood immobile beside the sink, blinking back tears. Her throat constricted, nearly choking her. "I didn't realize. I didn't know how you felt—that you really wanted children. I thought it was just a phase you were going through, like a toy you'd play with and forget. I never thought—"

"I'm not quite that shallow. You know how much you want a baby right now? Well, that was me a few years ago. Only you said no."

Anne whispered. "So, you're going to say no, now, forever?"

Philip's shoulders sagged as he turned from the sink. "The dream never completely died. But, and this is a big but, you can't change your mind. And I don't want you insisting that you'll only have one kid the day you go into labor. You've got to be willing to keep an open mind. Remember I'm the father. I may not give birth, but the baby would still be half mine."

Snatching a dishtowel off the table, Anne countered. "Feminists would have a problem with you. Some women might even say that you're too controlling. Your sister would for sure. She already thinks I am a—a wimp."

Philip waved the comment away. "To hell with Jackie." Philip moved towards Anne. "I'm talking about you and me and our baby.

This is our decision, and I want to make it together—just like when we make the baby." Philip's voice and eyes softened as he gazed on his wife. He stood over her and gently lifted her chin, so their faces were only centimeters apart.

With a sniff, Anne returned his gaze. "Yeah, I guess that makes sense."

Philip wrapped his arms around her, hugging her close. "If that doesn't make sense, then nothing makes sense. Besides, you might fall in love with this mothering thing and want a dozen kids."

Anne relaxed into her husband's embrace. "Let's just see what kind of a mother I make with one; then we can make plans for more."

After nuzzling the top of her head, Philip moved his mouth down the side of her face, tickling her as he murmured softly in her ear. "Always making plans, aren't you? You know what they say, 'If you want to hear God laugh—tell Him your plans.'"

Anxiety washed over Anne, breaking the moment. She pulled away, her eyes wide with momentary alarm. Rumors were traveling across the Internet that threatened their hopes, everyone's hopes. But no, she shook her head and relaxed back into Philip's arms. She wouldn't think about that now. After a releasing squeeze, Anne moved back toward the table and began clearing away the rest of the dishes, her mind still on what Philip had said. "God isn't malicious, you know. He gives us freedom to do what we want because He knows that's how we learn best."

With a chuckle, Philip returned to the sink. "Oh, I don't know. God might just surprise us. Maybe you'll have twins."

Anne put the dishes on the counter and smacked her husband's arm. He laughed a little louder. "Maybe even triplets."

As the last rays of sunlight faded, every glorious color dwindled into blackness.

County News–Fillmore, Illinois
**The Ladies Home-Making Society Embarks
on a New Mission.**

The Ladies Home-Making Society is taking up a collection for families in the area who have been struggling with infertility. Proceeds will benefit young couples unable to afford advanced medical treatments. Each of the families selected has been trying for five or more years to conceive and have not been able to. Adoptions have become more elusive as the number of available infants and adoptable children has decreased. So far, they have collected nearly eight thousand dollars and will offer the money to four chosen families. Anyone wishing to donate to this fund is welcome to contact Macy Mallard and make an offering to "The Next Generation Fund."

4

July
POSITIVE

With a hard twisting in her middle, Anne stood in her bathroom examining the shiny, new pregnancy stick, willing it to turn pink. A bird twittered at the window, its song accompanying the morning sunrise as Anne held her breath. Before she expected it, she saw the color change, and suddenly the knot in her stomach relaxed. She could feel her spirit soaring with invisible wings. Would it be ridiculous to take a picture of the pink line and post it?

Dismissing that idea, she tiptoed out of the bathroom and gingerly picked her way across the room. She gently rubbed her belly, amazed at the life growing within her. Could she hurt the baby by moving too fast? With the precision of a ballerina, she attempted to slip into her blouse and skirt. Viewing herself in the mirror, she could feel a light sweat on her skin. Her body did not show the difference, but she knew she would never be the same. At least, she hoped she knew. Doubt shadowed her joy.

Her friend, Saundra, at work, had thought she was pregnant and told everyone, only to discover a month later that it was all a mistake.

The doctor said she'd probably never actually been pregnant, just a false positive.

Anne ran back into the bathroom and, snatching up the testing stick; she noticed that the color had faded a bit. Was it just an illusion? Was she wrong to get excited so early?

A slanting beam of light fell across the wall, illuminating a picture of her and Philip together at a picnic on the beach during one of their romantic get-aways. *I can't tell Philip. Not yet. Not till I'm sure.* With that thought in mind, she stepped back into the bedroom and over to the side table. She had already done her research and knew the names of the best doctors in the area. Picking up a little notepad, she scanned the list and circled one.

Dr. Evans sat at his desk, staring at a piece of paper, one of the many scattered about. Some had been thrown to the side, while others lay arrayed in front of him like a huge jigsaw puzzle, but this one paper had absorbed his attention for several moments. It was a chart outlining the number of new patients in Montgomery Country over the last six months. He searched through a manila folder and found another paper with a similar graph for a neighboring county. He compared the two. Then after a bit of searching, he found a third paper with a third graph covering the same data for another county and laid that alongside the others.

He whispered, "Oh, Holy Mother of God."

His nurse, Loren, entered the room, saw the scattered papers and frowned. She waited a moment before she cleared her throat. "Doctor, your new patient is here."

Dr. Evans noted her disapproval and the heat of embarrassment burned his neck. He was usually well organized, but he couldn't worry about that now. He sensed the frenzy of his mind unbalancing him. He snapped, "What patient?"

Loren lowered her voice, her eyes darting to the doorway. "Mrs. Smith. You know, she called a couple of times asking prenatal questions. You spoke with her on the phone."

Dr. Evans tried to clear his mind. Yes, he remembered Mrs. Smith. His stomach tightened. They had had a very cordial conversation about detecting early pregnancy symptoms, and he gave the usual advice concerning preparing for a healthy pregnancy. He'd been giving that advice a lot lately, more like pep talks, actually. He stood up and put on his professional face. "Do you have her chart?"

Loren handed him the slim laptop as he crossed in front of his desk. "She's done the preliminary paperwork, and everything looks fine. Nothing unusual."

Mumbling, "There never is." Dr. Evans took the open file and passed his nurse, a frozen expression on his face.

Loren followed behind him as he entered the examining room.

Laptop in hand, he knocked and opened the door. With a practiced smile, he shook Anne's hand. "Mrs. Smith, it's nice to meet you. I am Dr. Evans."

Anne was dressed in a white paper dressing gown, her eyes just glancing off his as she took his offered hand. When the exam was over, Anne sat fully dressed in a chair waiting for the results.

Loren entered first, beaming.

Dr. Evans stepped in close behind. "Well, Mrs. Smith, it looks as if you're about two months along. Your baby is due on or around March 25th."

Anne's whole body relaxed. Her smile was apologetic. "That's wonderful. I wish Philip were here, but he had to work today—a project's overdue—and, well, I wasn't sure the news would be good."

Dr. Evans nodded. "You said you'd already taken a pregnancy test at home, but false positives are known to happen. It's always good to double check."

With adrenaline pouring into her system, Anne grinned like a giddy teen. "It seems that getting pregnant is a tricky affair these days. I've got friends who haven't been able to, and one of them thought she was but found out later she wasn't. I just wanted to make sure before I told Philip. He'll be so excited, you know."

"And you?" Loren was rapidly typing away.

Anne looked up, her eyes wide. She began twisting the hem of her blouse.

"I'm happy too, just a little worried. It's a big responsibility." Her eyes focused on Loren's fingers as she continued to type. "Can I ask what you're writing?"

Loren grinned. "Just notes. You know, in case we need to follow up later."

Sitting on the edge of her chair, Anne leaned forward. "Some of those questions you asked earlier seemed a little strange, even a little intrusive, like the one asking about domestic abuse."

Dr. Evans pursed his lips. "You'd be surprised what people tell us. Sometimes families need help, but they're afraid to ask."

With a little jerk, Anne sat up straighter. "So what do you do with that information, exactly?"

"Sometimes we can get help for the mother and the child, even the father. You never know. Like I said, people can be surprising. If you don't ask, you won't ever know."

"But is it really your business to know? I mean, frankly, I don't think you should ask about my personal affairs. If I have a problem at home and I want your help, I'll let you know."

Loren stopped typing, her eyebrows rose.

Dr. Evans shrugged off a sigh. "Well, that's entirely your prerogative, Mrs. Smith. I can understand your feelings, but these are questions any reputable hospital will ask. Babies and old people are the most vulnerable members of our society, and if they're at risk, I want to know. I'm sorry if you were offended, but please understand that when you're pregnant, you are caring for another person, and that person has rights, too."

"I thought conventional medicine taught that the baby wasn't a person until it was born?"

Dr. Evans reached out to shake Anne's hand. "If you want that opinion, you'll need to find another doctor." He walked toward the door. "Loren has given you all the directions for wellness care for the first months, and how to deal with any morning sickness you might experience. But if you have any problems, we're here to help. Just call. The receptionist will make your next appointment for mid-September."

The implicit dismissal ended any further discussion. Anne returned the quick handshake and mumbled her thanks. Following Loren down the hall, she was deposited at the front desk. With a confused frown, Anne turned and thanked Loren.

Loren patted Anne's shoulder and whispered, "Don't feel bad. Doctor Evans gets a little brusque sometimes, but it's just because he really cares about his patients. You wouldn't want him any other way, would you?"

Anne shook her head but said nothing as Loren checked the chart in her hand and called for the next patient. Anne faced the receptionist and tried to remember her schedule for September.

Dr. Evans heard Loren's attempt at diplomacy and sighed. It was only 11:00 AM, but he was exhausted. Returning to his office, he sat down, knowing full well that Mrs. Smith would be back, and he would have to deal with her again. He wondered why that bothered him so much. Was it because she seemed unable to grasp the privilege of pregnancy? Or did it have something to do with all the graphs and charts staring mercilessly up at him? Both, he decided.

August

Musings of K. J.
A Wanna-Be Mom

Unless you have struggled with infertility, you won't understand my suffering. My husband and I were married in our early twenties, so we decided to put off having kids until we were a little older and more settled. It seemed like the right thing to do at the time. Though if I knew then what I know now, I probably wouldn't have put it off. Time is running out, and I feel like I'm dying without ever having really lived. My mom tells me that motherhood just takes time, and my dad tells me I'm ridiculous to worry, but I can see their mounting anxiety, even in their smiles.

It has been eight years now, and I'm losing hope. I'll be thirty next month, and if I ever want to have more than one or two children, I need to get pregnant soon. I initially wanted four kids; now I'd be happy with just one.

Yesterday, I went temporarily insane and shared my fears with a lady at the doctor's office. It turns out she was there to get some kind of implant, so she'd never have to worry about pregnancy again. She suggested, very politely of course, that perhaps I was a bit selfish. "After all, aren't there more than enough people in the world anyway? Why don't you just adopt one of those unwanted kids from Africa or something?"

I guess she needed someone to lecture, and I opened myself up for it. She did a dandy job making me feel worse than I already do. Doesn't she realize that I already feel guilty?

I don't know exactly what I've done wrong, but I feel terrible all the same. I feel as if I offended the Powers That Be, and I'm getting severely punished for it. Do I believe God is punishing me? Maybe—sometimes.

Sometimes I wonder if it was the contraception that messed me up, or the additives in my food, or maybe something in the water. Sometimes I want to call the National Board of Health to investigate. Do they really know what the long-term results of generations of contraception will do to the human race? They say they do, but how could they? But every time I am ready to call in a team of investigators, I realize that even the investigators don't know.

So all I've got is guilt and questions and no baby. My husband is ready to adopt that kid from Africa, but it turns out there aren't so many available kids from Africa...or anywhere else. The infertility problem is hitting everywhere at once. Panic is setting in, and everyone who ever thought about having a kid is clamoring for one, while those lucky enough to get pregnant aren't nearly so likely to give them up. The list of waiting kids has virtually disappeared while the list of waiting parents grows longer by the hour.

I always thought that having children was rather easy, and hopefully, fun. It was a dream that everyone could enjoy, a right even. But now that hope is denied me and apparently a lot of other women, too. There is no one to call for help. My doctor is as worried and confused as I am. There is no one I can complain to or condemn. Knowing I am not alone in my suffering hardly makes me feel any better. Am I being selfish to want a baby of my own? I don't think so. I think motherhood is so right, so natural, that it's one of the greatest gifts in life. Only now the gifts aren't arriving.

Is God punishing us? Was it our complacency that cost us so dearly? If God was really that cruel, I don't think I could believe in him. I'd hate him. I'm not ready to go there. Not yet.

So the next time you see some woman staring longingly at someone else's baby, don't be too quick to judge. She might just be all of us...someday.

5

August
SUNDAY NIGHT

Cerulean sat with his arms spread wide over the back of the bench, his head back, soaking up the last of the day's warm sun.

Viridian sat hunched next to him, his head propped on a clenched fist, while one foot jiggled in furious repetition.

The park pulsated with the ebb and flow of visitors. A man threw a Frisbee to his dog, putting on quite a show. The majority of people strolled about the autumn grounds in pairs, or jogged along singly, trying to get in a quick workout before the evening light disappeared. One mother attempted to wipe dripping ice cream from her young son's face, only to have him push her away with a shrill, exhausted whine.

Cerulean opened his eyes, flicked a glance at his son's jostling foot, and gazed at the scene. *Parenthood is never easy.* The day had been hot and humid, but as August was coming to a close, a hint of summer's end wafted through the rustling leaves. He breathed in the earthy scent noticing the gray clouds building on the western horizon.

Cerulean tapped his fingers together. "You never realize humanity's struggles until you something goes wrong. When everything is in working order, you marvel at simple beauties. Amazing what people go through: colds, headaches, broken bones, diseases, mental disorders, even the natural process of growing up or growing old has its variety of suffering." He tipped his head casually toward his son and whispered, "Are you ready?"

Viridian slammed his foot on the ground and sniffed, "Ready to suffer, you mean? I've suffered since the first moment you brought me here. I just can't see what holds your interest. I've been all over the countryside and spent a whole month following a kid from the inner city, but I feel less admiration for them now than ever. They're either spoiled and whining or poor and ruthless. Nobody cares, and everybody complains."

Cerulean felt a flush creep up his cheeks. "There is some truth in what you say, but it's not the full truth." He glanced at his son and sighed. "There are other guardians besides me. Maybe it's time you went with someone else for a while."

Viridian's eyes brightened. "You mean with another race?"

"No...not yet. Opportunity is still before you. Eventually, you must make your own choice. I always thought you'd follow in my footsteps, but I can't force you...." He nodded to a man who crossed in front of him. "And perhaps this isn't right for you. Still, I think you should give them a little more time. I'm observing Anne, but there are whole nations and cultures you have yet to see. There are guardians all over. Do some research; discover where you might like to go next; make contact with a guardian from an area that interests you. You've got a whole world to choose from."

Looking across the park, Viridian pursed his lips. "I'd rather try another race, but if I have to stay here, I think I'd better go someplace else. I want to do something productive, and that's just not happening here." He crossed his arms; his hands balled into fists. Leaning toward his father, his eyes narrowed. "Will I be able to choose another form?"

Cerulean nodded and opened his mouth, but Viridian was quicker. "Good, I hate this one. I never considered how limiting humans' perceptions would be." Viridian gazed into the distance and shrugged.

"I'm certainly not learning much."

With a slow sigh, Cerulean stood and surveyed his environment. "Learning doesn't come from others; it comes from inside. But, perhaps it would be best to go where your father won't be tempted to lecture you so much."

Across the street, the door to the doctor's office swung open and Anne stepped out.

Cerulean watched as Anne buckled herself into her vehicle and drove away. "She's heading home."

Staring up at the sky, Viridian extended his hand. "It's going to rain. The park will empty in a minute. Should I leave now and make arrangements to try a different place?"

Anne's car disappeared around a corner.

Cerulean's gaze shifted to his son. "There's nothing to stop you. But aren't you even curious how the appointment went, what she'll tell her husband?"

Viridian shrugged. "She's pregnant. That's obvious enough. She'll tell her husband, and they'll be happy—for a while. It all seems rather pointless."

Cerulean cleared his throat with a raspy huff. "She's not so different from us."

"Humans are *very* different from us."

The first drops of rain fell as Cerulean forced his temper into submission. He looked Viridian in the eye and gripped his shoulder. "I hope your next venture is more to your liking."

Shrugging off his father's hold, Viridian nodded, his gaze fixed in the distance. "Me, too." He blinked away.

Looking around at the nearly empty park, Cerulean watched a couple sprint off arm-in-arm. A squirrel scampered to the safety of his nest, and rain-defying birds twittered their hearts out, refusing to be subdued by the impending storm. Surprise brought a smile to his lips as he realized that even in its lonely, rainy, late afternoon dimness, a playground still charmed him. He carried that thought with him as he disappeared from sight.

Anne arrived home just as the sun touched the horizon. The rain clouds had drifted north revealing a clear evening sky. Philip's car wasn't in the driveway, and she felt a pang of disappointment. She wanted to talk to someone. Taking a deep breath, she stepped out of the car and relished the last moments of the day. A cool breeze washed over her, making her dread walking into a stuffy house. She turned and meandered down the road.

They lived on a dead-end, country road with only two other families. An elderly retired couple, the Burdocks, lived across from a large field and a small creek, and a middle-aged couple, the Hoveys, lived just beyond them. Few cars traveled down their lane. Anne had fallen in love with the wooded site—nestled between large fields—the first time she saw it. Philip was a little dubious about living ten miles from town, but he agreed that the house was practically a steal with four acres surrounded by woods.

Anne strolled along leisurely, still trying to absorb the knowledge that she was pregnant. A joyful communion with the natural world pervaded her spirit. Passing the creek, Anne glimpsed Millie on her hands and knees in her front flowerbed. A plethora of marigolds crowded the garden with nary a weed in sight. Anne smiled with renewed awe at the sight of Millie's slight hands darting with efficient deftness, pulling up unwelcome weeds, and encouraging flower stems. *Where does she find the energy to keep up with the garden, her farmhouse, her dementia-struck husband, and her two grandchildren?*

"Hello, Millie!"

Mrs. Burdocks' eyes brightened at the sight of Anne. She braced herself and managed to get to her feet with minimal struggle. "Well, hello there, Anne. How are you on this fine evening?"

Anne's heart pounded with her news, but then her lips pressed together in hesitation. Would Philip be slighted if he weren't the first to know? *Oh, the doctor was the first, really. What difference could it make?*

Millie could tell something was afoot. She stepped forward, her brown eyes rounding in expectation. "What's going on?"

With a sly look, Anne glanced back toward the house and then turned to face Millie. "I've got a little secret." Her face cracked into a huge grin. "I'm pregnant! I haven't had a chance to tell Philip yet, but I know he'll be glad."

Millie's eyebrows rose. "Well, I should think so. A baby's wonderful news!" She stepped over and hugged Anne gently. "I only had the two, you know, but I wish I could've had more. I dreamed of a dozen kids running about the place. But, well...that wasn't meant to be. I was lucky to raise the ones I had."

Anne's heart melted. "You've been through a lot, Millie. How's Bernard doing?"

Tipping her hand in a so-so gesture, Millie answered. "Some days better than others. He forgets my name and calls me 'honey,' and then he talks about things we did when we were first married as if they happened yesterday. Other times he's as lucid as anything. Today he's great. Tomorrow—who knows?" A frown appeared as she studied Anne. "You doing all right then? Feeling well?"

"Oh, just a little tired. I considered taking a nap when I got home, but when I saw the sunset.... It won't be long before I'm shut up inside. I want to enjoy these last days before winter."

Millie blinked as she stared at the fading pinks in the west. "Yes, it's right to make the most of each day. They don't last. You'll find that out. The days are shorter than you think. Sometimes, I wonder if we're all just a pack of fools."

Anne froze. "Millie, you okay?" A dog barked off in the distance as the birds sang their goodnight songs. Anne simultaneously wished that Philip was home and that Millie's life hadn't been so hard.

With a look of ageless certainty, Millie confronted the woman in front of her. "You're just beginning, Anne. You can't possibly see how fast it all goes." Tears welled in her eyes. "It's like Sunday night. Remember, when you were a child and vacation ended? School on Monday was staring you straight in the face, and you had to get to bed. You wondered, 'Did I waste it? Did I waste my chance?' But nothing you did or said would keep Monday from coming."

Anne shivered. Millie and her husband had reached their sunset years. That was a fact. She wouldn't allow their sorrow to dim her joy.

A car crunched down the gravelly road.

Anne glanced over to see Philip's Lexus turn in the driveway. She patted Millie on the shoulder and tried to think of something comforting to say. "Anyone with a garden like yours shouldn't worry." Anne turned again. Philip's car door swung open. She faced Millie, anxious to think of a departing word. "Well, I need to go...."

Millie's gaze settled on Philip. She smiled and waved, as he looked in their direction. "Don't worry about me, child. I've got one foot in this world and one in the next. Sometimes I get a little flustered. You'll understand some day. But for now, hurry up and let Philip in on the secret. And, Anne, it is good news. As long as there's a baby left in the world, it means God isn't done with us yet."

Relief flowed over Anne as she began to turn aside. "Well, if Philip has his way, God'll be busy for quite a while!"

Philip stood gazing in her direction, his arms akimbo, waiting.

When Anne came close enough, she called out, "I've got news!" She reached out for Philip's arms and, pulling him forward; she kissed him. As they meandered toward the house, Anne murmured, "I'm so happy."

Suddenly, Philip stopped. "Oh, my briefcase." He ran back to his car.

As Anne stood waiting, she could see Millie picking up the last of her gardening tools.

There was a distant call, "Honey? Honey, where are you?"

Anne could barely make out Millie's response, "I'm coming, dear. Coming."

When Philip embraced her again, they turned up the path to the house. But Anne could not help one backward glance as Millie disappeared from sight behind the autumn flowerbed.

6

August
DOCTORS

The pitch-black of a moonless night cloaked the room. A single lamp illuminated the figure of Dr. Evans as he sat hunched over his desk studying a series of charts. His jaws ached from clenching his teeth, but he could not relax. Rubbing his hand across his bloodshot, weary eyes only made the sting worse. On the walls, certificates detailing his degrees and even a newspaper article about a case where he had saved an infant's life were blotted into obscurity, as were four neatly framed pictures of his family: his wife Sylvia, his daughter Carrie, and their two dachshunds: Roscoe and Rosie. His concentration centered on the clearly detailed charts that only confirmed his worst fears.

The number of pregnancies was dropping dramatically all across the state. Dr. Evans felt a shudder run through his frame. He was trained in long-suffering patience and knew how to consider the facts carefully before arriving at any conclusions, but there was little hope of reading this data wrong. The situation was grave. Despite the bleak state of affairs, his faith in an omnipotent God remained unshaken, though he would never attempt to explain God to anyone. He firmly believed that as he used his skills in accordance with God's will then he and God were working on the same side. No matter how painful things might become, God always managed to make everything balance out in the end. Rubbing his exhausted eyes once more, Dr. Evans tried to appraise the ramifications of a dropping population. What the hell was he supposed to do? And what in Heaven was God going to do? His cell phone buzzed, and he reached for it mechanically.

"Hello, Dr. Evans." His face relaxed as he heard his wife's voice respond. "Oh, hi, honey, sorry I'm so late. It's just that I've got a problem on my hands, and I'm getting a little—" His face clouded over as his wife broke into his explanation. His puzzled frown turned to alarm. "Are you sure? What did the officer say, exactly? Okay, an ambassador, whoever! Was he sure that Carrie was taken? Okay now, don't cry! Just hang on. I'll be home as quick as I can. Don't call anyone else; keep the phone lines open in case there's more news." Dr. Evans listened to his wife a moment and shook his head. "I know, dear, remember I warned her, but, well, never mind that now. Just stay calm…wait for me. I'll be right home."

Dr. Evans pushed the end button and got up from his chair, flinging his jacket over his shoulders. He ran out the door and then back in the room, grabbed his car keys out of his desk drawer, and began to run out the door again.

His colleague, Dr. Sung, strode toward him, a hand waving. "Hey, Frank, working late too, eh?" He strolled up. "I was just coming to see you. I've noticed something a little funny, and I was wondering if we could—"

Dr. Evans put up his hand as he continued marching forward. "Sorry, Bing, but I've got to go. An emergency at home. My daughter…you remember Carrie? You were at her send-off party before she left for her work-study. Well, there's been some big blow up or something; she's been kidnapped or caught up in some kind of protest." Dr. Evans struggled with huffing breaths as he hurried toward the exit. "We don't know the details. Sounds like all hell is breaking loose. Sylvia's nearly frantic."

Dr. Sung's eyes grew wide as he stared, nodding his head. He stopped at the exit. "I'm so sorry. Yes, get home…let me know if there is anything I can do—cover with your patients, anything."

With one hand on the door, Dr. Evans tried to speak over the lump rising in his throat. "I know. Thanks, Bing. I'll let you know as soon as I learn anything." Dr. Evans bustled through the doorway.

Staring after him, Dr. Sung mumbled to the empty doorway. "That's the third major blow-up this month. Add a couple of earthquakes, and it'll seem like the end of the world."

Dr. Evans' lamp glowed from the open doorway, so Bing strolled into his friend's office. Reaching over the desk, he felt for the off switch. As he did so, he noticed the graphs spread across Dr. Evan's desk. He plopped down in the chair, a long hum coming from deep in his chest. He studied the charts for a moment and sighed. He pushed up his wire-rimmed glasses and rubbed his eyes. "So…we're worried about the same thing. Question is—are we the only ones?"

On the twelfth floor of the Center for Advanced Research, a team of doctors broke from their meeting and streamed down a cream colored corridor, highlighted by a series of enormous glass windows. Dr. Peterson pounded ahead of his flagging constituents, the tail of his long, white, lab coat flapping behind him.

Dr. Mitchell jogged to catch up. "Hey, Greg, stop a minute. Let's get a cup of coffee and talk this out."

Halting in mid-stride, Dr. Peterson glared at his colleague. "Talk this out? What's there to talk about? There're entire cultures going extinct and those," a finger jutted out accusingly, "illustrious decision-makers are just going to stand by and let it happen. Native races have died before because we *couldn't* do anything. But now, we have the technology, the medical sophistication to save people. But it costs too much money! Who cares about aborigines in Africa, Native Americans, or little island communities? They can lose their place in a wildly changing world, and who gives a damn?"

Dr. Peterson stormed ahead again.

Dr. Mitchell hurried along, his mouth open to respond, but Dr. Peterson snapped his fingers in emphasis.

"We might as well be talking about a flock of birds." Emotion choked Dr. Peterson. "If you and the rest don't care, don't assume I'll just toe the line. I'm going to tell the world what a group of hypocrites and bigots run this hospital, and I'll push forward with my research." Dr. Peterson stopped and waved his hands. "There's a massive purge going on, and I won't sit down and shut up. I'll stop it!"

A hushed silence fell over the hospital corridor. Doctors, nurses, and other participants froze; all consultations ceased.

Dr. Mitchell looked around, attempted a reassuring smile, and steered his friend toward their office. "Come on, Greg. We can talk this out." He whispered. "I'm on your side, remember?" He nodded toward the doorway.

Dr. Peterson heaved an exasperated sighed. "You didn't sound like it in there. Reason isn't what we need, *Dr*. Mitchell. We need a little decent compassion." Dr. Peterson crossed into his office and walked straight to his desk. He sat with a heavy thud, forcing a loud squeak from the chair.

Pulling his well-oiled chair up alongside Dr. Peterson's desk, Dr. Mitchell leaned in and spoke softly. "Listen, Greg, this is a serious matter. I know our research will probably work someday, but we aren't a hundred percent sure, not quite yet. Let's not go around accusing people of crimes that can't even be committed."

Dr. Peterson pounded his fist on the desk. "If we know that we have the research within our grasp to save whole communities, but we refuse to do it because it's expensive, we have committed a crime, a crime of negligence."

"It isn't just the money, and you know that. People are uncomfortable with the whole concept of cloning. Cloning body parts and animals is one thing, but to clone a human being, well now, that's another matter. People get squeamish. Moral ground rules need to be laid."

"What the hell? We've been cloning people for years, but we've had to stop in the earliest stages of development to keep those moralists happy. Have you ever thought *that* was right? Moral ground rules! Oh, God! There're no ground rules when it comes to science. There's only forward or backward. If I don't do the research, someone else will. At least I give a damn about the people I'll be cloning. I'm not doing this to create some slave race or something."

Snorting, Dr. Mitchell leaned back, folding his hands behind his head. "You wouldn't, but once you've gone forward, as you say, then anyone can copy what you've done, and not everyone cares like you do. That's what those hypocrites and bigots, as you call them, are afraid of. They don't want to let a genie out of a bottle they can't put back. Some genies can get pretty mean." Silence hung in the air a moment. Dr. Mitchell sat up. "Besides, you never told them the whole truth. Right now, we can't keep a cloned rat alive."

Dr. Peterson scooted closer to his desk, squeaks of protest again rising from the frame. "It's just a bump in the road. We'll figure it out. Must be the rats we were using."

Rising to his feet, Dr. Mitchell strolled over to the coffee machine, poured himself a cup, and stirred in three mounds of sugar. "I'm not so sure. I was doing a little checking, and we're not the only ones who hit this particular bump. Pretty much every top researcher doing cloning experiments has been having trouble. Not every experiment has gone sour, but the vast majority. It seems we have a real mystery on our hands, and we aren't the only ones getting frustrated."

"We have a problem, alright, but it's no mystery. It's the oldest problem known to humanity. Some people think they know what's best for everyone. It's called sabotage."

Sipping his hot coffee, Dr. Mitchell grimaced. "Sabotage? There you go again, accusing people of crimes that haven't been committed yet. But even if that were the case, it shouldn't be too difficult to get around it. There are lots of researchers in the world, and many of them don't have anyone looking over their shoulder. Perhaps we just need to find the right place to do our work, the right partners to help us."

Dr. Peterson eyed his colleague critically. "You know, I'm beginning to wonder who the senior doctor is, *Dr.* Mitchell."

With a grin, Dr. Mitchell smirked. "Senior doesn't mean smarter."

Dr. Peterson's gaze moved back toward his computer as he sighed. "And to think, I gave up swearing for you."

September

Sun Rise News
Why Can't I Get Pregnant?

Disappointed women all over the country are beginning to ask the same question: "Why can't I get pregnant?" OB/GYN's are scratching their heads, wondering why their waiting rooms are emptying of pregnant patients. Business is booming for fertility clinics, but without the success they are accustomed to.

What do all these situations have in common? A sudden and alarming drop in pregnancies. Doctors and researchers throughout the nation are scrambling for answers. Over two hundred support groups for would-be moms have sprung up recently, and even social media fans have joined in to find a solution, with prenatal advice becoming the number one trending topic this month.

There have been a number of researchers studying this sudden and inexplicable change in pregnancy rates. A group of doctors in New York are calling for a complete review of recent food additives and advise anyone wishing to become pregnant to eat only organically-grown foods. Scientists in Colorado are initiating a fact-finding committee that will take water samples from every major city in the US to investigate whether there has been intentional sabotage of our water systems. A cloning expert in Florida is reaching out to researchers in the UK and other European nations to discover whether cloning could become a viable alternative form of human reproduction.

There are numerous reports from countries all over the world that they, too, have witnessed a similar decline in viable pregnancies. So far there is not enough information to reach any certain conclusion about what is causing this dramatic shift in pregnancy rates, but for the near future, we will keep hearing the question: "Why can't I get pregnant?" and see a lot of head scratching in response.

7

GOD, I NEED HELP

The sound of their footsteps echoed down the long, empty hallway as Loren led Anne to the ultrasound department and introduced her to the technician, a young woman in her early twenties. She greeted them warmly and took Anne into a small, dimly lit room. Anne did exactly as she was told and in a matter of minutes she was lying on a firm bed, her mid-section bare. Her heart leapt at the sight of her baby's form on the monitor.

After taking several measurements and performing specialized tests, the deftly skilled technician asked, "Do you want to know what gender it is?"

Anne's face lit up. "You can tell?"

"Well, it is a little early, but with this view, I have a pretty good idea. I don't have to say—if you want to be surprised."

Without hesitation, Anne responded, "No, I want to know."

"You are most likely carrying a baby girl."

A tear slipped down Anne's cheek. Her heart raced at the sight of her daughter's beating heart. "Her heart's beating awfully fast. Is she all right?"

The technician remained silent a moment. When she spoke, her voice was low. "She's the most perfect baby I've seen in a long time."

Anne couldn't sit up, but she turned her head so she could look at the young woman. "You sound sad. Are you sure she's okay?"

The technician nodded. "She's fine." The young woman sniffed. "I shouldn't say anything, but it's been months since I saw a baby this young. I'm sure you've heard how things are. Everyone's worried. The administrator is even thinking of cutting my position."

Weariness enveloped Anne. "I'm so sorry. How long have you been doing this?"

The young woman shrugged. "Only a couple years, but I fell in love with my job the first day. Every baby is amazing. But now…there just haven't been as many. Seems people aren't having any. I'm afraid something's really wrong." She took the wand off Anne's tummy and straightened up. "I shouldn't be talking so much." She attempted a smile. "Your little girl is just perfect, Mrs. Smith. I'll send the report to Dr. Evans this afternoon."

Sitting up, Anne took one last look at the frozen image on the monitor. "Thank you." She dressed and left the hospital. An image of her baby floating in her uterus, rocking gently with her every move, filled her mind.

Throughout the long afternoon, anxiety began to work its way into the crevices of Anne's mind, displacing her earlier joy. A soft light bathed the kitchen, muting the scenic pictures into mere shadows.

Anne prepared dinner with mechanical efficiency, a wrinkled frown marring her face.

The front door slammed, and a heavy tread marched across the room. Philip dropped his briefcase on the counter and offered his wife a quick hug. "How was your appointment?"

"Fine. The baby's perfectly healthy." She forced a smile as she placed two pieces of warmed-up fried chicken on Philip's plate, then scooped up some instant mashed potatoes and canned green beans.

She set his plate at his usual place. Next, she pulled out a bowl, poured in a little cereal and milk, and finally sat down.

Philip frowned. "Hold on, now. You've got to eat better than that. Here, take a piece of my chicken." He wiggled it in her direction.

Anne's stomach churned. "I can't. I'm still a little nauseous. Once I've cooked something, I can't even think of eating it. Cereal is about the best I can do. Maybe I'll feel better later."

Biting into the chicken leg, Philip admonished her as he chewed. "You don't know what you're missing. This is terrific, best thing I've had all day. It'd be good for you." He continued to munch contentedly.

Anne sat with her head propped on her hands. She stared vacantly ahead, the image of her baby still in her mind.

Philip's chewing slowed as he watched Anne. Finally, he swallowed, straightened up and wiped his lips. "I thought you said the baby was fine."

"She is fine. But there's a problem; I just can't figure it out. It all seems so strange."

The chicken leg dropped from Philip's fingers. "*She*? You know it's a she, and you didn't think to tell me?"

Coming out of her stupor, Anne blinked. "Oh, yeah, sorry, honey. It's a she. I was thinking about names on the way home, but...I'm worried." She surveyed the room and leaned in to whisper. "I don't know what it is, but I have this terrible feeling, like maybe the baby won't live, or I won't live, or something awful is going to happen."

After wiping his hands on his napkin, Philip stood, walked around the table and hugged his wife. "Oh, that's just your hormones talking. You know how you get when things are out of whack. You're just feeling out of sorts. Every pregnant woman goes through this. It'll pass."

Anne watched Philip return to his seat, resenting his hug and the coinciding rise of nausea. Tears welled in her eyes. "Dang it, Philip, it's not hormones. We need to talk about this."

Philip shook his head. "Nope, I don't want to. You said the baby's fine. That's all I need to know."

Getting out of her seat, Anne snatched a towel and wrung it in her hands. "But there is a problem! It's on the news every day; everyone's talking about it. Even the technician doing the ultrasound is worried. Her job may be cut, but I don't think that's what's worrying her." Anne's throat tightened. "She's awfully young. She might never…."

Philip washed down his last mouthful with a sip of water. "That's not your worry, is it? I mean, so what if a hospital cuts a position? It isn't the end of the world. And as for the news, well, people are freaking out before they know what's going on. Population levels go up and down all the time. So maybe the US is at low tide, I bet China isn't. India? They'll never be in want of babies. Just wait, things'll turn around. Before this baby is born, there will be a hundred women lined up to take your place at the doctor's office."

Anne rubbed her temple. "It's not that simple. This is bigger than you think. Even Dr. Evans is worried. His office isn't so full anymore. He hasn't said anything about it, exactly, but it's obvious. He's distracted, and he's lost weight. He seems older somehow. The nurse told me that he was worried about his daughter who was detained over some protest-or-another, but he's definitely preoccupied. He asked me a lot of questions he's never asked before."

"Questions? Like what?" Philip retrieved a beer from the refrigerator and snapped it open with an angry twist.

"He wanted to know if I did anything unusual when I got pregnant and whether we lived in the country or the city, and what kind of food we ate, and what kind of work you did, things like that." There was a catch in her voice. "You could see it in his eyes. He knows something's wrong...something big."

"If his daughter was caught up in a protest, he should be worried. That whole part of the world is on edge." Philip put his beer down and collected his dishes. "Maybe he wants to write a paper for some medical journal, and he just needs the data to fill in his charts."

Dizziness overwhelmed Anne. Gripping the back of the chair, she closed her eyes and struggled to keep on her feet.

Philip rushed over. "Hey, none of that. Here, you're going straight to bed. No more worries, all right? I don't want little Miss Margaret to get knocked off her feet before she's even born."

Comforted by this attention, Anne let herself be directed up the stairs. "Margaret? Where did Margaret come from?"

"Oh, I don't know. I just like the sound of it. I'll try out a bunch of names, and we can see what we like. Margaret, Mary-Jane, Griselda—"

"Ugh, Griselda? I think not! I'm already feeling sick, don't make it worse. And please, whatever you do, don't make me laugh."

With careful maneuvering, they sidestepped a laundry hamper, a multiple of unmatched shoes, and stacks of books. Helping his wife gently into the bedroom and onto the bed, Philip practically crooned. "Now, don't you worry about anything. I'll maintain a perfectly sober disposition. Just relax."

He slipped off her shoes and socks and helped her lie down. "I'll clean up downstairs, and then I've got a little paperwork to finish. You just rest. If you get hungry, let me know. There's still some chicken and stuff left."

Anne stifled a groan. "Thanks, I'll let you know." She slipped under the covers, pulled them tight under her chin, closed her eyes, and prayed for sleep.

In the morning, a sharp wind hit the windows, and cold air slipped in under Anne's blankets. She kept her eyes tightly shut, pulled her blankets closer around her body and tried to remember what day it was. *Saturday, thank God.* The wind rattled the windows again. A heavy rain slashed against the house.

Philip's voice carried up the stairs. "Aw, damn it!"

A sudden smash made Anne sit up. "Philip? What happened? Did something break? Are you alright?"

Philip's irritated voice answered back. "Oh, it's nothing. I just opened the door to check the mail, and my papers blew all over the place; a few got wet. Dang it! I need these." There was a pause and then, "Hey, can I use your hair dryer?"

Fearing for what further damage might be done, Anne decided that she had better get up. She lumbered out of bed and tried to remember exactly how she had managed to get into her nightclothes. Oh yes, Philip came in.... She moved forward and suddenly felt a flutter in her belly. The baby had moved—vigorously. Lowering herself onto the chair, she sat on a mound of yesterday's clothes. She put her hand on her tummy and waited. The kick came again, not so violently, but definitely a kick.

"Hey, honey, come up here! Hurry."

Philip rushed into the room, a wet dishrag in his hand, his hair disheveled, and a wild look in his eye. "What's wrong? Did you fall—?"

Anne reached out, her frown doing battle with a grin.

He forward cautiously. "What?"

"The baby kicked. I could feel it." Anne shifted her nightshirt a little, and they both stared at her rounded belly. Suddenly, Anne squealed, and her face glowed with happiness.

Philip knelt down. "This is too cool. It's like something from a sci-fi movie. A little alien—"

Smacking her husband's arm, Anne frowned. "Stop it or I'll really hit you, and then I'll have something to report to Doctor Evans alright. This baby is as human and perfect as you and me."

Philip rubbed his shoulder. "Hey, I'm the father, remember." He put his hand on his wife's belly. "It's just so weird, you know. I never got this close to a pregnant woman before. Nobody in my family has kids."

"Considering your family, I'd say that's a good thing."

"Not fair. They're just as good as anyone in your family. A few personality issues maybe, but hey, no one's perfect."

Anne leaned her head on her husband's shoulder. "I got the pick of the litter."

Gently rubbing his wife's belly, Philip whispered, "Too true."

The phone's ring tone chimed. With a groan, Philip rose to answer it. The storm had calmed and rain now pattered lightly against the windows. "I'll get breakfast. Just hang on." He reached for the cellphone on his bedside table. "Yep, Philip here."

Anne continued to wait for another kick, but there was none forth-coming. She straightened her shirt and sifting through her clothes, she rejected yesterday's and moved toward the closet. Pulling a pair of sweat pants and a sweater off the shelf, she stepped toward the bath-room.

Philip spoke sharply into the phone, gesturing with his hand.

Anne glanced at her husband's frown as she tiptoed across the room.

Philip shook his head, one hand running his fingers through his hair, his eyes unnaturally large.

She stopped in concern and waited while Philip continued to listen intently. She stepped closer, trying to surmise who had called. His sister from Kentucky? Jackie was always getting over one catastrophe just to find another. *What has she gotten mixed up with this time?* Anne dismissed the thought and shuffled toward the bathroom again.

Philip raised his finger to stop her, but then his eyes flared and a red flush suffused his cheeks. He waved Anne on. Putting his hand over the receiver, he called, "Take a shower, honey; I'll fix breakfast."

Philip listened as Anne turned on the shower, then he brought the phone to his ear and growled. "Listen, I don't know if this is your sick idea of a joke, but I don't care who the hell you are; you could be the president of the United States and I'd tell you the same thing, my wife's pregnancy is none of your business. Stay away from here and don't even think of calling again. I happen to work for a very powerful attorney—"

The voice on the other end attempted a soothing tone. "Mr. Smith, if you'd just listen a moment, I could—"

Philip shook his head. "Go to hell!" He punched the end button. After tossing the phone onto the dresser, he stalked to the bathroom door. The shower spray pelted against the stall. He knocked, waited, and then asked, "Anne, you okay?"

Anne called through the rushing water. "Yeah, I'm feeling lots bet-ter. Don't worry, honey. Just give me a few minutes."

Philip hesitated and then called out, "I'll be downstairs. Take your time."

The room was a disheveled mess. With quick, snatching motions, Philip picked up a large bundle of crumpled clothes. He tossed them onto a pile by the door, then grabbed the bed sheets and pulled them straight. Finally, he spread the blankets over them and tossed the pillows at the head of the bed. Satisfied, he strode to the door, picked up the pile of clothes and walked out of the room.

When Anne meandered into the kitchen, the washing machine in the basement was whirling through the last of the rinse cycle, and the smell of frying bacon wafted through the air. Since her nausea had abated, she could enjoy the pleasant scene. "What's all this? You decided to take over?" She put up her hands and laughed. "Don't worry; I don't mind. Anytime you want to take over is fine with me."

Reading a slightly damp paper with an assortment of others spread out on the table, Philip frowned in concentration.

The smell of bacon burning wafted through the air. Anne tottered to the stove and turned the frying pieces. She cleared her throat. "You know, when you start something like this, it's best to keep your eye on it. Bacon burns pretty quickly."

No response.

"Philip? What's got into you?"

Philip looked up, his mouth open. "Huh? Oh, yeah, the bacon. I almost forgot. Thanks." He picked up one of the damp papers and shook it. "I was trying to sort these out." He slapped them down on the counter, then went over to the coffee machine and poured a cup. He snatched the creamer out of the refrigerator. "Not such a great morning." He swallowed. His hands trembled as he poured the creamer into his coffee. He paused and glanced at his wife. "You got a call earlier."

Moving the bacon onto a waiting plate, Anne tried to imagine what on Earth Jackie had done this time. She pulled the egg carton from the refrigerator. Without looking at Philip, she kept her tone neutral. "Yeah, who from? Jackie asking for something?"

"No, not Jackie." He drummed his fingers against his cup. "It was some reporter. He's been following up this story, about the drop in pregnancies. From what he can figure out, the drop has been occurring slowly for the last few years. Suddenly, last year, it took a dramatic shift and dropped off even more, that is, until about June."

Anne stood frozen. A picture of Millie picking up her gardening tools suddenly appeared in her mind, but then she shook herself, picked up an egg, broke it, and dropped it onto the hot frying pan. The sizzling spray made her step back. She broke another egg and studied her husband who was standing next to the counter gripping his coffee cup too tightly. Anne braced herself. "So, what happened in June?"

"Nothing. No pregnancies anywhere in the US. Maybe across the globe."

The spatula slipped from Anne's fingers. Her stomach twisted and the nausea returned with a vengeance. She limped toward the table, sat down and put her hands over her eyes. "Now *I* don't want to talk about it. I don't want to even think about it. Oh, God! What can it mean?"

Philip picked up the spatula and flipped the eggs. His jaw tensed as he replied, "I don't know." He slapped the spatula down and rubbed his forehead.

Anne frowned as she mumbled. "So why did the reporter call here? What did he want?"

"He wanted to talk to you. When I asked him who he was, he went into this long song and dance about how he's been following this population story. He said he got interested a couple of years ago when his wife couldn't get pregnant. He tried to make it sound like some personal crusade or something but—"

"But what? You think he's making it up? You think doctors and hospitals and people all over the world are getting upset about nothing? Everyone's got a case of overwrought hormones?" Anne's voice sounded shrill even to her own ears.

Philip sniffed and turned to the pan. "Damn. The eggs!" Before she could warn him, Philip grabbed the hot frying pan by the handle and then dropped it almost immediately, waving his hand in pain. Eggs spattered across the floor.

Anne motioned him to the sink. "Put your hand under cold water, would you? Don't worry about breakfast. I'm not hungry anyway."

Philip stomped to the sink, flipped on the cold water, and let it pour over his hand. "I was."

"I told you—we need to talk about this."

Slamming off the water, Philip faced his wife. "Don't you get it? This is too big for us. It's not our problem anyway, and besides, there's nothing to talk about. The more we worry about it, the worse we'll make it. Our baby is fine. That's all we can deal with. I don't want reporters asking questions; I don't want you worrying. I don't want to take on the troubles of the whole world. I can't fix this!"

Anne wiped away the tear that had slipped down her cheek. "No one is asking you to fix it." Her body trembled. "I just need you and me to be together in this. If you pretend that everything's alright, well, then…I'm alone." Anne placed her hands over her middle. "The baby is starting to show and people are beginning to stare. If things get any worse, I'll feel like a freak. Philip, I need you!"

Moving over to Anne's side, Philip bent down and embraced her hunched shoulders. "I can't stand thinking about something happening to the baby. I feel bad for all those other people, but this whole thing's so crazy; no one knows what's happening. Everyone's getting panicked, and I don't want to go there." He looked Anne in the eyes. "I want to focus on the baby and us. I don't want to care about the world when it just makes me sad. We have a right to be happy."

"You forget; our baby will inherit this world. We better care, even if it makes us sad." Anne forced herself to her feet. "Besides, maybe if we understand better, we'll learn something that can help."

Philip sighed and squatted to pick up the mess. "Well, I guess I better start breakfast over. At least we can eat something before we take on the world."

After wiping her face with a tissue, Anne blew her nose and forced on a cheerful mask. "I'll make some toast." As she opened the cabinet door, the phone rang.

They both froze and glanced at each other. After a couple rings, Philip snatched up the receiver.

"Philip here." Philip listened, and relief flooded his face. "Yeah, she's here. Just a minute." He looked at his wife, who was still standing frozen, a loaf of bread in her hand. "It's your mom." He handed the cordless phone over.

Anne took it, handing him the bread, and sat down on a stool by the counter. "Hi, Mom. What's going on?"

Philip fried eggs and made toast, ate his breakfast, and washed up his dishes by the time Anne was done.

"So, I take it your mom wants to come for a visit?"

There was no use denying the obvious; it was as real as the cold breakfast lying in front of her. "Yeah, and Mark is coming too. Mom can't travel alone, and he has a little vacation time."

"Wonderful! I suppose they'll be pleased to stay here?" Philip's sarcasm stabbed the stillness.

"No. Mom said she didn't want to put us out. Mark will make arrangements for a hotel in town."

"Oh, well…." Philip averted his gaze and folded his arms over his chest. "He doesn't have to. I could clear out the extra room for your mom, and he could sleep on the couch for a couple of days."

Anne sighed, though it pleased her that Philip looked a little ashamed. "Mom's really pushing herself to do this. I told her that she could stay here, but she said no, she'd feel better at a hotel. She just wants to see if I'm alright and spend some time with us."

Philip glanced at his watch. "I promised I'd go in for a couple of hours, but I'll be back before lunch. We can do something fun then, okay?"

The smell of bacon still pervaded the room, and her renewed nausea was calming to a mild throb. "Yeah, fine. I've got plenty of stuff to do around here." Anne sat down to confront her breakfast.

Philip kissed her before he left. "Just do me one favor? I'll try to worry a little more; you try to worry a little less—deal?"

Anne nodded as she let him go. After cleaning up the kitchen, she straightened up the living room. Next, she decided to go downstairs and deal with the laundry. As her foot touched the first step, it slipped on the edge, and she lost her balance. She tried to catch herself, but her hands grabbed thin air. She stumbled, clutching helplessly at the wall and landed at the foot of the stairs. A sharp pain throbbed in her back. Attempting to sit up, she cried out. After a moment of near-hyperventilation, she surveyed her position. She was alone in the basement; Philip was gone, and there was no one to hear if she yelled. Anne let her head fall back against the wall. "What a day! What a lousy, terrible, stupid, awful, horrible day! God, I need help!"

"Hello?"

Anne heard the voice, but she could hardly believe it was real. Someone was knocking on the kitchen door. A man's voice repeated the call. "Hello? Anyone at home?"

November

BBC NEWS
The United Nations Declares a State of Emergency

Repeated attempts by various experts to solve the medical emergency now known as the Human Extinction Threat have come up with no single viable explanation for what is causing the complete loss of fertility in women around the globe. All that is known for certain is that the pregnancy rate has dropped to the point where it is virtually nonexistent. The UN has established committees in every nation on every continent, with several countries having multiple committees working on various aspects of this crisis. In the US alone there are 235 committees investigating air, water, and soil conditions; poisons, pesticides, insecticides; and various large farming and livestock operations. There are committees investigating the possibility of sabotage, ethnic cleansing, and even alien intervention. Panels and boards have been put into place to deal with the overwhelming psychological stress related to fears concerning mass extinction. Hospitals all over the nation are reporting an increase in mental disorders, and various departments are reporting unusually high absentee rates among workers.

As of this reporting, there is little solid evidence to direct researchers. "It is the very normalcy of the world around us that is so baffling," said P. T. Scott, a top-level spokesperson for an international coalition appointed to look into the fertility crises. "Animal, as well as plant life, appears completely unaffected. Animals of all kinds are reproducing at normal rates, and there does not appear to be any unusual decline in farm production or plant viability. There is, of course, the continuing concern over the melting ice caps due to global warming, but even that wouldn't account for this sudden and dramatic drop in human pregnancy rates. It is truly baffling."

Top researchers at cloning labs all over the world are increasing their efforts to assist by attempting to clone the first human from conception to birth. The laws of various nations normally forbid this form of research, but the UN council has decreed that in this state of emergency, all forms of research must be allowed to go forward. There are religious groups, including the Roman Catholic Church, condemning this action and insisting that fertility is an act of God and that cloning does not respect the full rights of a person to be born naturally with a mother and a father. The UN says it will take the Catholic Church's position into consideration, but maintains that under the circumstances, cloning is a legitimate form of human reproduction.

If you learn of anything that might be helpful to researchers, please contact their hotline: 1-Extinction. For faster service, call your state and local health departments.

November
FAMILY

Hoping that she wouldn't slip and break something, Philip eyed his mother-in-law through the window as she stepped onto the porch. She was a thin, tiny woman with a neat bun of gray hair wrapped on the top of her head. Every inch of her proclaimed an inner dignity, though her clothes were a cheap imitation of better quality goods, and her shoulders were permanently stooped. Philip realized once again that he was rather in awe of the woman, a woman who, Anne informed him, was secretly scared to death most of the time. Before she could knock, he swiftly opened the front door.

"Marylou, Mark, hi! Come on in. You know you're always welcome, no need to knock."

Anne's mom stepped across the threshold followed by her son, Mark. She looked at her son-in-law, blinking. "Well, I hate to barge in. I thought Anne might be napping or something."

Mark, a stocky outdoorsman, stepped in behind his mother and with a firm grip, shook hands with his brother-in-law. "Mom's been worried the whole drive down that we'd interrupt a nap. You'd think that Anne spends her whole life sleeping now."

Marylou shuffled forward, inspecting the living room in one appraising glance. "You know how I am. And besides, Anne does need her rest. All pregnant women do."

Leading them into the living room, Philip took their coats, and gestured toward the large, over-stuffed couch. "Please, take a seat, relax. Anne'll be down in just a bit." Philip laid the coats in the spare bedroom and reappeared. "Actually, you are more right than you know, Marylou. Ever since Anne had her little accident, she gets tired easily. I tried to tell her to slow down when she first got pregnant, but she thought she could handle everything, same as usual. Turns out she's wrong. And what's more, she actually admits it!" Philip grinned as Anne walked in the room.

A moment of silence hung in the air as Anne went up to her mom and offered her a gentle hug. She hugged her brother, too, though more forcefully. "Hi, Mom, Mark. How was the drive down?"

Overriding the question, Marylou stared at her daughter. "You never told me you had an accident. What happened?"

Anne darted a silent, wide-eyed accusation at her husband.

Philip began speaking quickly. "Hey, Mark, you probably want to stretch your legs. How about I show you around the place, and you can help me a bit?" Philip patted the larger man on the shoulder and laughed. "It's near enough to five to have a beer, don't you think?" The two men started through the doorway.

Philip glanced back at Anne, grinning at his narrow escape.

Motioning for her mom to sit down, Anne sat in the recliner next to her. "Sorry, Mom. I thought about telling you, but I was afraid you'd worry. Besides, I just slipped." Anne chuckled. "But then I was rescued. It was rather amazing, actually. Philip had just left for work and I was going downstairs to start the laundry when I slipped, and I landed right on my bottom. I wasn't hurt, just scared. I got the wind knocked out of me, and my back bruised a little. Nothing to get upset about."

Marylou shook her head. "So why did you need to get rescued?"

"Well, I didn't actually. But a rescuer showed up just the same." A far-away look filled Anne's eyes. "I was just about to burst into hysterics when I heard this guy yelling from the back door. He said he'd been out front and heard a cry, so he got worried. He started calling to me, and when I called back, he came in and found me." Anne grinned. "He really was the nicest man I've ever met, except Philip, of course. He was middle-aged, brown hair streaked with gray, brown eyes, just your average guy, but he had the nicest manners. He asked if he should call for an ambulance, and I told him I'd just slipped but my back hurt a little. So he came right down, and he helped me to my feet, and I realized that I wasn't really hurt, and suddenly, I did the stupidest thing in the world."

"You started to cry."

"Yeah! How'd you know?"

"It's what any mother would do who's worried about her baby. You weren't just frightened for yourself; you were scared for the little one. That's how it is when you're pregnant." Marylou's eyes glistened.

"Well, you're right, Mom." Anne chuckled. "I made an idiot out of myself, and this poor guy had to stand there and watch me have a meltdown." Anne looked off into the distance. "He was so nice about it. He took my arm and helped me up the steps and offered to call Philip. But I told him I was fine, so he just said that he should be going, and he left. But his eyes! I'll never forget those eyes." Anne sighed. "I never even asked his name."

Marylou peered at her daughter. "It seems to me that you forgot something else."

Anne's brow furrowed with incomprehension.

Marylou folded her hands. "You didn't ask him why he was at the door."

Folding her hands in contemplation, Anne pursed her lips. "You know, at the time it didn't even enter my mind. I thought about it later, but I figured he was just one of those guys who sells organic meat, door to door, you know—Pasture Perfect. They come around every fall. Frankly, if he had asked, I'd have bought a whole cow off of him.

I can't explain it, but there was something about him. He was electric, if you know what I mean." Suddenly feeling intimate, Anne leaned toward her mother, her hands clenched together and her voice low. "Do you believe in guardian angels?"

Marylou answered slowly, "Maybe." She paused and began again. "You know how it was with me. I've spent most of my life being terrified, but that stopped a few months ago and I can't explain it, other than to say I was healed. I don't claim that an angel came down from heaven and healed me, but something happened, *someone* healed me. And at the time, it felt sort of electric, though I can't say exactly what I mean."

"Maybe it was just a change in your medicine?"

"No. Haven't changed my medicine in years." Marylou waved the thought away. Her eyes were wide with honesty. "Too scared to, you know. No, this was sudden and unexplainable. After all those years of being afraid, suddenly the fear was gone. I'm not exactly brave now; I'm still timid about things, ask Mark. But the terror is gone." She smiled at her daughter and reached out for her hand. "Some things are just good, and they don't need to be explained. Perhaps it was someone's prayers that did it; I don't know. Just be happy your guardian angel had the sense to show up when he did." Marylou glanced at her daughter. "But you know, there are scary things happening in the world, the news reports.... How are you handling that, Anne?"

Anne tried not to stiffen. She wondered if an ironic laugh would be appropriate. "How am I supposed to handle it, Mom?" Anne got up, her round tummy protruding noticeably. She rubbed her back. "You know how I always wanted to be strong and independent, never afraid of anyone or anything." Anne turned and stared at her mother. "I always wanted to be different. While you were always trapped by your fears, I wanted to be free, even if that meant being a bit selfish. I figured it was worth it. No one was going to lock me in a cage."

"Is your baby a cage, Anne?"

"No, and that's the mystery of it. It should be. I mean there's all the responsibility and the wear and tear of having my body serving anoth-

er person. Sometimes I think my body likes this baby more than me."
Anne clenched her hands into tight fists. "But I don't care! I really
mean that. I don't care, or rather, I care so much; sometimes I feel like
a wild woman. I'd kill anyone who tried to hurt my baby." She sighed,
running her fingers through her hair. "Philip wants nothing more than
to shut the world out and take care of us—I wish it could be like that.
But the world's not about to go away. I'm worried about everything
at once. People are acting so strange around me, staring and gawking,
asking me ridiculous questions that are none of their business. Mom,
I'm all mixed up, I don't understand what's happening."

"I wonder. Does anyone really understand?"

Anne's voice began to rise. "No, I'd guess we're pretty damn pa-
thetic right now." She stepped toward her mother, one hand rubbing
her forehead. "Sorry, Mom. I'm not mad at you, just not covering my
weakness so well. You can't imagine how tired I am."

Philip and Mark entered, each with a drink in hand. Philip put his
arm around his wife. "The lasagna is almost ready. You guys want to
eat now?"

Marylou stood up. "I'm ready whenever you are. Besides, I'm sure
that Mark is famished. He only stopped once, and that was just to get
gas."

Mark shrugged. "I was afraid we'd get caught by that storm that's
heading in. I heard you're supposed to get snow tonight."

Philip stepped to the window and looked out, expecting to see a
snow-covered field, but van lights met his eyes. "What the hell?" He
strode to the front door and yanked it open, stepping out onto the new
fallen snow.

Mark stepped out beside him. "What's going on? Those look like
reporters."

Handing his beer to Mark, Philip mumbled. "Yeah, that's what
they look like, alright. Dang it!" Philip gestured for Mark to wait and
walked up to the first van. He met two men standing outside as snow
swirled down on their bare heads. He edged up slowly. "Hey, saw you
through the window. Is there something I can help you with?"

One of the men put out his hand. "Hi, you must be Mr. Smith. I spoke to you on the phone some time ago. You probably don't remember me, but my name is Gerry—Gerry Farris, and I'm with the local news station in Centerville. I've been following up on that story I mentioned. Well, I've been doing some checking, and it turns out that your wife is one of the last pregnant women in this county. I was wondering if she was aware of that, and if I could get her reaction. Is she home? My boss," he hitched his thumb back towards another man who was now stepping forward, "would love to talk with her. I'm sure you've heard of Mr. Roberts. He's the producer of "The Newest News Show." We're doing a special on the pregnant women left in this state. A kind of follow-up piece, sharing their experiences so to speak. Oh, and you'll be compensated for your time, don't worry."

Philip opened his mouth ready with a retort, when Mr. Roberts stepped forward with his hand out. Philip did not take the bait as he appraised the sleek coat, the expensive boots, and the man's take-charge demeanor.

"Hello, Mr. Smith. I hope you'll forgive this intrusion, but we had some other interviews to do in the area, and when Gerry told me that you guys lived so close, I thought we'd just stop by and see if we could work in a little interview with your wife. If it isn't convenient now, maybe we can arrange another time."

While flakes mounted on his head and arms, Philip realized that his throat had gone dry. He swallowed and tried to speak.

Mark had edged closer and was staring at the men. "I'd better go ask Anne."

"No, don't bother. I already know what her answer will be." Philip stared at Mr. Roberts, trying to keep his breathing even. "Listen, my wife hasn't been feeling well, and she needs her rest. Her mom's visiting, and this isn't a good time. I'm not sure there's going to be a good time. We're private people, okay? She's just having a baby, for God's sake; it's not like we're hiding an alien from outer space or something." Philip stuffed his hands into his pockets. "I'm sorry, but we can't help you."

Mr. Roberts' smile was well practiced, his deep, gravelly voice calm and reassuring even as it grew a little louder. "I appreciate your position, Mr. Smith. You just want to protect your wife, and if my wife were pregnant right now, I'd feel very much the same way. But you see, I'm a reporter. I know how people get when they're worried. If you think you can keep the world away from your door, you're wrong. I know you'll find this hard to believe, Mr. Smith, but I'm here to help. If people hear what your wife has to say, there's a chance they might be satisfied and leave her alone. But if things continue to go along as they are, and she tries to go shopping, or to work, she's going to get some odd reactions. She's not safe, not the way things are now. But she can share her story and ask for respect and understanding, and maybe—just maybe—she'll get it." His gaze remained firm and focused.

Philip felt the cold seeping into his bones as his courage began to fail. "I don't know. Really, it's Anne's call, but I see your point." He turned and looked at Mark. "Mark, would you tell Anne we've got guests?" He turned back towards Mr. Roberts. "Just give him a moment, and we'll go in. You can ask her yourself."

Mr. Roberts nodded. He turned to his men. "You guys stay here. I'll go in and see what Mrs. Smith thinks. If she's okay with it, I'll call for you."

Rubbing his frozen nose, Philip mumbled, "Thanks."

Anne stood in the doorway. The light from behind put her form in a silhouette so he couldn't distinguish her features. He could only guess at how she felt.

December
SCHOOL

The steel-framed plastic chair pressed against Anne's backbone, forcing her to shift in her seat. The austerity of the principal's office offered not a particle of comfort, but Anne hadn't expected it would. She wondered how it was that she, a teacher of good standing, had been called in like a naughty child to have a conference with the principal. Rubbing her cold hands together, she tried not to stare at the imposing, polished table directly across from her.

The kids had left early, and the staff Christmas party would begin at 2:30 PM. She had always enjoyed the annual Christmas party, but this year she felt more anxious than excited. Though she had kept up with her rambunctious class and never missed a day except for a couple of doctor appointments, her reputation in the school had changed. From being a well-liked teacher and a respected colleague, she had become the center of attention and gossip. Her fifth-grade students were ten to eleven years olds, and it wasn't her job to teach them the facts of life: that job belonged to someone else. Yet recently, she had become the resident expert on pregnancies, babies, and all things having to do with human reproduction.

At first, the kids who raised their hands to ask about her baby had mystified her. She knew they were the brave, daring kids who liked to show off their audacity every chance they could, but then even the meeker kids started ranging off the topic, asking pointed, even scary questions. They wanted to know what pregnancy felt like and if she was having a boy or a girl. Then they wanted to know *how* she had become pregnant, and Anne could only blush and say that they needed to get back to the subject at hand. But the questions persisted—questions and comments, stories even. The kids started sharing about their moms' experiences with pregnancy, as if they had been discussing it recently and the memories were fresh in everyone's minds. Then things got awkward. There were questions that sounded more like accusations.

"How come you got pregnant so quick when my aunt has been trying for years?"

"What'd you do different? You got some kind of magic pill or something?"

"Can't you help my sister? She's been wanting kids a long time."

"What makes you so lucky? It's not fair."

When Anne shrugged helplessly, these kids who respected her enough to be the authority on history, science, math, and English, looked at her as if she was holding something back. Anne felt afraid of her students for the first time. They were losing their implicit trust in their all-knowing, good-hearted teacher, and it shook her.

Anne stared at the still-life painting of a fruit basket adorning the wall, undoubtedly drawn by a child, a very young child. Had it been a gift? She heard the handle turn and the door swing open as Mr. Erlandson entered the monotone, painfully Spartan room. His gray suit and gray eyes matched the room perfectly.

"Sorry, Anne, I didn't mean to keep you waiting. I just had to take care of a little matter." He strode over to his desk, hesitated, and then dragged his chair in front of Anne. He sat, leaning in, hands clasped contemplatively, his gaze locking onto Anne's eyes. "You know why I called you in, don't you?"

Where could she begin? Her hands had turned white from wringing them so hard. She didn't want to look Mr. Erlandson in the eyes, so her gazed moved to the fruit basket on the wall.

Mr. Erlandson, unfazed, was undoubtedly used to difficult conversations. "Well, Anne, it's rather simple, actually." He paused. "I'm worried about you." His tired eyes and paternal expression said more than his words. "Yes, that's pretty much the situation, isn't it? You see, Anne, I've been the principal here for almost twenty-five years, and I feel like an old grandfather to everyone, kids and teachers alike. I want the kids to get a good education and the teachers to have satisfying careers. It isn't about the money or the prestige. Good heavens, I could have moved up the ladder years ago. But no, that's not what it's all about for me. I love education, and kids, and teachers who know how to work hard and love hard. And right now, I'm having to love you pretty hard, Anne." Mr. Erlandson put his hand on Anne's trembling fingers. "I think it would be best if you didn't come back after the winter break."

Tears filled Anne's eyes. She blinked but didn't say anything.

Mr. Erlandson gave her hands a little squeeze, and then leaned back in his chair. "I was afraid this would come as a shock, but then, I thought surely you could see the problem, and I wouldn't have to spell it out."

"Problem? You mean about the baby? This isn't the 1800s, Mr. Erlandson. Women can be pregnant and still teach effectively. I've proven that. Thousands of women have proven that."

"Yes, of course, and in normal circumstances, I wouldn't be concerned. But, Anne, you know things are far from normal. The world is on edge in a way it's never experienced before." Mr. Erlandson removed his glasses and rubbed his eyes. "My God, Anne, the human race is facing extinction."

Anne gasped. Everyone was saying it. Reporters flashed it in the headlines. Cults prophesied it, but no one had said it to her face. No one she trusted and respected so much as this venerable, old man in front of her had spoken that fear out loud directly to her. Doom crawled into her mind. She must speak, but she didn't know what to say. It was the same silence she felt when her kids asked her to help a relation who wanted to get pregnant. Because she was pregnant, somehow everyone expected her to know something, to be able to fix the problem. But Anne felt helpless.

"I know. It's what people are saying, but I can't believe it. Not now, not yet! Besides, that doesn't mean I can't teach. I'm still a good teacher, Mr. Erlandson. Maybe the kids need to see that I'm not some sort of freak. I'm just a normal woman and my baby is a normal baby, just like them. Maybe they need the hope that my baby brings."

With a sigh, Mr. Erlandson tapped a pencil against his desk calendar. "I'd like to believe that, Anne. But it's not fair and frankly, it's not true, not anymore. You're not a normal woman, and your baby surely won't be just like everyone else and your hope — her hope — might be lost on us. You're set apart by circumstances, not ones you chose, but that doesn't make any difference. You're still set apart, and everyone knows it. For some reason, you've been chosen to carry a baby through one of humanity's darkest hours. I can't explain it or defend it, I can only worry and try to keep you safe."

Mr. Erlandson stood and picked a sheaf of papers off his desk. "I've already taken the liberty of discussing this matter with the school board. I've written out a temporary leave of absence for you, a medical leave so you can keep your insurance, and you'll still get your monthly check. But I can't let you keep working here. As this problem grows, people will get more panicked, and you and your baby will become the center of unwanted attention. All mothers need privacy and security. I'm giving you that. Don't reject this, Anne. I'm older than you and I've seen people in some pretty troubling situations, and they don't always act reasonably. I don't want you to get hurt, not under my watch." He paused and looked out the window. "Maybe in a year or so, we can reconsider the situation—we'll know better how things stand, okay?"

Anne stood and looked at the papers in Mr. Erlandson's hands. She took them and reached down and picked up her purse, trying to control a sudden trembling working through her body. "Can you give my apologies to everyone at the party? I think I'd better go home now."

"Why don't you stay and say goodbye? I think everyone would like that. I've heard there's even a shower planned. Don't shut them out just because I'm trying to keep you safe. They're your friends. Remember that." Mr. Erlandson attempted a reassuring pat on the arm.

"I'm not afraid of facing them. I'm afraid of crying and ruining the party. I just need to think things over." Anne looked at her principal and put out her hand. "I appreciate what you're trying to do. I'm just not sure it'll do any good."

Anne let the door shut softly behind her.

December

Last Chance Survivalist Group
Now Accepting New Members

Do you know how to grow your own food? Or treat an injury? Fix a faucet or replace a faulty electrical wire? How will you manage when there are no more electricians, carpenters, plumbers, doctors, nurses, or farmers in your area?

Everyone knows that without a next generation to carry on the skills and technology necessary to keep our lifestyle alive, the entire world is about to go through an enormous reversion back to the earliest ages of civilization. As each generation passes away, there will be fewer people to work the machines and manage the technology necessary to maintain our society. Everyone who survives these coming years will have to be more practically educated and skilled than ever before.

For those wanting to survive humanity's impending crisis, we are now beginning survivalist training and coaching on how best to prepare for an uncertain future. The LCSG has compiled resources from around the world relating to the very latest and most effective means to survive any natural or man-made disaster. We have lists of supplies you will need, the best places to get high-quality materials, classes where you can learn lifesaving CPR and other medical skills that you will need in the coming years.

The LCSG is not a religious cult prophesying doom and gloom for humanity. We are skilled laborers and professional men and women who want to share our expertise with you so that we will all be better prepared for an uncertain future.

For more information visit us on the web at xyz.LCSG. com or e-mail us at LCSG@yihaa.com. Make your future the best it can be. Join us today.

December
LOVE

Leaning against Anne's windowsill, Cerulean pondered his existence. She slept blissfully ignorant of his presence. Philip had risen early and gone to work, leaving a note that he'd be back late. The swirl of flakes as they fell from the white sky seemed to appear out of thin air. Cerulean admired the silent perfection of their simple duty, trying to shake off his anxiety by absorbing the glory of the moment.

Anne stirred in her sleep.

He turned towards her. What did she dream about? He tried to imagine her thoughts but failed. As Cerulean reached out to touch her, his heart pounded violently. He pulled his hand back to his side, realizing once again, the tremendous cost of loving deeply.

What would his father say if he were alive and could see him now? There was so much training involved in becoming a guardian that such indiscretions as falling in love with a subject were supposed to be rare. Still, he did not feel guilty, and he refused to allow it to affect his judgment. Being in love did not mean he lost his reason. He knew that Anne was married and that she loved her husband and that he had no place in her life. Cerulean merely admitted his passion to himself as a fact that he would not run from. He admired her strength and felt endeared to her weakness. He saw her struggle, and he understood the level of concentration it took for her to maintain her presence of mind. She was changing, growing. Even in the few months since he had been back, he could see how much she had altered.

Anne was no longer as selfish and single-minded as she had been. She recognized gray areas now and was more patient with other people's faults and weaknesses. He had especially admired her composure during the interview with the reporter who had asked her a series of pointed questions: "What are you going to name your baby? What do you think about the drop in pregnancy rates? How is your husband handling things? Are you getting enough support from family and friends? Will you have a natural birth? What are your plans after the baby is born? Do you have any opinion about abortion? How about cloning?"

Cerulean had stood invisibly by throughout it all. He had watched and admired Anne's calm demeanor as she fended off each question like a gladiator blocking the blows of a fierce and deadly opponent.

Anne's eyes opened and she blinked at a sudden flash of light. "What the—?"

Cerulean reappeared outside in the snow, grimacing at his near escape. Viridian sauntered up to him. They nodded to each other, and Cerulean motioned toward a grove of trees. They strolled silently toward a sheltered spot.

"It took you long enough. I've been waiting—"

Cerulean waved Viridian deeper into the woods.

Viridian cleared his throat. "I've been sent to tell you—you're needed at home."

With a deep sigh, Cerulean waited. He had been wondering when this would happen.

A sudden gust of wind blew up as Viridian shook his head. "It's no use. The human race won't survive this. I'm being sent to prepare for another planet. They're just emerging, and Sterling says that I'll find my skills better utilized."

With a nod to cover the collapse of his dream, Cerulean brushed a bit of snow off his son's shoulder. Then he touched Viridian on the chin and lifted his face toward the rising sun. His eyes narrowed. "You certainly have taken another form."

Viridian straightened his broad shoulders, a haughty gleam in his eyes. "Yeah, I'm considered pretty good-looking now. I asked for advice, and Roux suggested I take on a stronger build. He works with Olympic athletes, and he wanted me to fit in." Viridian flexed his muscled arm.

Even through the heavy leather jacket, Cerulean could see the definition of a fit young man. He stared at his son's crystal blue eyes as the boy flipped back his wavy hair and grinned. Cerulean's expression darkened. "The look fits you."

He nudged his son further into tangled wood. The black trees contrasted sharply with the white snow that speckled their bark. Old, broken trunks jutted from the hillside while branches lay strewn across each other. Gray-green moss grew thick on the old wood while prickly vines scratched at pants and unwary arms. Cerulean made a path and sat on an old log.

Viridian tucked his hands inside his coat pockets, shifting from foot to foot.

"I'll stay until the baby is born, then I'll return." Cerulean ran his fingers through his hair. "I know what they're concerned about, but they needn't worry. I won't interfere. I always knew this day might come. I won't betray anything." Cerulean shrugged. "Besides, what can they be afraid of? The human race is no threat. It never was."

Viridian leaned against a black trunk, a sneer creeping across his face. "I'm not sure they know what to expect—from you, I mean. The other guardians seem to think that you get too involved. They say there was a scandal once. You revealed yourself?"

Cerulean expression soured. "They like to talk, don't they? Besides, I had a good reason. I reported it to the council, and they agreed with me. The matter was closed."

"Closed maybe, but not forgotten. There're some who think you should leave and never come back. They're afraid you'll try to give hope where no hope lies."

Cerulean breathed heavily as he rose to his feet, his hands clenched. "There is always hope! Even if everything happens for the worst, if Anne is one of the last, if her baby grows to face a dying world, and this land sees the death of humanity—still—there is hope."

"How can you say that?" Viridian slapped his hand against a tree. "Hope? Here? Now?" The youth turned and began to mount the hill, but he stopped and looked back at his father. "You're too involved. That is what they told me, and I agree. I think you should listen and go home, now, before it's too late."

"*After* the baby's born. And then I'll come back, as I always planned."

Viridian shook his head, his hands returning to the warmth of his pockets. "Well, don't say I didn't warn you." He turned and marched away.

Cerulean stood silent and alone as a few flakes of snow swirled through the sleeping branches and landed all around him. A vision of Anne sleeping, her baby safe in her womb, tugged at his heart. "I won't abandon you." He whispered.

The snow-covered woods stood as a mute witness.

December
CHECK-UP

Once again, Anne was sitting in Dr. Evans' office but this time her brows furrowed as she realized that things had changed. Pale rectangles on the walls stood in stark contrast to the posters of the reproductive system and various ads for contraception that once hung there. Why hadn't Loren found something pretty to cover the accusing empty spaces? Perhaps they hadn't quite decided what to do with the room, much less the walls.

Dr. Evans strode through the doorway, his hands clutching a small laptop.

Warmth spread into Anne's cheeks.

When the exam was over, Dr. Evans tapped on the keyboard as he spoke. "Well, you look in the peak of health, though I'd like to run a couple of extra tests, just to be on the safe side."

Scrunching her face, Anne chuckled. "Everyone's so worried about me, though everyone has to admit, I'm just fine." She paused, mustering her courage. "What kind of tests?"

"Oh, nothing unusual, just some blood tests, double check your sugar levels, heart check, an extra ultrasound, of course."

"Doctor, I know you mean well, but I don't think that's going to help."

Dr. Evans looked up from his notes. "Hmm, what's that?" He peered at Anne over the rim of his glasses.

Anne laughed and then tried to make her voice sound convincing. "You can do all the tests in the world, but it won't make you feel any better. You won't know why I'm pregnant and other women aren't. It'll just be a waste of time and money."

Dr. Evans adjusted his glasses and put down his pen. He leaned against the counter. "Tell me then, what can I do to help?"

Anne shrugged and pointed to her shoes. "Can I put them back on?"

Nodding, Dr. Evans bent down to retrieve them. "May I?" He helped to slip the right shoe onto her foot.

Blushing, Anne took the other shoe he was holding. "Thanks." She tried to make the laborious process, which felt more like advanced acrobatics, look easier than it was. "Really, Dr. Evans, you're doing great, there's nothing more you can do. Everyone seems to think that because I'm pregnant, I've got answers. I don't. More tests won't help. I feel fine, the baby's fine, and if I don't go falling down any more stairs, we should live through the next few months without any problems. But worry sure isn't helping. You know, even my principal ordered me to take a leave of absence. For my own good, of course."

Dr. Evans returned to his laptop and continued typing notes. "Well, I have to agree with him. I think that was a smart move, and I'm happy you're off the streets and away from any trouble." Dr. Evans stopped typing. Tucking the laptop under his arm, he gazed at Anne. "Listen, Anne, you're young and you're just starting this parenthood journey. I've been a father for a lot of years, and I'll tell you, I never lived through such hell as the months when I didn't know what had happened to Carrie. It was like a part of my heart was being strangled. I can't describe it, but I wouldn't wish that feeling on my worst enemy." He sighed. "You'll never regret taking good care of your baby. If you miss out on her life, if you take risks and something goes wrong, you'll hate yourself. Trust me, there's nothing so hard to bear as regrets, especially about your kids."

Anne scooted gingerly off the exam table. "So how's your daughter doing?"

"Oh, she's fine. Had some wild stories to tell, some of which might have been a tad exaggerated." His eyebrows rose, "but for the most part it was a pretty tough experience. She wasn't treated badly, thank God, but she could have been, and I think she knows that. The world's not a safe place. And when things blow up, innocent people get hurt."

After pushing her arms into her coat sleeves, Anne attempted to button it. "You don't think she should quit trying to help people, do you? I mean, she was there to help, right?"

"No, her ideals are wonderful, but I guess she'll think twice next time about the risk involved. You know, some people wouldn't mind blowing up the world, themselves included."

Anne gave up on the last button and stuffed her hands in her pockets. "Yeah, I suppose. Though I can't help admiring her spirit. Your daughter has the right attitude."

Dr. Evans scribbled on a notepad. "I'll see you in two weeks. And we'll do another ultrasound if anything worries me."

In a silent truce, Anne accepted the paper with a nod.

Dr. Evans smiled his goodbye and began to walk away.

Anne turned toward the front desk, shaking her head. Did Dr. Evans have any idea how much he and his daughter had in common?

January
CLUELESS

Chewing his lip with a shiver down his back, Philip stood outside the bathroom door, knocking violently. "Anne, are you ready yet?" He glanced at his watch, a warning tone in his voice. "Everyone'll be here soon."

Anne mumbled, "I'm coming! I'm coming! You have no idea how hard everything is now. I feel like a blimp trying to put on a wet suit."

Philip's mouth felt too dry to laugh. "Well, that may be, but my mom's not known for her patience and my sisters really want to see you. They made a point of asking about you. You're the star of the show, you know."

"Oh, dang it, Philip! You know your mom and sisters don't even *like* me. They tolerate me okay, but they're not coming all this way to check on me, they're coming to get front-line gossip. Oh heck…. Do you think anyone would notice if I came down in my pajamas?"

Philip rubbed his face and then scanned the room. A crumpled mess of clothes covered the chair. "Hey, your jumper would work. Why not try that?" He went over and pulled the jumper out of the pile and tried to smooth down the wrinkles.

Anne's voice came from behind the closed door. "I've been wearing that for days. It's comfortable but not too clean. Oh, yeah, your mom would love that! Go look in my closet. Millie brought over a bag of stuff from her daughter the other day, and I never went through it. See if there's anything in there."

Striding to the closet, Philip yanked out the overstuffed shopping bag and dumped the contents onto the bed. He sifted through it and with a relieved smile, walked back to the bathroom, jerked open the door, and held out a dark green jumper with a matching long sleeved sweater. "Here, this should work. See if it fits and get out of there." Exiting, he whined over his shoulder, "You know how hard I have to work to make conversation with them. I wish it was your family coming over, not mine." His steps echoed down the stairway.

A few minutes later, the doorbell rang. Anne cringed and frantically combed out her hair, hoping to braid it before Philip called for her again.

Standing ramrod straight, Philip plastered on a smile, pulled open the front door, and faced his family. His father, James Smith, his mother, Caroline, and his two sisters, Susie and Jackie, stood shivering on the porch. Jackie glowered in a black leather jacket, while Susie sparkled in white faux furs. Philip cracked his smile as he waved them forward.

"Hey, come on in. It's cold out there! Here let me take your coats." He led his family toward the living room, pausing only to unceremoniously drop their things in the side room. He returned to find them huddled in the middle of the room.

With shoulders back, Philip marched toward his dad, his hand out stretched like a gauntlet. "Hey, Dad, how was the drive?"

Mr. Smith, a tall heavy-set man with jet-black hair and swollen features, accepted his son's hand and let it be pressed. With a twisted grin and a quick glance at his wife, his voice boomed, "Well, your mother was afraid the weather wasn't going to cooperate, but I told her we could charge through just fine. I checked the weather report; everything looks clear for the next week or so. Besides, it's been too long."

There was nothing else Philip could do but nod agreeably. His frozen smile still in place, he shifted toward his mother.

Caroline waved an imperious hand. "You don't happen to have something hot to drink, do you, Philip? My hands are freezing. Your father keeps telling me that I should dress for the weather, but there aren't clothes made to keep out this kind of cold. Really, couldn't you have moved somewhere a little more temperate?"

"It's not always this cold here, Mother. Besides, I wouldn't exactly call Florida temperate, at least not in the summer."

He turned again and swept his gaze over his sisters. "Hi Jackie, Susie, how are you two? I'll fix Mom some hot tea; you want some?"

Susie's eyes lit up as she waved her brother off. With her fashionably blunt cut blond hair, bright blue eyes, and a bubbling personality, she practically defined charming. Taking efficient control, she crooned, "Here, let me get it. Mom's got very specific tea needs. You don't happen to have any stevia, do you? She hates Twice-As-Sweet and wouldn't be caught dead eating real sugar. I'd love to sneak a peek at the kitchen; always getting new ideas that way, don't you know."

Philip practically staggered under the onslaught of his sister's niceness. "No... we've only got real stuff, but maybe brown sugar would work? It's not very strong, and I hear it doesn't make you fat."

Behind him, Philip could hear Jackie's snort. "Ha! Sounds like something Anne would say." Jackie, a slim, tanned, and dark haired specimen of womanly beauty pursed her lips as she scanned the room. "Where is she? I've been dying to see her. She huge yet?"

Philip's eyes narrowed as he nodded. "Yeah, she's gotten pretty big, or rather, the baby has."

Caroline sat upright on the sofa, her back ramrod straight and her unwavering gaze scrutinizing every detail of the room's décor. "I like the way you've decorated, Philip. Early American?"

Philip turned to lead Susie to the kitchen. "Yeah, early something. Anne picks things up from the local antique stores. I just go along to lift and carry."

Susie pinched her brother's shoulder and motioned toward the kitchen. "Lead on, Philip. Mom can't go too long without her tea or she turns into a dragon."

Philip braced himself and led the way.

Knowing that an escape to the outer regions of the galaxy was not an option, Anne crept down the stairs, appraising the scene before she made her appearance.

James had plunked himself on the couch beside his wife, forcing her to adjust her seat so that she didn't sink in his direction.

Jackie stalked around the room, arms folded across her chest, inspecting the pictures on the walls. Her eyes instantly brightened as Anne stepped into the room. "Well, there you are! I was wondering if you were ever going to show yourself."

Anne plodded forward. "Oh, it just takes me a while. You have no idea how challenging the simplest things have become! Just getting shoes on is a major ordeal. A baby changes everything."

Jackie's good humor disappeared. "I suppose. I'll never know, will I?"

Anne blinked, stunned by the bitter tone. She forced a turn toward James, who had grunted noisily to his feet to greet his daughter-in-law. Anne waddled over to him and took his hand and then looked to Caroline who remained sitting. "I'm happy you were able to come. Philip's been looking forward to seeing you and showing you around the place." Out of the corner of her eye, she could see Jackie appraising her pregnant body. Anne swallowed. "You've never been here before, have you?"

James plopped onto the couch again. "Nope, it's too far for us. We don't like going long distances and this is a quite a hike." He shifted his weight and stammered, "But then again, it's never too far to visit family!" With rapid breaths, he hurried on, "Caroline's been so anxious about you and the baby. We would've come sooner but—"

Caroline put up her hand. "We hardly wanted to add stress to an already difficult situation. But Philip assures me you're doing well, so this seemed like a good time." Caroline surveyed Anne's strained features. "Please, sit down, dear."

As Anne perched on the edge of the nearest chair, she noticed Jackie's face twitch in expectation. Anne pictured lions at feeding time.

Caroline interceded. "You do look well—considering." She paused before adding, "Philip tells me that you've quit your job. Do you think that's wise? Teaching positions are hard to come by, so many teachers and all."

Anne clasped her hands about her round tummy and shrugged. "It wasn't really my choice. My principal thought that I'd do better to stay home for the duration. He's like a grandfather; he worries a lot." She braved a smile through an awkward silence.

Jackie sat on the arm of the sofa by her mother. "So, you'll start up again in the fall then?"

Anne sighed. "I'm not really sure. I took a leave of absence, and at first I assumed I would go back, next year, maybe. But lately, I've been thinking about staying at home and never going back. It might be kind of fun, you know, being a homemaker. Philip makes enough, so there's no worry there."

Jackie's face pinched in disapproval and wagged her finger. "You'll be bored within a month, I guarantee it. You're used to doing what you like, when you like, and babies are no joke, let me tell you. My friend, Karen, had two and lived to rue it. They slept in her bed, interrupted her every move, and got sick every time she turned around. It was a full-time nightmare." She stretched her skinny, jean clad legs. "Besides, you'll only have one and when it goes to school you'll have nothing to do. You don't want to lose your position, Anne. Think about your future. I agree with Mom, you should keep your foot in the door, at least."

Masking her feelings behind the barest "hmmm" possible, Anne found relief in tapping her fingers together. She barely acknowledged Philip when he and Susie reentered the room with a tray.

Philip glanced at Anne and then carried the tray over to a side table. He took a steaming cup of tea and offered it to his mother and then looked toward Jackie. "You want one?"

Jackie cleared her throat and waved him off. "Not a tea person. Thanks."

Susie picked up the other cup. "Here's your coffee, Dad. Philip likes the good stuff too, so don't worry." She handed her father the hot mug.

James grinned as he accepted it. "Oh, good. I didn't want to ask. I was afraid you drank that swill people call instant." He took a sip and sighed his satisfaction. "Yes, this will do. Thank you, my dear."

Philip darted another glance at Anne. "Well, if you'll excuse us, we should see about dinner. Anne's got everything just about ready; we just need to check the oven." Seeing Anne labor to get up off the chair, Philip stepped over and lent her a hand. He leaned in. "You alright? They'll love what you've cooked up."

Anne nearly snorted at the irony of her being the evening's main course. "I'm fine. It'll just take me a minute." She pressed his arm as she stood. "You stay with your family, they've come all this way to see *you*."

Philip swallowed, watching her waddle out of the room. He sighed.

Susie moved in and put her arm around his shoulder. "Don't worry, little brother. She'll be all right. Anne's tough. No matter what people say, she hasn't done anything wrong. It's not like getting pregnant is a crime or anything."

Philip stared at his sister and shrugged her arm away, "What does that mean? Course it's not a crime. Who said it was?"

Jackie sprang off the couch arm. "Well, there are those who wonder how you two managed it when no one else can."

Philip glared at Jackie. "You've got to be kidding! We were blessed with a child. Why are you making it out like we *did* something? We didn't *do* anything but make love, like every other mother and father in this whole d—" Philip caught himself and struggled to regain his composure. He took a long breath. "Listen, we've been interrogated by the best. Reporters, Anne's doctor, my co-workers, even people on the street stop us and ask *how we managed it*. But listen to me, and listen really well, because I don't want you giving Anne a hard time, we didn't *do* anything! Babies are—" Philip groped for words, "Damn it, why is this so hard? Babies are gifts. That's all. I can't explain it. I don't decide who gets them and who doesn't. We were lucky. Lots of other people deserve one just as much. But it wasn't exactly our choice."

Jackie sidled up closer. "But that's exactly what it was—a choice. Babies are a choice and you made yours. Frankly, I don't understand what all the fuss is about. Most women don't even want to get pregnant, and if that guy out east can figure out how to clone us, so much the better. One way to rid the world of trouble and pain."

"You'd have babies conceived in test tubes, grown in factories like robots, wouldn't you, Jackie? Just go in and pick out the color and size you like and let someone else take care of the messy stuff. God, what a world we'd live in if you had your way!"

Caroline put up her hand. "Stop it, you two. I was afraid of this. You never could get along." Her frown focused on Philip. "But, Philip, you're going to have to do something about Anne. She's not going to be able to handle everything. That's why I came, really. I enjoy talk shows and I know what people are interested in. Right now there's an absolute obsession with pregnant women. Some people are a little unscrupulous. They might even try to barge in when she's in labor. I'm not trying to be crude, but I've heard some of these women talk and they're pretty far-gone. You better take care, Philip. Anne could get hurt." She looked him straight in the eye. "Have you ever considered adoption? I mean, there are a lot of people who'd take the baby in a heartbeat and then you'd be free. I'd love to be one of those mothers, who coos at you and assures you that you're very blessed, and perhaps in some eyes you are, but I'm afraid that's a shortsighted outlook. Really, you have no idea what your life is going to be like from now on."

Philip's hands balled into fists, his face frozen stiff with impotent fury.

Anne waddled back into the still, tense room. Everyone's gaze centered on her. "What?" She looked down at her clothes. "Did I spill something?"

Jackie's sarcasm gave vent to her fury. "You are so clueless, Anne, it's not even funny."

New Now
Democrats and Republicans Reaching Across the Aisle

At this climax in human history, leading Democrats and Republicans are reaching across the aisle to embrace an uncertain future. Though specialized UN committees have not yet reached a consensus as to the best way to approach the decline in birthrates, they have decided that further research and analysis to decipher the cause and effect of the immediate situation should be considered. Already hospitals all across the nation and around the world have been forced to shut down their prenatal and birthing departments and mothball all plans for expansion. Doctors are looking into furthering research into geriatric care so as to prolong life expectancy another 10 to 20 years. Brain research departments have been given extra funding to consider such options as uploading human personalities into data banks that can be retrieved at a later date. NASA has upped its efforts to discover if there is any alien influence acting in this unprecedented period in human history.

"There is no point in arguing about who is right and who is wrong," said leading Democrat Fred Haley in a January 12th press conference, "just so we can solve this problem and get things moving in the right direction again. We need to work together and stop trying to find fault. This is a humanitarian crisis of the first order and humanity must work together to face it."

His words were applauded and echoed by leading Republicans who also called for a cease-fire in all contentious issues. "With the exception of abortion," said leading Republican Max Martin. "We are facing the extinction of the human race and the last thing we need to do is kill off the last of our kind through voluntary murder. Republicans have always supported the view that all life is sacred, from conception to natural death, and now that there have been no new recorded pregnancies for months, it seems clear that there are no 'unwanted babies.' Democrats can reach across the aisle all they want. They just can't go back and give us back the population we lost through all the years of legal abortion."

Despite some protests, Republican Martin's views were met with approval by a prominent group of Democrats while Rights for Women groups have vigorously protested any infringement on their freedoms. "After all, when all is said and done, how do we want to face our end? By demeaning women? Don't you think that women are capable of making the best choice not only for themselves, but for society as well? If you don't think women are capable of even that level of intelligence, well then, there isn't much worth saving, now is there?" said Sandra S. Glick, president of Women for Women Forever.

Some extremist groups are insisting that this crisis is a judgment of God for the sins of humanity. One group, Save Humanity Now, even proposes that any women found to be pregnant should be separated from the general public to offer them and their babies the best possible chance of survival. In their view, all children born during this crisis should become wards of the state.

For now, though the rhetoric is about union and solidarity, it seems that there are still a variety of opinions about how best to come together.

City Sources
Doomsday Event

Bombs have exploded in twenty-four cities around the world in recent months, foreshadowing what some are calling the Doomsday Event. Various extremist groups have banded together and formed what is being dubbed the Atonement Society. Their premise is that God has judged a sinful humanity and condemned it to extinction. The Atonement Society's creed includes the belief that only through a severe purging can the human race redirect the hand of God. The AS also includes the thinking of a variety of secularists who say that though they do not believe God is behind the sudden loss of fertility, they do believe that humanity needs to be "purged of unwanted elements." First listed for purging is the nation-state of Israel, then the Vatican, followed by various sects of both Islamic and Christian groups, the Atheist's Society, women's groups, pro-life advocates, abortion supporters, and militant minority groups. The list is as varied as its members, and those who are being targeted are faced with the same fate as their enemies: instantaneous annihilation.

The AS is still a relatively small fringe group with only limited financial support, but the public should stay alert for further news bulletins and report any suspicious behavior to your local authorities.

Psychoanalysts and cultural observers, as well as diplomats and leaders from various European, African, and Asian nations are condemning the AS's behavior as the actions of madmen. Psychologists are noting that under severe stress, people will attempt to find someone to blame. By destroying those perceived at fault, they hope to release themselves from their fears. It is also known as the "scapegoat effect." Researchers have applied the term Doomsday Event to such radical beliefs since the outcome of such thinking will just as certainly destroy humanity as the fate they are trying to elude.

February
CHANCES

Alone in the dark, silent medical lab, Greg sat at his desk and gazed at the whiskey bottle in his hand. A hard smack against the windows, a gust of wind blowing wet snow, snapped him back to reality.

Night already?

He poured himself another glass, propped his head on his hand, and took a sip. His gaze shifted, falling on the graphs before him. He grimaced. Slapping the glass down, he picked up one of the papers, leaned back in his chair, and studied it. He took another drink, slammed the paper down and leaned over his desk. Tracing his finger over his laptop's scroll pad, he brought up another page. He stared at it, rubbed his eyes, and swore. "There's no connection! Damn it; there's no pattern at all!"

The door opened and Mike shuffled into the room. "Hey, Greg, it's late. You should go home and get some rest." He paused. "We have an important meeting in the morning. You want to be fresh, right?"

Greg snorted.

Edging closer, Mike looked down at his friend. "How many of those have you had?"

"Not enough, not nearly enough." Greg leaned back in his chair again. "I still can't see what's happening, and I've been trying for months. I've tried everything: research, reports, I've sifted through piles of articles from doctors all over the world. I've conducted so many bloody experiments, I should be getting a blasted Nobel Prize for my efforts, but I come up with the same thing: cloning works, sometimes, on some animals, but never on humans. There's no rhyme or reason to it. Mistakes are running rampant. Mass insanity is hitting labs all over the world." Greg tipped over his empty glass with an emphatic gesture. "I've done all this stone sober." He picked up the fallen glass and lifted it, "So now I'm trying to get drunk enough to help me think. Maybe if I see a few pink elephants, I can make sense out of all this." He flipped his fingers through the loose papers.

Pulling up a chair, Mike sat next to his friend. As if in respect to the tomb-like quiet of the environment, he kept his voice low. "You're making yourself crazy and that's not going to help anybody. We don't have the answers we want, but we have a lot more information than we had before. All this research is helping. We know that human cloning has failed systematically, but animal cloning is still relatively effective. There must be a reason. We just need to figure out the core difference, and we'll be able to move forward."

"Core difference? What does that mean? Even animal cloning has become erratic. One doctor is able to affect a perfect clone but another doctor following the same procedure, even in the same office, isn't able to get the same result. You know scientific theory—if the experiment isn't reproducible—it isn't viable evidence. It's as if some giant cloning god has taken the puzzle and thrown the pieces to the wind, and just when we think we've got them all back in order, we discover that he ate a few."

Chuckling, Mike eyed the half-empty bottle. "That's pretty good. Remember that for tomorrow's meeting. The reporters will eat it up."

With an irritated wave, Greg poured himself another drink. "No, not me. I'm not going to that meeting." He saluted his friend with his drink. "You think I'll stand there in front of a pack of reporting zombies and try to appease the masses by saying I don't know why cloning isn't working—go ask the gods?" He snorted. "Yeah, that'd be about right." He took a large swallow.

Mike sighed and reached for the bottle. "I think I'll take this for a while. After all, you might really start seeing pink elephants, then where would we be?"

"Bring on the elephants! Hell, I could handle an elephant better than another rat." Greg attempted to stand but lost his footing and lurched to the side. He gripped the desk. "Damn it. I want a baby! I don't care about rats and elephants. I want a baby! God above, I can't even make a multi-celled fetus!" Greg's voice broke. He tried to snatch back the bottle.

Mike let it smash to the ground. Neither of them reacted to the splintering crash.

Greg rubbed his hands across his numbed face. Swallowing hard he could hear the beseeching cry in his own voice. "I can't save them!"

"No, maybe you can't. But don't kill yourself over it." Mike circled around the desk, stepping wide of the broken bottle and reached for his friend. "I know just the place for you. My wife is the best cook in the country, and I'm pretty sure she can fix you a little something that will make life worth living again."

Greg nodded, allowing himself to be drawn away from his desk. "Damn it, I took up swearing again, think she'll mind?"

With his arm around Greg's shoulder, Mike led his colleague along. "Oh, I think she can handle it okay."

In the morning, Greg woke up with a groan. He ran to the bathroom, and after a series of retches and flushes, he returned to the bed and flopped down. When Mike walked into the room, Greg threw his hands over his face. "How big of an ass did I make of myself?"

"Not too noticeable." Mike came and stood by the bed, a change of clothes in his hands. "These will be a mite too big, but it's the best I could do. We need to leave pretty soon, so heave ho, if you don't mind."

"Oh, Lord! Don't say the word *heave*, please, I beg you."

Mike grinned and shook his head as he walked out of the room. "Five minutes, Dr. Peterson."

Greg's assent was barely audible.

An hour and a half later, a team of doctors and researchers sat at a large table in a nondescript boardroom fielding questions from a phalanx of reporters. Photographers took pictures while the doctors attempted to maintain their assured demeanor. Finally, a reporter directed a question to Dr. Peterson.

"Dr. Peterson, you are one of the country's foremost cloning researchers. What's your take on current events? Can we reverse the drop in fertility, or is there any possibility that cloning will become the next viable form of human reproduction?"

Blinking in the glare of strong lights, Dr. Peterson rubbed his jaw. "Yes, to both questions. I believe we can reverse the fertility drop, but it will require a better understanding of human genetics to do so. Cloning is a workable solution, but even that has limits. As generations of humans are cloned, the genetic variations will decrease and thus the very mutations we usually think of as potential problems actually become the source of our strength. Without enough variation, a single disease could wipe out an entire generation of clones. We'll need to add to our genetic bank, so to speak. Everything we learn about human fertility will assist us to clone better and everything we learn about cloning will help us understand fertility better. Though they are two very different processes, we need to focus on the link, the commonalities, between the two."

Another reporter jumped in with a follow-up question. "Why do you say that, Dr. Peterson? Why must they be linked? One is concerned with a biological union between a man and a woman while the other is a matter of copying DNA code. What kind of link are you looking for?"

"I am looking for any kind of link that will explain what's going on. As human fertility has dropped, so cloning has begun to fail. We can clone certain animals but only erratically. We can still clone particular cells for the purpose of regenerating limbs, but for reasons we cannot explain, our experiments on human cloning have begun to fail, and we can no longer create a viable fetus. So you see, to have both fail at approximately the same time, suggests a link. I want to find that link and solve this mystery—before we run out of time."

A stunned silence permeated the room before another reporter threw out a question aimed at a different doctor. Dr. Peterson rose to his feet, his shoulders slumped. He inched his way toward the door.

A reporter stopped him. "Dr. Peterson, before you go, what do you think of humanity's chances of surviving the next hundred years?"

Dr. Peterson stared back at the room full of listeners. "Unless I can get back to work, not so good." As his image and words were soberly recorded, he turned and swept out of the room.

14

February
CHURCH

The slanting afternoon light poured in through the stained glass windows, adding a golden color to the white walls of the small church. Anne hadn't known what to expect when she decided to stop. The outdoor sign boldly written in neat gothic letters, St. Anne's Catholic Church, quite literally had her name written on it. She felt destiny called, but as she surveyed the interior, she felt weak and dizzy. The wooden pews stood in rigid rows, a solemn testimony to the parishioners, who came and sat there, listening, watching, and praying.

Raised to think for herself, Anne had grown up separated from any detailed knowledge of religious creeds. She vaguely remembered mysterious scenes from her childhood when her parents attended Mass. If anyone asked, they would say they were Catholic, like her grandparents, though Anne saw little evidence that the creed mattered much in their daily lives. She didn't know how far back her roots clung to the old religion, for she had never inquired, and her mother rarely spoke about her religious beliefs.

Marylou used to recount stories about renowned ancestors who lived in the long, dim past: a heroic legend named Aram and a descendant of his named Georgios, who sojourned to the Celtic isles. There was even a renowned Briton named Melchior, who had a famous son, but they were just tales meant to inspire young minds. As it was now, Anne felt neither young nor inspired. The thread tying her to the ancients had snapped long ago.

Peering to the right, Anne saw the little, red light above the door. She knew that signified that someone knelt in confession to the priest. Anne shivered. She would never go in there. Her problem was not guilt but confusion. No man in the world could seriously hope to understand a pregnant woman standing on the edge of a dying world.

Anne stepped forward, and clutching the back of pew, she slid onto a smooth seat. She bumped the kneeler with her toe and wondered about protocol, but then rubbing her aching back she put that thought aside. Why did they kneel anyway? Surveying the altar, she noticed directly behind it, the ornate gold box that housed the Host, the tabernacle, her mother had called it. She knew what they thought: there lies the presence of God on Earth. Anne wanted to smile, but tears came to her eyes. Why was this so difficult? Why had she even come?

Anne leaned against the pew and gazed toward the ceiling. Mighty, sword-wielding angels painted on the ceiling made the tears flow. She brushed them away with one hand and stared up. Why did the image of a golden warrior-angel bring a lump to her throat? The groan that swelled up from her depth startled her. She knew. It was the very idea of a glorious being coming to her rescue, saving her and her baby from a hideous fate. Oh God! Why was *she* pregnant? Why was everyone suffering so? She wanted her baby to live, but her hopes and dreams were smashed to bits every time she realized that her child had no future. What kind of life could her baby have with everyone dying off and no new generation to continue the race? Anne covered her face with her hands and tried to stem the heaving sobs that racked her chest.

As she sat there, the perplexed, desperate face of a young woman in the grocery store came to mind. She had parked her shopping cart in front Anne as Anne had tried to decide which kind of chips she wanted. The young woman's cart contained only a few items, and she wasn't looking at the shelves. She was staring at Anne's protruding belly. When Anne grabbed the corn chips, she had noticed the woman's expression. She tried to smile, to pass off the awkward moment with a laugh. "Sorry, am I in your way?" The woman had shaken her head and started talking. Fast.

She related her life story, how she had been married for three years and how she and her husband had wanted children right away. He was a farmer, and they cultivated over five hundred acres. They owned a big house and had plenty of money. Both their parents were looking forward to grandchildren.

Anne felt as if the woman was trying to sell her something, as if she was trying to pitch her perfection for motherhood. She didn't know what to say. The woman never said her name, just talked on and on about her hopes for a family, breathlessly, relentlessly. Anne couldn't get past her cart or her steady stream of words.

Suddenly, a middle-aged woman rolled her cart near and wanted to pass. Anne saw her chance; she backed up and turned around. After mumbling, "Have a nice day!" she left. She didn't even finish her shopping. She just wanted to get out of the store as soon as possible. But she knew that when she got home there would be phone calls, visitors, and a steady stream of interruptions until Philip came and blocked out the world for a while. She couldn't even read her mail or check her email without being reminded of her fate. The look on the young woman's face, the frantic efforts to explain her position, how suited she was for motherhood, how she deserved it, left Anne emotionally drained.

She closed her eyes in the quiet church. The click of the door signaled that the parishioner had exited the confessional. Looking around, she noticed that now only one other person waited in line. Parishioners were beginning to filter into the pews. Anne checked her watch. Mass would begin in fifteen minutes. She didn't want to stay, but she didn't want to leave either. She felt safe here. She watched as an old woman came down the aisle. The matron wore a conservative blue skirt, a neat blouse, and a scarf around her gray curls. She stepped up to a front pew and then, staring straight ahead, she said something under her breath and bowed so formally that Anne was taken aback. It was like a scene out of movie, so powerful that there should have been soaring thematic music. But people don't bow to a box, do they? Catholics might, she remembered. She felt awed by that stately bow. The door clicked again and the last person left the confessional.

The overhead lights came on and the church was filled with a bright glare, illuminating the statues and icons. Anne resented the intrusion. It had been so peaceful, so calm, and beautiful. She stood and moved out of the pew. Stopping a moment, she wondered if she should genuflect, but it felt awkward, and being so big now, she wasn't sure she could get back up without falling off balance. She took another step and felt an odd hesitation, like when she had steered her cart away from the woman in the store. She knew she'd been rude, but she didn't know what else to do. She waddled to the back of the church, wrapping her winter coat more tightly around her expanding middle, and pushed open the heavy oak door. She stepped out into the cold air, admiring the beauty of the evening light as it slanted across the churchyard. The trees were bare and black against a gray sky, stately in their naked simplicity.

Moving aside as parishioners began to mount the church steps, a few looked her way, but most seemed more intent on pushing their way through the winter cold than anything else. She lumbered to the small parking lot across the street and was just about to get in her car, when a voice behind her spoke.

"Linda's leading the Rosary today. For all the good it'll do. You'd think if anyone was listening things would've changed by now." Two middle-aged women moved passed the row of cars. The faint murmur, "Why won't God hear us?" ringing in Anne's ear.

Good question. Surely all these faithful people were honest worshippers. Yet He had not answered their prayers, at least not the way they wanted. Anne shrugged. She wasn't sure what she believed. If God didn't hear the prayers of the faithful, He wasn't likely to hear hers. Heaviness settled on her chest as she got in her car and drove home.

February

Mike's Debatable Blog
Guess We're Not God

I've been blogging for several years now, and I always enjoy the variety of responses I get from readers. As you know, I usually throw out some kind of debatable question, offer a few positions, and then let you take it from there. I'm no coward who shrinks from tough issues. I've tackled such monsters as abortion, homosexuality, pornography, child abuse, the debt, and sticky international and foreign policy issues. So you know, generally speaking, that nothing surprises me. That is—until yesterday.

I proposed a question, which I am sure has been weighing on a lot of minds lately: "Has God abandoned us?" Now for me, the question isn't merely rhetorical. I believe in God, and I really want to know what you think. So I threw out some opposing opinions I've heard from family and friends and even a guy I met in the elevator last week. I mentioned how some people are saying that God has nothing to do with the fertility issue, it's purely a scientific puzzle, and medical researchers are going to have to figure out the answers for us. Some people feel that God is warning us because we have been living immoral lives, kind of like the Israelites of old who always got in trouble when they started hanging out with false gods and summarily got annihilated in battle or sold into slavery. Some people are attempting to downplay the infertility issue. They say this whole thing is a publicity stunt created by the government to distract us from other issues. Crazy, eh? Others are claiming this is the end of the world; God just surprised us—not by coming

93

after us with thunder and lightning, but by letting us come to Him, one by one, in silence.

Being such a pertinent question, with so much controversy surrounding it, I expected a thousand comments this morning. But to my amazement, there was only a handful. Two people wanted to know why I bothered to ask an unanswerable question. Another person said I was working for the devil trying to scare everyone. There was a dating service ad offering me unlimited pleasure if I signed on today. And one—get this—only one person actually wrote a serious, thoughtful reply.

It was a doctor from India. He said that though he wasn't a believer in the one God as Jews, Christians, and Muslims were (he is Buddhist, by the way), he said that he knew there were forces in the universe that far surpass his understanding. He believed that all life was a gift, even though he could not name the giver. Pure reason led him to believe that no one had to give gifts forever and that to assign guilt or blame to the giver for not continuing a long-standing pattern showed a lack of reason and bloated pride. He believed that the kindness of the past did not bind one to a slavery of gift giving. Whoever had given humanity the gift of fertility had offered us a gift whether we deserved it or not. Now that same force was withdrawing that gift, whether we deserved it or not. So, in his mind, it was not useful to question or debate the point. What was useful was to appreciate the gifts we still had.

So now, I am sitting here at my desk wondering if this guy from India sees better than all the doctors and researchers and ranting talk-show hosts. In his simplicity, does he see the honest truth? That there is a gift giver, I call Him God, you can call Him what you like, and He stopped giving for a reason we can't understand, and that having fits and tantrums isn't going to help.

But now I am left with a sinking feeling that there is nothing we can do. The only fun in debating an issue is to come to some understanding so that we can hope to do something to make matters better. For once, I feel completely powerless to debate the issue, which is why I think I had such a lack of response. You feel it too, don't you? If fertility really is a gift from God, then all we can say for sure is: Guess we're not God.

March

ConnectUs Post
Jobs Today

Looking for a job? There are a lot of opportunities if you know where to look. But one temptation is to think that tradition will keep jobs open despite a world in flux. As the population crisis develops, future employment opportunities have been adjusted. Though certain fields will still grow for some time—think geriatrics, home health care, & nursing—there are significant numbers of career options which may be extinguished within the next few years. For example: midwives, labor coaches, nannies, prenatal nurses, & preschool teachers are all professions on the verge of extinction. There are a lot of changes going on in the world—make sure you aren't caught preparing for a career that doesn't exist.

Jobs Are Our Business—Find us at: jobsfortoday.com

15

MARY'S BIRTHDAY

Anne jostled Philip awake. It was time. The contractions were coming regularly, and she wasn't sure how long before the baby would arrive. Instantly alert, Philip rushed around getting everything packed in the car and drove like such a demon that Anne was half amused and half frightened out of her wits. But when they finally jerked to a stop in the parking lot, all amusement fled as a whole battalion of nurses and doctors met them at the hospital entrance. She could have been the Queen of England giving birth to the heir to the throne the way everyone acted. Anne dutifully changed into a white gown, monitors were attached, and every contraction was recorded with serious attention. An intravenous tube was put into her arm, and she was told to rest until they had determined that everything was all right with the baby.

It seemed like hours before she was able to get up and walk around, but all too soon she didn't feel like walking anymore, and before she knew what was happening, she felt sicker than she had ever felt in her life. The power of those contractions amazed and alarmed her. She began to seriously admire her mother and every woman who had ever given birth. Dr. Evans had given her the option of taking pain medication, but he advised her to go as natural as possible to avoid complications. Knowing that the baby's health mattered more than anything, she decided that she could handle whatever came her way, but when the contractions got mean, she began to question her decision.

Philip stroked her arm and encouraged her. "You're doing great, honey, keep it up."

Anne, sweating fiercely, wanted to tell Philip to take a flying leap when Daisy, the head nurse, leaned in and looked her in the eye. "When I tell you, push like an Olympic medalist. You can do this, Anne."

Anne took the experienced nurse at her word, and the baby was born a few moments later. Relief flooded through Anne's body. As soon as they laid her baby on her breast, all memory of the pain vanished. She just stared at her baby and smiled weakly. She was too exhausted to cry. The baby fussed and then snuggled its bare body against her bare chest. Anne thought she would die of happiness.

A few hours later, exhausted and exhilarated all at the same moment, Anne lay back on her hospital bed, holding her precious sleeping bundle and reviewed the last few hectic days.

Millie had come for tea and regaled Anne with stories of her first baby, Tim, named after her husband's brother. She had recalled how she worked around the house during her early contractions and only when she couldn't distract herself anymore, had she finally decided to go to the hospital. Millie could have had a home birth, but Bernard was squeamish and insisted that she go to the hospital, which was fine with Millie.

Anne smiled, remembering Millie's placid expression as she recounted her birthing experiences. She said it hurt like heck, but then God blessed her with amnesia the moment she saw little Tim's face. Millie's eyes had glistened when she said, "Children are worth every bit of suffering you go through." Patting Anne's hand, Millie had sipped her tea, sitting upright on the couch.

During that glorious afternoon, Anne had silenced her phone, turned off the computer, and sunk back onto the couch cushions, reveling in the expectation of seeing her baby soon. Millie had nibbled on homemade, chocolate-chip cookies and shared her memories, joking about the early days, and how it had been a miracle her children survived. She had been told that nursing a baby was unhygienic, but she felt that was ridiculous, so she nursed her babies for a full twelve months. She had been told that babies should sleep in their own cribs from the first day or they get too dependent, but Millie couldn't bear to hear them cry so she had ignored that advice too. Her children grew up to be fine, strong, independent people, so she figured she hadn't gone too far wrong. She figured that what mistakes she did make, she amended with love.

But then, she warned Anne, shaking her finger, "That doesn't mean you can let them talk back or skip out of their fair share of the work. Why, if they sassed me or tried to wiggle out of their chores, I made sure they had twice as much the next time, and I made sure they knew why too. It isn't all about them, you see, and they've got to understand that, just like a mother has to understand it isn't all about her and the father, just the same."

Millie had laughed, practically cackling at how Bernard used to handle the kids, trying to bluster them with his authority and then would turn around and buy ice cream to make everyone feel better. "He's a gem, that man, an absolute gem." Millie eyes filled with tears then, and Anne had reached out and grasped her hand. They had sat together, holding hands, trying not to cry.

A nurse came in and took the baby for a few tests. Her reverie broken, Anne decided to sneak in a quick shower. When she crawled back into bed, her hair and skin still damp, the sensation of cleanliness refreshed her. Noticing how long the shadows had become, she wondered when the nurse would bring her baby back. As she surveyed the adorable photos on the walls and the patterned wallpaper with sprays of roses and wild, rambling vines climbing toward the ceiling, Anne realized how much work it had taken to transform this hospital room into such an inviting place, a room where a baby would be welcomed, and a mother's heart would rejoice.

Footsteps stopped at the door, and Philip called out cheerfully as he walked in. "Hello, little mama! How're you feeling now?"

Rather than responding with the happiness she had so recently felt, a lump swelled in her throat. Tears filled Anne's eyes. "I just realized—this might be the last time these walls witness a birth, or that anyone ever gets to experience what I have at this moment—not even our daughter."

"Oh, Lord! You have to think about that right now?"

"But it's true."

Without another word, Philip came over and sitting on the edge of the bed, he held her, and they both cried. After a time, Philip regained his composure and wiped his eyes. "I'll go see where she is." He got up and started for the door.

"Philip, I know what I want to name her."

"Yeah, I thought we agreed on Miriam."

"No, if you don't mind, I'd just as soon call her Mary—Mary Ann." There was a pause. "I can't explain it, but it feels right."

Philip's hands flapped to his sides. "You're the one who gave birth; I guess you can pick the name. Besides, Mary Ann Smith sounds nice."

Clearing her throat, Anne continued. "You know, now that we have a baby, we might want to start going to church. It might be good to raise her to believe in something."

Turning away, Philip frowned, "I already believe in something. I don't need to go to church to prove it. Besides, we won't be taking her anywhere unless I find her." With that, he left the room.

The sunny day had dimmed into twilight. Anxiety warring with the expectation of holding her baby again, Anne murmured to the silent vine-covered walls, "Oh, Philip, we can't do this alone."

Centerville Dailey

March 25th at 3:33 AM, Philip and Anne Smith of Centerville became the proud parents of a baby girl. Perfectly healthy and with dark brown hair, the baby weighed in at 7 lbs. 6 oz. She is the first grandchild of Anne's living mother, Marylou Saunders, who currently resides in Wisconsin. Anne's deceased father, Fred Saunders, was a police officer for over twenty years. This is also the first grandchild for Philip's parents, James and Caroline Smith, who presently reside in Florida. James is a retired tax consultant for IAM Consulting. Philip Smith works for N & O Law Firm. Anne is currently on leave from Evergreen Community School. The family wishes to extend its gratitude to everyone for all the cards, flowers, gifts, and well wishes, which have poured in from all over the world.

March

AMERICA TODAY
A Baby Is Born

A baby girl was born in Centerville, IL yesterday, and contrary to the usual display of pink or blue banners and exuberant announcements, this birth was met with awed silence. Philip and Anne Smith have asked that there be no visitors at the hospital or at their house for the next several weeks to allow them the privacy and peace needed to adjust to this momentous change in their lives. Under normal circumstances, it would seem unusual to make such a request, but Anne explained to reporter Fred Lipton of America Now that they had already received numerous requests for interviews. Anne charged certain media personalities with insensitivity and invasion of privacy and insisted that her baby was no different from any other, and the massive attention focused on her family was unwarranted. When reminded that this baby is one of only a few being born across the globe, Mrs. Smith merely reiterated her request that her family be left in peace.

Though <u>America Now</u> did respect Mrs. Smith's petition, not everyone has been so kind. Five different attempts from national and local news agencies were made to enter her room under false pretenses. One unidentified woman, apparently working alone, did manage to slip into her secured room disguised as a nurse. She took several pictures of the mother and baby while they were sleeping. The pictures went viral as soon as they hit the web. The police arrested the unidentified intruder, but Mr. Smith has said that no charges will be forthcoming as no actual harm was done. He did repeat his wife's plea that reporters and the public respect their need for privacy. A local businessperson has taken the precaution of hiring a bodyguard for the young couple for the next several weeks to protect them from any further incidents.

March

Centerville Hospital News
Remodeling Expected

Early this spring, the birthing rooms on the first floor will be remodeled as extended care rooms for the geriatric department. Personnel with assignments in the birthing and geriatric departments, please read the bulletin for further details or ask the hospital personnel supervisor, Kelly Karr, for further instruction. There will be a meeting on Wednesday at 9:00 AM in the boardroom with the latest information on remodeling and reassignments.

16

AS THEY LAY SLEEPING

A beam of light entered the hospital room. Though he was hidden, Cerulean was acutely aware of everything in his surroundings. As he watched Anne sleeping, an unknown woman slipped into the room and stood next to her. When the woman pulled something out of her pocket, his brilliance intensified. When he realized she was positioning herself to take a photo, he relaxed. At first, her sharp movements appeared angry, but as she stood by the bed and adjusted the camera angle, her expression softened. She put the task aside for a moment and mutely stared at the mother and child.

Anne slept on her side with her baby tucked under her arm. Tightly wrapped in a blue-and-white striped blanket, Mary's little face was perfectly serene, her thumb mashed up against her bright red mouth and her eyes closed. Her fair skin contrasted sharply with her dark hair. Reaching out to touch the baby, the woman abruptly stopped herself. With trembling hands, she readjusted the camera. After taking five pictures, she pocketed her camera and left.

Cerulean stayed, watching over Anne, remembering the day his own son came into being. He had felt so proud. His wife had embraced their child in much the same manner as Anne, eminently secure in her motherhood. She had been a perfect mother. Some years later she became pregnant again, but this time she did not survive the experience. It was a poignant reality that their species had learned to live with— that mothers often died bringing forth new life. Existence was precarious. The males who survived infancy usually lived for thousands of years, but they were acutely aware of their species' vulnerability.

Cerulean continued to observe the confident intimacy of the mother and child as they lay blissfully intertwined and realized once again the similarities between his species and humans, despite their physical differences. Humans would say that Cerulean, a being of light and energy, could never comprehend the biological realities they faced on a daily basis. A fact many Luxonians would agree with. He had often heard other guardians exclaim that humans were too different to fully comprehend, and their job was only to record the necessary data to appease the Supreme Judges on their home world.

Cerulean was aware that his people were endangered; there were few of them and procreation was dangerous, but he had never forced this understanding on his son. Their people had learned to be proactive against anything that might threaten their existence. Once they mastered space travel, they had pushed against their boundaries, attempting to create an ever-larger safety zone where there would be no surprises, no unexpected dangers. Various roles had been assigned to everyone, and guardians were sent out into the universe to watch and to learn—to guard their people from any threat, near or far.

As Cerulean observed Anne, he remembered his own wife and their loving embraces. *It was a long time ago.* But still, he longed to hold a woman as Anne held her daughter. He wished he could protect Anne from the future she must face. He looked at the little baby and tried to imagine how different the child would look the next time he saw her. He would have to leave soon. His allotted time was spent, and he could face charges of treason if he disobeyed the one-year rule. Almost one year had passed since he had returned to visit Anne. Ten years would pass before he returned again. Viridian had already left. The judges who dictated the various assignments would be alarmed by his emotional attachment. The particular judge, Sterling, who ruled over this jurisdiction, would probably insist that he give up his assignment. Viridian would undoubtedly agree.

A wave of intense grief welled up inside as Cerulean realized that he and Anne were facing the same kind of loneliness. She was facing the end of her kind, while he was no longer one with his. Though he had watched humans through many centuries, he had never before felt so desolate at the thought of leaving them. Going home felt more like going into exile. He wished he could wear his physical body when he got home, though he knew that would hardly be appropriate. There were a few, odd guardians who went native and maintained the shape of their subjects, but they were considered eccentric and often shunned by proper society. In such cases, the judges determined that they should be reassigned. A few escaped to live among the races they had chosen, only to become outsiders of both worlds.

Cerulean considered the possibilities. Would he become an outsider if he chose to live among humans? He was perfectly capable of maintaining the human form for as long as he willed it, but there were risks. What if he was discovered? Medical tests were advancing at a precipitous rate; at some point humans might be able to detect the difference between him and an actual human. What would they do? How would they react? Most importantly, how would Anne react? What would she think of him? His light dimmed.

The soft tread of feet shuffled outside the door. He must end his agony quickly. For one brief moment, he took on physical form and bent and kissed the baby's soft cheek and then Anne's warm forehead. Before the door opened, he vanished.

17

ANNE'S DIARY

Black rectangular windows mirrored the single lamp, which lent the kitchen its mild glow. Anne bent over the wooden table, one hand flattening the notebook that served as her diary. All was silent except for an occasional hoot of an owl and the chirping of tree frogs.

Who am I writing to? I don't know. You, reader, whoever you are. I feel so solemn and bottled up. I want someone to care as I care, see what I see. Does anyone understand what's happening? So much has changed.

I go outside, and though the Earth and sky appear the same, whenever I step near the road, I realize that it connects me to a vastly different world. Even the road itself is altered. There haven't been repairs for so long that grass grows in zigzagging tufts through it. No one has mowed the edges in years. It's rather beautiful in its wild state, but it sure makes for rough riding. And I'm not particularly thrilled about meeting another car—there's so little room to move over nowadays, at least on these backcountry roads. When the spring rains come, everything floods, and the pavement is further washed away. But there's little hope for repairs any time soon.

There's little budget for improvements. Though the government still manages things in theory, it's been up to individuals to fix problems for the most part, though few can do anything about major highways and broken bridges. Everyone has to make do with alternate routes or not travel much. And as for the poor, well, they get poorer, and everyone has to get used to taking in family and neighbors. It all comes down to personal relationships. It never was the government's job to take care of us. I guess we see that now.

It's funny how I once believed that the government and science had all the answers. Advancements made the government look good. But now the technology and all its rewards have slowed to a near stand-still. Who cares about the next breakthrough in communications and transportation when we're struggling just to keep ourselves fed every day? Store shelves contain meager pickings as trucks and planes have had to scramble to keep up with skyrocketing oil prices and replacement parts are hard to come by. No more looking for the latest fashion or trendiest food. Survival is a full-time job.

Gangs flourish since the government can't give people what they want and the police are understaffed. There are whole sections of cities under siege. I guess its Darwin's law of survival of the fittest—whoever has the biggest gun or the best black-market scheme wins. Businesses and private industry can only do so much. Their resources, as well as their numbers, have shrunk drastically. Call in the military? Who wants a military state? Even the military doesn't want that. Thank God. There are enough countries that exist under military control. We haven't fallen that far. At least—not yet. If we don't keep to the ideals of a republic, we're sunk. So far it's been our ideals that have held us together. There're a lot of individuals trying to help, trying to keep order and peace, but it's a tough road to walk. Murder used to be headline news. Now wholesale mass murder or mass suicide is common. Oh, my heart aches. I wonder about the suicides most. Did those people really have a choice? Or did some idiot who charmed them into a vision of Nirvana push them into it? It hurts too much to think about.

Well, it's still relatively calm in my little world. I have my family and neighbors to think about. I can't fix the world. I can only love what's in front of me. That'll have to be enough for now. Good night, reader. Time to dream....

Aware that disagreeable tasks must be faced head on, Anne sat at the kitchen table with an open fifth-grade math book between her and her daughter.

Mary, a thin girl of medium height, pale complexion and short brown hair with bangs running riot over her forehead, slouched next to her, one hand propping her head, a frown burying her better nature. Exaggerated sighs punctuated every step as she worked through an algebra problem. She excelled in school, except for math. Hunching her shoulders like a storm trooper facing the enemy, Mary finished the problem and slapped down her pencil. "I don't see why I even have to do this. I mean some kids aren't even going to school anymore. Carrie's mom says that since the whole world's going to die anyway, there's really no point."

Anne, tired from a full day, didn't want to debate the merits of higher learning. Her eyes narrowed in shocked irritation by the casual manner in which Mary referred to the end of the world. Anne had always maintained that they did not know for sure if the world would end. The possibility always existed that human fertility could return. Perhaps scientists would make a breakthrough, and they would have a future once again. She would not admit defeat. There was always hope. Putting up her hand to stop any further commentary, she rose from the table and stepped over to the woodstove. She shook the kettle to see how much water was inside and, satisfied, she put it back down directly over the hot top. "You want a cup?"

Mary shook her head. "I'd rather have cocoa."

"You know that's not going to happen."

Mary stretched and stood, wandered over to the refrigerator and took out the stainless steel milk container. "Yeah, but I like to share my deepest yearnings with you, Mom." She grinned. Mary often used that line when she was told she couldn't have something.

Anne's wry smile turned into a pucker. "You know how I feel about your education." She grabbed a metal cup out of the cupboard and handed it to her daughter. "I don't care if the world ends tomorrow; I still think learning matters. What else do you want to do with your life? Spend it like one of those street bullies, threatening and cursing the world around them? Or would you rather be a mindless zombie, lost to a world of drugs and games? They aren't living—they are dying, every stupid day."

Snorting, Mary poured the milk. "Spare me, Mom. I get it. I just don't like it. I mean, why on Earth did you get pregnant in the first place? So you could have a kid who'd watch everyone else die?"

Anne's hand darted out and smacked Mary. She immediately regretted her impulse and rushed in to replace the slap with a hug. "Sorry! Oh, Lord, why do you have to say things like that?" Tears burned her eyes. "It's not my fault. It's not anyone's fault."

Pulling back from her mother's tight embrace, Mary rubbed her face. "Yeah, I know. I didn't mean it, either. I just hate; well, I hate algebra. It always puts me in a bad mood."

Anne sniffed her tears away. "You aren't alone there." She looked at the clock on the shelf and reminded herself to wind it before she went to bed. "Have you checked the seedlings today? It's going to be cold tonight." The sun nearly touched the horizon, and dark gray clouds rolled in from the west.

Mary's shoulders sagged. "No, I'd better put the tarp down. Is it supposed to rain?"

"Not tonight; tomorrow, maybe. The temperature will be up and down all week, but it's not supposed to go below freezing."

Mary snatched her sweater off the back of the chair and started toward the door. "That's what you thought last year, remember? And all the tomato and pepper plants froze. Just because the weatherman says something, doesn't mean it's true. You put way too much faith in them." Mary swung open the back door. "I prefer to use my senses, more reliable." She strode out the door, letting it bang behind her.

Anne watched her go with a pang in her chest. She couldn't explain how it used to be, how hard lifelong habits were to break. Before Mary was born, there were working satellites in the sky that could image the world's surface, making it possible to predict the weather with uncanny accuracy. But since the most recent debt crises, the economy was in a tailspin. There was little funding for satellite repairs, space technology, and exploration. Weather satellites among many technological tools had become unreliable as equipment aged. Funding was diverted almost exclusively into discovering the cure for infertility and disease control, life prolongation research, and attempts to find other forms of procreation to sustain human existence.

In today's world, there were more funds for mind transference, where a human brain's synaptic map could be uploaded onto a master computer thereby preserving a human's unique intellect from extinction, than weather prediction services. Brain transference had once been considered science fiction, but as the population crisis worsened, extreme ideas were embraced with a new openness. Even cryogenics became popular among the elite who wanted to outlast extinction by freezing their bodies for a millennium, to be thawed when the world was a more receptive place.

Anne couldn't explain to Mary how she had been conditioned to accept the weatherman's predictions, how she still sometimes expected bananas and cocoa to be readily available in every store, and how she had never doubted that the human race would go on forever. Extinction had never entered her darkest dreams. Now it was her daytime reality.

Anne peered out the window.

Mary stood with her shoulders hunched against a sudden, driving wind. The sky had darkened considerably. Fighting the heavy tarp, Mary struggled to keep her balance.

She's never going to get those plants covered. Grabbing her own sweater, Anne flung it around her shoulders and rushed outside. A thick, wet scent hung in the air. Yes, it was definitely going to rain.

She ran up to her struggling daughter, the tarp wrapping itself about her legs.

Together, mother and daughter gripped the tarp and flung it over the shelving unit that held their precious seedlings. A backyard garden had provided them with basic foodstuffs through the long winter, and even if things got worse, they would not starve, not soon anyway. Anne looked over her shoulder as she tucked the ends of the fabric between the shelf and the south wall. Most of the chickens had retreated into the henhouse, but their feed buckets stood exposed under the cloud-laden sky. Cramming the last fold into place, Anne gestured to her daughter. "We should get the feed under cover, or it'll get soaked."

Mary nodded and ran ahead. She dragged one of the five-gallon buckets toward the chicken coop and hung it on the receiving hook under the eaves.

By the time Anne arrived, there was only one feed bucket left, and she lugged it into place. She grinned at her daughter as the first drops began to fall.

Mary ran around in front of the chicken house, ushering in the last of the straggling hens and then slammed and barred the door so it wouldn't blow open during the night. Mary circled back, took her mother's hand, and swung it up high. "I love storms!"

The wind picked up, the clouds darkened, and rain slashed at them. A quick flash of lightning streaked across the sky as they dashed for the house. Then a sudden crack of thunder crashed against their ears. They both raced up the porch steps and rushed into the warm embrace of the kitchen, laughing and panting. Water was dripping into her eyes as Mary flung her wet hair back out of her face. "That was fun! I'd much rather outrun a storm than do math!"

All her former anxiety dissipated as Anne took off her wet sweater. She switched on the light and felt warmed by the soft yellow glow, which enriched the room. They were safe and cozy and dry now. Beef stew simmered on the woodstove, and the ingredients for corn biscuits lay out on the counter. She checked the woodstove and threw in a log. "How about helping me make biscuits?"

Rushing toward the counter, Mary grabbed the bowl and spoon. "I can do it, Mom. You go and rest a bit. You must be tired. Besides, Dad should be home soon, and you'll want a chance to talk."

Anne ruffled Mary's wet head. "You are such a mix of—I don't know what!" She wanted to hug her daughter, but the sudden memory of their earlier altercation stopped her. Mary must grow up in a vastly different world than the one she had known and become her own unique person, but at least they had something in common—they both loved spring storms.

The door slammed as Philip walked into the house. Dark circles underlined his eyes and a frown bore testimony to his mood. Anne knew better than to ask him what was wrong. She shifted her gaze out the window.

Philip had put on a few pounds and was less active than he had been in their early marriage, though he occasionally enjoyed doing an outdoor project. When they decided to keep chickens, he had suddenly discovered a latent love of building. He had declared he would build the best chicken coop known to mankind. As Anne had surveyed the end result, a tower-like structure with its shingled roof, multilayered perches, planked sides with a little weathervane at the top, now protected from the storm with a thick tarp, she realized, he had come very close.

The trick had been teaching Mary to collect the eggs every day and remembering to label the cartons correctly with the current date. It had been a learning experience, as had been the garden. If it hadn't been for Millie's unflagging support, Anne doubted she would have been able to keep a single seedling alive for more than a week, much less maintain an entire garden. Having to care for plants, water and weed, harvest and store, was a completely unexpected demand on her time and attention. As it was, Anne learned to love the process, though she found it humiliating when she found some worm or unnamed critter had chewed its way through her zucchini, corn, or tomato plants.

Philip had cheerfully regulated most of the garden work to her. He was a lawyer not a farmer; he often reminded her. His job was to come out on summer evenings and point to the weeds she had missed or question why they had twenty squash plants but only two rows of corn when they all liked corn and only she liked squash. Trying to explain that it was pure luck, which seedlings lived and which died was like trying to explain the art of magic to an electrician. His mind simply did not comprehend the world of unpredictable vegetation.

When Philip slumped into the kitchen, Anne appraised his thickening waist, his stooped shoulders, and his pallid skin. He certainly didn't look healthy. Or happy. Philip reached for a beer. Anne pulled out a kitchen chair. "Sit down, Philip. The stew's almost ready. Mary is fixing biscuits."

Philip flopped down on the wooden chair and took a long swig from his beer.

Anne's brow wrinkled. She disliked beer and could never comprehend his desire for it. Of late, it was the first thing he reached for when he got home. He never drank more than two or three, but this new behavior was disconcerting nevertheless.

"Tough case at work?" Anne asked.

"No, not particularly…. Work's pretty much the same as usual." He eyed his wife. "What've you been doing all day?"

Laying the spoon aside, Anne sat down in her usual seat opposite her husband. "What haven't I done? It seems like I start the morning with a list, and as I work through it, the list gets longer instead of shorter." Her lips twitched. "I know my day isn't as stressful as yours, but sometimes even laundry issues can get a little hairy, believe me."

Philip's exaggerated nod and a subsequent long swig of his beer irritated Anne. *He has no sense of humor anymore.* She dusted some crumbs off the table, attempting to look busy. Her innate desire to settle problems overwhelmed her good sense. "I hate to pry, but is something wrong, Philip? You seem…unhappy, or something."

Philip's eyes darted toward his daughter who was just filling the muffin tins.

Anne followed his gaze, and without thinking, she asked, "Did you butter them first, Mary? They'll stick—"

Mary groaned. "Oh, damn it! I forgot."

Anne jumped in her seat, and Philip's frown deepened. Anne stepped over and started directing Mary to put the filling back in the bowl, wash the muffin pan out, and then after buttering them, to fill them again.

Mary grumbled but did as directed.

Philip rubbed the outside of his beer bottle with his thumb in a meditative manner. He waited until Anne sat back down and then asked, "So when did our daughter take up swearing like a sailor?"

The scrubbing sound ceased as Mary froze.

A hot blush warmed Anne's face. "She doesn't normally; it was just the heat of the moment—"

Philip waved her explanation away. "I really don't want to hear it. I hear lies all day long; I don't need them here too."

"What does that mean?"

Philip took another long swig from his drink, and after a moment of heavy silence, he drained the bottle and got up. Leaving the empty brown bottle standing on the table, he shuffled toward the refrigerator, grabbed another beer, slowly twisting it open, and looked from his wife to his daughter. "You'd think everything was alright, that the world was doing just dandy, and we had years of happiness ahead of us." He waved one hand in the air dramatically. "It's not as if there's a black hole staring at us, coming closer every day, taunting us, ready to swallow us, miserable person by miserable person. We might as well be insects."

Philip sipped his beer, his hands shaking. He stared at his daughter. "Damn is right, Mary. We're all damned. We just like to pretend it isn't really happening, kind of like the Little People, damned by God for being cowards!"

Gripping the edge of the table, Anne stood, her voice high and strained. "Philip, what has gotten into you? We decided that we wouldn't give up; remember? We promised that as long as we had each other, we'd hold on to hope. There may be a cure; something may happen to turn things around." Anne attempted to soften the accusation in her voice. "What's happened to make you give up, Philip? What in God's name?"

Philip slammed down his beer. "God? Don't talk to me about God." He rubbed his eyes. His hands trembled even more. "You remember Steve? The guru-guy who can fix anything?"

"Steve?" Anne shook her head. "Yeah, he came for dinner a couple of times and helped you on a project. What about him?"

"He committed suicide."

"Oh, hell."

Philip swallowed and tried to control his voice. "And he didn't go alone." His eyes darted toward Mary again.

Eyes wide with fear, Anne followed his gaze. "Maybe we should go in the other room." She ignored the bottles on the table. "You can tell me—"

"No, there's no hiding anymore. Mary needs to know as much as anyone. People will only get crazier as time goes on. She needs to be prepared for the worst."

Anger warring with anxiety, Anne frowned. "I don't think that's the approach we should take, Philip. We should hope for the best!"

"We better prepare for the worst!"

"Philip! I won't have you scare her. She's still a little girl."

"She'll be grown-up before long." Philip walked toward his daughter, who was wiping her sticky hands on a towel. "Listen, Honey, I'm not trying to upset you, but I think you should know what's happening. People are getting—"

Mary put up her hands, her tears held in check by rage. "You know, Dad, I'm not stupid. I know what people are like. Don't I go to school? Don't I meet kids and teachers every day? Don't I go to the store and watch movies and check the news and stuff? I know more than you think. If you've just figured out that people are despairing, then you're behind the curve."

Philip stopped his forward momentum. "Say again?"

Mary slid off the stool and jerked the muffin pan off the counter. "You know how to ruin things, Dad. I know how it is; I don't need to be reminded!" She glared at her mother. "Or treated like a child!" Thrusting the refilled muffin tin into the hot oven, she turned and faced her parents through tears. "I don't know about you, but the kids in my generation figure that if you guys hadn't messed everything up, with chemicals and wars, murder, and stuff, we'd all probably be doing a whole lot better. But you and your parents didn't care too much about our future. Your debt has ruined our economy, and your stupid ideas have ruined our lives. Don't try to protect us now—it's a little too late. Should've thought of that ages ago!"

Mary stomped off. Anne and Philip listened as her footfalls mounted the steps and her bedroom door slammed. Philip took a long swig from his beer bottle. He gestured to his wife. "You want one now?"

Anne shook her head as she whispered, "Oh, bloody hell."

Philip nodded. He spoke over his shoulder as he left the room. "You got that right."

18

HOLD ON

Though there were scenic pictures of mountains and running streams on the wall and even two obscenely large fish mounted on wooden frames, Anne felt boxed in, isolated from humanity. She couldn't care less for mountains, streams, or even fish, except as a main course with lemon and butter.

It feels like a cage.

Squirming in her chair, Anne realized how foreign the dentist's office had become. She had not been here for years, and everything appeared dusty and stifling like a room that had was only opened a few times a year. No one really belonged here or cared about this particular place in the universe. The dentist only opened this office once a month. His main practice was two hours south.

Anne ran her tongue over her chipped tooth and winced. She wouldn't be here now except for the fact that she was worried that the chip might lead to something worse. Besides, she reflected, it was about time Mary saw a dentist. Anne felt guilty she had waited so long before having her seen by a professional. When she was a child, she had had yearly check-ups. It showed how things had changed. No one went to dentists regularly anymore. Doctors and dentists were for emergencies—much like everything else. Anne squirmed again.

Mary had already gone in, and Anne was doing her best to wait patiently. The television was rerunning an old talk show, and the inane conversation stretched Anne's already thin nerves. She looked around the bare room. There was only one other person there, and she was reading a book. Anne watched as another woman entered the room, signed in at the window, and after surveying the options, came and sat next to Anne. The newcomer was well dressed. Her blond hair, beautiful and wavy, smelled like lilacs. It was as if someone had opened the window and blown life back into the stagnant room. An odd sense of relief surged through Anne. She didn't want to stare, so she looked around and spied the magazine rack.

The other woman had smiled at Anne, and they laughed when they both started up at the same moment, heading for the same dog-eared magazine.

"I hate coming here." The woman motioned for Anne to take the magazine. "I always forget to bring something."

Anne murmured, "Me too." They both sighed at the array of well-thumbed survivalist and hunting magazines and sat back down. "Though I shouldn't mind it so much; the nurse and Dr. Sutter are perfectly nice. I never have any problem."

The other woman laughed. "Me either. I was born with perfect teeth, or rather the buds of them, though I'm terrified of losing them. My mom had false teeth when she was in her forties, and they never fit right. I'll never forget how traumatic that was."

With sympathy in her eyes, Anne wasn't sure what else to say, though she sensed that this woman would be happy to keep chatting. She realized that she didn't want the conversation to end.

Suddenly, the woman put out her hand and introduced herself. "Hi, I'm Eve. I work at Evergreen Community School."

Anne stiffened, flummoxed. She took the offered hand and felt the soft, cool fingers press her own. She had lost touch with everyone at

Evergreen after Mary was born. She never went back and rarely even thought of it now. "I used to teach there." She folded her hands on her lap. "I haven't been back in a long time. Is Mr. Erlandson still there?"

"Mr. Erlandson? No, he retired a couple years back. He said the closings were too much for him." Eve studied Anne carefully. "What did you teach?"

"Fifth grade. My daughter goes to a school closer to our house, Middleton Central. Do you know it?"

Eve shook her head. "No, but that's what I teach—fifth. I love it. I used to anyway."

Anne frowned. "Used to?"

"Fifth grade, eleven-year-olds—you know—the last of their kind." Eve clasped her hands together. It almost looked as if she was going to pray. "My contract will be up in a couple of weeks, and I'll be out of a job and, well, that's that. I shouldn't complain. I was able to keep my position longer than some. The preschool people were out ages ago."

Anne nodded. Someone called out a name. She glanced up. The third woman shoved her book under her arm, rose heavily to her feet, swung her purse strap over her shoulder like a soldier going into battle, and entered the inner sanctum.

Anne's reply was a soft murmur. "I'm sorry."

Eve looked out of the corner of her eye at Anne. "So, what's your name?"

"Anne Smith."

Enlightenment suffused Eve's features. "Oh, you know, I've heard of you. You left a couple of years before I came, but I got your room. People talked about you."

Anne resisted the temptation to follow up that remark and tried to think of something else to say. "So what are you going to do next?"

A deep sigh issued from Eve's chest. "I don't know. Maybe I can get something in the medical field; they still have positions: nurse's aide, geriatric care, whatever. I don't know what's wrong with me—I can't seem to look ahead, much less reinvent my life right now."

Anne struggled to think of a safe question. "So, what do you do for fun?"

With a bit of a smirk, Eve snapped her fingers. "Well now, there's a good question. I like movies, fun dates, and delicious food. But you know, the movies are pretty gritty these days, dates are becoming a bit of a bore—not too many men interested in my brilliant mind. And as for delicious food, well, I like to cook, but since my mom passed on, I haven't done much, except for the aforementioned guys, and they don't seem to care if I make lasagna or peanut butter sandwiches. Cooking for myself just isn't a whole lot of fun."

Anne shook her head. "And I'm at home every day wishing someone else would make a meal once in a while!" She chuckled. "I know what you mean about movies. The last one I saw made me cry, and my husband wasn't exactly thrilled with that." She pursed her lips in thought. "There aren't many places I can relax and have a good time, except home, and I'm surrounded by work there."

"Well, if I want to relax, I go to church. There's a beautiful little chapel not too far from where I live, and the priest is nice enough to let me have a key, so I can go in and sit for a while. I can't say it is fun, but I must admit, I'm always in a good mood when I come out. It's better than most dates."

Without another word, Anne unzipped her purse and after digging for a few moments, she pulled out a small pad of paper. She scribbled her phone number and handed it to Eve just as her name was being called. "Here's my number. My family and I live close by, and we appreciate good cooking. It might be fun to get together sometime. I'd love to see that chapel. I could use a little peace myself. Call me anytime."

Eve's eyes widened in disbelief. "You don't even know me."

Anne stood up, grabbing the strap of her purse. "Seems to me, we can change that."

Eve smiled and folded the note, putting it in her bag as her name was called. She stood and looked Anne in the eye. "Yeah, I'd like that."

Two weeks later, Eve stood on Anne's porch attempting to knock on the door while balancing a large casserole wrapped in bright kitchen towels.

The door swung open, and Anne stood back to let Eve come in. "Hi! You found your way, I see."

Eve laughed as she stepped into the cream-colored interior. She could see the kitchen, painted in butter yellow, directly ahead. "Yeah, it wasn't hard." She gestured. "You want me to bring it in there?"

With a quick nod, Anne led the way. "That'd be great. I'm so glad you were able to come. But I feel kind of guilty, a guest bringing the main course."

"That was my price, remember? I had to experiment on you guys—I love Amish cooking but their recipes are huge, and I needed a whole family for this one."

Anne followed behind, wiping her hands on a dishrag. "Well, I hope you don't mind, but you'll be feeding a couple of extra people. My brother, Mark, and our neighbor, Millie, are both coming. Mark's about Philip's age, single, and works in a research lab, and Millie's husband died a few years back, but she's been teaching me the secrets of country living."

Eve slid the dish on the counter. "Great. I enjoy meeting new people." She looked around the country-style kitchen. Noting the framed drawings hanging on the walls, she strode over. "You do these?"

A flush crept up Anne's cheeks. "A couple. But the best ones are my grandmother's. She was the real artist. Meanwhile, I dabble in the arts, though Mary, my daughter, is getting quite good." Anne pointed to a winter evening scene with a farmhouse in the background and a barren field in the foreground. She then turned toward another and pointed. It was a picture of a ship on the sea at mid-day. "That's my grandmother's. There's a difference between their styles, but I think they're both very talented."

Eve surveyed the walls. "Which one's yours? No, wait; let me guess." Eve stepped around the room, peering at each picture. Some were charcoal, another was pencil, a few were oils, and one was watercolor. She stopped at one that depicted a close-up of a sleeping infant. "Yours?"

Anne stepped next to Eve, staring up at the sketch. "Yeah, it's the only one I ever did of Mary. She hates having her likeness taken, even photos. I tell her I'm not going to steal her soul or anything, but still, she resists. I think it's because of all the media attention she got when she was little. Things have died down now, but for a while there, it was like the whole world was chronicling her every step. It got pretty obnoxious, and Mary resented every photo." Anne's gaze flittered across the room out towards the open fields in the backyard. "I can't blame her. Though I wish she'd let me draw her once more. I long to recapture that feeling of holding time still."

"I can understand." Eve wiped her sweaty hands on her long denim skirt and crossed her arms as she leaned back against the counter. "I rarely tell anyone this, but I like to write. I've been working on a book for five years now, and though it'll never get published, I like the feeling I have when I am writing. It's like what you said, like I'm holding time still, holding the world back."

Relieved at the change of conversation, Anne reached for two tall glasses and filled them with ice. "Tea?" She moved to the refrigerator and took out a pitcher. Pouring the amber liquid into two glasses, she handed one to Eve. "I love good stories. They take me away from reality." She sipped her drink slowly. "I seem to appreciate my life more after I've been away for a while. I even love fantasy and science fiction—though don't tell Philip. He thinks science fiction is stupid. He'd much rather read a dreary biography about warring kings than about made-up people who live in an imaginary world."

Eve's eyes sparkled with delight. "I knew you and I had a lot in common, but I never expected this. I love science fiction, too. That's what my book is—an alien race that comes to meet humanity and the main guy, he looks human, I couldn't make him reptilian or anything; it just wouldn't work for the story, well, he falls in love with this woman, but they can't be together because she's vowed to become a nun."

Eve chuckled. "Sounds crazy, I know, but it's a lot of fun to write. I even threw in a mystery: the nun's best friend is murdered, and she's afraid that whoever killed her friend will come after her next."

With an unexpected jolt of excitement Anne asked, "So does the alien help her?"

"Well, of course, he's a futuristic knight in shining armor. I never got into little green men and evil monster-types. I like aliens who have just as much decency as the best of us. Besides, I think that if aliens ever did come, it might be wonderful."

Anne's eyebrows rose. "You really think aliens exist?"

"Let's just say, I don't put limits on God."

Philip called from the living room. "Hey, Anne, your brother is coming up the driveway."

Anne laid her glass on the counter. "Come on, Eve, you'll enjoy this. Philip can be a little stuffy at times, but he'll love your cooking—which means—he'll love you. And as for Mark, well, he's shy but... you'll see."

Gripping her glass with both hands, Eve followed Anne into the next room.

Philip was running up the stairs. Anne called after him. "Hey, Philip, this is Eve."

Philip looked momentarily indecisive and then turned around and came back down the steps. His wrinkled suit was sweat stained, and his cheeks were flushed. He offered his hand to Eve. "It's nice to meet you." Gesturing at his appearance, his blush deepened. "No air conditioning. I feel like I've just put in nine hours in the Roman baths. Hope you don't mind, but I'll go take a shower and change."

"Please, get comfortable. I hate to see a man suffer."

Philip nodded his gratitude and turned back up the steps, tugging at his tie as he went.

Anne turned at the sound of someone on the porch. There was a murmur of voices. Anne walked to the door and watched as Mark took Millie's elbow and helped guide her up the last steps. Millie clutched a large salad bowl.

Lurching forward, Anne reached for the bowl. "Oh, Millie, you didn't have to bring anything."

Millie made it to the landing and smiled at Mark as she released the bowl into Anne's hands. "I couldn't very well come empty handed. Besides, I've got more lettuce than I can eat."

All four moved into the living room. Eve took the salad bowl and gestured toward the kitchen. "I can take it. I should check the casserole anyway."

"The casserole? It'll be fine. Now, wait a minute. I want to introduce you." Anne gestured from Millie to Eve. "Millie, this is a friend of mine, Eve Preston, she's a teacher at Evergreen school. Eve, this is Millie, my neighbor, kitchen-coach, and garden-guru." She looked from one to the other. "I'm sure you two will have a lot to talk about. Eve's quite a cook. She brought the main course tonight."

Eve shrugged and attempted a chuckle. "Well, if everyone comes down with stomach cramps, you can blame me."

Anne shifted her attention to Mark who was appraising Eve with a grin. "Mark, this is Eve. Eve, this is my brother. He's a technician at one of the medical labs up north. And, good man that he is, he takes care of mom."

Her eyes wider than usual, Eve shook Mark's hand and then, almost tripping over herself, motioned toward the kitchen. "I better put this in the fridge and check that casserole."

Trying to cover her friend's clumsy behavior, Anne motioned Mark and Millie toward the couch. "Philip's gone up to change, but he'll be right down. I'll get drinks. You want some iced tea, Millie? Mark?"

Millie nodded her acceptance while Mark waved the offer off. "I'll wait for Philip, thanks."

As Anne headed for the cabinet, she glanced at Eve. "What do you—?"

Before Anne could finish, Eve interrupted. "Where's your daughter?" She leaned against the refrigerator, her eyes wide. "I was looking forward to meeting her."

Anne darted a look at the clock. "She went to visit a friend, but she's supposed to be back by now. In fact, she was supposed to be home an hour ago." She stared at Eve's flushed face. "Hey, what's going on? You okay?"

Eve's whispered voice became accusing. "You didn't tell me your brother was so good looking." She rolled her eyes. "You could've warned me. I was ready for a geeky technician, not a drop-dead hand-some, Greek-god-type."

Anne snorted. "Mark? My Mark?" Easing Eve out of the way, Anne removed a pitcher of ice tea from the refrigerator and peered into the vessel. "Is there more to this concoction than meets the eye?"

Eve hissed, "Don't *you* think he's good looking?"

"I think he's great looking and a really nice guy to boot." Anne puckered her lips. "Why do you think I invited you here today?"

Eve's whisper turned dangerous. "To try my delicious Amish cas-serole!"

"Well, occasionally I have secondary motives."

Eve's gaze bored into Anne. "You know, it's dangerous to tick off a writer. I could create a character just like you—and kill her!"

Anne laughed as she filled another glass with iced tea. "Just re-member *Greek-god* was your expression, not mine. Philip will be so pleased."

Eve threw up her hands. "What? Philip was in on this?"

"He's the one who thought of it." Anne pulled a bag of rolls from the cabinet and refilled Eve's glass as she motioned toward the living room. "Shall we?"

Another hour passed and Anne decided that dinner couldn't wait. She gestured toward Philip who followed her into the kitchen. Millie, Eve, and Mark were getting along nicely, but Anne's stomach was be-ginning to rumble. A puckered frown mounted on her forehead as she slapped a hot pad on the counter. "I called the Dewitt's house an hour ago, and there was no answer. I tried again a few minutes ago but still nothing." She glanced at Philip, who was sipping his beer in a white t-shirt and jeans. He looked good today, and she had to admire the fact that he was always a kind host. "I'm worried. She knew we had guests today. It's not like her to be so late and not even call."

Blowing air between his lips, Philip put down his beer with a decided tap. "I'll drive over there. You go ahead and start dinner. It'll only take a half an hour or so, and I'll be back. I'm sure they're just outside or something and forgot the time."

"Don't yell at her. She'll be mad enough when she realizes we've been worried."

Leaning in so close that Anne could smell the beer on his breath; Philip barely controlled his anger. "If she blew us off, I'll tell her what I think, and she can have her little tantrum in the car. We have guests, and it was rude of her not to show up on time. Period."

Philip ran upstairs and a moment later came back jingling the car keys in his hand.

Mark looked up. "Hey, where are you going?"

Philip gestured with the keys. "To pick up a delinquent kid. You want to come along?"

With hesitation, Mark darted a look at Eve and then answered. "Uh, no, thanks. You probably want to have one of those important father-daughter talks." He grinned. "I'll hold down the fort here."

"Yeah, you do that, but leave some casserole for me, okay? And a slice of apple pie."

Mark lifted his glass in salute. "Done."

Within thirty minutes, Eve's casserole was in danger of being consumed before Philip returned, but Anne filled two plates with what was left and set aside a couple of rolls before she took out the pie and ice cream. Everyone had moved back to the living room while Anne cleared the table. Eve and Mark were in a serious conversation about the debt crisis while Millie relaxed on the couch, her eyes closed.

The phone rang. Anne went to answer it. "Hello...? Oh, hi, Philip. What's taking so long? We're about to cut the—"

Anne stopped talking and stiffened. "Why? What's happened?"

Eve and Mark both looked up and stared at Anne.

Anne gripped the phone with both hands. "Oh, God. Is he dead then? Where's Mary?"

Eve and Mark stood up at the same moment; their eyes fixed on Anne.

Anne continued to listen. She was near tears now. "Okay, just come home as soon as you can. Or do you want me to go there?" She listened again and nodded her head. "Okay, okay. But Philip, how about if…." Anne winced as a voice shouted over the line. "Alright, I won't. Just let me know as soon as you hear anything. I'll be right here." Anne listened again and then spoke quietly. "Bye." Anne put the phone down, staring at the floor.

Mark walked over to her while Eve stood back. Millie had straightened up on the couch. Putting his arm around his sister's shoulder, Mark asked, "Hey, Anne, what's going on?"

Trying to keep from trembling, Anne spoke softly, "There's been an accident, but Mary's not there. She's not anywhere."

Mark turned Anne around so that he could look into her eyes. "I don't get that. What do you mean?"

Feeling dizzy, Anne stumbled over to the chair to sit down. "Mr. Dewitt was going to drive her home, but he never made it. His car was found in a ditch, rolled over. Apparently, he hit something. A dead dog lay by the road, and the car was pretty smashed up. The police say, Leo, I mean Mr. Dewitt, was probably killed instantly. Philip saw the car from the road and stopped to help. He didn't know who it was until he got the door open, and Leo's body fell out." Anne covered her face with her hands. "Oh, God, where is Mary?"

Mark's jaw clenched. "She wasn't in the car?"

"No." Anne looked at her brother and then over at Eve. "But Bev, that's Mrs. Dewitt, she said that Mary left with Leo. He was taking her home. That's the last they saw of her—in the car with him, heading here." Anne closed her eyes, dizziness overwhelming her.

Millie spoke low and soft. "It could be that someone rescued her. She might be in a hospital, Anne. She might be fine."

Eve's reassuring voice chimed in. "It's more than a possibility. It's probably just what happened. You want me to call around?"

Anne clenched her hands together. "Philip said the police are already calling around. He's staying with them to help search, oh, God! What if she was thrown—?"

Mark sat down by his sister, putting his arm around her shoulders, hugging her. "There's no use thinking like that, Anne. We just don't know what's happened. You're going to have to live through the next few hours till Philip can get back with us." He looked at Eve, whose eyes met his in understanding.

Eve spoke up. "I'll clean things up a bit, and Mark and I'll hang out with you. Millie, would you like something?"

"No, dear." She looked out the window as the sun was setting. "It's getting late and though I wish I could help, I know I can't. The best thing I can do is get out of the way."

Anne wiped her eyes with a tissue Eve had handed her. Her voice was a forced calm. "Have some pie before you go, Millie. No use letting it go to waste."

Millie struggled to her feet. "This is no time for pie. We'll save that for when Mary gets home." She walked over to where Anne sat hunched. Millie put her hand on Anne's shoulder. "Don't worry, honey, I have a feeling that Mary will be alright. I think if she were dead, you'd have heard already." She looked once more out the window. "I'd better get home while there's still light to see by."

Mark stood. "I'll drive you. It's getting late, and the road is long."

Shifting her gaze from Mark toward Eve, Millie's expression was sympathetic. "That's very gallant of you, Mark. I always appreciate a gentleman, but no. I've walked this lane more times that I can count. Don't worry; I'll be fine. A good stretch of the legs will be just the thing for me." Millie gestured toward Eve. "Thanks so much for dinner, Eve. I hope we'll meet again under happier circumstances." When Anne stepped up to say goodbye, she took Anne's hand. "Remember, there's more to this world than meets the eye, Anne." Millie managed the steps herself and started down the lane.

Anne stood on the porch watching her friend leave as Eve turned to clean up the dishes.

Mark's hand clasped his sister's shoulder. "Hold on, Anne, don't give up."

Anne's stomach hurt as if she had swallowed a stone. "Oh, God, this so hard."

July
HUMANITY'S WORTH

Cerulean felt sweat trickle down his back as he clenched his jaw. He didn't often lose his temper, and he had no plans to start now. For one, it showed a lack of self-control; for another, it was dangerous.

One of the most influential judges, Sterling, had accompanied him back to Earth without the slightest warning. He was not one of the ordinary judges who presided over the vast array of irregularities that always occur when dealing with alien beings. Those judges were merely bureaucrats trained to intercede for calm order when temperaments and opinions clouded issues. Those judges were commonplace. Supreme Judges were altogether different. And Sterling was in a class by himself.

They both watched, paralyzed, as a car swerved to avoid a dog, skidded out of control, and then rolled over a steep embankment. Cerulean began running.

"Where are you going?" Sterling placed his hands on his hips.

"I can't just stand by. She might be hurt." Cerulean plunged through the thicket towards the overturned car.

Sterling shook his head; his shoulders slumped. "There you go again."

In the very beginning, judges acted as assistants to the guardians. They had been appointed to help discern the cultural and intellectual qualities of alien life. A judge accompanied every guardian on planetary visits, and the two worked in tandem to discern whether a particular alien life was, or at any point in the near future might become, a threat to their own fragile society. Later, the judges began to feel that the stress of travel and the needs off the home world outweighed their value as companions, so they stopped accompanying the guardians. They stayed at home, read reports, interviewed returnees, and took counsel together. They became a separate and very powerful force unto themselves.

And of the judges, there was the highest caste, those of Supreme Judge. There were only twelve, and they held immense power for their word was law. If it was suggested that a planet study should be abandoned, the Supreme Judges reviewed the case and made the definitive decision. No matter how complicated the case, they needed to reach a unanimous consensus. Sometimes this took years. But once their minds were in accordance, they could never be jarred apart. That would be heresy.

Rumors had swirled about Cerulean since he had assumed his father's place. It had been discovered that his father, Teal, had revealed himself to a young man who was on the verge of suicide. Teal had observed this young man for a number of years and realized that he was brilliant and had the potential to do great things, but since he had suffered through a series of demoralizing setbacks, he had ceased to believe in himself. When his mother had been killed in an accident, the young man decided that life was mere random chaos and that nothing he did would make any difference. Teal had stayed the youth's hand before he pulled the suicidal trigger. The youth, though terrified, had wits enough to realize that it was impossible for a man to simply appear out of thin air. So Teal revealed enough to assure the young man that he was not mad, but on the contrary, he would likely live to do wonderful things, if only he did not give up. The youth did not kill himself that day or any day thereafter.

When Cerulean accepted his father's position, he also accepted his history. Cerulean, in turn, revealed himself, not to a young man, but to a madman who was about to destroy something that would save humanity from immense suffering, a cure that would make the difference between life and terrifying death for millions. Cerulean, like his father, made the decision to interfere, and the cure was not destroyed, it was discovered.

In these two cases, father and son had broken a time-honored rule: that no one of their race was to reveal himself or herself under any condition. But in both cases, the Supreme Judges had reviewed the particulars and decided that a minor revelation could be allowed in the service of an alien species. Still, they let it be known that guardians were not to make such decisions on a regular basis. There was a formal protest by other guardians who complained that this breach of secrecy made visitations dangerous for everyone. The Supreme Judges agreed and decided to punish Teal by releasing him from duty before his time. In turn, they punished Cerulean by insisting that his son, Viridian, be trained to take his place, just in case.

Cerulean realized his danger, but he knew that he must continue his work. He was not concerned that humanity was a danger to his people, but rather, that his people were becoming a danger to themselves. He felt that by observing how humanity faced its end, they could learn a valuable lesson, perhaps a lesson they could learn no other way.

Cerulean lifted Mary free from the overturned vehicle.

Sterling grimaced. "Do you think that's wise?"

"She'll die if I don't do anything."

"Humans have a long history of persecuting what they don't understand." Sterling pointed to the child. "Is she worth the risk? I know you have strong feelings about humanity, but they aren't worth your life…or mine for that matter."

Cerulean began to check Mary's vital signs.

Sterling shook his head. "What are you going to do?"

Sweat beading on his brow and a strand of hair falling into his eyes, Cerulean looked up at the passive face of the neat, elderly man standing in front of him. "I just need a few minutes."

"It doesn't look like you'll get them." Sterling gestured with his chin toward an oncoming car.

Philip's car slowed as it came around the curve.

Cerulean swiftly picked up the child and carried her down the steep embankment. He found a level spot and pressed his hands over her leg wound. He watched Mary's eyes flutter as he spoke to Sterling. "Go up and watch. Just give me a minute to get her stable. If they don't come this way, appear to be a bystander and lead them here."

Sterling sniffed, doubt in his eyes. "Who will I tell them I am?"

"They won't care! Just make something up."

Mary moaned.

Cerulean squeezed the gash on her leg. The slippery blood pulsed against his fingers. He gestured angrily.

Sterling thrust his hands into his pockets and began the ascent up the embankment. A car door slammed shut.

Mary's eyes fluttered open. She groaned and then reached out convulsively as if she still thought she could brace herself for impact.

Cerulean's voice was gentle. "Shhh, it's going to be alright. You've been in an accident. But you'll be okay."

Squeezing her eyes shut, Mary moaned. "Oh, my leg, it feels like it's broken."

Cerulean swallowed and attempted to clear his choked throat. "It probably is. But you've got to stay still until someone reaches you. A car just stopped up ahead; I'm holding the bleeding back." Cerulean looked around but found nothing he could use to help bind the wound. He let go of her leg for just a moment, and he tore off his shirt.

Her blood spurted. Mary whimpered as she watched with wide, terrified eyes.

Cerulean wrapped his shirt around the wound and bound it tightly. He surveyed his work and realized that the shirt would only hold back the bleeding for a few moments before it became soaked. His voice was strained as he forced himself to keep his breathing even. "Tell me your name. You live around here?"

"Mary—" She began to sob.

"Tell me something else...where were you going? Help will get here soon, promise."

Mary's shoulders shook as she covered her face with her hands.

Sirens wailed in the distance. Cerulean sighed in relief.

Philip stood on the shoulder of the road, shouting Mary's name.

Cerulean wrapped his fingers more tightly over the wound and realized that Mary would lose consciousness again.

Sterling was nowhere to be seen.

Breathing heavily, sweat trickled down the side of Cerulean's face.

Mary's eyes opened suddenly, her gaze focused on him. She didn't say anything but her look was so imploring, so desperate, that Cerulean's heart gripped him in a tight, painful squeeze.

Car doors slammed.

Cerulean began to shout. "Here, down here! Help!" As soon as he was certain he saw someone begin to slide down the embankment, he grabbed Mary's hand and spoke rapidly. "Here, put your hands here, over the wound. You've got to squeeze hard. You hear me? Don't let go."

Mary's eyes were red-rimmed and wide, but as Cerulean removed his hands, she clamped hers over the wound, swaying as she sobbed.

Cerulean disappeared.

Mary shrieked.

Footsteps crunched through the dead leaves coming toward her. It was a police officer. He shouted and other men came running. Philip ran toward his daughter crying out her name. Everyone was talking and medical assistants were gripping her leg. The last thing Mary remembered was the flash of light.

Cerulean stood on the edge of the ravine off to the right. Sterling stood next to him. Still breathing heavily, with a frown mounted across his forehead, Cerulean brushed twigs and leaves off his pants with sharp slaps "Where did you go? Why didn't you lead them to her?"

Sterling hunched his slight shoulders. "I'm not as comfortable with humans as you. I wouldn't have been able to explain myself, and I certainly wouldn't have been able to slip away like you do. It might have led to something—unpleasant."

"She could have died."

Sterling snorted. "She most certainty will die."

"Someday, yes, but not today. No thanks to you."

"Humans die every day. Would you save them all?"

Cerulean eyed the Supreme Judge with cold fury. "You've lived too long. You forget what it is to die."

Sterling's voice deepened. "You live too close to humans to remember your place. They're impulsive and that's what gets them into trouble. This accident should never have happened. The man swerved to miss a stupid animal. If he had merely stayed on the road, he would not have died."

"You don't understand humanity's sensitivity at all. They don't like to kill things. Not if they can help it."

Sterling's chuckle was laden with irony. "Really? I happen to know as much about their history as you do. They've done quite a lot of killing in their time. I haven't noticed a high level of sensitivity."

Cerulean clenched his hands into fists. "That's because all you know is what you've read. You don't *know* them. The official records only detail the peaks and valleys, not the intimate thoughts and feelings of a man or woman on an ordinary day. Many people do generous and caring things every day, but no one notices because it *is* so ordinary. Humans may be contradictory, but they have some very respectable qualities. They are sensitive and merciful and amazingly adaptable. There's a *reason* why they were created. Their place in the universe matters."

Inching his way carefully down the embankment, Sterling moved away from the scene. "Not for long. Their end is near." He exhaled loudly. "One wonders why they were created at all. Even with all their good qualities, as you say, still, their life spans are so short. No individual can ever learn enough to make a serious contribution. They're like these ants," Sterling kicked at a colony as he began to climb the next rise. "They only have merit through accumulation. It takes centuries for humans to learn anything, and then in one generation they can forget it all." He stopped on the peak of the next ridge, overlooking a small town. "They are so fragile and helpless, so confused and misdirected. One has to wonder—what was God thinking?"

Cerulean's brutal laugh echoed through the tangled woods. "Now isn't that just like you, to question God! You wouldn't even save an injured child in a dying world! And you wonder about humanity's worth?" Cerulean began to hurry down the hill. "I don't know why you came, but if you think I'll abandon these people, you're wrong. I can't change their fate, but damn it, I can care!"

Nearly stumbling, Sterling threw his arms wide as he awkwardly followed Cerulean down the hill. When he got to the bottom, he sighed. "I'm tired of walking. We'll speak of your future—later."

Cerulean turned away. "Fine. I'm going to see Anne."

The two beings, facing different directions, vanished at precisely the same moment.

Mary awoke to the blurry sight of her mom bent over her.

Her mom's red-rimmed eyes looked haggard and wisps of hair fell free of her ragged ponytail. Her lips trembled. "She's awake."

Her dad came over and leaned over the edge of the hospital bed. He, too, had dark circles under his eyes and his clothes were rumpled.

Mary's throat felt thick and sore. "Where—?"

Her mom patted her hand. "Don't try to talk. You're in a hospital. Daddy went to pick you up, and he found the Dewitt's car overturned. It took a little while, but they found you and brought you here. You'll be okay, sweetheart, though you might not feel so good for a while."

Mary blinked and tried to speak again, but searing pain caused her to clutch her throat.

Philip barked, "Nurse!"

A woman dressed in white appeared at Mary's bedside. "Oh, good. I'll let Dr. Maynard know." An assistant came in and recorded Mary's vital signs and adjusted the drip line going into her arm.

"Can she have some water?" Anne smoothed back Mary's hair. "I think her throat is dry." A large plastic cup was brought, and Anne carefully helped Mary take a sip.

Mary lay limp and exhausted. She looked from her dad to her mom. "That guy, the one who was with me.... Where'd he go?"

Anne's hand went to her trembling lips. "I am so sorry, honey, but he died."

Trying to focus, Mary frowned. "Died? He was helping me. How could he die?"

Tears slipped down Anne's cheeks. "I am sure Mr. Dewitt tried, but he had a severe head wound. You were thrown and luckily you had the presence of mind to put pressure on the wound. I give you a lot of credit, Mary. That was a smart move."

Mary shook her head slightly and immediately winced in pain. "I wasn't thrown. I was carried. That man who saved me; he carried me. He tied his shirt around my leg and then made me hold back the bleeding just before—"

Philip straightened up. He glanced at the nurse who was just finishing her notes. She shrugged. Philip stepped back a pace and whispered. "A dream?"

The nurse scratched her chin and studied Mary. "Don't know. Possibly. I doubt anyone'd go to the trouble of helping her and then just leave. Doesn't make sense."

Philip rubbed his hand over the stubble on his chin and returned to where Anne sat on the edge of the bed.

Patting Mary's hand, Anne spoke softly, "Well, I don't know who you saw, but I do know that you're alive, and you're going to get well. The doctor said it was a close call, though." She glanced at Philip. "Thank God, no matter who else."

Philip agreed, his eyes glistening with fresh tears. He lightly caressed Mary's bruised face. "You want anything, sweetie?"

A weak smile crept across her face. "Do you think they have any ice cream?"

Philip's face lit up. "If they don't, I know where I can get some."

The nurse called from the back of the room. "Oh, I think we can find a few bowls of ice cream around the place. What kind?"

The words, chocolate, strawberry, and mint were all spoken at once. The nurse grinned. "I'll see what I can do." She stepped over and took Mary's hand. "For such a brave little lady, I'm pretty sure we can find something you'd like." She winked at Anne. "Besides, my brother works at a Dairy-Sweet just down the road." She picked up her laptop and left the room.

Mary yawned and closed her eyes. "My head hurts."

Anne stroked her daughter's forehead as Mary's eyes closed. "You just rest, honey. They're giving you some strong medicine, and you'll need every ounce of strength to recover." She nodded toward Philip. "Your daddy and I'll be right here. Sleep now."

Mary nodded off, whispering, "I liked his eyes."

Philip led Anne to the chair in the back of the room. His brow furrowed. "It seems strange."

Anne slid into the chair with a long sigh. "What?"

"The police officer said that he couldn't see how she had been thrown where she was; the car wasn't at the right angle and—"

Anne stared up at him through weary eyes. "And?"

"There was a bloody shirt wrapped around her leg."

Anne sat up, her eyes widening. "You mean someone helped her and then—left?"

Running his hand through his hair, Philip shook his head and snapped. "But why he left...I can't imagine. He saved her life for God's sake!"

Anne suddenly remembered a pair of kind eyes belonging to a man who had come out of the blue and disappeared almost as suddenly. She felt a tingling sensation spread across her body. She looked at Philip but no words came.

Philip gazed down at Mary as she lay sleeping. "Well, it doesn't matter. Whoever it was must have had his reasons. It's best to just be grateful and leave it at that."

Anne wanted to agree, though she wondered if it would be left at that, or if perhaps someday, she and Mary would see those eyes again.

FATHER THOMAS

The white-stone chapel stood in the middle of an open square, surrounded by garden beds blooming with end-of-the-season flowers. Modern, towering edifices surrounded the ornate gardens. If pedestrians focused only on the small, white structure, they could imagine themselves transported back to the Middle Ages. There was something contradictory, almost mystical, about the petite church's serene existence in the center of the modern, bustling world.

The large wooden doors creaked as Eve pulled them wide enough to slip inside. Anne followed close behind into the surprisingly bright interior. Large, peaked, stained-glass windows marched in stately rows down each wall. The artistry was magnificent. Peace embraced Anne. Twelve rows of cherry-wood pews stained a shiny brown stood at attention on either side of the central aisle.

Her rubber-soled shoes glided across the stone floor without a sound as Anne made her way forward. The gold tabernacle was encased in a large marble structure that looked very much like a miniature church with an ornate cross gracing its peak. Candles to the right and left glimmered in the golden light. Her eyes were drawn upward toward paintings of saints and angels on the ceiling. Anne felt mesmerized. Though the churches she had visited before were just as ornate, she felt something here pulling her forward. Realizing that she was standing in front of the tabernacle and that Eve had knelt down in the pew on the left, Anne nodded her head in a show of respect. Without being sure what else to do, she slipped into the pew on the right. Closing her eyes, Anne folded her hands together and attempted to pray.

Oh, God. I don't really know You, so I don't know what to say. I've called on Your help a few times but.... Anne's attention strayed. Mary was at home, and Philip had gone back to work. Everything should be normal, but everything felt different. The world was a mess. Her life—

A strange discomfort informed her that someone was watching her. Even when she and Philip were alone together, she would sometimes sense someone else's presence. She glanced about, but there was no one else. Anne closed her eyes and tried again.

Philip has been struggling at work, God, and his health's not so good. He's tired all the time but when I try to help, he just gets mad and tells me that he doesn't need another mother. What am I supposed to do?

Anne realized she had opened her eyes and was staring at the tabernacle. She squeezed her eyes shut again. *Are You really there?* She opened her eyes again, almost afraid that she might actually hear a response. There was nothing but the quiet presence of Eve across the aisle. She stared at the gold box. *I don't know You, but I'd like to. Who are You? I can't imagine how You might look. Would anyone recognize You?*

Eve moved out of the pew as a priest approached from a side room. "Hello, Father. I'd like you to meet a friend of mine, Anne Smith."

Anne quickly slid out of the pew and stepped up to where her friend and the priest were standing.

Smiling, Father Thomas held out his hand. Taking Anne's hand in his, he pressed it warmly. "Hello, Anne. It's nice to meet you." He darted a glance at Eve. "So, how do you like the paint job?"

Eve's eyes glowed. "It's beautiful. Really brightens up the space."

With sage agreement, Father Thomas nodded. "Yes, even churches can get dark without proper care. The building that is…though—" he smiled, "I'm sure the same can be said for souls."

A giddy sensation muddled Anne's composure. Her words came out in a tumbling rush. "Thank you for letting me visit, Father. I'm not really a Catholic, though my parents were once, at least I think they were. They never really talked about it, some kind of family secret maybe, like a skeleton...." Reddening slightly, Anne tried to recover her composure. "It's just that—"

Father Thomas grinned. "That's okay. I wasn't a Catholic the first time I walked into this chapel either. You don't have to show your papers or anything."

Anne swallowed. "Oh, I'm not sure I could ever become Catholic. Philip's not too thrilled with God, though I'd like Mary to see this place. She likes art. I mean—" Anne shook her head. "I'll shut up now."

The twinkle in Father Thomas' eyes matched his demeanor. "Would you like me to show you around? No conversion necessary, alright?"

Anne's shoulders slumped. "Yeah, sure, I love art and history."

Eve chuckled and gestured toward Father Thomas. "Well, then you're in the right hands. Father Thomas happens to be an art historian. Middle Ages, right, Father?"

"First love of my life." He motioned toward the tabernacle. "But Someone stole my heart away, and I've never been the same since."

Anne shivered. Someone stood off to the right, just outside her field of vision, though when she darted a look, there was no one. She glanced back to the priest. "You believe in angels, right?"

Father Thomas had begun to walk toward the back of the church but now, as he turned toward Anne, he opened his hands in a welcoming gesture. "Certainly, a foundation of my faith. But remember, not all angels look alike."

"But, do they look like *someone*?"

"If God wants them to." Father Thomas stood under one of the stained glass windows near the back of the church. "Look here. This is an image of what someone thought an angel might look like. We don't know why the artist picked this face and form. We can tell a lot from the symbolism, but it was something from deep inside the artist that created this picture. We're visual creatures. We need to see to understand. Yet God asks us to envision another world—to see without eyes. Still, He knows our weakness. He knows how we struggle and He allows us to catch glimpses of the unseen through the seen. Like in this picture."

Anne considered the stained glass window and felt conflicted. "No, it's a nice picture and all, but the angel I saw looked like a real man. He acted like a real man too. But in my heart, I've always wondered if he was an angel."

Father Thomas didn't appear unduly disturbed by this revelation. "Well, as I said, God allows us to see the unseen through the seen. And just because angels aren't tied down by our mortal frames doesn't mean they can't look human. History is replete with angels coming to assist men, or women, as the case may be, in human form."

As if someone had just lifted an enormous weight off her shoulders, Anne grinned in relief. "Maybe I will convert. After all, I don't know anyone else who would have believed me and not thrown me into a loony bin."

Eve put her arm around Anne's shoulder. "Don't worry, Anne. I won't tell. Besides, I'd belong right there beside you in that ol' loony bin. I believe in angels too."

Father Thomas' gaze pierced the golden tabernacle. "Belief in God and His angels is not crazy. I firmly believe it is one of humanity's sanest acts."

September

Windy City News
Buildings in Lower District to Be Torn Down

The city planning council voted unanimously last night to raze all abandoned buildings from 5th Street to 101st

Street, between Adams and Jackson. They hope to turn this city section into a nature wilderness park within the next five years. The park will be open to everyone, free of charge. This has become the trend among city developers, who now face a dearth of housing needs and large sections of abandoned buildings.

The few residents who still live in the project area are being asked to consider relocation, with monetary assistance to help with the costs. For those unwilling to make the change, the city council has decided that those residents may opt to live within the confines of the wilderness park, although with no special services afforded to them. Residents will be responsible for road maintenance, emergency transportation, and postal services at their own cost.

Recent efforts to bring communities closer together, thus affording more cost-effective materials and services, have encouraged many residents to make similar property conversions in their cities. So far, major districts in New York, Los Angeles, Chicago, Milwaukee, St. Louis, and Kansas City have completed their first projected closures and begun the transition to wilderness parks.

As Sally Jefferson, director of The Eden Project, said in a recent interview, "Our hope is to repair some of the damage done to Earth. Humanity bears a heavy responsibility for the scourge of pollution and destruction we have inflicted on this planet, and we wish to make amends. The worst parts of our cities are emptying, and we have the choice of abandoning them or using our ingenuity and integrity to re-wilderize these sections for everyone. A variety of native plants will be reintroduced, as will a balance of animals so that neither predator nor prey will have the upper hand. It will be a place of harmony, allowing people from the city to come and rejuvenate their spirits."

Not everyone is happy about the Council's plans. A long-time resident of Chicago's south side, who preferred to remain anonymous, said the whole idea is as ridiculous as colonizing Mars. He said, "There's a lot of different kinds of wildernesses in the world, and Chicago's been pretty wild for a long time. No trying to change us now. You just can't pretty some things up!"

But Milwaukee resident, Phyllis Ladtrome, felt a little more sanguine. At 80 years of age, she believes it's about time we decided how we want to leave things. "It's like when you move out of a house, you don't know what'll happen next, if someone will love it as you did or if it'll just get torn down. Still you owe it something for being your home for so long. You just can't help yourself. You sweep it out and tidy it up before you walk out the door for the last time."

At present, there are 102 cities considering the Eden Project. No one knows for certain what may come of this new effort to deal effectively with our diminishing future, but as Phyllis stated before she left her house for the last time, "It was sad to go, but we all have to go eventually. Might as well make the most of it. Fewer regrets that way."

November
DISCONNECT

Heavy winds slammed against the old farmhouse, but the thick walls bore the assault in stoic stride, the windows rattling only slightly. Anne had checked weeks ago to make sure that every frame had been locked securely in place. She laid braided rugs against every door to catch any fierce winds and double-checked the wood supply. As the season changed from late autumn to early winter, she was not worried. Philip barely even noticed the shorter days and rarely commented on the weather except as it caught him going to or from work.

Saturday morning, Philip sat on the only easy chair in the house, a three-year-old magazine in his hand. He was reading when Anne stepped into the room. Looking up, he watched Anne as she began to dust the furniture. He smirked. "You know, I could hire you out, you're so good at keeping house."

Anne straightened up, not sure how to take the comment. "Well, someone has to." She tilted her head to read the cover of the magazine. "Mountain Men? What on Earth? Are you thinking of taking up rock climbing, Philip?"

Philip dressed in sweats with a towel near at hand, laid the magazine on his ample stomach. There wasn't a beer in sight. It was Saturday morning, but sometimes on the weekend he had been apt to start early. Philip eyed her. "We don't have much of a life, do we?"

Anne stiffened. The rag in her hand hung limply, the bottle of wood oil resting against her leg. "What does that mean, exactly?"

Tossing the magazine aside, Philip maneuvered the chair to an upright position. After huffing to his feet, he spread his arms wide in a humble, innocent gesture. "I just mean, we don't make love anymore. We have sex, but what does that mean? It's good, okay, but not exciting. It's like scratching an itch or getting a drink when you're thirsty, but there's no spice, no passion, nothing to sink your teeth into."

Anne sucked in her breath. "So, you're basically saying, I'm boring?"

"I'm saying *life* is boring." Philip waved his hand in impatience. "Look, Anne, I am not trying to hurt you. It's just, well, look at it from my point of view. I'm nearly 40. My whole life is slipping by and I've never done anything exciting. With the way things are at work, I'll probably never rise any higher. I'm at my peak and it's nothing special, no glorious views, believe me. We're not about to have half a dozen kids or even one more. There're no wars to fight, no invaders to battle…. Life's just a long series of days to get through. Mary doesn't need me; she has you—no one needs me. My life, as it stands now, is meaningless."

The glint in Anne's eyes should have warned him, but Philip had just finished reading an article about a 65-year-old man from Michigan who had "taken back his life" and was now—or three years ago had been—climbing the highest peaks in the world, had rafted down some of the most dangerous rivers, and was pictured with a beautiful woman at his side. Her name was Gina, and she confided that they had "a powerhouse sex-life," details on page 24. The man from Michigan didn't need to confide anything. His smile and the twinkle in his eye spoke for him.

Anne felt a throbbing in her ears. She didn't need to read the article to know what Philip's head was filled with. She had recently talked to

Philip's mom who was eager to tell about the family goings-on. Jackie had a new boyfriend, a band member who traveled a lot. She related how Jackie was sure that this was the perfect relationship. Jackie's new guy worked at night and slept during the day while Jackie had the opposite shift. But they met every afternoon for great sex. Caroline didn't seem embarrassed to pass along this tidbit. In fact, she seemed confident that Jackie would be pleased if Anne knew. Besides, Caroline crooned, Jackie had had so many disappointments in life; no one could begrudge her a little happiness. When Anne had related this news to Philip, he had just snorted, saying that sex would only take Jackie so far. After all, she was getting older, and soon her biting wit would dig a hole and this relationship would fall in, just like all the others. Anne had kept her opinion to herself.

"I never imagined that you...." Anne stared blankly ahead. It was true though. They had fallen into a rut. They didn't go anywhere or do anything special. Mary was pretty much the center of her existence. Keeping the house, the garden, and the recent additions—they had acquired three cats along the way—was about all she could manage. Besides, Philip had willfully withdrawn emotionally, and she was angry with him.

"I don't know what you want from me, Philip. I'm sorry you're bored and unhappy, but you know, happiness comes from within. Father Thomas says that—"

"Oh, hell, Anne, don't start with your Father Thomas stuff. You've told me the highlights, and I really don't want to know anymore. If I wanted to get to know Jesus, I'd have introduced myself a long time ago!" Philip picked up the towel and wrapped it around his neck. "No, what I want is life. A *real* life!"

Anne's eyes narrowed as she clenched her teeth. She had no words.

"I'm sorry, Anne, but you're so complacent; I don't think you can understand. I'm a man. I'm built differently. I need more." He slapped his belly. "I've decided to get in shape and go off someplace new. I'm going to travel and have an adventure."

Anne sniffed. "By yourself?"

"No, a couple of the guys and I are working on something. We're thinking of heading south—maybe all the way to Central America. That'd be cool. Just think of it!"

Anne felt repulsed. Her husband was a child, an irresponsible kid, wanting to play while the world fell to pieces. He cared for no one, not even his own family. Her tone remained icy. "How? When?"

Philip shrugged. "We'll find a way. Spring maybe. I need to work off this gut first. I want to be fit to climb mountains and hack my way through a jungle trail." He strode over to a table and snatched up his jacket. His tennis shoes were cracked and squeaked on the floor. "One of the guys from work built a home gym, and he said I was welcome anytime. I'll be gone till later, okay?" His expression softened. He strode over to her, his chest out, his voice gentle as he caressed her stiff arms. "I didn't mean I don't love you. Course, I love you. I'm just going through some stuff. I need a little something to help me through. But I still need you, too. You know that, don't you?"

Refusing to respond, Anne merely watched as Philip accepted her silence and walked out the door. She heaved a long sigh. *He loves me? He needs me?* Anne eased herself down on the edge of the couch. *What does that mean?*

Philip's dad had begun to have kidney trouble a couple of years back, and Caroline had summarily put him into a nursing home. Caroline visited him regularly, and James didn't seem unduly upset by his change in fortune. But Susie had informed Anne that Caroline had acquired a new friend, a wealthy widower who liked to take her out for "a little fun." He was teaching her *things*, Susie had said. Anne didn't doubt the truth of it. And now Philip was in the mood to learn something new.

She sighed and closed her eyes. She felt it again: the presence of someone watching her. Remembering what Father Thomas had said, she didn't open her eyes. She spoke softly. "I don't know who or what you are, but I have the feeling I'm not alone. If I'm right, and if someone is here with me, well then, pity me. I feel like an utter fool." The room remained silent, but Anne smelled something—like rain on a spring day, earthy and comforting. She sat up and looked around. The doors were closed, not a breath stirred. She shook her head. "I'm off my rocker."

A knock sounded on the kitchen door. Anne rose heavily, went to the door and opened it. There stood her neighbor, Mrs. Hovey. She backed up, opening the door wider. "Oh, hi, Erin. This is an unexpected pleasure. How are you?"

"Hi, Anne, I'm fine. I can't stay. I just wanted to tell you. You may not have heard, but Millie was rushed to the hospital. They say she's pretty bad. Her heart, I think."

Anne's hand flew to her chest. "Millie? Why, I just saw her the other day."

Erin's eyes glistened. "Yeah, I know you're good friends, that's why I stopped by in person. I didn't want you to hear about it from... well, I just thought you'd like to know. I saw an ambulance drive up about four this morning. Her daughter said Millie suddenly called out in her sleep, and when she went to check in on her, she wasn't breathing right." Erin handed Anne a slip of paper. "Here's her room number. I thought you'd like to visit. I've got some errands to run in town, but I'll stop by and see her this evening."

Accepting the slip of paper mechanically, Anne forced a smile. "Thank you, Erin. That was thoughtful of you." She looked at her clothes. "I'll need to change, and let Philip—oh, never mind. I'll take Mary with me." She nodded as Erin said goodbye. Anne turned and considered the state of her life. "Well, forget the cleaning."

Anne climbed the steps, calling for her daughter, "Mary? Where are you?"

Mary stuck her head out of her bedroom doorway. "I'm in my room. What's up?"

"We're going to go visit Millie. She's in the hospital."

Mary sighed long and loud. "Now? I've just got started on a report for—"

"I don't care about any report. This is important. Millie has been a good friend to me, and to you as well, and you sure as heck can get your little body out of your comfort zone and come with me to say hi—or goodbye—as the case may be."

Mary stepped into the hallway as her mother reached the landing. "Do you think she might die?"

"She's an old woman, and they brought her to the hospital in an ambulance. That makes me worry. No one gets to live forever, you know!" Anne's eyes flooded with tears.

Rubbing her nose with the back of her hand, Mary darted back into her room. "I'll be ready in a minute. You want to bring something?"

Anne stepped into her room and grabbed a dress from the closet. Her voice softened. "Like what?"

Mary came running into her mother's room, her jeans and sweatshirt looking neat and clean. "I don't know; I just thought maybe she'd like something. But what do you bring someone who's dying? It's not like they can take anything with them."

After straightening the shoulders of her dress, Anne peered at her daughter. "Yes, that's true." But then she thought of the miniature of the St. Michael figure that Father Thomas had given her. "Get that little statue off my dresser and wrap it in the blue tissue paper from the present box."

Mary snatched the statue off the dresser, disappeared a moment, and then reappeared just as Anne was ready to go. She handed her mom a little packet of blue tied with a yellow ribbon with a tiny white flower stuck on top.

Staring, Anne asked, "Where'd you get the flower?"

Mary turned and began to run down the stairs. "It was right there on the dresser by the present box. I thought Daddy left it or something."

Anne didn't ask where Philip would get a flower at this time of year. She felt a chill go up her arm. Clutching the present, she grabbed her purse and ran down the steps after her daughter.

"She's very weak," the nurse whispered, unfolding an extra blanket and draping it over Millie's still form.

Mille lay on her back, her closed eyes, and a peaceful look on her ashen face.

Mary and Anne stood side by side in the middle of the room, afraid to step closer.

The nurse gazed at them and offered a sad smile. "It won't be long."

Anne sat down beside Millie's bed and took her limp hand.

Mary stayed in the background, watching.

In a few moments, Millie's eyes fluttered open. It took a while for her to focus, but when she saw Anne, she offered a weak smile. "Oh, I'm so glad you made it. I was afraid I'd leave without being able to say goodbye."

Tears coursed down Anne's cheeks. "Oh, Lord, Millie. Do you have to go? I don't want you to leave."

Millie's weak fingers attempted to squeeze Anne's. "It's the way things are, dear. When my Bernard came down sick, I was glad I was there for him in the end. It helps, you know, to face your end when you've faced some others."

Anne rested her head on Millie's bedside and tried to control the sobbing that was aching to be let free. Finally, she raised her head and wiped her eyes. "When my mom died, you sat with me and held my hand, but I didn't feel so bad then. I was ready to let Mom go. She'd had a hard life and when it was her time to leave, I didn't feel *I* was being left. But now, with you, it's like my heart is being wrenched away."

Millie's face glowed. "I know. Funny how it is. God gives us family and all, but it's the ones we chose for ourselves that really make the difference. I was blessed. I was close to my family.... Best friends." Millie sighed. "But the world's changed. I always loved nature, things that can be tended and loved...and let go." Millie paused to get her breath. "I'm waxing poetically; you'd better stop me."

"I love listening to you, Millie." Anne's lips trembled. "You make so much sense."

"I wish I could help you through the years ahead, dear. They'll be lonely ones. You'll face some hard times."

"I can't. I don't want to."

Millie's eyes gleamed. "You won't be alone. As Mr. Shakespeare said, 'There is more to the universe than is dreamt of in our philosophy'…something like that. He knew. Look at the stars; there are worlds out there, Anne, worlds upon worlds."

Sniffing back tears, Anne raised her head. She attempted a joke. "Don't tell me you're a science fiction buff. Eve would be thrilled."

Millie spluttered and coughed. "Nothing of the kind. Don't even know what that means." She gripped Anne's hand. "There's more, Anne. Lots more." Her hand went slack, and she coughed again. The nurse returned, frowning. Millie coughed heavily, and the nurse moved Anne aside.

Anne stepped toward Mary and gestured to the door. "We'll come back later."

The nurse nodded, but all her concentration was centered on Millie.

Anne took Mary to a little food station on the first floor. They had tea and biscuits and attempted conversation, but it was sporadic and disconnected. An hour later, Anne decided to go back up and say goodbye to Millie. They took the elevator to the fourth floor and passed through the stark white corridor toward Millie's room. When they got near, they saw a line of people standing outside the doorway. Anne's stomach clenched. She started forward, but Mary grabbed her hand.

"Mom, this is Millie's family. It's their turn now. We should stay out of the way."

With a frown, Anne decided that Mary was right. She stepped back toward the end of the corridor and leaned against the wall watching the line of people filing in and out of the room. Millie was exhausted, and all these people coming in and out couldn't be helping her. Irritation flooded through Anne as her cheeks began to flush. *Doesn't anyone care how Millie feels? Has anyone asked her what she wants? Or is everyone just trying to sneak his or her last peek at a dying woman?* Anne squeezed her eyes shut to control a growing rage. She felt a tug on her arm.

Millie's daughter stood before her. Her red, swollen eyes peered at Anne through glinting tears. She reached out and pulled Anne into a fierce hug. Anne accepted the smothering embrace as the woman, many years her senior, whispered, "Oh, Anne, God help me. She's gone now, and I don't know how I'll live without her."

November

Poetry Contest Entry #369
Tiger

Loneliness gnaws like a tiger that eats my soul.
It munches slowly, determinedly, and then bites off whole chunks of me.
I run away, but he follows wherever I go.
I hit him, smash him, hate him, but he grows stronger like a storm.
Once when I was little, I was loved.
Mother cuddled me. Father held me on his knee.
Sister thought I was funny and often laughed with me.
Then the laughter grew silent.
Time was a tiger too.
Mother was busy.
I was too big for Father's knee.
I am the last of my kind.
No more little ones dangle on anyone's knee.
Some cry that we have earned our doom.
But I know better, true.
I know it is the tiger that eats at me.
I'll never be free of him because hope is the key.
As long as man is doomed—there is no free to be.
Grandma died last week. Mama will die in time.
I'm left with a thousand like me and then there's only nine.
Loneliness gnaws at my bones, biting at my soul.
Hope is a matter of the will.
But only the tiger eats his fill.

THE IDEA OF PEOPLE

After a long stretch and a cavernous yawn, Dr. Mitchell rose and meandered over to Dr. Peterson's desk, the slight squeak of his shoes making the only sound in the room. The desk was a mess. "Typical," Mike murmured, "never could keep his stuff straight." Frowning, he stared down at the various notes. "Man, oh, man. He's into everything!"

Dr. Peterson's staccato-like step as he entered, accompanied by his sharp, intense tone, warned Dr. Mitchell that trouble was brewing.

"Mitchell? There you are. Have you checked on that report from India-Tech?" Dr. Peterson frowned at Dr. Mitchell's slow response. He rotated his hand for emphasis. "You know, the brain mapping, mind-uploading information, remember?"

Pursing his lips, Dr. Mitchell mumbled. "Oh, yeah, here we go." He waited until Dr. Peterson crossed the room and stopped at his desk. "Yeah, I checked, and they don't have anything new. Well, I shouldn't say that. They have a ton of new stuff, but nothing that'll help us." He scratched his head. "I don't get this big interest in brain research. I mean, we're cloning experts, remember?"

Dr. Peterson slipped into his chair, grabbed a stack of papers, and then thrust them off to the side, flipping on his laptop. "Who says I can't do both? Besides, we've hit a dead end. Brain research is more promising right now. If we can just get the map laid out, we'll be able to upload human intelligence onto artificial devices. If we can't keep the human race going, we can at least keep human knowledge alive. Humanity deserves that, don't you think?"

"Humanity? What exactly defines humanity, Greg? We're not just data carriers, you know. What's the point of information without humanity to make something of it?"

"Oh, please, don't start. I'm not a philosopher. I don't care how you define humanity or what you think of our purpose of existence. I just don't want humanity to go extinct."

"It's like a fox hunt with you. The chase. That's what you love."

"Oh, go to—" Dr. Peterson looked around. "Where's Ellen, the new girl? I told her to come in early so we could start on a project."

Dr. Mitchell pursed his lips. "I believe her name is *Helen*, and she's married." He watched as Dr. Peterson's eyes scanned the computer screen. He had lost him. Dr. Mitchell shrugged as Helen came running in, flinging her lab coat over a short, tight dress. Dr. Mitchell side-stepped out of the way.

Helen stopped by Dr. Peterson's desk. "Sorry I'm late. Frank wasn't feeling so good this morning so—" Anxiety formed creases around her eyes.

Dr. Peterson didn't look at the woman who was now standing next to him. He spoke sharply. "Did you get that information on robotics I wanted?"

Like a frightened rabbit, Helen's eyes darted to her desk. "Yes, of course. I've got the files downloaded to my email. Do you want me to get them?" Her expression appealed to Dr. Mitchell for reassurance.

Dr. Peterson merely scooted a couple of inches over on his chair and ordered, "Sit down next to me. You can transfer your files to mine from here. But first, I want to see what you've got—if it's worth my time."

Helen squeezed herself onto the chair next to Dr. Peterson and was forced to lean across him as she pulled up her email. "I just went to these sites, see, and I researched over—"

Feeling very much like a third wheel, Dr. Mitchell walked away.

Later in the day, Dr. Mitchell sat at his desk, sipping a cup of artificial vanilla-mocha brew. He smiled as he alternately bit into a peanut butter sandwich and sipped the hot drink.

Dr. Peterson strode into the room, his hands visibly shaking. He seemed to want to make an announcement, but the room was nearly empty.

Helen had left early after a call informed her that her husband had gone to the hospital with severe abdominal cramps. Dr. Mitchell had peered appraisingly at Helen when she asked him if it was all right to leave. She squirmed under the glare of his scrutiny, but after a moment he merely said. "It's where you ought to be, Helen. Go take care of your husband." She had scurried away like a mouse that's been freed from a cat's paw.

Dr. Mitchell had decided that he deserved a cup of the best drink available and then, in a fit of health consciousness, he grabbed a peanut butter sandwich to go with it. He had chuckled to himself when he thought that perhaps this woman might escape the overmastering power of his colleague's magnetic attraction. His wife had once said, "Greg gets women the way a spider gets flies." Mike had to agree. His eyes narrowed as he watched Dr. Peterson stand in the center of the room, looking around. Was he looking for Helen? *Probably doesn't even remember her name.*

"Something I can do for you, my friend?" Dr. Mitchell tried to keep his voice light though he felt the tension rising like an overstretched rubber band. The other two lab assistants suddenly decided they had business elsewhere and left. Mike decided he wasn't going to take the bait. *Let him come to me, if he wants. I'm tired of it.*

Dr. Peterson walked over to Dr. Mitchell and stared down at him, an odd look transforming his face, sending a cold shiver down Mike's back. Dr. Mitchell felt as if he had just been measured for a casket. A decision was made, Dr. Mitchell realized, but what decision, he couldn't guess. He sipped his drink and pointed to another chair. "Sorry, this seat's taken, but you can have the one over there."

Propping his hand on the desk, Dr. Peterson leaned over his friend. "I've got it."

Dr. Peterson's acrid breath curled up Dr. Mitchell's nose. Mike wiped his hand across his face, brushing a bit of peanut butter from his lip. Sitting up, he pushed away a rising sense of claustrophobia. "What now?"

"I know what to do. I just need a few volunteers."

Dr. Mitchell froze. His mind raced over all the recent territory that Dr. Peterson had been covering. After cloning had failed to satisfy, he had dabbled in brain uploading research, robotics, and even freezing people so they would last a millennium. He had no idea what Greg was talking about now, but he knew, with a shiver, that he wanted as little as possible to do with it. "For crying out loud, Greg! You've always *got it*! It's always something new. Here I've spent the better part of my adult life studying cloning, and you've run all over the place trying to find a shortcut. To what end? So you can hold death off a while? You know, if there is an answer, we'll find it. But if there is no answer, we're out of luck—end of game. There's no use trying to cheat. You'll just hurt people in the end."

Dr. Peterson's chin clenched as his expression froze. His tone dropped to a whisper. "There is no right or wrong anymore. The moral code burned to cinders the moment scientific law stopped applying. I don't care what you believe, in God or Zeus; there are no more rules. There's only going ahead or going back, and I am sure as hell not going back."

Mike felt the weight of his friend's body too close to his own. He tried to shift his position so that Greg would back off. "So, what're you going to do?" Forcing his way out of his chair, he moved past Greg, and stepped across the room. He refilled his cup, realizing too late that he just mixed decaffeinated swill with his luxury drink. "Damn!"

He turned in exasperation. "Really, Greg, I don't know what's gotten into you. You used to be a pretty good doctor. You really cared about people, at least the *idea* of people. But now—now?" Mike's heart was pounding rapidly. "I hardly know you. You're jumping from cloning, to brain research, to robotics. You aren't doing reliable studies; you use people like toys. You don't care! Damn you! You don't care about anything, not really!"

Dr. Peterson straightened up, his hands on his hips, staring at Dr. Mitchell without appearing in the least disturbed. He merely restated his earlier point. "I have the answer this time. I can fix things. I just need a couple volunteers."

"For what?"

"I'm going to upload their brains onto a computer."

"You mean a brain map?"

"No, I mean the whole brain's consciousness."

Dr. Mitchell rubbed his chin. "Is that possible? And more importantly, is it safe?"

"Sure, I've already done it on rats."

"A man isn't a rat, Greg."

"That's why I need to do this."

"But what about the man involved? How can he have his brain in two places at once?"

"He can. It'd be like having a twin."

"More than that, I think." Dr. Mitchell stepped away. He didn't want his brain's consciousness in the hands of the man in front of him. He didn't know who would. "I'm sorry, Greg. This is a little too much for me. I could handle a clone. But this? This scares me. We haven't thought it through enough. Once this is done, there's no going back."

Greg slapped the desk in front of him. "This is no time to micromanage our morality. We need to save human intelligence. No matter what!"

For the first time, Mike realized that he was no longer communicating with his friend. There was no friend to communicate with. The word "possession" flashed through his mind, and he blinked in the chaos of conflicting thoughts. *I don't believe in that kind of thing.* Dr.

Mitchell squared his shoulders. "I don't know where you're going to find any volunteers around here. Despite your absence of moral code, the rest of us still believe in ethics and we're going to live, and eventually die, by them."

Dr. Peterson grinned mischievously. "That may be...that may be."

Dr. Mitchell put his ruined drink down and turned toward the door. He suddenly knew how Helen felt. "I'll be seeing you, Greg." He flushed, hurrying down the stark white corridor. "Damned, if I'm not a mouse with a cat on my tail."

January

Universal News
Weather Report

Recent weather patterns have shifted so dramatically that some scientists now claim that a new ice age is upon us. Contrary to all expectations, the Earth has been growing colder for the last ten years, suggesting a serious shift in future ecological patterns. Despite global warming, which was shown to have caused some of the worst meteorological changes in human history, this recent shift cannot be accounted for by mere human activity. In fact, evidence indicates that the sun is cooling at an alarming rate.

Solar studies have always been incomplete, and though scientists have been able to make fairly accurate estimates as to the age of the sun and its natural lifespan, researchers are beginning to wonder if perhaps they have missed some vital information concerning solar health.

It seems, according to Dr. Gretchen Grinnell of the Solar Institute, that there are still a number of mysteries when it comes to star life. "We have been watching the stars since humanity began, but serious study of star life had been a mere blip on the historical chart. There is so much we don't know. I feel very much like the caveman of old, scratching his head, wondering what's going on with the sun. All we can say for certain is that there has been a measurable drop in solar activity. At first, we believed these changes were due to natural flux and would balance themselves out with increased temperatures at a later date, and of course, that still might happen. But humanity is so fragile that a few degrees can alter our lives significantly. The sun is so massive, and the convolutions it might experience are so enormous that we might not survive to take measurements, much less find a solution."

That evaluation has been echoed by weather stations across the world as forecasters struggle to accurately predict tomorrow's weather. "We do the best we can with what we have, and the rest is guesswork based on what has happened in the past," said weatherman Harold Healy of GKRD news.

So, once again, we are left with an uncertain future. It seems that's about the only thing we can be sure of these days.

EYES

"I hate Good Friday services. They're so depressing." Mary, her arms crossed in front of her, stood watching Anne slip on her dress shoes.

It had been a tough day with fasting and three hours of stony silence. What else would go wrong before the day was over? *Easter can't come fast enough.* "It's not meant to be fun. It's about something real, and real isn't always fun."

Mary tapped her foot. "Well, let's get it over with. Is Dad coming?"

Anne stood and ignored the question. They both knew the answer, and she didn't like delving into Mary's motivation for asking. *Does she want to rub it in or make it clear that I am dividing the family?* Anne picked up her beige shawl and wrapped it around her shoulders.

"You look so old fashioned in that thing." Mary scowled. "I'd think you'd want to look as young as you could."

Anne strode towards the door, trying to keep her thoughts on her present mission: to get to Mass and remember what the day was about. Eve was going to be there. Straightening her shoulders, she descended the steps carefully, her heels clacking on the wood. "You don't really know what you are talking about. There are a lot of ways of looking young, Mary. I'm trying to find my way."

In a matter of minutes, they sat side by side in the cold car driving down the broken road toward church. Anne gripped the steering wheel tightly. After glancing at her daughter who sat in a slouched heap next to her, Anne tried to focus on the road. "You know, when I was younger, much younger, a friend and I strolled along the beach. A woman in shorts and a halter top walked ahead of us, a slender figure with tanned legs and a long, blond ponytail." Anne's eyes flickered back to Mary who was in the midst of rolling her eyes. "And so, you know, I just assumed she was young, probably about my age, twenty-something."

Mary sighed.

"But then, someone threw a ball in that woman's direction and it went over her head, so she turned around to catch it, and there she was, right in front of me, and she wasn't 20 at all—she was closer to 70. She had on heavy eye make-up, but nothing could change that face. She may have had surgery, but it couldn't hide the age in her eyes. She'd never be 20 again." Stopping at a light, Anne looked at her daughter. "I was horrified when I saw what she really was. That poor woman was so worried about looking old that she tried to fool people and act like she was something she wasn't. I vowed then and there that I'd never do that to myself. I'll grow old as gracefully as possible, but I'll never pretend I'm something I am not." Anne pressed the gas pedal as she moved out into traffic again. The two were quiet for some time.

After a few moments, the church steeple peeked above the buildings.

Mary spoke up. "I guess that's really what today's all about."

Anne turned into a parking spot and shifted into park. She looked at her daughter, puzzled. "How's that?"

"Well, God died and if God can die, everyone will die. Death is inevitable."

After pulling the key out of the ignition, Anne stuffed it into her purse. "True, but you've got to remember, we don't stop there. Good Friday is followed by Easter Sunday. God rose. We'll rise too."

"That part sounds nice, but I'm not so sure. I mean, God can do what He wants; He's God. But does He really want to bring *us* back to life? We're not so great. Besides, if He really had some kind of big plan, wouldn't He fix us so we'd act better? Seems like there's an awful lot of things He could change, if He wanted to."

In the distance, parishioners shuffled into the church. Anne kept her voice low. "Mary, we don't get to run the world, and God doesn't run us; we're not robots." Anne struggled against a feeling of doom. "Perhaps God doesn't refuse to help us, so much as He forces us to help ourselves. It's true, we get into a lot of trouble, but maybe He wants us to figure out how to get out of trouble and face our limits."

Stepping out of the car, Mary adjusted her skirt. "Yeah, whatever. Still, it'd be nice if God offered a helping hand."

Anne nudged her daughter's back as they walked forward. "Maybe He does, we just don't realize it."

Cerulean watched the crowd enter the church. A cool breeze blew against skirts and hair. Sunbeams reflected off shiny shoes and glasses. Cerulean, standing under a blossoming hawthorne tree, sighed. He could remain here no longer. Duty called him home. His time was up. He had to deal with the mess the Luxonians were making for themselves. Sterling had sent word that trouble was brewing. A revolution was building, and Cerulean wasn't sure how to brace himself for the impact.

Seven Supreme Judges had broken away from the twelve, insisting that their traditional system of government had become too stifled, and their race had become too afraid of changes. Three of the seven were planning an invasion of one of their weakest neighboring planets for the sole purpose of creating a working class that would better meet their future needs. The other four were advocating intermarriage with compatible races, insisting that they would allow the offspring of these mixed relationships special privileges so as to encourage the new breed to settle on their planet, bringing new life to their tired world.

Guardians all over the planet had taken sides, some forming secret liaisons with other beings to share their resources. Others were more mercenary and had imagined a system of surrogate parents who would breed in confinement and be paid for their services, much like animals are bred for their strength and intelligence. These biological parents would have to be screened, tested, and monitored, but that would only create more industry for the emerging population.

Cerulean grimaced as a man about Sterling's size and weight stepped into the church. He knew that Sterling had written an unfavorable report about his work on Earth, but in the escalating tide of revolution, his case was of little importance. No one really cared what he did. Humanity was dying, so Earth was of little concern.

As Cerulean moved in closer and watched the men and women with bowed heads step across the threshold, dip their hands in a dry font, and make the sign of the cross, he wondered if these particular humans grasped something his people were missing. There was humility in their expressions that he no longer saw in his own people. Luxonians, faced with danger, had turned toward invasion, technology, and now even slavery to escape their fate. It would always be so, Cerulean decided. As long as there was a chance to remake their world, they would do anything, even if it involved anarchy and madness.

It was time for him to leave, but he didn't want to go. Anne had just entered the church with Mary. She was as lovely as ever. He had seen Anne's developing devotion to God, and he admired it, though he could hardly understand it. He knew the Christian creed as he knew the creed of a hundred other faiths, some of which had faded into myth and legend. But he wondered, why had this creed survived so long? And why was Anne so drawn to it? Cerulean placed no borders on God, yet he did not have a creed of his own. To Luxonians, God's existence was a merely an ancient theory that had little bearing on daily life. Few of the beings he knew had had any faith, and those who did carried out their religious duties with remorseless punctuality, not with devotion. Not like Anne.

Cerulean was the last to walk into the church. There were no seats left, and several people were standing against the wall. Cerulean found a spot between the wall and the steps leading up to the choir loft. He was tall enough to see everything.

An hour later, the congregation was on their knees. The door to the central tabernacle was open, and the altar had been stripped bare. The reserved host had been placed in a tabernacle off to the side. Two candles were burning, and the smell of the incense hung like a canopy over the assembly.

Cerulean felt peace pervade his soul.

One by one men and women began to rise from their knees and file out of the church.

———————————

Eve and Anne were still on their knees. Mary sat perched on the edge of the pew ready to leave.

Eve nudged Anne and whispered, "I'll be staying a while, but you better go. Mary's tired and Philip will be wondering."

Nodding, Anne turned toward Mary. She picked up her purse and walked to the back of the church right past Cerulean. For one brief moment, she raised her head and their eyes met. Stifling her surprise, Anne caught her breath. She knew those eyes—that smile. Mary nudged her to keep moving, and Anne continued forward.

Cerulean stepped away from the wall, bowed, and left.

Anne stood beside her car, peering at the church doors. Evening darkness covered everything. The early stars were sparkling and the air was decidedly cold. She pulled her shawl tight over her shoulders. Mary was already in the car. Anne waited. Surely, he would come out soon. She saw the door open and then a twinkle of light brightened and disappeared. Anne felt her heart pounding as she slipped into her car.

24

HOME

Winter should be over, but spring had not yet arrived. Anne felt ancient as she knelt on the cold ground. She rubbed her back as she slowly rose to her feet. The ground was still frozen. It was traditional to start seedlings in April, and though the winters were longer and harsher than ever, she believed that the Earth would welcome new life in its usual course. It was early morning, her feet felt numb, and her fingers chilled. The gray sky hinted at coming snow. "Oh, God, surely we'll get one more spring. Won't we?" She hated to beg, but she could not help the small strangled, "Please?" that followed. April was too early to start anything this year. She would have to wait and start her seedlings next month, tend them carefully, and then, by late May or perhaps early June, the ground would be ready. It was not much of a difference. The plants would still have enough time to grow well. They always did.

Even Philip admired her green thumb. He would walk out occasionally in the still, warm evenings and comment, "Your garden's not much to look at, but boy, it sure does produce."

Anne smiled wryly at the recollection. There were so few things she and Philip could talk about these days. Most often, they seemed to merely pass each other with barely a word or a nod. At first, Anne had suspected he was having an affair, but after a while she decided he couldn't be committed to anyone seriously enough to be a threat to her. If he had found another woman, he surely wasn't giving her much.

Anne sighed. She heard the roar of Philip's motorcycle as he drove off to work. No goodbye kiss, no "See you tonight, honey." Nothing. *He just straps on his briefcase, grabs his precious gym bag, and drives off at top speed.* The lump in her throat where her disappointment used to lodge each morning had melted into resignation. He did need her, in his own way, though she had to admit, she needed him less and less. When Philip had announced that he was buying a motorcycle, she actually liked the idea. The price of gas had shot up so much that travel, except for the most necessary occasions was untenable. He had managed his schedule so that he only had to go in to the city three days a week, and he worked at home the rest of the time. His friend's gym was only a couple blocks from work, so he'd just run over there when he had time. Anne had wondered: *Why can't he work around here for exercise?* till she was tired of the question. It was no use wondering why Philip acted as he did. They lived in different worlds.

Anne walked toward the house. With the overcast sky, the house looked dark and foreboding, as if it was brooding over some menacing secret. She looked at the sleeping flowerbeds, all brown and dead looking, but she knew that under the soil there were a myriad of bulbs. *Sometime those bulbs will come back to life, and there will be color and beauty again.*

Mary was calling for her. Mary had received a nursing degree and was working at a local hospital and nursing home, though she still lived at home.

Anne trotted forward. "I'm out here. Coming."

Mary stood on the porch, her arms crossed. "Have you seen my coat? I was sure I left it on the armchair in my room, but it isn't there now."

Anne nodded. "Yeah, I put it in the wash. There was that big splash of mud from the other day. I thought I'd get it done before you had to go to work."

"So, it's in the wash?" Mary's tone was incredulous. "I need it now! Next time, Mom, just let me take care of my own clothes, okay?"

Anne stopped in her tracks, her irritation rising. Just because Mary was a working professional, she seemed to think that she now held a higher status than her mother. She refused any advice and was often bent on correcting any bit of information Anne shared with her. It was as if Mary decided that she was now the mother, and Anne was one of her elderly patients who ought to be handled with a firm hand. *How did I ever end up with such an arrogant, angry daughter?*

But then she remembered her visit to the nursing home. Mary had forgotten her satchel one day, and Anne had brought it to work for her. When she arrived, Anne was directed to the dining room. She had stood back and watched Mary and was struck dumb with surprise. Gone was the angry, morose child she had come to know. Suddenly, her daughter was a different person altogether. Her motions were gentle, there was not a hint of condescension in her tone, and an expression of love radiated through her eyes. Mary appeared to have had no difficulty facing an infirm, old woman, smiling, and holding her hand as she helped her grasp her fork. Laughing at something the old woman had said, Mary's face shown the first glint of beauty that Anne had seen in a long time.

Tears sprang to her eyes at the memory. How she would have loved to have been that old woman and have Mary look at her like that. But when Mary caught sight of her, everything dimmed. The light went out of Mary's eyes; her cheeks flushed a deep red. Marching across the room with her hand out to receive her satchel she mumbled her "Thanks" not even looking at her mother. Anne had managed a soft, "See you at home, honey," before she left, but she had no idea if Mary had even heard her.

Here stood that same imperious woman who she knew was capable of love and kindness, but would offer none to her. For years, Anne had felt guilty, assuming that she had mismanaged their relationship. She had failed as a mother.

Mary had accused her of allowing reporters to harass her, but Anne knew she was helpless to stop the media. They were an insidious beast that would appear when she least expected them and demand an interview with: "Just a moment of your time...." and take three hours. They would insist they had recorded the conversation accurately, but then they left out important parts and included things Mary had never said. Often the articles and news reports were linked to special events: closings or the population countdown. Every time a landmark was reached there would be a rush for interviews: "How do you feel, being one of the last? What do you think your future will be like? Have you any advice for others like you?"

Mary grew furious during these "interrogations" as she called them, and spoke sarcastically, even insulting the integrity of the interviewer so that the session would be cut short. At the last meeting, Mary had managed to walk away in record time with a smug smile. She had gotten the interview down to fifteen minutes before the infuriated reporter threatened that he would never speak with her again. Mary had clapped, saying, "I hope you keep your word this time. You guys make promises but rarely keep them." Mary was so strong-willed that she invariably made enemies. In a world with fast dwindling resources, Anne dreaded Mary's future.

Controlling her resentment and ignoring her daughter, Anne marched up the last steps to the kitchen door. She stopped on the threshold; though she didn't turn around for fear that Mary would see the glint of tears in her eyes. "For your information, I washed it, dried it, and laid it on my bed. I just hadn't gotten around to putting it back in your room. I've been busy too, you know. No thanks expected—it wouldn't be like you." She stalked into the kitchen, trying not to slam the teapot on the stove after she refilled her cup.

Mary walked in behind Anne and said nothing. She retrieved her coat and then returned with her satchel thrown over her shoulder. She stopped and stared at her mother who sat at the kitchen table, sipping a hot cup of tea. "Sorry, Mom, I appreciate what you do."

With a quick shake of the head, Anne shrugged off the comment. "No, I don't think you do, Mary. I think you and your father merely see me as hired help, and you couldn't care less what I think or how I feel."

"That's not true. Dad loves you; he's just going through a lot. He's kind of lost himself."

Anne controlled the impulse to laugh. "Yeah, and while he's been losing himself, he lost pretty much everyone who ever cared about him. Don't make excuses, Mary. You, who hate hypocrisy, let's not pretend that we *care* anymore. At least it'll be more honest."

Mary stood stiff, her shoulders rigid. "You sound bitter."

Anne sniffed back tears. She would not let them fall. "That's because I am."

With unrepentant stoicism, Mary responded. "Not much I can do about that, is there?"

Anne slammed down her cup and it shattered. Hot tea splashed across the table and on her faded dress. "Like hell! You like to say things like that, how everything is beyond you, you can't be bothered to care, except when it suits you. You see yourself as a victim who ought to have a better life, a better world, and you punish everyone for reality being what it is. You blame me for everything! I know you do. Yet, Mary, my girl, if you really were so bloody smart, you'd realize that every generation has hard times, everyone has troubles. No one's exempted from grief in this life."

Mary bent forward and hissed. "Not everyone is born into a dying world!"

Anne slammed her hands together. "We *all* are. It's reality, Mary. We all live awhile and then we all die. The end was always coming; we just liked to pretend it wasn't. Some people have lived with far worse persecution than you'll ever know, but they still managed to craft lives of meaning! They lived—really lived—while they had time."

Anne reached for a towel and began swabbing up the mess she had made. "I feel sorry for you, Mary, not because you might live to see the end of our race, but because you never really got to know our race. You've been angry and judgmental, never seeing the good side of what you have. I suppose you simply pitied the old people because they are so close to their end. But really, if you look at them, they aren't any better or worse than the rest of us. We all have our appointed hour, Mary, even me."

There was a moment of brooding silence before Mary regained her composure. Her voice reverted to its deadpan calm. "I suppose you got me there." Glancing at the clock, she began to step forward. "I'd better get to work; another day, another dollar. Hate to sound mercenary, but I haven't quite got the hang of your meaning yet. Maybe when I'm old and have no one left to blame—I'll get over it."

Anne whispered. "Don't wait till then, Mary." She threw the shattered pieces of cup into the trash and wrung the tea-soaked rag in the sink.

Mary strode out the door, the storm door clicking shut behind her.

Anne turned and sat back down, refusing to let her tears fall. She always felt drained whenever she lost her temper. She had resolved over and over again to manage her emotions better, but she wasn't that holy, not yet. Closing her eyes, Anne considered what to do next.

Suddenly, Mary appeared in the doorway.

Anne looked up, startled. She didn't want to see Mary again so soon. They needed some space to cool their tempers. She frowned. A police officer stepped in behind her daughter. Mary moved aside and allowed him to walk further into the room.

The officer faced Anne, his cap clutched in his hand. Sorry, Mrs. Smith, but your daughter told me you were here. It's about your husband." He cleared his throat. "We just found his motorcycle overturned by the side of the road. He's in pretty bad shape. They're taking him to Memorial. You might want to hurry, just in case."

Anne stared right through the officer. She didn't speak. She stumbled up to the bedroom and snatched her purse off the arm of her chair. As she started down the hall, Mary yelled. "Grab your coat, Mom, it's snowing." Anne swung back and opened the closet. She tried to pull her coat off the hanger. The hanger caught so Anne pulled harder, and the plastic snapped and fell as Anne yanked her coat forward. She didn't bother to shut the folding door.

Out under the snow-filled sky, the police officer offered to take them in his patrol car, but Mary gestured to her Ford. "I'll have to get to work and explain. I'll take you, Mom. We'll see what's going on, and then we can decide what to do."

The police officer nodded as he slipped into his car. "Sorry again, Mrs. Smith."

Anne dropped into the front seat beside her daughter, her mind numb. They didn't say a word until they reached the hospital.

Rushing through the doors, Mary called back to her mother, "Let me ask; I know everyone. They'll know what's going on." Mary conferred with an emergency room attendant for several moments, and then came back to her mother. Her eyes were bright with unshed tears. "He's in the emergency room. They're still working on him. We'll have to wait."

Anne nodded and looked around the dingy waiting room. On this snowy, cloud-laden day the walls looked gray and stagnant.

Gesturing toward a chair, Mary asked, "You want to sit down?"

Anne shook her head. She leaned against the wall and thought of nothing at all. A little while later they were called into the emergency room. A curtain hung in front of the bed. Philip laid there, his face badly bruised and scraped with signs of dried blood around his neck and chest. His clothes had been cut off him; a white sheet lay over most of his body. Tubes streamed from his arm, and a ventilator hose was stuck in his mouth.

Anne almost gagged. She stumbled forward and held back the scream that tore at her throat. "God, oh, God!" was all she could whisper over and over again.

Mary stood on the other side of the bed, sobbing. "Don't go, Dad. I still need you."

Philip made no motion, but Anne lifted his hand and squeezed it gently, saying his name. She felt a sudden gentle twitch as if he knew she were there.

172

The doctor came in, checked Philip's vitals beeping on a monitor, and then stood and watched Philip's forced staccato breathing. "We're doing everything we can, but he's pretty banged up. I'd like to get him to a better equipped hospital, but...." Silence filled the moment.

A nurse walked in with a clipboard. "Do you want us to call anyone?"

Sniffing, Anne tried to wipe away her tears. "Yeah, could you call Father Thomas at Sacred Heart?" She looked at Mary. "I'll call Caroline myself, later."

The nurse nodded and left. The doctor shook his head. "Bad time for a motorcycle ride. I see it all the time."

Mary glared at the doctor. "Are you blaming him? He might die for his mistake, don't you think that's enough?"

Anne jerked. "Mary!" She looked at the doctor. "You're right. But knowing Philip, he undoubtedly thought he'd be okay."

The doctor pressed Anne's hand. "I am truly sorry."

Anne's gaze fell on Philip again. She couldn't think of what to say. They had left so much unsaid, and there wasn't time now. She heard the rhythmic hum of chanting in her head. She pulled up a chair and clutching Philip's hand, she bowed and repeated every prayer she knew.

Mary sat on the edge of the bed, sniffing back tears. She sneered. "He wasn't a believer, Mom. He's not going to start now."

Anne leaned in a little closer. "Even if he never had sense to pray for himself, it never stopped me." Her blurry gaze fell on her daughter. "It matters to me, Mary."

Twenty minutes later, Father Thomas walked in the room, followed by Eve. Eve stepped over to Anne and hugged her. "Oh, Anne, I am so sorry. Father Thomas called and told me. I ran over to the church, and we came together." She glanced over at the bedside.

Father Thomas put on his stole and arranged his prayer kit, but Anne reached over and whispered, "He's gone."

With the solemnity of the moment, Father Thomas laid his hand on Philip's forehead and made the sign of the cross, whispering his prayers. After a moment, he made another sign of the cross and turned toward Anne. "What can I do for you?"

Anne trembled. "Nothing right now, Father. The funeral director is coming, and I have to sign some things. Then I think I'll take Mary home. Maybe later you can stop by."

Mary lifted her tear-stained face from her hands. "They're short-handed because of the snow. I'm already here; I might as well stay."

Anne wanted to resist, but decided not to argue. Exhaustion enveloped her.

Eve frowned. "Mary, you've had an awful shock. Don't you think you should go home awhile?" She glanced at Anne. "Besides, your mom might need you."

Mary stood up and, patting her father's arm one last time, she spoke quietly, "No, Mom needs *you,* she doesn't need me. I'll be home to-night." She stepped past her mother and for a brief moment their eyes met. Blinking back her tears, Mary tried to smile. "Don't feel too bad, Mom. Dad died living the way he wanted."

Anne's chest ached. Her daughter's words weren't true, but she couldn't explain why.

Mary pulled the curtain aside and walked away.

Eve sat down near Philip's bed. "Well, he doesn't look like he suffered."

Anne swallowed hard. "The doctor said he was probably brain dead almost immediately."

"So he never said anything?"

Anne shook her head. "Nothing."

An hour later, the funeral director stepped into the room. He was courteous and kind, and Anne numbly went through the necessary formalities. Eve clutched her hand and when it was over, they walked past the curtain. As if waking from a stupor, Anne suddenly asked, "How will we get home? Mary brought me, but she'll need her car. Father Thomas is staying to make his rounds."

Eve nudged Anne forward. "Don't worry. I thought of that." As they exited the building, Catherine and Lydia, two volunteers from church, stood waiting for them by a small, blue car. They didn't say anything, but their expressions spoke their compassion clearly.

As Anne leaned back in the seat, her body fell limp in surrender. "I just want to go home."

June
GUARDIAN ANGEL

Standing by Philip's grave, Cerulean recalled the first time he ever saw Anne. He pictured the sullen child trying desperately to be stronger than her mother. He saw her courage fighting against overwhelming fear and her spirit yearning to be free. Then he remembered the day, ten years later, when Anne met Philip. Their attraction had been obvious: he had guessed the outcome. While he had been gone, his theory was proved right: they had married and planned their life together. Anne became a teacher; Philip became a lawyer—they became professionals, lived in the country, made a lot of money, and took trips whenever they wanted. They lived their dream.

Cerulean picked up a brightly colored stone and placed it at the peak of the fresh mound. Anne was no longer the girl she had been. He could see a lot of Anne in Mary, though Mary was not attractive, and he wondered at that. Cerulean stepped back and stared at the gravestone. There, carved into the center, was an angel holding the host aloft. Cerulean blinked in the strong light. Philip wasn't a believer. But then he noticed that Anne's name was on the stone also. Her name and her birthdate were clearly marked with a blank spot for her death date. Yes, that made sense. If Anne were going to make a tombstone for them both, she would include angels and God. *But who will bury Anne,* he wondered.

The Earth's population had plummeted dramatically since the last time he had visited. The weather had grown harsher, and climatologists estimated that it would grow nearly intolerable before long. Virulent diseases had carried off great portions of towns and cities. Africa had been especially hard hit, as had been China, India, and great swaths of the Pacific Islands. It seemed that these scourges were immune to the best antibiotics available, and too few researchers had the time or the resources to discover cures. He had assumed that Mary would outlive her mother. But as things spiraled out of control, on Lux as well as on Earth, he realized that no one knew the future, or who would survive the next few years. The end might come sooner than anyone expected.

A woman approached, thin, composed, forty-something. She strolled from a blue Ford parked under a large spreading maple tree, her coat buttoned to her neck, her hair bouncing with every step.

Anne? Cerulean drew back, his heart pounding against his ribs. He had seen her go home earlier. What was she doing here, now?

Anne's gaze swept across the cemetery, then her eyes locked onto him.

Cerulean sucked in a breath and glanced to either side. The flat landscape and low headstones offered no hiding places. He met her gaze.

Anne stopped and stared, apparently uncertain as to whether she should come closer. Then just as suddenly, she began walking forward again. Stepping up to the gravesite, she looked at the stone a moment before she peered over at Cerulean. A breeze rustled the leaves on a nearby tree.

Anne spoke first. "They did a good job—don't you think?"

"I uh...uh—" It had always been Cerulean's experience that humans started with an introduction of some sort, but then, he knew he didn't need one. But didn't Anne? Cerulean cleared his throat and tried again.

"Yes, beautiful. I was just admiring the…the…art work." Cerulean cringed.

Anne peered at Cerulean a moment. "Do I know you?"

Cerulean swallowed. How could he answer that question? "Ah, no, probably not, though I have seen you. I knew Philip, of course." He tried to make his voice sound natural, exuding a confidence he didn't feel.

Anne's stare persisted. "You worked with him?"

"Something like that."

Anne knelt by the grave and dug her fingers into the loose earth. She crumbled the dirt in her hand and sprinkled it over the mound. "I never went to many funerals in my childhood…but now…too many." She examined the gravestone with a puckered frown. "In old movies, you'd always see the wife sprinkle dirt over the coffin and it seemed to mean something—acceptance maybe. A powerful image. After all, there comes a time when we have to accept. We live. We die. It just is."

Cerulean stepped to her side and he, too, knelt down. He scooped up a small handful of earth and spread it over the mound, gently.

Anne's eyes followed the stream of dirt as it spread over the grave in a thin covering. Then her eyes followed the curve of the arm up to Cerulean's shoulder, over his neck, and finally to his face. She remained absolutely still as she whispered, "I know you."

Head bowed, Cerulean whispered. "If you do, it wasn't my intention. Though, if I had been free to choose, I would have chosen you… as a friend."

Anne swallowed hard and sat down, her hands beginning to shake. "Tell me."

Cerulean surveyed the environment. Seeing no one, he also sat down on the grass next to the grave. He stroked his chin. "Do you want the truth—or something to make you feel better?"

Anne's eyebrows arched. "Generally, the truth makes me feel better."

"Yes, for you, that may be true." Cerulean plucked a blade of grass and tossed it to the wind. "My name is Cerulean, and I come from a long way off. Your people have not even explored my part of the universe, but we are travelers, among other things, and we visit distant planets."

Anne remained frozen in place, her eyes widening.

"I am a guardian, a protector, of sorts. Despite our advantages, our people are vulnerable and we want to know and understand other races, so as to guard against future threats. At least that was the idea, long ago, when the guardianship was first created."

Cerulean glanced at Anne, and observing her frigid expression he hurried on, his expression grim. "I came to Earth long before you were born, and I observed humanity, noting its strengths and weaknesses. I saw a great deal to concern me," his voice softened, "and a great deal to admire. It has been a work I've grown to love."

Anne looked up toward the sun, blinking back tears, her voice shaky. "I thought you were my guardian angel."

A shadowed smile crossed over Cerulean's face. "I can't be that. God's domain, not mine."

Shaking her head, Anne slapped her forehead. "This is absolutely insane—yet I can't help but believe you. I've seen you out of the corner of my eye countless times, always in the background." Anne suddenly sat upright, pointing her finger. "You helped me the day I fell down the stairs." As Cerulean opened his hands in admission, Anne leaned forward. "And you saved Mary?"

Again Cerulean nodded. He gazed at Anne as the sun lit up the streaks of gray, which ran through her hair. He forced himself to look away. "Do you understand what's happening to your race?"

The awe in Anne's expression faded as her gaze fell upon the tombstone. "Yes. Humanity always knew there would be an end; we just refused to think about it. We assumed it would always be on someone else's watch." Tears flooded her eyes as she stared at the figure of the guardian angel. "I always hoped that perhaps, if we learned our lesson, if we got better, maybe God would relent, like He did with Noah, and we'd have another chance." She studied Cerulean. "But you don't think so, do you?"

Cerulean shook his head. "It's not for me to say. But, Anne...there is more to this world than you realize. There is more than humanity realizes. Oh, your scientists say they can measure to the outer limits and they know a great deal, but they don't know nearly enough. They don't know what really matters."

Anne wiped her eyes with the back of her hand, her words choked. "What really matters?"

"That we have this chance." Reaching out, Cerulean touched Anne's arm. He felt the softness, the vulnerability of her skin. "Anne, you're not alone. You never were. Humanity was never alone. Don't you understand? This is our chance to find out who we are, what we're made of, who we belong to."

Anne's eyes shifted from the image of the angel to the host. "You believe in a God?"

Following Anne's gaze, Cerulean nodded. "There's only one."

Anne rubbed her hands up and down her arms where goose bumps had broken over her skin. "With Philip gone and only Mary left to me, even with God, still, I am alone. You say I'm not." Anne frowned. "But really? I've spent too many nights crying myself to sleep. No one comforts me; no one holds my hand. I'm alone in my own head trying to think, trying to understand, scared and confused—I am alone. We all are."

"That is the paradox. Luxonians are made of light, and we can move at will and take on different appearances, but even with all of that, we are all separate identities. We each have unique minds and individual wills. We can choose good or evil, civilization or anarchy." Cerulean's momentary smile disappeared as he frowned at his clasped hands.

A sour look crossed Anne's face. "So, this appearance—your looking like a man—it isn't real?"

"I wouldn't exactly fit in as a being of light, now would I?"

Anne snorted. "No, I guess that might be a dead giveaway. But, really, why don't you just show yourself? Why don't you tell our government or religious leaders the truth? Surely, we couldn't hurt you?"

Rubbing his temple, Cerulean chuckled. "If you knew just how many laws I'm breaking having this conversation with you.... Remember, my people are vulnerable; guardians are supposed to protect our race by finding out information without being seen."

"So, you're basically a spy."

"Well, I wouldn't put it that way. I'm an observer, a guardian of both my people and yours." Cerulean flung a little stone aside. "I'm not a spy. I care; I believe in humanity."

Bitterness crept into Anne's voice. "So what do your kind think of us? Do they still see us as a threat? Have you told them all about my stupid life, and how I can't even manage my own daughter? That should amuse your celestial friends."

Cerulean spoke softly. "No. When I describe you, I tell them about your strength and kindness, your enduring love." He did not look up though he could feel Anne's eyes on him. "But you must understand, there are several guardians on Earth, 36 to be exact, and they have not all had good experiences. Some report evil things, and some report the mundane and silly. Everyone has their own perspective, but it is up to the judges to discern the truth." Cerulean sighed. "But right now, humanity is not of much interest to them. The Supreme Council has other problems to think about."

"Who are these beings that dare to judge humanity? I mean, isn't that God's job? If you know about God, surely they do."

"They simply judge whether you are a threat to us, so that we can develop strategies to meet that threat. So far we have been able to make ourselves more secure by being ready for sudden aggression. We've found ample means only because we've learned so much about our enemies."

"Enemies? So—we're your enemy?"

"In the Judges' eyes, possibly. They look at everything in the universe as possible allies or possible enemies. So far, we have few allies and lots of enemies."

After a pause, Anne shifted her weight and started again. "You said that your people have a lot of problems and they aren't worried about us now, so what's going on? Have some of your enemies attacked?"

"The worst enemy of all—the one within."

Anne's next question died on her lips as a small group of men strode toward them. Anne rose to her feet. "They worked with Philip. Nice enough but…er…well, it doesn't matter now." Anxiety engulfed her face as she stiffened.

Cerulean moved to her side and his hand brushed against hers. He offered a comforting squeeze and then parted, standing off to the side.

Anne stepped forward, squaring her shoulders. "Hey, Jack, Sam… Anthony. It's nice to see you, though I wish it were under better circumstances." Anne held out her hand.

Sam and Anthony reached out and shook her hand in turn while Jack stepped forward and pulled Anne into an engulfing hug. He whispered something in her ear.

Anne blushed and stepped back, gesturing for Cerulean to come forward. "This is…a… cousin…of mine. He came to visit."

Cerulean maintained his impassive gaze in the face of Anne's quick lie and stepped forward, shaking each man's hand politely.

Jack nodded his salutation and took control of the conversation. "We're so sorry, Anne. I went to the hospital as soon as I heard, but it was all over by then. Philip'll be sorely missed. He was a great guy."

Anne murmured, "Oh, yeah, true." She shook herself and looked back toward the gravestone. "They just put it in," she said, pointing. "Did a nice job."

Jack stepped forward and knelt down by the mound. He reached out and patted the earth as if he was trying to comfort his friend.

Anne's frown deepened.

Cerulean's gaze followed every dramatic motion that Jack made. He watched as Jack stood back up. His suit was neatly pressed, a perfect fit. He was an attractive man in good condition. The other two men standing off to the side wore neat suits and looked every inch the professionals mourning for a departed colleague.

Jack stepped over and grasped Anne's hand. "I never thought I'd find you here, just lucky, I guess. But you've been in my thoughts—a lot—and I've wanted to tell you how sorry I am and how much Philip's friendship meant to me. You've got a rough road ahead, but know that I'm here for you, Anne. Call on me, please."

Anne's hands trembled as she looked off into the distance.

Slowly, Jack let her hand down, a soft smile played around his lips.

Anne's return smile was quick and efficient. "Thanks, Jack. I appreciate it." She nodded toward the other men. "I'm grateful to you all. The flowers you sent were beautiful. I still have the plants. Mary took one."

A new light kindled in Jack's eyes. "How is Mary handling all this?"

Anne shifted her weight onto her other foot, barely suppressing a sigh. "Well, she's been through a lot and though she's familiar with death, working in a hospital and all, this was really hard. But she's handling it." Anne's gaze darted toward her car.

Jack's eyes remained fixed on Anne. "Tell her that I've been thinking of her, and if she has any problems, anything at all, I'm available."

Murmuring her thanks again, Anne glanced back at Cerulean, whose expression was stone-like. "Come on Cer...Stephen, I'll take you home."

Anne stepped in front of Jack, nodded a polite goodbye to Sam and Anthony, and began walking down the gravel path toward her car. She shivered.

Cerulean moved in step beside her. Within a few moments, they were in the Ford and driving away. Cerulean adjusted the rearview mirror.

Jack remained standing in place, watching as their car rolled onto the main road.

Cerulean's eyes narrowed.

August
ANNE'S DIARY

I don't know why I am keeping this journal, but I figure that anyone who manages to survive might find it interesting—maybe.

I'm so lonely.

Philip is gone, it's true, but he wasn't much of a friend these last years. I really shouldn't miss him so much, but I do. I miss what we had. I miss the dreams we dreamed and the hopes we shared. I miss his wanting me and my wanting him. I miss being young and making plans. I'm growing old. We should be obsessed with death. But I'm not. Life is still my obsession.

Mary doesn't understand me. She's been kinder since Philip died. It's as if she finally realizes that I'll be the next to go, and she should enjoy our time together. She has taken to cooking, which surprised me. Suddenly, she is looking up old recipes and serving delicious dinners. I wonder if she has met someone. She'll never tell me, of course. She always says that marriage is an outdated idea. But the other day, when my anniversary date arrived, she handed me a little picture of the three of us and said, "Here you go, Mom. Just because Dad's not here to celebrate doesn't mean we should forget." I was amazed. But I think there is a guy somewhere.

Cerulean. I made him promise never to watch me without letting me know. He solemnly agreed, though I could see it cost him something to do so. I'm not sure what a promise is worth in his world, but I believe he'll keep his word. He told me that he only gets to visit every 10 years and that he'll have to leave again in April. My heart froze. Why? I suddenly felt like I did when Millie died.

I guess, even though I only saw a flicker of him every now and again, I made up so many imaginary ideas that I was comforted. Now that I know he's really an alien who only visits every ten years, I'm a little bereft. I like him more than—what? Is it wrong to feel attracted to an alien? Good Lord, how would that sound in confession! "Bless me Father for I have sinned. My sins are—I'm attracted to an alien?" Poor Father Thomas. I couldn't do that to him. Could I?

I'm in love. There, I said it. I've only met him a few times but my heart pounds when he is around, and I feel so happy. I wish he were human. But then, if he were a man, he wouldn't be Cerulean. He would die with the rest of us. I don't want that. I want him to live. He said something about trouble on his world, but he doesn't want to talk about it. He said the less I know about them, the better. But he did say that his people could learn a lot from humanity. I wonder what he meant. I suspect Luxonians could teach us a thing or two. But Cerulean doesn't think they could save us, even if they wanted to, and they don't seem inclined to. I can't help but thinking that he's lonely too. Despite his being able to travel at will and visit worlds beyond my imagination, still, he's lonely.

Oh well, I have him until April and that's still months off. We can see each other as often as we like, though Cerulean says he doesn't want to be "known" by the general public. I think he wants to be with me as much as I want to be with him, but he sees danger where I want to become reckless. I don't care if you read this, Cerulean—I love you. I even love your name. It's for the color blue, isn't it? How perfect.

I wish I could tell Eve. She'd be thrilled, though Eve's been go-

ing through a lot lately. She doesn't date anymore; she's quieter and spends a lot of time in church. Father Thomas and Eve have a special relationship. Some people like to whisper nasty things, but I know them too well. They are both too in love with God to hold with any rival.

Still, I'd love to see the look on Eve's face if I told her I've met an actual alien. She'd probably pull my arms off trying to get me into church for an exorcism. But Father Thomas? I think he'd believe me. He'd just ask me to bring Cerulean to church on Sunday. Only problem, Father's so obvious. He'd shake Cerulean's hand after Mass and say, for the entire world to hear, "So, you're that nice extra-terrestrial Anne was telling me about." Deep sigh.

I hear Mary's car driving up. She's home early, and I haven't been to the garden to pick the lettuce and tomatoes yet. I promised her I'd make a salad. We should do more canning. The pantry and freezers are about to burst, but I can feel a change in the weather and the garden won't last much longer. I need to get busy out there. Winter's no joke and what we can't use, a hundred other folks can. Oh, God, help me.

August

City Slicker Magazine
Food Shortages, Disease, Early Winters, Make a Deadly Combination

The World Population Report harbors some grim statistics. Because of a dramatic drop in population due to infertility, a series of deadly storms that have hit coastlines all over the globe, and the scourge of two new diseases, the human population declined to near decimation. The northern half of the US experienced an early winter with snowfall beginning as early as September for states that normally do not see snow until December. Even the southern states have recorded lower-than-average temperatures. Fruit crops have been severely damaged from recent climate changes, and further damage is on the horizon.

Farmers are working to devise better and bigger greenhouse solutions, but due to a lack of manpower and materials, only the largest companies have been able to make much progress, though the resurgence of backyard gardens has proven to be very beneficial for everyone. Current statistics estimate that forty-six percent of foodstuffs are now being grown through backyard and small farm efforts, and as the crises deepen this number will only increase. If you haven't started a backyard garden, see backyardgarden.com for information. They have tips, information about local suppliers, and general advice on how to make your backyard garden a success for you and your community.

The Centers for Disease Control and Prevention are working on identifying and controlling the recent outbreaks that have devastated whole sections of towns and cities. Mutating bacteria have built up immunity to every known antibiotic. This bacterium, nicknamed the Super Bug, seems able to change according to its host and attack an individual's immune system, much like a virus might run through a computer's hardware. Doctors and researchers are working around the clock to come up with a vaccine, but as of today's report, there has been little success.

Local and state authorities are advising everyone to do what they can to stretch their food supply until spring, which, if predictions are accurate, should arrive in early June. Make plans to expand next year's garden now and remember, always practice good hygiene. Wash and preserve your foodstuffs carefully. Do not mix with large crowds, and doctor yourself with home remedies whenever possible. There are numerous resources available for self-care, covering everything from the common cold to broken bones. Visit "cureyourself.com" for more information. As our problems escalate, the public will have to become more self-reliant. The ratio of healthcare professionals to the general population has widened to an alarming rate. A large number of veterinarians have been called into hospital service just to cover the growing need.

So make a difference in your neighborhood by educating yourself. Remember the keys to survival: food, water, shelter, and healthcare. Learn all you can and practice good stewardship to make the world a better place.

And while you're at it, you might want to offer up a prayer.

December
ISOLATION

Dr. Greg Peterson slumped against the wall in exhaustion. The stark cell padding didn't keep him from hurting himself. Bruises on his arms and legs and a slash across his face where a guard had raked him in a fight highlighted the circles under his eyes. The drugs they were giving him rarely knocked him out completely, but they made his world hazy, like a dream. He had asked the guards for alcohol, insisting that it would have the same effect, but he'd enjoy it a whole lot more. The guard on duty had sneered. "You're not in here to enjoy yourself, idiot."

A disturbing grin further disfigured his already damaged face. Greg had conceded the point. No, he wasn't. He was locked in a padded cell because a judge had declared him insane and a danger to himself and others. *Why didn't they just kill me? It would've been so much easier and saved everyone a whole lot of trouble.* But he knew the answer to that, too. With the drop in population, the very idea of killing anyone, even a convicted criminal, had gone heavily against public opinion. Polls showed that few people favored the death penalty before the population drop, but now it was a point of zealous honor not to kill anyone for any reason.

As if that would fix anything. Greg had snorted in irritation when he read the quote in the paper. He had begun screaming at the walls, "Oh, God, these stupid, mindless, animals! They aren't worth saving. *I'm* not worth saving!" He had raged periodically for the first several weeks of confinement. But now, as Greg leaned wearily against the wall, his shallow breathing barely making a sound and his eyes drooping in sleepiness, he remembered his past.

He had found the perfect answer. There was a way to upload the brain onto a computer, but the brain functions had to be active—you couldn't upload a dead brain. There were several people willing to have their minds made immortal, but Greg knew that he needed minds of the highest quality. They would be the survivors, heirs to humanity's wealth of knowledge. He needed men who knew what he knew, men who could rule from a computer armature. He felt a frenzied need to hurry, and when he tried to explain his hopes to his colleague, Mike had only laughed in that inane way he had and remarked that he didn't want to live forever.

Greg felt driven. Once it was done, Mike would understand. He'd come to believe. It wouldn't hurt, and Greg sincerely believed there was little risk. The animals he had experimented on had survived. But animals were of no real use. It was impossible to tell what exactly you were recording from an animal. He needed a human mind to see if the person's intellect and will could be uploaded. So one evening….

—— A Year Ago ——

Mike glanced at the drink in his hand. "Wow, this whiskey is—" His gaze lifted to Greg's, panic in his eyes. "What'd you put in it?"

Greg smiled. Wanting Mike to remain relaxed, he had a lie ready. It hadn't been necessary. Mike's head slumped forward, and the glass slipped from his hand and fell to the floor.

Greg took a breath, and slid into action, loading the body into his car, speeding to the hospital. A team of doctors awaited him. They needed to open the skull to get direct access to the brain.

He'd no sooner drilled the first pilot hole into the skull than there was a bustle at the door and armed security guards rushed in and put a stop to everything.

Apparently, Mike had shared his concerns about Greg with his wife, and when her husband didn't answer her calls, she alerted the authorities, who had heard whispers of Dr. Peterson's new experiments. No one knew what they would find, but the investigation that followed was enough to convict Dr. Peterson and his zealot accomplices of unlawfully using hospital materials and personnel and of endangering a colleague's life.

The last vestiges of Dr. Peterson's carefully controlled personality snapped in the courtroom. He remembered the raw feel in his throat, how it ached as he screamed at the judge and jury. He couldn't remember exactly what he said, but apparently, it wasn't nice. He was sent to prison, a review for parole in twenty years—if he lived that long.

Snorting at the memory, Greg leaned his head heavily against the padded wall. Raising his hand to his lips, Greg felt something slithering down his chin; he was drooling. He tried to wipe the saliva away, but gravity pinned his arm to the ground. He remembered his near escape and his eyes once again glazed over.

—— Two Months Ago ——

One of the guards, Joe-something, enjoyed hearing details about his research. The fool considered himself a budding scientist, and Greg spoke to him like an equal, using all the big words and fancy terms he could think of. Joe became more and more awed by Greg's brilliance. Finally, Greg invited Joe into his cell, telling him that he was going to share his secret, the key to humanity's survival so that maybe he could smuggle it out to the waiting world. Joe believed every cock-eyed word and entered the cell, never considering that a man as emaciated as Greg could be a threat. Besides, they were friends. As it turned out, Greg's strength was enough to smash an unwary man into an unconsciousness heap.

He stripped Joe, took his clothes and the keys, and then stepped sedately along the corridor. All too soon, he found himself face to face with another guard who was not so enchanted with him. He observed the ring on the man's meaty finger. When the guard approached and told Greg to hold still, Greg warned him that he had outside connections who could make a visit to his wife. To Greg's amazement, the guard was not intimidated. Snorting, the guard stunned him and laid him flat on the ground. When Greg attempted to struggle, there was a brief scuffle before he was well and truly subdued. It was during that struggle that he had acquired his scar. Despite his failure to escape, he was rather proud of the scar. The authorities transferred him to isolation. After an attempted suicide, he was placed in this padded cell. He wondered how he had managed to maintain his sanity.

A gurgling laugh bubbled to the surface. *I've never been sane. Anyone who thinks he can save humanity is hardly sane.*

At the sound of the door sliding open, Greg's eyes fluttered. He forced his eyes wide in an attempt to clear his fuzzy vision.

A dark-haired man in a white lab coat stepped into the cell.

Greg smiled inside. Oh, yes, his one and only friend, Dr. Mitchel, had come for a visit. He showed up every now and again, always around some holiday. Greg tried to lift his arm in salute. "Nice to see you, Mike. Have a seat." His gurgled laugh sounded grotesque as he patted the floor.

Mike wore casual pants with a thick turtleneck sweater. He stepped into the room, making no sound. Looking down at Greg, who struggled to sit upright, Mike reached down and helped to steady him.

Greg's vision cleared, and he stared, attempting to speak without the gurgle. "How long's it been?"

Mike shrugged. "I was here a couple of months ago. Tried to rouse you. I guess you were too doped up. They said you'd been agitated, so they gave you something extra." He looked Greg over. "You seem better now."

"Don't know. I'm no doctor. Never was. Just pretending." He raised his hand. "How's the wife?"

"Fine. She asks about you sometimes." Mike's eyes darted around the gray, stained walls, while his mouth remained in a straight, uncompromising line. "She still prays for you. Says it's your only hope."

"Hah! I'm well past hope. You oughta tell the truth. Don't lie. If ever a man was damned, I'm that man."

Crossing his legs, Mike sat on the floor. "I'll never believe that. Even after you did…what you did. Still, I know you better. That's why I worked with you for so long. Yeah, you can be arrogant…and incredibly stubborn, but deep down, you care about humanity, even if it's only the idea of humanity. Still… that counts for something."

Greg put up his hand as if blocking too bright a light. "Don't be stupid. I was a fool. I thought humanity was worth saving. I may be locked up, but I still know better than you."

"Listen, Greg; we don't have much time. Truth is, things have gotten worse. Some places are running short of supplies. There may not be enough food, not in the prisons anyway. Some people are talking about making—hard decisions." His eyes glinted at his friend who sat slump-shouldered against the wall.

"So what do you want me to do? Kill myself? I tried that; someone came along and stopped me. Weren't too nice about it, though."

"I just thought you should know. I can bring some foodstuffs, but I don't have a lot myself." Mike shifted his weight and looked at the blank walls. "I thought that maybe…you'd want to make yourself ready."

Greg shrugged as he forced himself into a straighter sitting position. "Ready for what? For judgment? Don't you think I've been judged enough? Damn, if you won't let me die in peace." He blinked and then squeezed his eyes shut against a sharp pain in his head. A trickle of sweat rolled down his face. His eardrums threatened to explode. "Listen, I know you care. Always did. You see things I never could. I looked to the future, to possibilities, that was my god. There's no future now, not for me, not for anyone." Despite his agony, Greg tried to pat his friend's arm, but he couldn't lift his hand off the floor. "You mean well, but I'm sick of living. I'm looking forward to a nice, black hole that'll swallow me up."

"What if—" Mike hissed, "What if there isn't some nice, black hole? Maybe, there's more than this." He waved his arm, encompassing the whole prison. "Heck, Greg, you thought you could upload a man's brain into a computer because you believed that there's more to a man than his body. There *is* something more, and it's beyond all the synapses and stuff we try to map out. Don't you think you might try to believe in—well—whatever it is that comes after, that part of us that lives on?"

Frowning at the numbness in his arms and legs, Greg slurred his question, "Why?"

"Why not?" Mike leaned in a little closer. "Listen, it's not over till it's over. You can always say you're sorry for acting like an idiot, and you can try to care honestly, not to fix everything—but to wish humanity well—no matter what happens."

Thick phlegm bubbled up in Greg's throat, enhancing the gurgling noise. He swallowed hard, but he couldn't get past it; he couldn't breathe. Alarms exploded inside his head. He needed to breathe. To swallow. To answer. "Fool!" He squeezed the words out. "Look at me." He'd only managed to suck in a hint of air. His face burned, bright lights filtered across his vision.

Mike rushed to the heavy metal door and began banging on it with both fists. He looked back to where Greg had fallen on his side, jerking in a fit. Running back, Mike laid his friend's head back so he could get more air. He felt Greg jerk and stiffen and then go limp.

Greg's eyes stopped rolling, and he lay motionless, staring at nothing.

Two guards marched into the room, batons ready. Taking in the scene, they strode up closer. The larger man scowled. "Hope he's dead."

Mike stared at the remains of his friend and felt tears slipping down his cheeks. "Your hope—never mine."

JACK AND MARY

As evening fell, only a single bulb illuminated the kitchen. The room was shrouded in a golden aura, making Anne feel like she should whisper. She had heard what Mary said, but she had a hard time believing it. Staring at Mary, Anne's mind went blank. Finally, she managed to stammer, "J-Jack?"

Mary wrapped her fingers around her lukewarm cup of tea. "Yeah, he was a friend of Dad's, and he's really nice. He called me at work a couple of weeks after Dad died. At first, I was a little put-off, I mean, what do I need with a lawyer? But he was so sincere; I realized I was just getting defensive for no good reason. So, we had lunch together."

Anne couldn't define her fear, but her stomach knotted. Why would a man nearly twice Mary's age want to have lunch with her? She tried to make her voice sound casual and unconcerned. "How did it go? Did you have a nice time?"

Mary glanced away, shifting her weight on the kitchen stool. "Yeah, I had a great time. He's a good man, very caring."

Anne blurted out her next question, her hands flying "How old is he, exactly?"

"I didn't ask, and I don't care!" With a reproachful sigh, Mary continued. "You know, Mom, you have got to give up some of your preconceived ideas about things. Yeah, Jack's a bit older, but in a world that's on the brink of extinction, I hardly think that matters." Her eyes stared accusingly. "How would you feel if you were interested in someone and I asked how old he is?"

An image of Cerulean flooded Anne's mind, and she looked away. "You have to understand, Mary, I just want to protect you. There are predators in the world, and sometimes they come in the guise of friends."

"Such an unchristian sentiment from you, Mom! I'm surprised. You always want me to be more open, not close myself off, but here's a man who finally takes me seriously, and you condemn him as a predator." Mary waved her hand in dismissal. "You think I'm pretty stupid." She slid off her stool and swept toward the doorway.

Weariness enveloped Anne. No matter how she tried, she could rarely approach her daughter correctly. Were they doomed to misunderstand each other? "I don't think you're stupid. I love you."

Over her shoulder, Mary answered back, "You have a funny way of showing it."

With her hands clasped in front of her, Anne pictured Cerulean's compassionate face. At their last meeting, he had reported that there had been trouble on Lux, so he was returning home immediately. He'd promised that he would come back as soon as possible, but if he didn't make it back before spring, he might have to wait for the next cycle. She had nodded her head; barely comprehending the idea that ten, maybe twenty years would pass before she would see him again…if ever.

Anne attempted to pull herself together. Cerulean was not human. He didn't owe her anything. *Desperation blinds me.* As she appraised the empty room, she realized that she was the loneliest she had ever been in her life. Her gaze shifted out the window and down the lane toward Millie's empty house. Her mom had died, then Millie, and finally

Philip. With a shudder, Anne suddenly understood that this was her future, saying goodbye. She would probably get a whole lot lonelier before her turn came.

Staring at the vacant space where Mary had sat, Anne wondered why they couldn't get along. Mary had become much kinder after Philip had died, but then, without warning, they were back to square one. Obviously, her relationship with Jack was Mary's number one interest. She'd brook no interference.

Her shoulders slumping, Anne rubbed the small of her aching back as she considered the wood stove. It was getting late. She had spent the day foraging for wood in the tree lines between fields and splitting what she could. She had hauled a fair quantity to the woodshed and then spent the evening filling the stick boxes. Their supplies were running low and since the winter had been so frigid, they had run out of cut wood early. Anne looked gratefully at the heat radiating off the surface. Thank God for the Amish. They're the ones who came up with this cross between the old and the new world. She had even managed to bake bread in the side oven. The only challenge lay in keeping it supplied with the right-sized wood and sticks.

Heaving a deep sigh, Anne recognized the telltale ache in her legs and arms that warned of a rough night. "One problem at a time," she murmured as she moved off her stool and turned off the light. Mary would be up early for work, and she had to keep the fire strong or the pipes might freeze. Tossing another log on the glowing embers before she went to bed, Anne thought of Cerulean and prayed that he was all right, not having as much trouble with his son as she was having with her daughter.

The planet Lux was vastly different from the planet Earth, reflecting the beings that lived on its surface. Their sun was in closer proximity to the planet with the light so bright it would damage human eyes. But this was not a problem for Luxonians, as light was a primary part of their substance. Their homes, gardens, pets, and the environment, in general, were as varied as their creative natures allowed.

As he reentered his spacious living room, Cerulean tried to keep his mind clear from all distractions. He frowned. Viridian was due to arrive at any moment. He didn't need to see his son to know that he would probably lie to him.

There were rebels who wanted to abolish the Supreme Judges altogether and create a new governing body based on their ability to make progress. Progress was measured by how fast new solutions could be implemented. Previously, the Supreme Judges had worked on a system of data collection, discussion, and finally, consensus. They would investigate an issue from every angle until they felt they understood it perfectly and then agree on a solution. But the process sometimes took years. Viridian, like the rebels, understood that time was not on their side. Since they did not have enough women able to produce healthy children, their population was at risk. But since they were more advanced than many of their neighbors, they also had power.

Viridian openly suggested that an invasion of neighboring planets would alleviate their troubles. They could conquer an alien race, take as many inhabitants as needed to help keep their labor force strong, and work out a compatibility program where those able to produce viable offspring would be allowed to do so. It would mean the end of their race as they knew it, but Viridian was not opposed to that idea. His favorite chant, "We've been stuck in the past far too long!" reflected his races' yearn for change, and he would lead the way.

As soon as Viridian appeared, Cerulean felt his energy fading. How could he fight his own son? "So, how have you been, Viridian? I've heard a lot about your hopes and plans for our race. Your speeches arouse many passions."

Viridian's colors glowed. "Don't flatter me with your observations. Why have you come back? You love the humans more than your own. Let *us* take care of things. You don't belong here now, Earthling."

Cerulean kept his colors muted. "You don't believe that." Cerulean glided toward his son. "I understand your aim, and though I can't agree with your ambition, I respect your passion. I only wish that you'd tell me the whole truth. You want me to leave because you're afraid of what I might find out.... What I might do."

Viridian's laughter reverberated in taunting echoes. "I am not one of your chosen specimens, Father. I am a citizen of this world, and I have more interest in what will happen here than you, I'll outlive you by generations. I wish to make room for new growth and more—"

Swinging aside, Cerulean cut off Viridian's speech. He gazed at their home, a bright space filled with the glory of life. Plants of wildly divergent shape, size, and brilliance glowed around the room. An insect buzzed; its rainbow figure zipped past.

Cerulean morphed into a man's figure; his light remained muted. He perched on an outdoor ledge high above the surrounding city and gestured to his son. "Relax. You're going to wear yourself out."

Viridian glided nearer. His colors glowed like flames.

Cerulean raised his hand to stall him. "You might be right. I don't have as much interest in what happens here as you, but then I'm not trying to forge my way. You're embarking on a mission you don't understand. Before you remake a world, it helps to know the world you are remaking."

"I know—"

"You are young, Viridian. You've heard a great deal of talk and the old order has been shaken. You hope to remake the world according to your idealized dream and become a hero for doing so." Cerulean saw the flash of indignation rise from his son. "I am not trying to insult your integrity, but I was young once too. I judged my father, and I was right to some degree. But you know, Teal had his own wisdom. It took me a long time to see it. Real wisdom is not something we make or acquire; it is something we rediscover. We just keep forgetting it."

Viridian gazed over the blaze of a multicolored sea. Controlling himself with effort, he faced his father. "You have your mission in life; I have mine. You're a pacifist. Go back to Earth—and stay there."

Cerulean shook his head, recalling the day in the snowy woods when his son told him to leave Earth and return home. His essence dimmed and then his colors flared. "I'm still your father. Make no alliance unless you discuss them with me first. The judges are in chaos, so I will judge what is best for you. Do you understand?"

The sneer in Viridian's voice was palpable. "You have no authority over me."

"You're ignorant, Viridian, and that is my fault. But I still bear responsibility for you. If you abandon me, you will set yourself adrift in a merciless world, suffering the fate of all anarchies: defeat by the very force you thought you controlled."

"Anarchy is like fire, Father. Every ruler has to pass through to reach the other side."

"Fire can purify, but it can also destroy."

Viridian swept in closer to his father, his colors muted to a soft glow, defined, and human-like. Reaching out, he touched his father, their colors blending. "You think you're helping me...but I know what I'm doing." Viridian drifted away. "Fire destroys what is old and worn first." He flashed out of sight.

His colors dimming once again, Cerulean chuckled in bitterness. Two planets, both on the brink of annihilation, but neither of them knew how to face their fate. He looked over to the welcoming bed where he used to lie with his wife and closed his eyes a moment. Sighing, he threw up his hands and opened his eyes. "I'm from this world. I'd best start here." Striding forward, Cerulean blinked out of sight.

Mary sat opposite Jack; a blush flamed in her cheeks. They sat cozily in an intimate corner of what had once been someone's living room and now served as a converted diner specializing in "country-cooking." Jack waxed poetically about her looks. No man had ever told her how beautiful she looked, not like this anyway. When his eyes roamed over her, her blush deepened. She luxuriated in their intimacy, even from across a table. His gaze seared her soul.

"So, tell me about your day, your life, your hopes and dreams."

With an embarrassed grin, Mary twirled spaghetti on her fork. She had no intention of putting it in her mouth. Her stomach had tied itself in knots. "I can't imagine why you are so interested in me. I'm no one special. Just a fairly competent hospital nurse who—"

Jack leaned in. His smile devoured her. "You're chosen, Mary. Not only are you beautiful and endearing, you're chosen by God for a holy—"

Mary's fork dropped onto her plate. The knots squeezed painfully. Those words sounded like an echo of the past, "A Chosen One," "Last of Her Kind." She remembered the class photos where the press would line them up according to age. She was always the youngest, always the last of the last. How she hated them for that. For reminding her. For rubbing it in. Mary stared into Jack's sky blue eyes and tried to read his mind. "What the—?"

Jack's passion rose. "Listen to me, Mary, I know how things are. I was a theology major before I became a lawyer. Do you realize that this is not the first time God chose to end the world? But every time He *seems* like He is ending the human race, He actually renews us. I believe you have been chosen for that renewal."

Mary shook her head; she doubted that the knots could get any tighter. "I don't understand. I know about Scripture. Mom made me take catechism classes, even when I was way too old for it. We didn't learn much, but there was this old lady who mumbled Bible stories at us. I know all about Adam and Eve, Noah, Abraham, Moses and all those guys who played along with God's game-of-the-day, but I never thought it was so great being one of His chosen ones. God has a way of tormenting those He professed to love. Look what He did to His Son."

His eyes glowing, Jack pressed his fingers pyramid style. "You don't understand. How much history do you really know? I bet you don't realize what ancient times were like—it's hard to understand. But God has plans and when He is about to change things, He always prepares the way by molding certain people for their special roles." Jack's voice trembled with intensity. "Great men and women almost never realize just how important they really are. It's only later, when things can be seen from a distant perspective that humanity comprehends and is grateful to them." Jack reached across the table and grasped Mary's hand. "I believe you are a very special woman. You may never see it that way, but God surely does, for you were born to renew humanity."

Mary snorted. "How can a barren woman renew anything?"

Jack glanced at the stares that Mary had attracted. He leaned in and whispered. "You won't always be barren. I believe that—"

With a small notepad in hand, the owner approached, a woman in her late sixties with circles under her eyes. "Anything more I can get you guys tonight?"

Jack declined with a wave, and Mary looked dumbly at her full plate.

The hostess pointed to the spaghetti. "You want me to get you something else?"

Mary shook her head.

The woman shrugged and moved off. "If you need me, just ask. I'll be in the back, cleaning up. It's slow tonight."

Clenching her hands under the table, Mary squeezed her eyes shut.

Jack's intense whisper deepened, "Listen to me; I know what I'm talking about. It scares you. It would scare any sane person. But, Mary," Jack reached out for the place where her hand had been, "you'll never be alone. I promise you that. I'll never leave you to face the future without my help. I know your strength, your goodness, and your endurance. From the first moment I saw you—I knew—you were the woman for me."

Opening her eyes, Mary stared at Jack. She winced at the fanaticism in his voice, but his expression was so honest and sincere, just like an ordinary guy, like a guy in love. She averted her gaze and tried to breathe more evenly. "I don't understand. I like you, but I'm not interested in becoming anyone's savior. I'm not made of heroic stuff. I don't care what ideas God or anyone else may have. I'm just me, Mary Smith. If you can love me for who I am, an ordinary woman living an ordinary life, albeit, in a dying world, well then, we can continue seeing each other. But if you have any grand ideas of my becoming a second Eve," her voice rose a decibel, "you're out of your blinking mind."

Straightening up, Jack placed his hand next to his empty plate. "I can respect that. I shouldn't have scared you. Sometimes I get a little carried away. I love the old stories and I wish they were true. Maybe you're right; you're just an ordinary woman. At least as far as the world is concerned. But," Jack managed a small grin, "you'll never be ordinary to me."

Mary felt the knots loosen a little. Appraising the spaghetti, she wondered if she could get a to-go box. "Thanks, Jack. You're special too."

Looking at his watch, Jack pushed himself back from the table. "It's getting late, and I don't want your mom to worry. How about if we get that put into a container, and I take you home?"

In a few minutes, they were driving away from the diner. The moon glowed, a large, white disk surrounded by bright stars. Jack's eyes glimmered in the dim light. "One of these days, I'd like to take you for a drive in the country."

"I live in the country. I've seen it already."

Gripping the wheel a little tighter, Jack responded lightly. "Oh, but there are some wonderful places you haven't seen." As they turned onto a country road, they passed a bucolic farmstead on the right. "I'd love to move into one of those old farm houses someday and live off the land."

With a shake of her head, Mary tried not to laugh. "That's a far cry from being a lawyer, or a theologian for that matter."

"Not really. When you study things deeply, you realize how inter-connected everything is. Living off the land is one of the sanest things man ever did."

"One of the hardest too. Mom works our little farm, and it's no joke. That's why I went into nursing. I'm no farmer."

Jack nodded, his eyes fixed on the road ahead. Finally, he whispered, "Yeah, but I think you'd love the place I have in mind. It'd be perfect." His hand slid over, and he rubbed her thigh gently. "Trust me."

With a shiver of pleasure, Mary leaned back into the soft leather seat. She enjoyed being the center of a man's attention, but Jack was a puzzle. She needed to get away and sort out her feelings. "I'm scheduled to work next week. So, I'll be tied up for a few days. You can give me a call on the weekend, and maybe we can take a drive then, alright?"

Jack turned into her driveway and parked the car. "The house looks dark. Is your mom still up, you think?"

"No, she's probably exhausted. She works pretty hard keeping this place up. Bees are jealous of her industry." Mary peered out the window to the dark outline of her home. "I really should help more. She rarely complains, though."

Jack slipped his arm around Mary's shoulder and pulled her into an embrace. He caressed her cheek and then cupped her chin in his hand, staring intensely into her eyes. "I enjoyed our time together, and I want to see you again…soon."

His aftershave mingled with his masculine scent sent a thrill through Mary. She relaxed into his arm, her eyes closing. As his fingers caressed her jaw and neck, her voice grew huskier than normal. "Even if I'm just plain old Mary and not a new Eve?"

His lips brushed hers. "Just the way you are."

Mary let herself be kissed, responding in turn, relishing the pleasure of his warmth and strength straining against his expensive suit. After a memorable goodbye, she slipped into the dark house, still feeling the tingling sensation of his lips on hers, his touch vibrating through her body.

The floor creaked as she tiptoed passed her mother's room. She stopped a moment and listened. The house was silent. Her mother never snored. She quietly opened her bedroom door, imagining Jack in bed and wondering if he did.

April
ADAM AND EVE

Mary heard her Beethoven's Seventh ring tone blaring from deep inside her purse. Since it was break time, she took the call in the lounge. Only a couple of other nurses sat across from her, deep in discussion. As she propped her head on her hand at the oval table, Jack's smooth voice reached through the phone and rippled through her mind. She could barely control the idiotic grin on her face.

They had taken several drives together, one ending at his apartment. He had shown her his extensive library, his handcrafted artworks, and his old movie collection. He was a man with varied interests. "You're a renaissance man," she had remarked.

Jack had grabbed her around the waist and kissed her, passionately, with the words, "I want to add you to my collection."

Remembering that embrace, Mary's grin spread across her face. Her co-workers had stopped talking and began ogling her. They had commented often enough on the various gifts Jack had given her and the almost non-stop attention he lavished upon her. "Did he call *again*?" Deciding that they were jealous, she ignored their pointed remarks, including sentiments like: "Only fools rush in...."

Mary wondered where he wanted to take her now. They had visited a number of places she hadn't even known existed in her part of the world. They had sipped a luxurious Chardonnay at a backyard winery, visited a local trade center, and strolled through the remnants of a deserted part of town. Jack never seemed to want to do or buy anything extravagant, though the watch, the sweater, and the dress he had given her were of good quality. Mary was past trying to figure him out. She had learned to trust his kindness and love his impetuous nature. He loved her, and that was all that mattered.

"Hey, love, I've been thinking about you too." She rose from the table, leaving her co-workers' stares in the dust. Leaning against the wall with the phone plastered tight against her ear, she tried to catch his every word, blocking out the murmur of conversation in the background. Mary hunched her shoulders, hugging herself. "Yeah, that'll work.... Yeah.... So do I." Mary's blush deepened. "Love you too." She slipped her phone back into her purse with a sigh, refusing to engage in eye contact with the other nurses. She peeked at her watch and grumbled. "Another three hours."

One nurses' mouth twitched in sympathy. "You'll live through 'em. Just keep busy; that always helps."

With a sigh, Mary made her rounds again and found odd jobs to take up the slack. The hours crawled away. After slapping down the last file, she walked outside to the dark parking lot to find Jack waiting for her. He was dressed casually, but his eyes glittered in expectation. Caught off guard, she almost tripped as she ambled toward him. "I thought I was going to meet you at your place?"

Jack got out and snapped opened the passenger door, glanced around, and waved her in, like Cinderella's coachman taking her to the ball.

The car's back end sagged lower than normal.

After she was safely tucked into her seat, Jack winked. "Hope you're up for a surprise. I found a place. It's beautiful."

Huffing humorously at his impromptu move, Mary grinned at the spontaneous game. *He belongs in another age, traveling the seas with Christopher Columbus or conquering the Aztecs like Cortez.*

Jack slipped into the driver seat and thrust the car into drive.

She was about to wave to a friend, but he zipped off before she could.

They drove for hours, and by the time the sun was coming up, Mary realized she had fallen asleep and a new day had begun. She raked her fingers through her tousled hair and blinked at the wide-open fields and the breathtaking view. Hills dotted the horizon. Her mouth fell open in astonishment and despite the warm morning, a chill ran over her arms. "Jack, where in the world have you taken me?"

Jack stared with a glassy gaze at the horizon. He reached out and caressed her hair. Smiling, his eyed fixed, he pointed up ahead. "We're going to those hills. I've bought a place. It's perfect."

Mary paused, trying to let his words sink in, but she couldn't grasp what he meant. "You bought a place? You mean, like a house?"

"Not just a house, a whole farm. There is an orchard, a huge garden, cows and chickens, a couple of hogs, and even a dog and cat to give the place proper atmosphere."

Mary stared at him, incredulous. "You *bought* it?"

Jack's gaze did not swerve. "Yeah, I bought it. I've been saving up for a long time. This has been my dream, to bring my wife to our perfect home."

Mary rubbed her temple, a frown mounting. "Well, if that's your idea of a proposal, I think you need to reconsider. A woman likes to be asked, you know."

Reaching over, Jack grasped her hand and rubbed her fingers between his. "I asked you the first time I took you in my arms, and you didn't resist. I've asked lots of times. You never said no. As far as God in Heaven is concerned, we're man and wife, just like Adam and Eve. We'll finally start our family."

Dizziness engulfed her, like someone had just kicked her in the head. Family? Had he said family? Did he mean he'd bring her mom up here, or his parents? Lord, she didn't really know anything about his family. "Do you have brothers and sisters, Jack?"

"Nope. My Mom died of cancer when I was five, and my dad was killed in a plane crash when I was thirteen."

Mary gave herself a little shake. How come she had never known this? How had it never come up? It had never seemed that important. Suddenly, his past loomed like a storm. "So who raised you?"

Jack's jaw jutted out, his eyes narrowed, and his tone frosted. "An uncle."

Mary swallowed a lump in her throat. "So was he nice?"

"Nope."

As she stared out the car window, her stomach in sudden revolt, Mary tried to guess their destination. "Where are we? In what state, I mean. Kansas? Nebraska?"

Jack chuckled. "You sure wake up asking a lot of questions. I guess I'll have to get used to that. Listen, honey; you don't need to worry about anything. I'll take care of you. I've got everything planned."

Mary's throat tightened and her heart raced. "Are we getting married, Jack?"

A frown mounted as Jack's mouth straightened into a tight line. He forced his words out as if he were explaining difficult matters to a stubborn child. "I already told you; before God, we are married. I'm just taking you home."

Mary sat very still. She licked her dry lips; her hands clenched in her lap. "Home?"

"Yeah, home." Jack glanced at Mary before returning his fixed gaze on the road. "I'll keep us safe. The rest of the world can do what it wants. We'll make a fresh start."

While her heart pounded in raucous disagreement, Mary tried to absorb all of this. There was no fresh start for anyone. Madness prevailed like her Dad always said. "What about my mom?"

They entered a narrow road with huge trees bordering the lane. The ride became rougher. Jack's gaze turned toward Mary for a moment as he spoke in a soft tone. "I know it'll be hard at first, but this was going to happen eventually. You were going to be parted from her when she died. She's an independent person, you said so yourself. She doesn't really need you, and you don't need her. Let her go…make your own life. She's made her choice. You have to make yours."

But I'm not making any choice, she screamed inside her head. She pursed her lips tightly together. First, she had to understand what Jack was doing, or what he *thought* he was doing.

Mary stared at the rising sun and tried to smash down the tide of panic that pounded on her brain. This couldn't be happening—not to her. She had always been protected and well cared for. After all, wasn't she one of the last? Wasn't she special?

Oh, Lord, that's what Jack thought—that she was special. That she was chosen. But he had decided what Mary was chosen for, while she had no idea. *Oh, Lord, save me.* She wished she had called her mom to let her know that she had a date with Jack. Maybe Mom would know what to do—call the police—call someone. But who knew anything about him? Jack had kept himself and his plans a mystery, and here they were driving into some hills she couldn't name, in a state she couldn't identify. Mary leaned back in the seat and squeezed back tears.

Jack caressed her hand. "That's right, honey, you just relax. I'll take care of everything. I've been planning this my whole life."

Mary didn't doubt a word of it. But she wished, more than anything in the world, that she could see her mom.

Ten Years Later—April
ANNE'S DIARY

This is the nicest spring we've had in years—early, too. I've already planted the potatoes and onions, and I think I'll do the lettuce next. The kale survives the longest but it's so tough; I'd like something a bit easier to chew. At fifty-seven my poor teeth aren't what they used to be. It's been so long since I've seen a dentist. I can't even imagine what he would say if I suddenly showed up. Silly of me to think like that. Medical care is for the sick, not the healthy, and I'm still as strong as a horse, thank God. Still, I'd like more variety. It seems I've gotten in a rut these past few years planting the same things over and over. I rotate the crops and all, but I'm sick of beans, corn, potatoes, onions, and cabbage. I think I'll try some peas, cauliflower, and perhaps a few melons and more pumpkins. I can trade for the seeds, so that won't be a problem. I've got enough fruit trees, and they generally do well, except for the peaches; the late frost always knocks them out. Maybe not this year though, everything is warming up so nicely.

I'll have to check on the roof. I heard squirrels rummaging around last night, and I'm afraid they've gotten into the eaves and made a nest for themselves. I'd better get them out before they have a brood of little ones. If they've already got family moved in, I'll never be able to throw them out. Silly? It's just that they get into the attic and start chewing and building and pretty soon I'll have a menagerie on my hands, or over my head, as the case may be.

———————

I took up my pencil to write out my feelings—I've been as moody as a wet cat all week. I don't know what's wrong with me. Well, that's not true. I do know. I just don't want to face it. It's been ten years now since I lost Mary, and I still can't bear it. I feel as if my heart will never mend. I've endured so many losses, from Mom and Millie, to Philip and a hundred other friends, but losing Mary has always been the hardest. I wish we'd been on better terms.

Thank God, I still have Eve. She's the most remarkable woman I've ever known. I can't understand why she doesn't become a nun, but she says that isn't her calling. You'd think it was, the way she acts. She is practically Father Thomas' right hand. She manages the food and clothing pantry, and the way she looks after the sick and dying, it's like she's a modern Mother Teresa. The woman wears me out just watching her. Father Thomas is getting old, though his spirit is still young. He relies on Eve for the home visits, though. They're a remarkable team. I wish I were a part of a remarkable team. But I do the garden work, which produces a quantity of food, much of which Eve gives away. I also help by passing along messages from the few folks left around here, but those are simple jobs. Still, I shouldn't complain. It's what I'm good at.

I still miss Cerulean, though not so much as when he first left. I realize now that I was infatuated—too needy. He has his world; I have mine. He did me one invaluable service, though; he showed me a glimpse of Your grandeur. If anyone else had told me that there were aliens living here, I would have backed away—slowly. But now that I've known Cerulean, the existence of aliens seems perfectly natural. Cerulean promised he would come back, but so much time has passed,

I've given up. There was probably some kind of trouble. He might have died for all I know.

I must learn to accept. I am a lonely woman in a dying world. I have my consolations, though. My little home comforts me—older and worn—it's true, but so is everything. I can do without modern conveniences. I live more like my ancestors now. But I don't mind. It's all in what you get used to.

Well, there's no use worrying about the past. It's the future I must look to. Odd, isn't it? A woman with no future looking forward, not back. But that's the only way to live. I can't believe You made us to simply perish with no meaning. I won't believe that. If it weren't for losing Mary, I'd be content. She's the only loss I can't reconcile myself to.

My light is fading; I should go and put everything away now. Then off to sleep...perchance to dream...ah, there's the rub....

Mary stumbled over a tuft of grass in the road and barely caught herself before she sprawled across the broken pavement. It was dangerous, traveling on these lonely roads, but she had endured it for months now, and her panic-ridden fears had quieted to a wary acceptance. Her whole life these past few years had prepared her for this journey. Looking up, she realized that the sun was fading, and she'd need to find a place to rest.

The road was so cracked and rough it was hard not to trip in the daylight, at night it would be a nightmare. Most people lived in small communities and got along as well as they could, trading, sharing labor and goods. Occasionally, travelers would come through like the bards of old, and they would tell the news from the next town or describe in vivid details what was left of the cities they had passed through. There usually wasn't much to say about the people. At least not much anyone wanted to talk about. Fresh graves didn't inspire conversation. The only joy was in the moment of *right now*. The past was useless. Wishing for what didn't exist was worse than useless.

Mary rubbed her eyes. They were sore and she knew that she had an infection, but she also knew that she had little hope of finding a doctor and nothing to offer, even if she found one. She had only two goals: go home and see her mother one last time, and then, die in peace. She realized now how much she loved her mother; heaviness pressed on her chest every time she thought about it. She knew her mother must have missed her, worried about her, been alone and afraid. But she couldn't have gone home if she wanted to, and she hadn't really wanted to, at least, not until recently.

Jack had been good to her. He was deluded, she had understood that, but she also knew that he had every intention of taking good care of her. He had a dream, a wild inspiration that they were going to reconcile God to humanity and thus renew the face of the Earth. Jack refused to give up, even when it never happened. Her initial anger subsided as she watched his manic attempts to make his dream a reality.

He worked the farm with devoted care, and he managed to forge out of the earth and an old country house, a home and garden. They were as happy as any deluded couple could be in a dying world. They gathered eggs and pastured the cows, they tended the garden and did all the things her mother had done, more even, but they had done it together, unlike her parents.

When she thought about running away, she wondered where she would run to—*what* she would run to. Her fury grew quieter every time Jack promised her a new world. She discovered she pitied as well as loved him. Though she had once been an independent woman, she found she slipped into a new role with Jack. The price of the enticing lie was to allow him to rule. He didn't like her to go anywhere without him. He said that he wanted to protect her from prying eyes and rude questions. Mary rarely ever saw anyone besides him and a few helpers who came by once in a while. When he did bring in someone to repair a pipe or help calve a cow, she was there, but always in the background. After a while, Jack couldn't find anyone to help, so he invented his own solutions. Unfortunately, they lost some animals in the process. Mary convinced herself that it wasn't really Jack's fault. He tried hard—desperately.

Mary stumbled and then righted herself. The memories never stopped. She knew that Jack had tried beyond all reason and strength. Reason did not rule his life, and it did not decide his death. She closed her eyes against the wave of nausea that hit her as the haunting memories flooded back.

Two men had approached the house after dark one night and Jack, ever cautious, went out to meet them. There was a discussion, and Jack had come back into the house looking more irritated than Mary had ever seen him. When she questioned him, he just said that the men were not welcome, and he had sent them on their way. He told Mary not to step out of the house until he told her she could. Mary felt perturbed by his command and even more irritated by the men who had prompted it. She knew that there were thieves running loose and little law enforcement to stop them. Still, they had met so few people that she had never seriously worried about her safety before. But Jack's expression spoke differently.

Later that night, they awoke to the sound of their cow, which had calved recently, mooing in angry distress. Mary had sat up, her heart pounding, while Jack had jumped up and grabbing his old, patched jeans, ran out of the room. She didn't hear anything else for what seemed like an hour but must have only been a few moments. A yell sounded from the barn followed by a series of angry shouts, and what she thought might have been Jack calling her. She looked out the window into the dark night and imagined she heard someone running away down the road. She pulled on her bathrobe and hurried down the steps. Looking out the door, she listened and waited. At first, she could hear nothing, but then she thought she heard Jack's voice, very faint, in the barn.

She ran barefoot across the yard toward the barn and saw the calf standing in the doorway, obviously confused. Her mother was standing right behind her, just as confused but angrier. Mary swallowed her fear and ushered the calf and the cow back into their pen and shut the gate. She then heard a faint moan, and circling around, she found Jack huddled up against the back barn door. When she reached down and touched him, he lurched back in agony. She pulled her hand away from something slippery and wet on her fingers.

She had no memory of how she got Jack back to the house. She helped him drop on to the couch and tried to make him as comfortable as possible, but they both knew he was fatally injured. She wanted to wash his wound, but Jack wouldn't let her lift his shirt. He had been stabbed and was bleeding profusely, but beyond cleaning and comforting him, she didn't have many options. Even with all her nurse's training, she wasn't skilled enough to tend a wound this serious. Jack faded very quickly. The stab had been too near the heart and gone too deep for her to stop his life's blood from draining away. When he stopped breathing and lay completely still, Mary leaned on his bloody chest and cried through the rest of the night.

The next day she was ill and unable to attend to anything, half-crazed with grief. It was not until the following day that she could think clearly. She deemed it fate that he should be buried near the garden he had loved so much. After making that decision, she then went and freed all the animals. Whether they would forage for themselves or wander into some other lonely family's homestead, she had no idea. It no longer mattered. If men could be driven to stab a man for a cow, then the world was insane, and she wanted to go where there was one person, at least, who remembered decency, even after insanity struck.

Her internal compass turned Mary toward her childhood home. She packed up a change of clothes and some food and smashed them into a satchel. Three days after Jack's death, she stepped out into the bright autumn day. That had been months ago. She did not want to remember all she had endured of late. The freezing cold, the uncomfortable stops with strangers; some welcomed her kindly, some weren't so kind. The satchel was almost empty now. She carried it because she was used to carrying it and because occasionally someone would give her enough food to last the next day or so. Only twice had she become desperate enough to steal. But she had been nearly out of her mind at those moments. She didn't want to think about that now. She was very close to home. If nothing stopped her, she should be at her mother's house before the night overwhelmed the day one more time.

As familiar sights came into view, Mary's mind wandered back to various events of her childhood. She remembered the press interviews; the senseless exuberance some people expressed when they met her, just because she was one of the last. She had been born famous, and she hated her fame. But as the excitement died down and the controversy settled into cold acceptance, she felt a hard spot of annoyance that she had been made so much of and then dropped like an old toy. If she was so special as to be one of the last children born, then why wasn't she special even now? Mary shook her head. She knew: because *everyone* was one of the last now. There was no differentiating between young and old, race or religion, man or woman. They were all the last of their kind. The great equalizer. Funny to think of it, but their mortality became humanity's strongest bond.

Mary's arms ached. She was so tired. Blinking in the April sun, she realized that it would be an early spring this year. She probably would not live to see another. Her eyes filled with tears and the broken road blurred, but her feet knew their way now. The trees were swelling with springtime, the farmlands were over grown, the Earth and sky seemed closer, but she recognized enough to assure her that this was her path.

Mary saw her driveway, what was left of it, the big white garage, and their wide front porch. The steps sagged, but someone still cared for the place. The grass had been cut. There was even a hand mower standing silent inside the open garage. Mary limped around toward the garden. It was about noon, and her mom would probably be inside eating her lunch, but Mary wanted to see the garden first. The garden would tell her everything. She stopped by the well pump and stared.

There was Anne bending over a potato patch with a hoe, scraping at the weeds, drawing them away from the roots of the little plants. Anne's back was bent and she had on a faded jean dress, but her hair was tied neatly in a bun on the top of her head. Her face was calm, and there was no look of anger or anxiety. Everything looked and felt perfectly peaceful.

Mary swallowed. The tears would not stop. She wanted something so badly she could not say the word, but she felt the pressing ache. The word finally came. "Mom."

Anne heard a whisper, and at first, she thought it was the sigh of the wind in the fruit trees off to the side, but then something alerted her to a figure near the pump. Straightening up, she smiled her welcome. Anyone who had walked all the way to her lonely home would invariably be in need. She didn't have much to share, but she had enough. And anyone who wanted to steal could try—the garden was barely planted and the wood stove would be hard to walk off with. She stepped forward, using her hoe as a walking stick. Her smile reached out to the newcomer, and she spoke before she could clearly see the face. Her vision was not as perfect as it had once been; her cracked glasses sat uselessly on a shelf in the house.

"Hi there. Anything I can do for you? Beautiful day, isn't it?"

Anne continued walking forward while Mary stood dumb, aching, with tears running down her face. As her mother came nearer, Mary stumbled forward and embraced Anne, crying, almost laughing. "This isn't exactly how I imagined it, crying like this, but—"

Anne pulled back, her hands on her daughter's shoulders, staring at Mary's face, speechless for a moment. "My God! My God, is it you—Mary?"

Mary's throat constricted, her words choked. Finally, she shifted her satchel on her aching shoulder and wiping her face with the back of her hand, she answered, "Yeah, it's me, Mom. I went off with Jack. Been living up in the Dakotas...on a farm we had."

Anne blinked, attempting to take everything in at once. She pressed her daughter to herself once more, saying, "My God!" She pulled back and looked into Mary's exhausted eyes. "We have a lot to talk about. Let's go inside." She led her daughter forward realizing with each step how thin and emaciated Mary had become. That her daughter was not well crushed her initial joy.

After they stepped inside, Mary looked around in wonder, grinning like a child. "It's just like it was. Nothing's changed."

Anne poured water out of a large metal container into the teapot, which she promptly put onto the woodstove. She strolled over to a wood box and threw a few more sticks on the fire. Shutting the wood-stove door, she turned and appraised her daughter again. "Oh, a lot's changed, but probably not so as you'd notice. I've learned how to manage in my own way. I get up with the birds and go to bed when they do. I eat what I can grow or trade. Meat is scarce, though I can get fish from the Hovey pond anytime. They've been good neighbors."

Mary was astonished. "Are they still here?"

"Yeah, one of the few. But I shouldn't say that. They've got a whole passel of Hoveys living there now, relations of relations from far and near come and go. But, they've had their grief. They buried three children last winter." Anne frowned at the memory. "Miserable experience."

"Children?"

Anne shrugged as she got the teacups ready. "Well, not little ones, just the youngest of the family. It is hard to never say *children* again, so we adapted the word. But it seems that no one's spared. Age doesn't protect a person, no guarantees about anything." Anne pried open a metal canister and placed a handful of leaves into a circular strainer. Putting the strainer over one cup, she opened another metal container and this time she turned toward her daughter. "I can't get over...but never mind that now."

She cleared her throat and tried to sound natural. "I suppose you still like your tea sweet. I've had good luck with stevia. I even bring the pots in the house during the winter. I'm so weak." She confided, "I'll go to no end to keep my little comforts."

Mary's eyes glowed with a pleasant memory. "Well, we didn't grow stevia, but I could brew a pretty decent herbal tea. We did have honey, at least sometimes. Jack wasn't exactly an expert beekeeper, but he did manage to harvest a little each fall."

Shivering, Anne straightened up. "I always figured it was him. I knew he disappeared at the same time, but no one would go looking. His uncle insisted that he had a right to follow his dream. When I begged him that he might be dreaming your dream without your permission, he ordered me to step out of the way. 'Leave 'em alone.' That was his motto. I never could reason with him. I suppose that's where Jack got the idea he could just spirit you away?"

Mary tried to ward off the image of Jack bleeding to death on the couch, but it hit her like a rock to the chest. Attempting to recover her breath, she answered. "Jack was the one who took me away—but he wasn't what kept me there."

She paused and looked at the afternoon sunlight streaming through the window. "At first, I was just plain scared. He had this crazy idea that we were meant to renew humanity, like we'd be a new Adam and Eve. I knew that was pure crap. I was afraid of him, but later, I realized I couldn't kill his dream. He lived for it. And he really did love me—in his own way. I never knew that kind of love before." With a sudden blush, Mary glanced at her mother. "I didn't mean that the way it sounded. I know you always loved me, but it was different with Jack. I was the center of his universe. He was strong and willing to create a whole world for me. He really believed he could. Some days I believed it too. I even hoped I'd get pregnant. But after a few years, I stopped fooling myself. But Jack couldn't stop; he worked from sunup till after sunset. He drove himself, but he achieved some wonderful things."

Anne poured the hot water over the strainer slowly, her hands trembling. The steam rose, and the smell of mint filled the air. She motioned toward the stevia.

Mary attempted a smile. "It's been a long time since I tasted anything sweet."

Tossing a sprinkle of the crushed leaves into the hot tea, Anne handed her daughter the cup while she poured some for herself. "Tell me. What did Jack achieve? Where is he now?"

Drawing in a deep breath, Mary carried the tea gingerly over to the table and nearly fell into the chair. Her satchel was left lying deflated on the floor. She waited for her mother to come and sit opposite her. They both sipped their tea a moment and then rubbing her aching eyes, Mary began.

"I enjoyed my new life, away from the routine of work and the glare of the world. Gradually I became convinced that Jack really was inspired, but then, as time passed and I never got pregnant, doubt crept in. I was afraid Jack would become disappointed and bitter. But he never did. He saw everything as a test, purification. If Abraham and Moses had been tested, then it was natural that we'd be tested too. It was not until the end that his belief finally stumbled. The men who stabbed him didn't know him or care about the lives they were destroying. Apparently, God didn't have any grand plan either." Mary stared at the ceiling.

"I tried to pray, Mom, but it was so hard. He'd thank God for things, he'd ask for blessings…it was all sort of random, sporadic, whenever he thought of it. I never thought about church or Mass. In our little world, all that stuff didn't seem to matter. That part of me had faded away with…well, with you and everything. I was different, and I figured God didn't care how we prayed."

Anne blinked back her tears. "It must have been awful, being alone with him, dying like that, praying to a God you hardly knew."

Wiping her hand across her eyes, Mary brushed her tangled hair away from her face. "I must have been in shock. I just sat there while his breathing got worse and worse. He was hurting, but I couldn't fix it. I even walked outside once; I couldn't stand it. I felt like I was going to break into a million pieces. But then I came back. His eyes were open, and when I took his hand, he looked at me and smiled."

Anne stared. "Did say he anything?"

Wringing her hands, Mary sniffed. "'It'll be alright.' And then he became still, and that was the end. I cried that whole day and through the night. Then it rained and I got a chill. I was sick for a while, but I knew I had to bury him so when the rain stopped, I went out intending to dig a grave. I was too miserable and exhausted to do anything of the kind, but I thought I could." Mary's gaze fixed on her mom.

"I know you won't believe this, but the strangest thing happened. I couldn't dig a grave, not in all that mud. I started crying again, and I prayed that I'd die too. But then this guy, a big, strong guy, came out of nowhere. He said he was traveling south, and he wanted to know if I had any bread to spare. I did, so I told him he could take it. I told him to go inside and get it himself. But he looked at me with the shovel and the pitiful hole I'd been trying to make and without even asking, he just took the shovel and started to dig. He didn't ask me why I needed a hole. He just dug a grave and then he went inside, and a few minutes later he came back out and said. 'That your husband in there?' I just nodded, and he went inside and came back carrying Jack's body over his shoulder all wrapped up in the bed sheets. He placed him in the grave and then, when he was done burying him; he got the bread, thanked me, and left."

Mary shook her head and looked at her mother. "I saw him carry a loaf of bread out of the house and I watched him walk away, but later, when I went to get something to eat, I still had my four loaves, right there on the pantry shelf. Maybe I was losing my mind, or maybe I miscounted, but I could have sworn that none were missing. It was like that story of the angel Raphael coming to help Tobias. I just accepted it. Besides, the grave was real enough." Mary rubbed her aching temples. "So then, I let all the animals free." She glanced away, "I figured someone would find them quick enough. I didn't want to be around to explain. I just wanted to come home."

Anne's eyes were wide with wonder. "What did the man look like? Was he average height, middle-aged, blue eyes?"

Mary shook her head, frowning. "No, he was tall, muscular, black eyes, I think." In sudden understanding, Mary's face relaxed. "He was nothing like the angels in books, Mom. No wings."

A wry expression crossed Anne's face. "So how long have you been traveling?"

"That all happened in the fall. I can't recall the date. I don't care much for dates anymore. I just packed up my bag and started walking. I met with some help, and I met with some trouble, but—" Mary swallowed and tried to sip her tea to regain her composure, "well, I'm home."

"Yes, you are. I couldn't be happier. I just wish I had known. All these years. I was positive you'd died. No one could trace you. And you never sent a word."

Mary propped her head in her hands. "Sorry, Mom. It must have been terrible. I can't explain it. It was like living in an alternate reality. I just figured you'd make new friends. You have a life here. I never doubted your ability to cope."

"Coping doesn't make a life, Mary! It doesn't mend a broken heart." Regretting her harsh tone, Anne reached out for Mary's hand, reconciling. "But the past is past. Let's move on. You look like you could use a dip and pour."

Mary snorted in exhausted puzzlement. "Excuse me?"

"Well, it's a cross between a shower and a bath, and it makes the most of your water. There's a large bucket beside the bathtub upstairs. Go on up, and I'll haul some water and fill it. When that's ready, you just get in the tub, use the little container, and you dip out a jug-full at a time. You slosh it all over, soap up, and rinse off. It works well and uses a fraction of the water that we used to." She peered at her daughter. "How did you do it up north?"

Mary stood, holding her empty cup. "Oh, that was one of Jack's successful inventions. He made a hose connection from a tub of water outside, that was filled by a hand pump to an inside tub. He had a way of generating enough power from a bicycle to pump the water from the outside to inside, and then he rigged up this shower drip thing so that you could stand under it, and it would sprinkle down on you. It was amazing." Mary's tone softened. "He was so proud of that thing." She shook herself. "But a dip and pour sounds good right now."

Picking up Mary's light satchel, Anne threw it over her shoulder. "Good, I'll put this in your old room. I turned it into a sewing room... but you can have it back. Your bed is still there. People sometimes wander through needing a place to stay for a night or two." She directed her daughter toward the steps as if she might not remember. "After you're all cleaned up, you can grab some clothes out of my dresser. I've got more than I need. I'll finish the baking. There's some cheese left, and we'll break into the pantry and have a little feast. You must be starved."

Mary labored up the steps. She was trembling by the time she reached the top. "Yeah, I should be, but I hardly notice it anymore." She moved toward her old room. Stopping at the door, she accepted her satchel. "Thanks, Mom. You're kinder to me—than I was to you."

"God knows what we've been through, Mary. Let Him take care of it. You just get cleaned up and rest a bit. Okay?"

Mary nodded as she stepped into her old room.

Anne turned and clumped down the steps picturing a loaf of bread.

Cerulean stood back, watching, as Mary entered the house with Anne. He didn't know what had happened to Anne or her daughter, but after what he had been through on his own world, he didn't need much imagination to guess that life had been hard. When the universe is falling apart, everyone gets hurt. He had spent the last few years trying to save his planet from self-destruction. Now it was his turn.

Deciding to stay out of the way for a while, Cerulean strolled toward the garden. A large, wood frame swing hung solid and still in the spring air. He plunked down, letting the fresh breeze blow over his body. It was good to feel the sun and wind again. Nature could be very invigorating. Humans received more than they realized from their fleshy forms. Biological bodies had limitations and disadvantages, that was obvious, but there were also senses that allowed a man to become aware of so many things at once: color, sound, smell, taste, and touch. It was all very stimulating. He leaned back and closed his eyes. He never wanted to go back. Flashes of the ceaseless arguments, the open warfare, battles, death—and the dismantling of the ancient traditions that once made him feel safe—were still raw in his mind.

The judges had not been able to come to a consensus. No one could remember the last time there was an absolute breach between the judges. Always, it had been in the best interest for someone to comply, to agree, to compromise. Always, they had put the good of the whole above the individual. But not this time. The three factions would not bridge the gap, and in time, the gap grew insurmountable.

Cerulean wiped his hands over his face, trying to stop the memories from rushing over him. Factions broke into fierce divisions, and before long everyone wanted to lead. What had so altered their fundamental character? Cerulean knew the Supreme Judges did not travel, so they were not as influenced by outside ideas. It had only been later that he learned the truth. New ideas had been brought to them. Like a seed, or a germ, transported from one land to another, so the seeds of different ideas had been transported into their world, into their imaginations. "Not all foreign ideas are wrong," Cerulean had argued. He carried new ideas himself. But these foreign ideas were dangerous, backward. These ideas fed egos and starved consciences. The Supreme Judges should have known better. They should have been wiser. Their whole lives had been dedicated to discernment. But this time, they failed. Why? Cerulean rubbed his face again. Burning rage and humiliation swept across him despite the cool breeze.

He knew the answer. It's why he decided to return to Earth. As he watched his people take sides and his son grasp at a sudden opportunity, he realized that wisdom is the fruit of humility. Viridian had once been embarrassed but never humbled. The judges had been considered wise so long they never questioned themselves. When new ideas sprang into their midst, they were unable to see clearly because they forgot the original vision which had kept them safe all these long years.

Judges used to be called the *Servants of Lux*, and the Supreme Judges used to be called the *Servants of the Servants*. They were chosen, not for their learning, but for their goodness. The changes that accrued like rust on metal ate at their integrity. It sheltered them from hard work and the messy part of living with other beings. No one questioned them, and soon they no longer questioned themselves. Pronouncements based on hasty, ill-considered evidence flew across the land, and when conflict arose, they had no humility to listen to anyone. The breach was inevitable.

Individuals and whole families were forced to accept roles they would never have chosen for themselves. Anyone who disagreed was exiled or killed. Killing became horrifyingly easy. There was no mercy because no one believed mercy was necessary. Suddenly, death was no longer feared. The judges no longer cared about the purity of their race. All that mattered was dominance—who would control the emerging new world. They were not worried about fertility anymore because they knew they could get other species to supply their needs. Once they accepted defeat of their original ideal—to protect their kind, their history, and traditions—they became determined to remake the world in reflection of a new image, a dreadful force of dominance.

The guardians and lesser judges grew nervous—then bold. It took a great deal of careful maneuvering and skillful negotiation, but after seven years of hopeless division and horrific destruction, he and a majority of the judges and guardians finally convinced the twelve Supreme Judges to come together again and discuss their future.

At first, everything seemed to go well, but then Cerulean noticed that after every session, there was a new surprise. Always one of the Supreme Judges would come back with new concerns or a baffling suggestion. Cerulean believed that slow appraisals and quiet introspection were one of their greatest assets. But suddenly, urgency pushed the Supreme Judges toward hasty decisions. Reports warned of steep population drops, devastating diseases and threats concerning their sun's health. At first, Cerulean, like many others, feared the worst. Perhaps they were doomed to suffer the same fate as humanity.

But when Cerulean investigated, he found that their population drop had not accelerated, and the other reports were just as false. It was not until later that Cerulean realized the truth. Someone was spreading those fears purposefully, using Earth as a template. Cerulean investigated, slowly, patiently. But he did not discover a connection—until last year.

Viridian had made many powerful friends. He was no longer destined to become a guardian. When Viridian announced that he was working closely with one faction of the Supreme Judges, Cerulean became seriously alarmed. Viridian was not qualified for such a responsibility. Besides, Judges could be very hard on those who did not live up to their standards. Viridian was setting himself up for a devastating failure. The youth was clever and ambitious, strong-willed and determined, but he was not a good listener, he was not humble, and he did not desire to serve. Viridian was definitely not a careful being. If one wanted to work with the Supreme Judges, one must be very, very careful.

Cerulean stopped the swing with his foot. He didn't want to remember anymore. He rose and meandered toward the house. He didn't want to frighten Anne, but he very much wanted to see her. Dearly wishing he had never made the promise not to observe her without her permission, Cerulean stepped up onto the porch and knocked on the kitchen door. There was no answer. A grunting sound came from the side of the house. Cerulean stepped off the porch and saw Anne lugging a five-gallon bucket from the well pump. He stepped over, and without saying a word, took the metal handle.

Anne was so intent on her work that she jumped when she realized what was happening. Stepping back, she choked out her words. "It can't be!" She whispered it again. "It can't be!"

Cerulean lugged the heavy bucket toward the porch steps. "I'm assuming you want this up here?"

"Yes, but, I still say—"

Cerulean grunted. "Listen, I may be strong, but I'm not terribly practiced in the art of water carrying, and I'm getting all wet." With a gesture to his soaking shoes, he asked, "Could we discuss this inside?"

Anne trotted past him and up the steps, shoving open the kitchen door. "Here, it's for Mary. She made it home today. Or do you know that already?"

With a huff, Cerulean put the bucket down on the linoleum floor. "I saw her. She's changed…a lot." He motioned to the bucket. "Where do you want it?"

"I need it upstairs for Mary, but you can't...."

"Oh heck I can't. I'll carry it up the stairs. You can take it from there."

Anne sucked in a deep breath as she envisioned trying to explain Cerulean to Mary. She nodded her agreement. After a few moments, they came down the steps together. Anne's face was flushed, and her heart pounded. It was wonderful, awkward, frightening, and electrifying to have Cerulean back on Earth, in her life, and even in her home. Attempting to walk into the kitchen as calmly as possible, Anne gestured toward a seat. "You might as well stay for dinner. I'm fixing bread and soup. I've even got a block of cheese." When she opened the refrigerator, it was clear that no electricity animated the appliance. Anne explained the small loss away, "Still works to keep things in." Trying to manage despite a dream-like dizziness, she began to bustle around the kitchen.

Cerulean seated himself at the kitchen table. He surveyed the room. "Not much has changed. At least not in here."

"No, not really. I still hang my onions and herbs, and I have the garden out back. I don't keep as many chickens, just a few. I don't need much. What I have extra, I always find a home for. I take care of the little things and the little things take care of me." Anne shut her eyes at the triteness of her statement. She didn't want to discuss her suffering.

Cerulean's smile turned brittle.

Anne brought him a glass of water. "It's hot. You're probably thirsty."

"Thank you." Cerulean took a sip, tapped the glass, and sighed. He appraised Anne carefully, his eyes taking in everything from her gray hair to her tattered shoes. "So, how does it feel, having Mary back?"

Anne's hands shook as she wiped minuscule crumbs off the table. "Not as good as I could wish. She's not well, you know. She's been gone for almost as long as you." She peered at him critically. "I don't know what you know. Have you been...around?"

"You mean have I been spying on you? No. I know practically nothing about your life since I left. Sorry it took me so long to get back. I am rather past my time, but…well…it's a long story. I do know what's been happening on Earth in general. Probably more than you do. There are a few guardians still here. We've discussed things."

Anne grimaced. "That doesn't sound too hopeful. But then, hope is what you make of it." Trite. Again. She pounded the bread dough. After a bit, she took a long breath. "So, tell me what's been going on out there. Did the Supreme Judges ever find out about us—our friendship—I mean."

Cerulean stared vacantly ahead. "Yeah, they found out about me—us—I guess you could say." He paused. "I lived through it."

Anne stopped kneading, her fingers resting on the soft dough. "Lived through it? Were they that angry? I thought it was a matter of personal discretion…like they left the final decision up to you."

"It became—rather complicated."

"I've lived a pretty bland life, might as well tell me about it and liven things up. It'll take a while for the bread to rise." She placed each ball of dough into a buttered bread pan. "Go ahead, talk. I'm all ears."

With the first hint of a smile, Cerulean nodded. "With that kind of encouragement—"

As the sun arched across the sky, Cerulean told of his return home, of the war that soon broke out, and his attempts to bring unity to the Judges. Finally, he described his son's treachery.

"Viridian worked with a group of guardians and ambitious minor Judges. They created false evidence to make everyone believe that our planet was dying and that radical changes had to be adopted quickly. I discounted the similarity to Earth because I believed that whatever was causing humanity's doom could be affecting us, but then I discovered that Viridian merely used Earth as a template. Their very lack of imagination was their undoing."

Anne blinked in dismay. "So you exposed him—your own son?"

Cerulean became rigid, his voice strained. "No, I confronted him. But he would not listen. The next day I was arrested for treason."

"*You* were?"

"Yes." Cerulean looked way and slowly exhaled. "I don't want to think about the rest. Suffice it to say that I was eventually freed, but my son was discovered. He and the others were held for trial. The Judges decided to convene a new council, and with an assembly of six thousand citizens, new Supreme Judges were chosen. There are thirteen now, and they have to make a decision, not by unanimous agreement, but by majority. It is a compromise that will work, at least for the time being. Peace has been reestablished, and our population problem is being addressed. There are several workable solutions that involve substantial help from alien races, but that is a path we needed to face a long time ago. Our biggest problem all along was our pride."

Anne sat on the bench at Cerulean's side. She wiped the last of the bread dough from her fingers on a worn towel. "So what happened to your son? Was he killed?"

"Executed."

"Oh my God!" Anne bowed her head and whispered. "How can you stand it?"

Cerulean let his hand fall on Anne's bent head, and he gently stroked her hair. "How did you stand the loss of your daughter all these years? How do we ever survive terrible things? We endure."

Anne laid her head in the crook of Cerulean's arm. "I missed you. But then I decided that God allows things for a reason. I can't say I am a better person, but I'm content." Cerulean said nothing in words, but warmth spread through her as he held her.

Mary stepped into the room and froze. Her haggard eyes widened at the sight of her mom—embraced by a stranger.

CONFESSION

It was a late afternoon in early May, the air chilled the skin, but hope bloomed in hearts like the first buds of spring. The dread of winter was over, and the enticement of summer promised a joy that had almost been forgotten. Birds chirped and fluttered from branch to branch as if they had already tasted the fruits yet to come. Their drunken-like abandon to all decorum lifted every heart that had sense enough to stop and live in this moment of joy.

With a calm demeanor, Father Thomas limped into the living room and greeted Anne with gentle warmth. A figure stood off to the side, but in deference to an unspoken request, he left the man alone for the moment.

Stepping in after Father, Eve hugged Anne in a vibrant embrace. "It's good to see you looking so well!"

Anne's heart lifted as it always did at the sight of her friend. "Well, I've been keeping busy, planting and all. Besides, this spring's been easier than most." She gestured. "Can I take your coats?"

Father Thomas shivered.

Eve grinned. "Don't try to part him from his single earthly treasure. He wears that thing everywhere." Her amused chuckle hinted at a secret. "It's a gift from a friend."

"Well, it's still a little chilly." Appraising Father Thomas in the slanting light, Anne frowned at his emaciated frame and sallow pallor. She wondered if he was ill, but then she remembered that Eve confided that he often fasted. A pang of guilt reminded her that she barely kept the traditional fasts, much less, imposed any extra penances on herself. *Life's hard enough*, she thought in rote self-defense before glancing at Eve, who was taking off her threadbare jacket. Anne's irritation grew. "Now, where's the coat I gave you? It was warm and had plenty of wear left."

Father Thomas laughed. "She gave it away. She gives everything away." His eyes sparkled. "Except my coat, of course."

Grinning in turn, Eve motioned toward the lighter, warmer kitchen. "Come on, Anne, let's get him something hot to drink, and you can regale us with all your adventures."

Eve's glance fell on Cerulean as he stepped out of the shadow. She froze. "Oh, hi! Sorry. I don't think we've been introduced."

Moving forward, Cerulean extended his hand politely. His voice deep and soft carried the hint of courtly manners. "My name is Sam. I'm staying over a few days to help Anne and Mary. There are roof issues that need attention."

Eve's eyes widened in interest. "Oh? You're a carpenter? Well, that's a handy skill. We could use someone to help us at the church. Prayers and duct tape can only do so much."

Anne nudged Eve toward the kitchen, gritting her words between her teeth. "He's not an *official* carpenter, and I doubt he knows anything about church buildings. Just a friend—"

Cerulean's grin widened. "I'd like to be of service—if I could. Show me what you need, and I'll try."

Glaring at Cerulean, Anne tried to redirect the conversation. "Sam, I thought you needed *a little rest?*"

Cerulean flexed an arm, inhaled, and exhaled as if to prove his fitness for tackling church buildings. "I've never felt better in my life. Besides, Father and Eve have come all the way out here to help you; we ought to do something for them."

Marching past Cerulean, Anne pushed Eve into the kitchen none too gently. "Like becoming a handyman?" She didn't wait for a response.

As she crossed the threshold, Eve snorted. "Oh, Anne! You remember the first day I came here with that stupid casserole, and I went all weak over your brother?"

Anne pulled four cups out of the cupboard. "I remember." After grasping the water pitcher, she suddenly stopped. "And I remember the rest of that day too."

"Oh yeah, sorry. I didn't mean to dredge up bad memories."

Shaking off a whirl of emotions, Anne tried to stabilize her mood. "It wasn't all bad. There was a lot of good in that day. And you weren't the only one smitten. Mark was pretty taken with you, as I remember."

Eve waved Anne's comment aside. "He's a good man, only, as it turned out, not mine. By the way, how's his wife doing? She was ill or something?"

"I haven't heard from them in an age. Last I knew, they moved down south to be closer to her family, but news travels slow these days."

"I can't believe he wouldn't keep you in the loop. You two were pretty close."

Anne slipped onto the bench at the table, folding her hands. Memories exhausted her. "Yes and no. Mom held us together. After she died, he focused on Pam and work and everything else in his world. I didn't fit in. Besides, he and Philip didn't see eye-to-eye. They exchanged angry words, and I don't think he could deal with what happened—Philip's death on top of so many others. Mark never even came to the funeral, just sent a card with some money." Rubbing a dirt stain on her hand, Anne whispered. "Things rarely turn out like you expect."

Eve's voice was husky. "No, they don't."

The two women exchanged an understanding before Father Thomas called to them. "Have you forgotten us?"

Eve rolled her eyes. "Lord, he can be so...oh, never mind. But sometimes I think the word "Father" hardly applies!"

"Eve!"

"Oh, tish. He's a human being. You know, it's warmer in here. " Eve rose but then stopped, tapped her fingers together, and cleared her throat. "Oh, Anne, before I go out there—is there anything you'd like to tell me?"

A flame rose into Anne's cheeks. She had known that she would have to explain Cerulean, but it was clear that Cerulean wasn't going to make that easy. "Tell you?"

Eve's eyebrows arched. "About Sam?"

Anne prayed for inspiration as Cerulean walked into the room leading Father Thomas.

Cerulean spoke first. "I thought it'd work better if we came and joined you two."

Eve softened her expression and glided toward Father Thomas. Practically crooning, she cajoled, "Here, Father, sit down. Your tea's almost ready."

She turned to Anne who had just put the pot on to boil and asked, "So, go on. Tell us about Mary. How can we help?"

Anne arranged the teacups on the table, her eyes flickering toward the steps. She lowered her voice. "I don't want you to *do* anything. It's just that Mary was sick when she returned, and she hasn't gotten any better. She's been through a lot—she's confused and she feels guilty. I don't want to interfere, but she needs guidance." She darted a glance at Cerulean. "But I may not be the person to give it to her."

Father Thomas shook his head. "Why not? You're her mother, and she came home to be reconciled to you. It seems to me she's expecting your guidance."

"She was. At least, I think she was. But she's been rather, well, I don't know how to say this, but she's been a little upset about Sam being here. She seems to think it's wrong...or something."

Father Thomas' expression remained deadpan as he looked from Cerulean back to Anne. "Is it?"

Cerulean raised his eyebrows.

Blushing, Anne shook her head. "No, it's not. Cer—I mean, Sam, is just a friend. He really has been helping me around the farm. He fixed the roof and evicted all the little critters—very nicely, by the way. He's been a great help." She stared Father Thomas in the eye. "But nothing more than a friend."

Folding his hands on the table, Father Thomas maintained direct eye contact with Anne. "Then why are you lying?"

Anne swallowed. The kettle began to whistle; she turned to take it off the woodstove. Without thinking, she grabbed the handle, felt the burn, and dropped it with a cry of pain.

Cerulean and Eve both ran over to her.

Eve put up her hand.

Cerulean stepped back.

"Here, water will soothe it." Eve snatched a bowl off the shelf, filled it with cold water, pushed Anne onto the bench, and immersed her hand. "Now, about this situation." She leaned in, her eyebrows arched. "Come on, Anne, you can tell us the truth. We're your friends; it'll be okay."

Father Thomas spoke up. "Not necessarily. Some things are not okay." He looked Anne directly in the eye. "What are you afraid of?"

Fighting for her dignity as well as Cerulean's safety, Anne rose, wiped her hands on a towel, picked up a hot pad, and carried the kettle to the table. Pouring water into a cup through the tea strainer, she sniffed back a laugh. "I suppose I am afraid you won't believe me. I know I wouldn't believe me. Not unless I had proof—but it's not my place."

She glanced from Cerulean's brooding eyes to Father Thomas' concerned expression. "Father, I have a secret, and though it is not really my secret, it protects everyone. Can you trust me to keep it a secret?"

Father Thomas turned to Cerulean. "I suppose it's really your secret then?"

Cerulean nodded, his face stern, masked.

Father Thomas waved his hand. "Well, as long as you can assure me, Anne, that you two are in good relationship with God and honoring the laws of the Church, I will trust you. But I don't particularly like secrets, except the ones I keep in the confessional."

Suddenly, Anne's eyes lit up. "Oh, now there's an idea. Father, you're brilliant."

Eve's brow's furrowed. "Hey, then I'd be the only one in the dark."

With a mischievous grin, Anne responded, "Not forever, Eve. Not forever."

Father Thomas stood. "How about we go someplace private, Anne?"

Looking out the window, Anne asked, "Would the backyard be alright? I mean, no one is out there, and I'm sure no one could hear us."

"Fine, whatever works." Father Thomas gestured to Eve. "Would you be a dear and get my stole?"

With lips pursed in disappointment, Eve disappeared out the kitchen door.

Cerulean intervened. "Anne, are you sure—?"

"It's alright. Father is bound by the confessional never to tell. But this way, he'll understand." Anne saw Cerulean's confusion and touched his arm. "You've trusted me this far; trust me now."

After passing around the rest of the tea, Anne stepped outside with Father Thomas prepared to act as a confessor.

Eve sat down and sipped her tea quietly while Cerulean strode to the window and watched as Anne and Father ambled toward the swing.

Finally, Eve spoke up. "So, just for the heck of it, why don't you at least tell me your real name?"

Cerulean looked back at Eve, amused. "Cerulean."

"Cerulean?" She repeated the name several times in different ways. "Yeah, now that seems about right. You would be a Cerulean. What, are you from another planet or something?"

Cerulean blanched, but Eve waved his expression away. "I'm just joking. But you are from someplace else. That much is obvious." Sizing him up, she exclaimed, "Russia?"

Cerulean said nothing, maintaining an impassive expression.

Eve peered at him intently as if she could glare him into revealing the truth. "No? Well, I never was great at geography." Eve tried again.

"So, just for the fun of it, let me play detective and try to figure out what really matters here." She drummed her fingers against her cup.

"You're a foreigner who needs help, but you've got a decent heart 'cause you're willing to help Anne out in exchange for food and shelter. Turns out, you like each other, maybe a lot, but you're are too smart to rush into anything…silly." She watched as Cerulean glanced back at the window.

Pushing aside the lace curtain, he spoke unemotionally. "You're right. I'm not from around here, but I didn't come because I needed anything." Turning around, Cerulean looked at Eve. "But that isn't really true." He paced back toward the wood stove. "I did need something. I needed to know that Anne was all right, that she hadn't died thinking that I had forgotten her. But why should that matter?" Cerulean's gloomy expression matched his husky whisper. "Why am I even here, exposing myself, endangering Anne…why am I taking this risk?"

Eve smiled. "You sound like a man in love. By definition, people in love take risks."

Cerulean's expression darkened. "So do fools." He paced back toward the window. "But I am not a fool when I care. Caring is an act of wisdom. That was the whole problem with my people. We stopped caring. We became passionless. Our hearts turned cold. We need—"

"Love?"

Cerulean stopped and gripped the back of Eve's chair. "Yes. And Anne can lead the way."

With a sigh, Eve folded her hands together. "It's hard to love someone you hardly know."

"Not really." Cerulean's gaze turned inward toward a memory. "I didn't really know Anne the first time I encountered her. But very quickly I saw something that made me care."

Eve leaned back. "What did you see?"

"Courage. Her mother was a frightened woman, and Anne had to be strong for both of them. She had to be something she didn't know how to be. But she did it."

Eve's brow furrowed. "You knew Anne when she was a girl?"

"I first saw her when she was seven—in a grocery store."

"Seven?" Eve's voice squeaked as she got up from her seat and put her empty cup in the sink. "How old were you at the time?"

"Older than you are now."

Eve appraised Cerulean's muscular frame. "That would make you eighty-some years old." She shook her head. "You've either had some major surgery or—wait—you're not one of those experiments, are you? One of those clones they were attempting?"

"No, I'm not a clone."

With a darting wave, Eve frowned, "So, what? You're playing with my mind?"

"Your mind is not to be played with. It's much too beautiful."

Eve glared at Cerulean. "Keep that up, and *I'll* have to go to confession."

With a creak, the kitchen door opened. Anne held it as Father Thomas stumbled through. His stole was slightly askew, and he appeared a little dazed. Tottering forward like a man in a dream, Father Thomas limed over and gripped Cerulean's hand in his own. "I've always wanted to meet—"

A strangled gasp issued from Anne.

Father frowned. "I was just going to say, I've always wanted to meet a man of your…er…quality." Taking off his stole, he turned toward Anne. "But about Mary. I think perhaps you should first ask if I could meet with her, and then we can have a little talk."

"I've already asked, and she said that it'd just be a lie." Anne sighed. "I don't know what to do. She doesn't trust me anymore."

"But she returned home. She came all that terrible way just to be with you. When there was nothing else, she knew you would take her in and love her as you always did. No matter what she fears, she knows better."

Anne faltered. "But I can't help her die, Father. And I'm afraid she will die…soon. She needs more than I can give. I want to be sure that Mary will be all right, no matter what happens."

Father took the cup that Eve handed him and blew on the rising steam. "I'll be happy to speak with her. But remember, it's her faith we're talking about. No one can have faith for her. And as for death and beyond…. We hope, we trust, but we can't know what conversations God has with souls after they leave here."

He lifted his cup. "Let me sip this tea a moment, and I'll go up and see her." He glanced from Anne to Cerulean. "I need to catch my breath. I must say—your confession was most original."

June

President Farrell's National Address
My Fellow Americans

My fellow Americans, I speak to you today to assure you that despite the troubles we have had to endure across our land, we are still united in mind and spirit. We are Americans invested with the idealism to meet every challenge with valor, every setback with courage, and every loss with renewed determination. Our loss, personal as well as national, is reflected in the grieving hearts of every human being around the globe. We are not alone, and in this unique moment in history, we have the opportunity to show the world just what Americans can do when faced with tragedy. I want to share with you, my fellow Americans, some of the successes of our friends and neighbors, ordinary people like you from families just like yours, who have shown exceptional courage in this—our hour of distress.

First, there is Frank from Alabama who discovered a whole town on the brink of starvation and in desperate need of medicine. What did Frank do? Did he run away or pillage their homes and take off, leaving those desperate people to die? No, Frank acted like a true American. Using old-fashioned ingenuity, he was able to establish a hospital out of the remains of their school building, and he encouraged everyone who was not too sick to assist him. He then brought in the sick and the dying and took care of the most desperate needs first. He rigged up a makeshift water system and scoured the nearby farms for food. In time, he and his friends were able to bring food, supplies, a doctor, and proper medicine to that beleaguered little town. Frank even managed to arrange for transportation so that the entire population could be evacuated to proper facilities for expert care. Frank is just one example of the selfless heroism that is occurring around the US even as I speak with you today.

There is the remarkable case of Janet, a wonderful woman in her seventies who stopped a gang of thieves from taking the last supplies from Newton Hospice Care Center. She faced these bullies with such courage and determination that the gang leader found he could not carry out his plans, and he gave back the stolen supplies. He and some of his gang even assisted Janet as she went her rounds serving the sick and the dying. Now there is true American grit at its best.

Finally, James Wilson cannot be personally thanked, for he gave his life in the performance of his duty. During a community hall fire, he risked and lost his life to save the members of a small religious group who met there for fellowship. James reminds us of all the thousands of others who have gone before him doing their duty, serving faithfully as policemen, firemen, doctors, servicemen, and many others who exemplify the best and the bravest in the human spirit.

My fellow Americans, as we face the trying days ahead, we must never forget our past and the noble spirit that gave rise to our nation. Despite tragic loss, we are still a blessed people. As your President and Commander in Chief, I have been proud to serve you, knowing that I serve with the best the world has to offer.

Never give up and never forget—you are an American. As long as the American spirit lives, there is always hope.

Good night, and God bless America.

July

Guest Opinion
"Hear Me, Oh Lord"

Throughout the ages, humanity has had to face many challenges. First, there were predators and the taunting specter of starvation. From its inception, the human species has never been completely sure we would survive. Even as we progressed up the ladder of developmental history from barbarians living in caves and killing our meat with primitive weapons to specialized barbarians who lived in better houses and killed not just animals but other humans in our battles for supremacy, so we always risked total annihilation. Extinction always remained a haunting possibility. But then we learned to cheat fate, and we forgot our vulnerability. It took plagues and natural disasters to bring us back to an awareness that the human race might not survive forever.

In ancient times, we believed in deities who controlled the forces of nature we could not understand. We named the elemental forces of thunder, lightning, and water and endured an uneasy alliance with the dangers around us. In time, the Israelites discovered themselves to be the Chosen People, the one race loved by the one God. But even in that uneasy alliance there was grumbling and murmuring against fates and fears. Later, God sent His Son to Earth, and we were calmed. There is another world for us after this one. We no longer had to fear the specter of death, for death had lost its sting. But as time passed, and we grew better able to protect ourselves, we turned inward. We no longer needed God. We thought we could be happy—alone.

Once we became explorers and moved beyond the boundaries that had caged us, once we became masters of the sea and eventually the air, we again forgot our frailty. Our advancement in skills and education so altered our understanding that eventually we worried that our demise might not come from our frailty, but from our strength. Suddenly, we worried we would overpopulate the Earth, and we rose up against our own to curb this dangerous trend. Under the auspice of preservation, we killed countless innocents. Under the banner of purification, strength, and freedom, remaking the world for the "wanted and the fit," we believed we were conquering the fear which had driven us since the beginning. But fear still drove us, though no longer from the outside. Now the creeping threat was inside us, in our minds.

Even when nuclear annihilation loomed, we still feared that we would grow too populous. Numbers scared us out of our minds and even out of our hearts. Whole nations took to limiting family size, and contraception soon became one of the most popular drugs on the market. But even as we slowed our population growth to a point where some nations risked extinction, still we were anxious. Even as technology developed and we emerged nearly emancipated from the grinding daily labor of our ancestors, enjoying the fruits of the highest standard of living ever known, benefiting from the best medicine, the quickest transportation, space-age communication systems, entertainment which took us far from reality—even then—we lived in fear. We did not fear extinction; we feared humanity itself. And we lost sight of our humanity in the process.

When conception slowed, no one realized the danger because we considered conception a threat. We were so imbued with inverse thinking that conception was no longer an achievement but a punishment. So today, we are a fraction of our former selves. We are about to face our biggest fear, which has chased us down through the dark passages of human history. This time, all our technology, learning, science, and ingenuity can't save us.

From the first, man cared not only about his own survival, but also about the survival of his wife, his child, and his neighbor. We have always been social beings. We are more than just single entities. How did we ever forget that? As we face the empty halls of our schools, the silent gardens where children used to play, can we now remember what we long forgot? We need to cry to someone. Man is not complete alone. Technology could never save us because it could never hear our cry.

It is a pity we learned so late what our ancestors knew so well—that our survival matters—even now when we can't survive much longer. I am seventy-seven years old and my days are dwindling. But even at my last moment, I will listen for the voice of humanity as it cries out to God— "Hear me, oh Lord."

August
FRIENDS AND RELATIONS

Mary lay still as death, dark circles under her eyes, her pale face sunken to the point of emaciation. Anne hated to wake her, but she needed to tell Mary the news. Leaning over the stained, wrinkled sheets, Anne nudged her. "Mary, Uncle Mark and his wife are coming. They'll be here soon."

Mary's red, swollen eyes blinked open. She rubbed them and tried to sit up, but she moaned in the attempt.

"Don't get up yet. I just got word. They probably won't be here for another few hours or so, but they're coming. I guess Pam's family wasn't able to help—they didn't get along or something. Anyway, Mark wants to move here."

Looking toward the open window, Anne spoke almost to herself. "They can use the basement and turn it into a private apartment, I guess. They'll have to do something about the windows though...." Anne imagined all the work it would take to make the basement livable. But then, she couldn't think where else they could stay. They couldn't very well camp out in the living room. And the sheds weren't that nice. Even with Cerulean's help, and she had to admit he was surprisingly handy, they would be hard put to make everything snug before winter set in.

Looking at her daughter again, she tried to keep the throbbing ache behind her eyes from building. "How're you feeling today?"

With a weak smile, Mary forced herself into a sitting position. She blinked at the strong light. "I'm feeling better. Maybe even a little hungry." She pushed away her blankets. "I need to get up. I'm sick of being in this room. I want to see Uncle Mark and Pam. I only met her at their wedding. She was nice enough though."

"I've enjoyed her company every time they've visited. Though that wasn't very often."

Swinging her legs over the side of the bed, Mary braced herself. She stiffened when Anne grabbed her arm. "No, I can do this. I need to use my muscles."

Anne smothered her reaction and stepped away to the bathroom. She took a quick survey and came back into the room. "I'll ask Sam to get some water, and you can freshen up."

Shakily, Mary got to her feet. Her voice grew strained and petulant. "Stop with the *Sam* stuff. I know his real name. I've heard you use it when I was out of the room. I don't know where he comes from or why you're keeping such stupid secrets from me, but that's your business. Just stop with the fake name. Did you just make that up on the spur of the moment?"

Anne's jaw clenched. "Yes, actually, I did."

"It doesn't matter. I've heard you call him Sir Illiad or something like that. What, was he in the military?"

The air felt stifling, and Anne had to control a smirk. "No, though I gather he knows a thing or two about battle. But his name is Cerulean. It's rather an odd name, and I thought people would be able to handle Sam better."

"I don't know who *people* are exactly, but I can handle Cerulean just fine. Were his parents foreigners?"

"Something like that." Anne watched as Mary made her way shakily across the room.

Suddenly, Mary stopped, one hand gripping the doorframe, and turned to her mother. "I know it's a lot to ask, but can you bring me the water yourself? It's not that I don't like your friend—Cerulean—it's just that he has this way of looking at me; it makes me uncomfortable."

Anne's eyebrows arched. "How is that?"

"I don't know. He reminds me of Father Thomas. It's like he is waiting for me to say something. But I have nothing to say."

"Father Thomas just offered to hear your confession, or to help you however he could. He wasn't trying to *get* anything from you. Nor is Cerulean." Anne swallowed her irritation, but it left a lump in her throat.

Still using the doorframe for balance, Mary turned back toward the bathroom. "No? I think they both have secrets, even from you. I think we all do."

"You're probably right." The urge to prop up Mary's tottering frame nearly overpowered her, but Anne held herself back. "Still, we can tell God anything, and He can help us."

Mary hobbled forward without another word.

Scowling, Anne surveyed the room. The bed was stained and rumpled. She glanced at the clock on the end table. With impetuous fury, Anne yanked the sheets free from the mattress, bundled them up, and stomped down the stairs.

Cerulean strode into the kitchen with a basket of eggs. His eyes lit up when he saw Anne. "I fed and watered the chickens. They're laying well—considering the heat. I thought they'd die out there."

A tight knot of anxiety twisted painfully as Anne snatched up the basket and bundled the rumpled sheets into his arms. "Chickens don't make a lot of sense. Neither does the weather. But I need to get these washed and dried before Mark shows up with his wife. I only have one other set of sheets, and I'll need them for their bed—wherever that's going to be."

A brief image of his deceased wife in one of her rare fits of temper flickered through Cerulean's mind as the bundle landed in his arms.

Anne counted the eggs. "You're right. This is perfect. We'll have a treat with dinner tonight. I'll make some deviled eggs and a salad with that new lettuce I planted." She sighed. "At least we can serve a decent meal, even though we don't have much else to offer." She eyed Cerulean critically. "You wouldn't happen to know how to kill a hen would you?"

Cerulean scrunched the sheets tighter and rubbed his chin. "The killing part wouldn't be hard. But I'm not sure what kind of shape it would be in when I'm done."

Anne nodded decisively. "Okay, I'll do that. You wash these sheets in the tub out there by the hose." She reached for a bar of soap by the sink. "Here, you can use this." She stared at his expressionless face, plunked the soap on the pile, and hurried on. "And then when you get them soaped and rinsed you can hang them on the line to dry. You know the one, by the wood shed." She frowned as Cerulean continued to stare at her. "What's wrong?"

Cerulean dumped the sheets back onto her arms. "*I'll* kill the chicken." As Anne received the bundle in surprised silence, he added. "You know, just for your information, I never signed up for duty here. I just got to know you as a friend. I don't remember saying I was a one-man labor force."

Blinking, Anne hugged the sheets in confusion.

Cerulean's face flushed with anger.

Guilt washed over her. "Oh, Cerulean— Sorry. I didn't mean— I wasn't thinking. It's just…with Mary being sick and now Mark—I told you about Mark, didn't I? I just got word. If Mark keeps to his schedule, he'll arrive today…." She dropped her gaze.

Cerulean continued frowning.

Tears sprang to Anne's eyes. Hugging the sheets, Anne sniffed and forced herself into competence. "I'll get these soaking, and I'll kill the chicken. It's my responsibility…. I shouldn't have thrown it on you. Sorry." She turned away.

Cerulean shook his head as he watched her trudge out the door.

After hauling the water up to Mary, Anne filled the outdoor washtub and began to lather the sheets with soap. A loud ruckus by the henhouse made her stop. With images of a fox making off with one of her treasured hens, she reached for a stout stick and rushed forward.

Cerulean stood by the hen house with a limp bird dangling in his hands.

Anne stopped in her tracks.

The expression on Cerulean's face was so peculiar that it brought a smile to Anne's face. She had a hard time maintaining her control. Clearing her throat, she tried to sound natural.

"Thank you, Cerulean. I appreciate your help."

Cerulean waved the dead bird in the air in a helpless manner. "I don't even know how I did it. I just grabbed it and—"

Anne closed her eyes; her hand flew up. "You don't need to give me the details." She reached for the bird. "I'll take it from here. I'll get some hot water, pluck it and…it'll make a great dinner."

She glanced at the descending sun. "Amazing how fast it moves. I'd almost swear—" She glanced at Cerulean. "You don't think…." She left her thought unfinished.

"The days are growing shorter? Who knows? God's prerogative, not mine." He started past her. "I'll haul the water and then…I need to be by myself awhile."

Her expression somber, Anne accepted his pronouncement with a nod of guilt. "I really do appreciate your help, Cerulean. Sorry again for the way I acted."

With a relenting smile, Cerulean shrugged. "I'm not angry with you. Since I'm no longer a guardian, I need to figure out who I am." He turned toward the water pump.

Anne walked into the kitchen with the dead chicken cradled in her arms.

Several hours later, a car rolled onto the gravel driveway. Mark parked in the back, nearest the kitchen door.

Wiping her hands on a towel, Anne noted the sheets on the line. They were about dry now and the smell of roasting chicken filled the air. Thank heavens for that breeze or they'd *all* be roasting.

Mary rested on the front porch with a cool drink, and Cerulean had not returned since he left for his walk in the woods.

Taking a deep breath, Anne braced herself. She stepped out onto the back porch. Mark climbed out of his battered, old Ford. Anne stifled a slight gasp. His hair was streaked with gray, and his shoulders were stooped like an old man. As Mark moved around the car to help his wife out, Anne felt herself sway. *Surely this couldn't be Pam?* She gripped the wooden post. As Pam made their way forward, she tried to make her voice sound joyful.

"Hi, Guys!" She almost tripped going down the porch steps, but recovered, and moved in to help Mark with the bag he was tugging out of the car. Pam leaned on the car. Anne stopped and hugged her brother and her sister-in-law before she reached for the suitcase.

Mark jerked the bag away. "Heavens, Anne, give me a break. I'll carry our bags." Appraising his sister with a sweeping gaze, he stopped in his tracks. "Except for the gray, you don't look like you've aged a day."

Anne widened her eyes in innocence. "All the fresh air and country living!" She cringed inside. "Come on in. I've almost got dinner ready. You'll see; you'll grow young here too. Practically a fountain of youth." Her stomach lurched.

Suddenly, Cerulean was at the door, taking the suitcase. He held the door open.

Pausing, Mark stared at the strange man, but Cerulean met his gaze evenly, and after a moment's hesitation, Mark stepped into the kitchen.

Anne followed behind and, with a quick glance, signaled for Cerulean to carry the suitcase upstairs. Cerulean lugged it away.

The door creaked once more as Mary walked into the room.

Mark turned around, and this time, the intake of breath was audible. Walking toward the thin, young woman, Mark gently hugged her. "Hello, Mary. You remember me?"

Mary smiled her answer as she put her hand out toward Pam's painfully thin frame. "Hello, Pam. Glad to see you again."

After the initial greeting, Anne began handing out cold drinks. "It's so nice to have you here. You can use my bedroom until we fix up a place."

Mark blinked back surprise. "I didn't mean for you to put us up. I was thinking that there might be someplace in town. That way we could come over and help out."

Anne waved her hands in frustration. "It doesn't work that way anymore. I don't know how it is down south, but here everyone is forming into communities. It makes life more manageable. Families and friends live together and share the work. If I had been thinking ahead, I would have built a little house next to this one or attached a new room or something. It just never dawned on me that you'd come here. I thought for sure you were going to stay in Florida."

Pam stared at the ground as she rubbed her fingers up and down her dripping glass. "Sorry we've come so unexpectedly. Mark wrote to let you know. He was sure you wouldn't mind."

Anne tried to smother her frustration. *Have I lost the art of communication?* "I *don't* mind. I'm thrilled that you're here. I just want to do more than send you off to live with strangers. I want you to live here. We just need to figure out how to do that. I have the basement, but it needs a lot of work."

Mark's eyes widened in alarm. "The basement? *Your* basement? Look, this is really kind of you, but I don't think that would work. Pam's allergic to mold and—she'd never survive down there."

Anne glanced at Cerulean who had quietly entered the room.

Mark saw the exchange. "Oh, and I didn't know you had other guests. I mean, look, Cerulean? Is that French? You were here before us. We're not trying to—"

Pushing away from the wall he had been leaning against, Cerulean gestured toward the backyard. "There's a shed out back that has solid windows and good siding. If we worked on it through the fall, we could insulate it and install some storm windows. There's a pile of wood in the barn that we could use for an added layer of flooring, and we could pick up some used ceiling panels fairly cheap. With all that, I bet we could make the place pretty nice, and as time went on we could add a room or two—whatever you want."

Mark's eyes lit up with interest. "You know much about building?"

Cerulean's glance skirted Anne's. "Well, I worked on the roof here and did a little work at the church."

His shoulders relaxing, Mark's expression softened. "I'd really appreciate the help. Pam's been through enough already. She lost—"

Pam stiffened and cleared her throat.

Mark rubbed her arm as he sat beside her on the bench. "Well, it doesn't matter. It's just that we'd like to be a part of a family again."

With the first sense of joy that she had felt in a long time, Anne marveled at the convolutions of her heart. "It looks like our little family is growing by leaps and bounds and I, for one, couldn't be happier."

Cerulean's gaze moved off into the distance.

Mary's eyes roved over to Cerulean.

Anne clapped her hands in exuberance. "The chicken should be ready by now. Let me just check the bread, and we'll eat. Mark, take Pam up to my room. You two can sleep up there until we get things arranged."

Mark stopped his sister. "Where will you sleep?"

"On the couch. I sleep there half the time anyway. The living room gets the most heat from the wood stove during the winter and the best breeze in the summer." She saw Mark's eyes stray toward Cerulean. "He sleeps in the room off the kitchen. It used to be an oversized pantry, but we turned it into an undersized bedroom. It's not much, but he's a simple man—person."

Mark nodded through an awkward silence.

Rising slowly to her feet, Mary motioned for Pam to follow. "You must be tired. I'll show you upstairs, and you can rest before dinner. I'll explain about the bath and everything. Living in the country must be different from what you're used to."

Pam stood, looking frailer and more exhausted than when she sat down. Picking up her small leather purse, her smile was the only strong thing about her. "No, not really. I've gotten used to doing things differently. I don't mind, as long as I'm not in the way."

Mary linked arms with Pam. "You're not in the way. At least, no more than I am. I'd like to hear about where you lived and what it was like. I was living in the Dakotas before I came home." Continuing to speak softly, Mary led Pam up the steps, and they were soon out of sight.

Mark turned to his sister, his face flushed. "You didn't tell me she was sick! You just said that she had come home out of the blue. What happened? She looks older—a lot older. Damn it, she looks older than you!"

With a sigh, Anne returned to the stove and checked the bread. Satisfied, she grabbed a hot pad and pulled the loaf out of the oven. With a barely controlled slap, she placed the bread on the table before answering her brother. "There's a lot to tell, but not all of it is mine to share. It's basically what I told you. She went up north with Jack, they lived on a farm, then he died, and she came home."

"How did he die?"

With a shake of her head, Anne returned to the oven, this time checking the chicken. "He was murdered, okay? Does it make you feel better to know that? He interrupted some thieves, and they stabbed him. Mary tried to save him but she couldn't, and he bled to death in front of her. Some guy came and buried him in their garden, or near it—or something—and then she just packed up a few things and walked home."

Mark's eyes widened as his hands clenched. "Walked home? From the Dakotas!"

"Yep, and why she did it that way, I can't say. There were saner ways of getting home, but I don't think sanity was much of an issue with her at the time. Jack had a lot of interesting notions and, well, it's for her to share if she wants to. I'm just here to help out as I can."

Anne lifted the chicken out of the oven and placed it on the stovetop. "I haven't asked you about Pam's family and what is going on there, even though I know there must be a story to tell." Anne waved Mark's reaction away. "I don't need to know. Not yet. When Pam is ready to share, she will. But for now, it's enough that she knows she's wanted. You and Cerulean," she tried to gage Cerulean's mood and when he stared back with a hint of a smile, Anne continued, "Well, you two can have whatever shed you need. Feel free. I'm just playing at this hostess thing."

Appraising the scantily laid table with disapproval, Anne darted to the refrigerator and pulled out a plate of deviled eggs. Then she turned toward the stovetop and snatched a small bowl off the warming shelf. "They could use butter, but green beans are good no matter what. Mark, get the seasoning off the counter and bring it over here."

As Mark obeyed, Cerulean sidestepped out of the way. "You'll get used to it, Mark. She tends to get bossy when she is worried. But if she ever hands you a live chicken and says it's for dinner—you can leave that to me."

Anne's relieved grin crinkled around her eyes as she darted a glance toward the steps. "Shall I get them?"

Mark shook his head as he started toward the steps. "No, I'd better go. Pam might not even want to eat."

Cerulean stepped closer to Anne and put his hand on her arm, his thumb gently stroking her skin. "You sure you're up for this? It means a lot of complications. Everyone might not get along, and you've got two very sick people on your hands."

Anne blinked, trying to ignore the sensation of his touch. "What would you have me do? Turn my daughter and my brother away? Why? So I can die alone and friendless?"

"You'll never be alone and friendless, Anne."

"Well, *they* might. Lord Almighty, how can you even think such a thing?"

"I didn't think it, Anne. I just asked to see what you're thinking."

"Well, if I turn people away now, I'll have to turn everyone away. We're all dying."

"I know."

"Good!" Anne marched around the table slapping down the spoons.

Cerulean stayed quiet a moment, and when he spoke it was nearly a whisper. "You'll take them all in?"

"Whoever needs me." Anne turned back toward the stove.

Cerulean watched as Pam hobbled down the steps with Mark at her side and Mary laboriously following behind. He mumbled under his breath, "You have no idea." But he found a place among them as they took their places at the table.

OF MICE AND MEN

With a little help from Mr. Hovey, Cerulean and Mark soon transformed a dilapidated outbuilding into a snug mini-home. Eve found someone with a work truck, and they scoured nearby thrift stores, buying useable furniture, which they loaded up, carried home, and carefully arranged.

Anne consulted Pam about curtains and how she would like to decorate, what rugs she wanted, and where to set the lamps. There weren't a lot of decisions to make as the options were limited, but Pam's face glowed with satisfaction at the outcome.

After Eve had left, Anne settled in with Pam while Cerulean and Mark returned the borrowed tools to the Hovey place. Anne straightened a doily on a side table where she had strategically set a lamp when suddenly Pam stumbled and cried out.

Anne ran to her, and, gripping her arm, she got her onto a rocking chair. "What happened? You alright?"

Pressing a tight fist against her chest, Pam gritted her teeth against a strangled smile. "I'm not alright, but that's normal with me." She leaned back, squeezing her eyes shut. "It's about time I told you the truth."

Dread enveloped Anne. Sitting hunch-shouldered on the edge of the bed, her hands clasped in her lap, she waited.

"My family didn't throw me out. They just couldn't handle my illness. Besides, we didn't get along." Her panting had slowed, and she was breathing more regularly now. Opening her eyes, she stared off into space, like a woman about to tell a story.

"My father was a strong-willed man, very proud and wealthy, and after Mom died, he decided that he was going to cheat fate. His name was Maximillian—if that tells you anything. When he realized he was dying, he decided to have his body frozen in one of those cryogenics labs." She sighed. "I tried to talk him out of it. As a matter of fact, both Mark and I made quite a nuisance of ourselves over it, but he was adamant, and my brother and sister thought we were being insensitive, trying to deny him his last wish."

Pam paused and took several long breaths before she continued. "That was a couple of years ago. Then I began to have weak spells, and when I was finally able to see a doctor, he diagnosed me with congestive heart failure, at an advanced stage. In better days I'd have a chance of survival, but the way things are now.... If I'm careful, I might survive a while, or I could die tomorrow. I don't know." Pam rocked, her eyes glazed and unfocused.

The sun glowed in pinks and oranges at the horizon. Anne stared through the newly washed windows and marveled at the sunset glinting between the trees, silhouetting black branches against a brilliant sky. A raw ache settled in her heart.

Pam rocked soundlessly. "It was my sister who suggested that I come here…the country air would do me good." She breathed through a long sigh. "I made Judy uncomfortable. She and my brother said that I ruined Dad's last days."

Anne frowned, puzzled. "I thought he was frozen. What does he care? Won't he be thawed in a millennium or so?"

Pam shook her head, her hands across her lap. "It was supposed to protect him for a hundred years. By then, everyone figured there'd be a medical breakthrough, and he could be revived, ready to live in a brave new world."

Anne heard the word "supposed" and pondered it with an arched eyebrow.

Pam broke into her thoughts. "But it didn't last a month before something went wrong. Some system or another failed. It was a mouse, someone said. A mouse had chewed through something."

There was a chuckle, and Anne lifted her gaze off the floor as she listened, her heart constricting painfully.

"Isn't it ironic? The best laid plans of mice and men? He was dead when they examined him on a routine visit—so were seven of the other fifty people frozen at the same time." Pam stopped rocking. "I doubt one of them will make it the whole hundred years. And besides, what if they do live, what kind of a world will they awaken to? Surely, it'd be better to be dead."

"Can't fault them for trying, I guess."

Pam turned her gaze on Anne. "For what? To become immortal? Don't be ridiculous, Anne. You know better. We're human beings, not God. It's not going to work. Just like everything else: cloning, brain uploading, robotic hybrids.... It's all pride gone crazy. It's unnatural. I tried to tell my dad, but he wouldn't listen. He really thought that he could buy a place in the future."

The room grew dark. Anne rubbed her temple. "You want to come inside and help make dinner?"

With shallow pants, Pam murmured, "I'm still a little weak. I better rest a while. When Mark gets back, he can help me in. Besides, you've been working all day. Why don't you take a rest?"

Anne slid off the bed, admiring the transformation of what had formerly been a shed. "I'll have time to rest later. For now, I better keep moving. Besides, the men will be hungry. Cerulean might not be human but he sure—" Anne caught herself and frantically tried cover her blunder. "I mean—"

Pam chuckled. "Oh, they're human alright. Don't go making saints out of them yet. You may've forgotten, but Mark can get into a pretty nasty mood when he's hungry and tired."

Relief washed over Anne. "Yeah, all the more reason I should make some biscuits and heat up the stew. Thank heavens the Hoveys are such good neighbors. We wouldn't have survived without them."

"From what old Mrs. Hovey says, you're a pretty good neighbor yourself." Pam sighed again. "Too bad it took such a terrible time to draw us together like this."

Stepping to the doorway and looking back, Anne asked, "Do you want me to light one of the lamps?"

"No, I like the fading light. It reminds me of being a kid and playing outside till dark. I loved it, the birds' bedtime songs, the changing colors. Why do we forget those wonderful things?"

Anne couldn't answer. As she stepped outside and saw the golden beams of sunlight slanting across the fields, she reminded herself that it was such details that frequently brought her the most joy. A sudden chill prickled her skin as the wind picked up. There were black clouds gathering from the southwest. *Oh boy, a storm on their first night in the shed.* She murmured a little prayer, *"Please, keep them safe. They're trying so hard."*

Anne had begun to fantasize about her friendship with Pam and how they might grow old together, sharing their thoughts and feelings, making each other less lonely. She had imagined pleasant chats at sunset and contented afternoons, cooking in the same kitchen, knowing that Mark and Mary were happy. But now....

Pushing against the growing wind, Anne hunched her shoulders, wrapped her sweater more tightly about her middle, and climbed the steps to the safety of her kitchen.

Cerulean and Mark returned wearing matching frowns. Thunder began to roll in the distance. After scarcely a minute, there was a flash of light and then, only a few seconds later, a crash resounded, shaking the house. Mark had brought Pam to the kitchen, and he squeezed her hand when she trembled.

With an exchange of relieved grins, they all assembled around the table and said grace. Cerulean had become so accustomed to this habit that he no longer hesitated. He didn't need to eat, but he enjoyed good food as much as any of them. The hard work had wearied him, and he wished he didn't have bad news to share.

On a recent stroll through the woods, he had been met by one of the last guardians on Earth. Roux had joined a community in South Carolina. In the form of a tall man with bronze skin, black eyes, and a muscular build, he had little trouble impressing the humans around him. But it was Roux's intrinsic honesty that finally won Cerulean's respect, and he was always pleased to see him.

Roux had approached from behind a fallen tree at dawn when Cerulean was usually alone outdoors. "Cerulean! I see you're looking fit and healthy. Must be all the fresh air and hard work. I always said that a little exercise wouldn't kill you."

Cerulean accepted this comment in the spirit intended, though he could tell that Roux's attempt at humor was forced. "It hasn't, not yet anyway. Though I must add, I'm not particularly fond of climbing on roofs or slaughtering chickens."

Roux's eyebrows rose in mock horror. "Roofs and chickens? Now there's story I'd love to hear, but not today. Truth is—you may be doing alright now—but I'm afraid that won't last much longer." Roux folded his arms across his chest looking very much like the Angel of Death announcing the arrival of doomsday. "I've heard rumors that sound pretty ominous and, sure enough, they're true. We're the last— you and I. Everyone else has left."

Cerulean's eyes widened. "Everyone? But humanity might live on for years yet, there's no reason to—"

"Oh, yes, there is." Roux appeared to deflate as he kicked at moss embedded on a fallen tree truck. "All hell is about to break loose, and every Luxonian with any intelligence wants to get away and watch the fireworks from a safe distance."

"You want to explain that?"

"What do humans do when they get desperate? They act like idiots." Roux slapped at an insect on his arm. "You know how it is. They have too much power, and they can't handle it."

Cerulean stood opposite Roux and propped his foot upon the same fallen log. He dismissed Roux's assessment with a wave of his hand. "That's not true. Humanity has been very restrained in the way they've handled things. Except for a few extremists, they've kept things amazingly quiet. In fact, there've been fewer wars in the last ten years than in all their history. I think humanity has done a remarkable job of staying out of trouble."

"Yeah, well, that's all about to end." Roux looked at Cerulean with a pleading expression. "Listen, I didn't want to be the one to tell you. I know how you feel; I love this place too. Humanity, despite all its crazy convolutions, has impressed me. I never expected to care this much. In fact, and don't you ever tell anyone, but I even wish I was human sometimes."

Roux stuffed his hands into his pockets and shrugged. "But that's not going to stop those bombs from exploding." He looked Cerulean in the eye. "The US and Europe are geared up for an all-out nuclear offensive against those crazy militant groups in the Middle East and plan to push Russia back to its former holdings. China says if anyone pushes a button, they'll retaliate. Russia insists that they can take on the world if need be. The other nuclear capable countries are claiming that they'll do whatever it takes to protect their own. This time, it will be Armageddon, and no one will survive."

"That's crazy! No one will survive, so why do it? I mean, they've made peace over and over again and survived so much! They've had their problems, but they've handled them without taking down the entire world. Why go nuclear now?"

"Everyone's tired of being scared and angry. They figure that if they have to go down, they'll go down fighting." Roux kicked the moss again. "Problem is, they'll just go down that much sooner, and there will be no one to hear their cry when they realize what idiots they've been."

"Humanity has been on the brink many times, but they always pull back." He looked at Roux. "They never cry in vain."

Roux took his hand from his pockets and reached out. "It's humanity's way of greeting, taking leave, and making a deal. I'll leave you to decide which one this is."

Cerulean clasped Roux's hand. He turned to leave, but Cerulean gripped his arm.

"Wait! So—you're leaving too?"

"I'll be watching. But from a safe distance." Roux climbed the little hill among the sunlit trees, and with a sudden flash, he was gone.

A peal of thunder crashed overhead as Cerulean sat among his friends. What should he say? Should he warn them? Was it his place to say anything? But then Mr. Hovey had heard rumors too, and he had warned Mark. He didn't know the details; he just suggested that they talk about making some arrangements. If a large-scale war broke out, things would become harder than ever. It would mean facing even more death and destruction, and Mr. Hovey wasn't one to be left without a plan.

Mark spooned up his stew without venturing a word.

Pam broke the awkward silence. "Listen, everyone, I know you're worried about me, but really I'm feeling much better, and who knows, I might live for years and become a meddlesome old lady." Her attempt at humor fell flat.

Anne looked up, as did Cerulean.

Mark stared at his wife a moment before he threw down his napkin. "Good Lord, Pam. It isn't all about you! I want to keep you safe, but, now it looks like there isn't a safe place for anyone."

Anne's alarmed gaze strayed from Mark's angry expression to Cerulean who had stiffened in surprise. Her eyes narrowed. "What's happened?"

Adopting a composed attitude, Cerulean tried to explain. "Turns out, there's a rumor of nuclear war coming."

Mark jerked back in surprise. "Mr. Hovey said war, he didn't say anything about nukes."

Cerulean kept his voice calm. "I've heard rumors too. Apparently, there's new international tension, and everyone's gearing up for an— event."

Mark spread his hands wide in surrender. "So what are we supposed to do? I mean, from everything I've ever heard, this is the point of no return. We all might as well dig our graves now and push each other in."

"Mark!" Both Anne and Pam exclaimed at once. Anne heard a crash from upstairs and rose to her feet. "Mary must have been awakened by the storm. I'll see." She stopped suddenly and turned around. "Don't tell Mary about this, alright? It'll just upset her."

Cerulean rose from the table. "I know how you feel, Mark, but it might be wise to start fixing up the basement anyway. We don't know what'll happen, but the basement is the most sheltered place."

Mark sighed and picked up his empty bowl. "You're probably right." He put his bowl in the sink and surveyed the empty bucket. "I'll get some water."

Pam protested. "But you'll get drowned out there! It's pouring."

Snatching up the bucket, Mark almost chuckled. "That's the least of my worries." He stormed through the doorway as the wind shuddered against the house.

Cerulean observed Pam's anxious expression as she watched Mark leave. "He'll be okay, Pam. Mark's got a strong will to live."

Pam whispered in a husky voice. "I just wonder how long it'll last."

34

October
AND MORE RELATIONS

A knock sounded on the door, but Anne was hesitant to answer it. Both Mark and Cerulean had gone to look for supplies, and Pam was resting in her little house. Mary slept soundly upstairs. There had already been three people come through that morning, asking for food. She had no idea if they were really hungry or if they had just made it their livelihood to beg. Begging had been revived as a new lifestyle choice. Anne sighed. *It works for them but not for me.* She considered not opening the door this time, but the knocking grew more persistent.

Anne stared at the lock that Mark had put in place because they had already had one thief come through, and he didn't want any others. Even Eve had reported a harrowing tale of the church being robbed at knifepoint. Neither she nor Father Thomas had resisted, and the thieves made off with several precious objects.

Anne hesitated, blowing air between her lips. She had already given away all the extra bread she had baked for the day, and she needed what she had left for lunch and supper. She had made it a rule never to let anyone see her supplies, but on two occasions visitors barged in to see for themselves. Cerulean, thank heaven, had been near enough to warn them away. This time she would have to tell them she had nothing to offer and suggest they go back to town. If only she could see through the door to tell whether it was a man or a woman. The pounding grew fierce. She decided to keep the door locked. No use getting into an argument.

Suddenly, a voice called Anne's name. Her brow furrowed. A vague memory rose in her mind. She pictured Caroline sitting on her living room couch, drinking tea with James and Susie while Jackie paced the floor. Why should that memory return now? Anne heard the voice again.

"Anne, for God's sake open this damn door before I kick it down!"

Anne unlocked the door with trembling fingers. There stood Jackie with a large, heavyset man directly behind her. The color drained from Anne's face. "Oh, heavens, Jackie. I didn't know it was you. Here, come in."

Anne's heart pounded as she stepped aside, and they stepped past her. The last time she had seen Jackie was at Philip's funeral. Jackie had neither cried nor spoken to her. She had walked up, offered a stiff hug to her and Mary, and then simply turned and marched away. Susie had whispered that Jackie was "going through some things." Caroline had died some years ago of a massive stroke while Philip's dad, James, had lived on in quiet oblivion in a nursing home until he passed away in his sleep. Anne had received a nice letter from Susie with a snapshot of a smiling James, as he looked the month before he died. Now, Jackie stood in her kitchen with some mountain of a man she had never met, and neither of them looked particularly glad.

Pulling off her gloves, Jackie stumbled over to the kitchen table, practically throwing herself down on a chair.

"Good Lord, I'm exhausted! What in the world took you so long?" Jackie laid her head on the table and, apparently in respect to some remnant of manners, mumbled, "Oh, yeah, Billy this is Anne. Anne, Billy."

Anne stared at the forlorn woman nearly lying on her kitchen table, and with an intake of breath, she turned to the man who had entered just behind Jackie. Bracing herself, Anne looked into Billy's eyes and realized with a shock that this huge man in front of her was still a child. He had the look of a bewildered and embarrassed kid.

He began to stammer. "So, so, sorry for intruding, Ma'am. Jackie, she said it'd be alright, and well, I've got nowhere else to go."

How, after all these years, could she still be so flummoxed by people? Anne moved toward the kitchen table and pulled out a chair. Eying Billy's massive build, she threw up a silent prayer that the chair would hold up under him.

Billy, obviously not trusting the spindly kitchen chair either, just leaned against the counter and took off his wet cap. "That's okay, Ma'am. I'm just glad to be out of the wind. It's near impossible to see when the wind gets in your eyes like that."

Jackie, her head resting on her arms, which were spread out on the table, volunteered, "Motorcycles aren't the best winter transportation."

Rubbing her temples at the onslaught of a headache, Anne tried to think what to do next. They looked exhausted, and she didn't have to work hard to imagine their hunger. "Well, I need to do some baking, would you two like a little bread and jam while I get things ready for lunch?"

Jackie lifted her head a few inches from the table. "I'd eat a porcupine right now and not mind the prickles in the least."

Billy guffawed. Apparently, he liked a little hyperbole now and again.

Anne's eyebrows rose as she made her way to the pantry. She grabbed a bag of flour, some baking powder, a small keg of lard and a canister of salt. She lugged them to the counter and pulled out a large bowl and placed it in the center of the counter. Then she returned to the pantry and picked up a loaf of bread on a tray wrapped in a cloth. Going to the refrigerator, she quickly snatched up a jar of homemade jelly and a bag of shredded zucchini. She put the loaf of bread, a knife, and the jam with a large spoon on the kitchen table. "Here you go; you can fix it the way you like it."

Abruptly sitting up, Jackie pulled the tray closer and quickly unwrapped the bread. Billy came nearer and pulled out the chair. Suddenly, he seemed to think better of it, and he turned toward Anne.
"This is mighty nice of you, Ma'am. I hate to take stuff without paying
for it, though I know you're a relation to Jackie. Still, I'd like to do
something. Could I help somehow?"

Anne stood frozen. The sincerity in the man's voice almost undid
her composure. She looked him over again. Yes, he was huge and he
was certainly closer to fifty than forty, heavyset with graying hair
hanging shaggy down to his shoulders, but he had the mannerisms of
an innocent, beseeching child. Anne tried to shrug off her confusion.
"Well, I could use some water from the well outside. Could you take
the bucket over there and fill it and bring it back in for me?"

Billy's gap-toothed smile enhanced his appearance more than Anne
could believe. He really was a dear, huge, man-child. He nodded, and,
sweeping up the bucket with one hand, he lurched out the door.

Anne turned to Jackie, who had sliced several pieces of bread and
was in the process of slathering them with healthy servings of jam.

"Where in the world did you find him? He's not the musician guy
your sister told me about— Is he?" Anne could no more imagine Billy
singing or playing an instrument than she could imagine a turtle at a
barnyard dance.

Ignoring the question, Jackie took one large bite of jam-laden bread
and groaned in almost indecent pleasure. Anne looked away in embarrassment. After Jackie had eaten one slice, she wiped her mouth with
her sleeve and motioned toward Anne, who had returned to her biscuit
preparation, stirring the zucchini into the mix.

"Do you have anything to drink?"

Silently returning to the refrigerator, Anne pulled out a metal pitcher of water and poured a full glass, setting it down with a firm tap in
front of Jackie.

Jackie sipped the water and then leaned back in the chair. "He
won't be gone too long, so I'll give you the short version. The musician ditched me when he found another woman better able to meet his,

uh…various needs. I discovered Billy when I was at a hangout and some guy got a trifle personal and I tried to resist. Billy just came up out of the blue and smacked the jerk on the back of the head and, voila, a new friend for life." Jackie's triumphant smile faded just as suddenly as it had arrived. "He's really a simple guy, nice, but not exactly the brightest bulb out there, if you know what I mean. Still, he doesn't ask for much. We've never even had—"

Anne cleared her throat. "I don't need to know everything. I'm not your confessor, you know." She turned back toward the biscuits and began beating the mixture vigorously. Returning to the refrigerator again, she pulled out a small plastic container of milk and poured a generous helping into the mix. She continued to stir. "I don't have a lot to give, Jackie. My resources are becoming slimmer by the day, but I'm not going to turn you or Billy away. Still, I need to know what you're thinking. Is this a just a friendly visit or…."

Resting her head on one arm, Jackie tapped the table with her fingers. "I'm not really sure, Anne. I'd love to say that I've got a husband waiting for me, or even a lover worried about my whereabouts, but I can't. Mom and Dad are dead, Philip's gone, and Susie told me that she's got enough problems; she can't handle mine. She's been in mourning ever since the love of her life committed suicide."

Anne turned and stared with shock. That was callous, even for Jackie. "What happened?"

"Oh, he got mixed up with some cult or another, and despite Susie's tearful entreaties, he joined them in a big ritualistic mass suicide. Don't ask me to explain it. Nobody can. It was all the news for a while." She looked around. "Though I suppose you don't get much news out here, do you?"

Anne shook her head as she filled the last muffin tin and sidestepped to the stove.

Jackie continued. "There's a lot wrong with the world, Anne, but I figure that if I am alive, I'm better off than some."

Anne pushed the muffins into the oven and quickly appraised the half-empty stick box. Closing the oven door, her gaze fell on Jackie once again. "Do you mean that life is better than death at any price?" Anne began to clean away the mess she had made. "Death is just a doorway, you know. There's more to life than what you see with your eyes."

Jackie slapped the table and sat upright, ready with a retort, when there was a skirmish at the door. Suddenly, the door flung open, and Mark and Cerulean came in with Billy's arms pinioned behind his back. The two women stared at the three men in shocked silence.

Jackie lost what was left of her affected composure and started yelling. "What the hell! What are you two idiots doing? Let him go this minute, or I'll tear your eyes out!" She screamed with such vehemence that both Cerulean and Mark stared at her with open mouths, but neither of them loosened their grip.

Rushing forward, Anne placed her hand on Billy protectively. "Sorry, Billy. They didn't mean anything by it. They live here and probably mistook you for a burglar or something."

Billy shook his arms free and hunched his shoulders as if he were used to the proceedings. "It's okay. They didn't hit me or anything."

Marching across the room, Jackie grabbed Billy's arm and tugged him to the table. "Here, eat something. It's the least they can do after you brought in their stupid water."

There was a slight cough, and Mary walked into the room. "Hi, I heard the commotion." Gazing around, she frowned before her eyes widened in surprise. "Jackie?"

Jackie's anger instantly melted into confusion as she stared back at the woman in front of her. "Mary?"

"Yeah. It's been a long time. I was…away."

Jackie scowled even more fiercely as she turned on Anne. "What? Are you starving her?" Impulsively, she took Mary's hand and pulled her into a hug. "It's good to see you, honey. Sorry I just barged in like this, but we, uh wanted to see some *friendly* faces." Her glare shifted to Cerulean and Mark.

Mary's exhausted eyes focused on Billy. "A friend of yours?"

"Yeah, a friend. Billy, this is Anne's daughter, Mary. Mary, this is my knight-in-shining-armor, Billy."

After a few awkward introductions, Anne decided to put lunch on as fast as possible while Mark lugged in the bucket of water. She arranged what food she had: leftover fish from the night before, the rest of the bread she had offered earlier, the homemade jam, plus some cheese, and a bag of roasted nuts. They all found seats though Cerulean and Mark sat on stools at the counter. Billy and Jackie began to dig in, but they stopped when Mary, with an inconspicuous cough, asked about Pam. Without replying, Mark slapped his forehead and ran out of the room.

Jackie looked to Anne for an explanation. "You'll have to catch me up on who-all lives here. I thought it was just you, and then I find your brother and some guy I've never even met are staying here, and then I find out Mary, who I thought was gone for good, has returned and now there's a Pam. Who's Pam?"

Anne slathered a slice of bread with jam and laid it on her napkin. She pushed the jar toward Billy, who looked distinctly interested in seeing it closer. She pointed to Cerulean.

"Cerulean is a friend of mine who helps around the house. He doesn't have any family living around here. Mark, as you know, is my brother, and Pam is his wife. Pam's got some medical issues, and they wanted to live close by, so they fixed up a place out back. Mary was living up north in the Dakotas with her...Jack, but he died, and now she's home." Standing behind her chair, with a headache pounding on her temples, Anne decided that was enough for now. She said grace.

Mark, Pam, and Cerulean joined in, and Billy bowed his head. Jackie sighed.

Anne gestured. "Pam might not be hungry. Go ahead." After taking her seat, Anne took up her bread and sighed in relief, as everyone assembled their meals.

Billy stuffed food in his mouth as if he had not eaten in months. Jackie put her hand over his when he grabbed his third slice of bread. "Don't overdo it, Billy. You don't want to make yourself sick."

Mary tossed her slice of cheese to Billy. "Here, I can't eat it. I always put too much on my plate and end up wasting it."

Billy stared at Mary a moment before he accepted the cheese with unfeigned relief. "Thanks; it's been a while. Sorry, I'm acting like a pig. I just get so hungry."

Mary gently pushed the peanut bag toward Billy. "We've got more peanuts than we know what to do with. A friend came through last month and traded for eggs. He thought the eggs were worth gold, so we got a lot of peanuts!"

Billy grinned, though Anne tried not to shake her head. They'd need every peanut they had to last out the winter. But as she looked around the table, she realized she couldn't argue the point. They needed to eat now.

The quiet of the mealtime was only broken when Mark came back leading Pam by the arm. Panting with her exertion, Pam plunked down on a chair with a sigh. "I told him I didn't need to come, but he insisted." Looking around, her gaze fell on Jackie, who was appraising her with curiosity. Pam introduced herself, "Hi, I'm Pam, I don't think we've met."

Leaning over Anne, Jackie took the offered hand. "I'm Jackie, Philip's sister. A black sheep, looking for greener pasture."

Pam's smile held firm. "Looks like that's why we've all come. Looking for green pastures in wintertime."

Finally satisfied, Billy sighed and patted his stomach. He leaned back in his chair, hardly hearing its protesting squeaks and grinned like a contented child. "That was good!"

Everyone laughed. Mark leaned toward Cerulean. "So, which shed will it be this time?"

Cerulean gestured with a nod of his head. "The old machine shed will work. It's a little too big to keep warm all winter, but we can partition off one end and fix it up alright."

Jackie stared at the two men and frowned, perplexed. "You mean you'd let us stay? Just like that? No big conference? No conditions?"

Putting down her glass of water and wiping her mouth with her napkin, Anne responded, "Oh, there're conditions alright. You two will have to do your fair share of the work, and unless you two are married, you'll be living in separate spaces. Mark and Cerulean can see about that when they fix up the place. And we'll have to go easy on the supplies, but if everyone pitches in we'll be fine till spring, and then we can make the garden a bit bigger, maybe raise a few more chicks, and trade work for things we need. There are always ways to stretch a budget."

Jackie blinked in stupefied protest. "Wait a minute! I told you about Billy and me. We're just friends. I don't see why you have to make it seem like more than that. I'm no predator." She looked at Cerulean, one eyebrow arched. "Besides, you never mentioned what you and your friend Cerulean have going."

Anne's headache returned with a thundering vengeance. "Our relationship is our business. But for your information, we're just friends. His room is off the kitchen here." Anne struggled to keep her temper under control. "I never said I thought you were a predator; I just believe that it's best not to put temptation in a person's way. The winters can get cold and lonely."

Mary's quiet voice broke the awkward silence. "I've got space in my room. Why doesn't Jackie just move in with me? Then Billy can have his own place."

Silence.

Jackie pursed her lips and gazed around the room, her eyes finding rest on Mary. She shrugged. "Yeah, sure, why not? It's not like I want to live in a barn." She looked to Billy, who was staring at Cerulean with interest. "Will you be alright, Billy, if they fix up a place for you out there?"

With a nod, Billy asked, "Can I help work on it? I like doing stuff like that. My dad used to say I was stupid in the head, but my hands are smart."

Cerulean strode across the room and deposited his plate on the counter. He stepped toward Billy and put one hand on the massive shoulder. "I sure could use your help, Billy. Mark here—he's got three thumbs."

Mark grinned, as did everyone else. Chairs scraped across the floor as they all stood.

Jackie wiped crumbs off the table. Her eyes roamed over Cerulean's muscular body, his half-grown beard, and his mysterious deep-set eyes. She sighed.

Anne watched Jackie and swallowed down the lump rising in her throat.

November
HEAVY BURDENS

Eve loved her life. She appraised the shabby living room, pleased with her efforts to create a home for the homeless despite her limited means. She rubbed her cold hands together and pulled her sweater tight around her middle. When the men came back from church, they would be able to sit down to a nice meal and relax in peace and security. Though things were far from luxurious, still everyone had a lot to be thankful for. She smiled.

She had already heard Father's sermon twice and almost knew it by heart. In all honesty, she could have written it herself. They were so alike. Sometimes it amazed her that she could feel so completely at ease with another human being, yet be so absolutely in love with God at the same moment. Her faith had soared to a height she could no longer describe to another soul, but she never had to try with Father Thomas because he was already up there, waiting for her. He loved God with the same fierce passion, the same complete abandonment, the same absolute trust. In consequence, they now loved each other more deeply, more intimately, than if they had been husband and wife.

She knew that some people liked to gossip about them.

"They're always together...."

"Laughing at jokes no one else understands."

"They even complete each other's sentences!"

Eve always grew quiet when some patronizing parishioner informed her, for her own good of course, of the scandal she was causing.

Father Thomas shrugged off the rumors. "You can't stop people from thinking evil things; it's a habit with some." He would point to the crucifix, and no further discussion was needed.

Eve glanced around the room once more, satisfied that everything was in readiness and clasping her hands together, she meandered to the window to watch the snowflakes cascading from a gray sky.

The sun had just set, and it would be pitch black by the time the men left the church. There were twenty-two of them now, and she loved each of them. There was another house a block away refitted for homeless women, many of whom were also at the same Mass. They would walk the opposite direction, away from the men but know that they had something uniting them. They were children of the same God...a God who reached out to them through the charity of a warm home and simple food.

She smiled at a memory of visiting an old Shaker village where all the buildings had a separate men and women's entrance. Eve didn't smile now.

Many of these men and women sincerely believed that physical intimacy was the height of human bonding. They believed that their bodies held the key to happiness. But as they got to know each other better, they learned that deep human love was in the simplest intimacies: talking, sharing a joke, holding a hand. It was as if this last generation would be the freest generation that ever lived, for their illusions were being stripped away, as time ticked off the moments of their lives.

There was a soft knock on the door and Eve turned, surprised. Mass wouldn't be over for another half hour. She stepped to the door. There was always room for one more. Pulling open the door, she saw a stocky man holding up a tall, thin, almost emaciated man. Eve took in the scene she had witnessed so many times before and reached out to assist. The stocky man led his companion to a couch and laid him down. The thin man didn't even open his eyes. Eve bent and smelled the familiar scent of homebrew. Looking up, she noticed the stocky man rubbing his hands together as he appraised the room.

He grinned at her. "Looks like you've got a nice setup here." He stuck out his hand. "My name is Dr. Mitchell. I work over at the hospital. This guy, Robert, comes in all the time and we do what we can… but I'm afraid there isn't room today and, the way he is now, I doubt he'll make it through the night. Ordinarily, I'd let him die in peace, but…."

Dr. Mitchell looked at a crucifix hanging on the wall, "He once told me that he was a believing man and wanted to die in the house of God—he has a Catholic medal on—so I figured, he's one of yours. He might as well get something for his last wish…."

Straightening up, Eve's smile softened. "It was kind of you to bring him here. Yes, I know Robert. I thought he'd come back, though I was hoping under better circumstances. He struggles with his faith, you know." She shrugged. "We all do…sometimes."

Dr. Mitchell appraised the couches and various chairs lined against the walls and the table laden with grand supper fixings. His gaze turned to Eve. "This doesn't look like the work of someone who has any doubts."

Eve's eyes glinted in the dim light. "Let me get him a blanket and a pillow. I'll be right back." She walked out of the room.

Dr. Mitchell strolled around the room, peering at the wall hangings and the statues in the corners, his eyebrows rising and falling as he stroked his chin. He stopped in front of a painting of the Virgin Mary cradling the infant Jesus. His gaze rested on the beautiful woman.

Eve came back, positioned a pillow under Robert's head, and laid a warm blanket over his prone body. She strolled toward Dr. Mitchell. "I love that picture too. It's one of my favorites."

Dr. Mitchell frowned as he turned to Eve. "You said, 'We all do.'

Surely you don't have any doubts about what you're doing?"

"Not really. That's not what I meant. Robert may struggle with his faith, but you *have* to have faith to struggle with it. Some people think that just because the struggle gets fierce, they don't really believe in God, but that's not true. It just means that they don't like the struggle—their will against God's." She gestured toward the tables. "Can I get you anything? It is not easy…bringing in a dying man."

Dr. Mitchell grunted as he waved away her offer. "Ah, no thanks, I'm not hungry. I've got a wife at home, and she's a pretty good cook." He started toward the door and stopped. "Can I ask you another question?"

Clasping her hands in her lap, Eve smiled. "Of course."

Dr. Mitchell rubbed his hands together, his face clouding. "The pastor of our church hasn't been doing too well. He's lost his wife and two kids, and he's nearing the edge himself." Dr. Mitchell darted a look at Eve's face. "Well, you see, I have questions, but I don't think he'd understand. He's got it all figured out. The good people will fly straight into Jesus' arms and everyone else will descend into the fiery pit."

Eve lowered her eyes, her expression sober.

Dr. Mitchell started talking faster. "But you see, I have doubts. I mean, I don't doubt that God is real, and I don't doubt that there is a heaven and a hell. I just don't know who's going where."

Eve smiled at this. She looked up into Dr. Mitchell's haunted eyes. "Anyone in particular?"

Dr. Mitchell cleared his throat. "Well, there was this other doctor, pretty famous…Dr. Peterson. He was one of the lead cloning researchers. He kind of went crazy, was sent to prison and…." Dr. Mitchell's eyes filled with tears. "He wasn't *all* bad." Dr. Mitchell rubbed his eyes and then ran his hand over his short, clipped hair. "I just wonder; does God make allowances for the good getting mixed up with the bad?"

Eve placed her hand over Dr. Mitchell's hand gently. "I can't tell you the mind of God, but I do know that He knows us better than we know ourselves. I am certain of one thing—that whatever does happen to Dr. Peterson, is what *must* happen to Dr. Peterson. Judgment may be less about going to a certain assigned place, but rather our returning to what we've chosen all along…." Eve sighed. "I wish I could be more helpful."

Dr. Mitchell stood and took a deep breath. "I've heard that Catholics believe in a place of purging where imperfect souls go to get cleaned up before knocking on the gates of Heaven. I always liked that idea. Cause, truth is, I know that no matter how hard I try, I'll never be clean enough for the likes of Heaven."

"Oh, I don't know. Heaven might be full of men like you…only they won't be carrying such heavy burdens."

Men streamed into the room. They had smiles on their faces and there was the happy chatter in anticipation of a hearty meal.

Eve turned back to Dr. Mitchell. "Are you sure you won't stay and celebrate Thanksgiving with us? After all, you did just fulfill a man's dying wish, and that is no small accomplishment."

Dr. Mitchell watched as the assembly flopped down casually on couches and chairs, obviously at home and in friendly company. "No. My wife…." His tear-glazed expression softened as one of the men knelt down beside Robert and started to pray. "My wife is waiting for me. I just wish I were as confident as that woman in the painting over there. If only I knew what she knew."

Eve opened her mouth to speak but a movement caught her eye.

An elderly man came hobbling into the room, thumping his cane at every step. "Hurry up, Eve, come on, Father needs you! The end is here. The world's on fire!"

Eve turned and stared at the old man. "Mr. Mason, what on Earth are you talking about?"

Mr. Mason stared at the now silent assembly and knocked his cane against the floor again. "It's true. The news is just in. War's begun, and fire is spreading everywhere. No one will escape this time. We don't need to descend into hell. Hell's coming to us!"

GOD TRUSTS YOU

Behold thou shalt conceive in thy womb,
And shalt bring forth a son;
And thou shalt call his name Jesus.
He shall be great, and shall be called the Son of the most High;
And the Lord God shall give unto him the throne of David his father;
And he shall reign in the house of Jacob forever.
And of his kingdom there shall be no end.
(St. Luke Ch. 1: Verse 31)

He is retired as noontide dew,
Or fountain in a noon-day grove;
And you must love him, ere to you
He will seem worthy of your love...
Come hither in thy hour of strength;
Come, weak as a breaking wave!
Here stretch thy body at full length;
Or build thy house upon this grave:
(A Poet's Epitaph – Wordsworth)

Cerulean sat on the edge of Mary's bed and held her hand, gently stroking her skin with his thumb.

Mary's breathing was heavy but steady. She enjoyed the sensation of Cerulean's gentle caress almost as much as she had once enjoyed Jack's passionate embrace. Her whole body felt warm now. Her mother had heated up a bath and helped her bathe. With Jackie's assistance, she had dressed and limped downstairs and to her bed, now stationed by the woodstove. She rested her hand in Cerulean's and enjoyed the sensation of his thumb and fingers as they stroked the back of her hand. His smile warmed her almost as much as the blankets. Her voice barely rose above a whisper. "Ironic, isn't it?"

Cerulean raised one eyebrow, still smiling at her.

Mary's smile reflected his. "You've been taught the ways of a proper gentleman, how to smile and gesture soothingly. Was your mother a teacher?"

Cerulean blinked, his voice low. "No, though she taught by example, you might say. She was a talented healer…always insisting that true healing was a gift to be received and passed on, not a right to be demanded. I'll always be grateful to her."

"How old were you when she died?"

"Old enough to live without her, but too young to lose her. My mother didn't believe that sons could outgrow a mother's care. She was unique, strong, and brave."

Mary pressed Cerulean's hand. "So that's where you get it."

Cerulean leaned in. "You said something was ironic; what did you mean?"

Mary turned her head to the side; her hand went limp. "Oh, I was just thinking how I always thought *I* would be the last. That's what everyone said. It took years before anyone was really sure, and maybe they were wrong, after all, it's hard to know, but…."

"But what?"

"Those reporters looked up every record available, and they compared and charted and graphed and did whatever it is people do when they're after a story. Anyway, they said that according to the records, I was the last child born on Earth. I was the last of the last."

Mary peered thoughtfully at Cerulean. "So I always figured I would die alone." A tear slipped down her cheek. "And it terrified me." She sniffed. "It wasn't till Jack took me away that I began to hope again, maybe for the first time. He assured me that I wasn't the last. I wanted to be what he wanted—the first, not the last." She attempted a breathy laugh. "Well, I was first with him anyway. That has to count for something."

Cerulean patted her hand again, frowning at how cold it had become. "I don't know exactly what God has in mind for you, but you aren't last with Him, either."

Mary's gaze moved across the room. "And you? Will you miss me?"

Cerulean swallowed. "Yes, I'll miss you. And I believe we'll see each other again."

Mary closed her eyes, dark circles disfiguring her child-like face. "Good. And you'll take care of Mom?" Her eyes flickered open. "To the end?"

Cerulean patted her shoulder as he stood, his own eyes filling with tears. "To the end."

The kitchen door creaked open, and Cerulean left the room.

Anne stood, brushing snow from her coat. Eve and Father Thomas stomped snow off their boots as they stepped into the kitchen. Anne called out, "Cerulean? Mark? Jackie?"

Cerulean stepped forward and took Father Thomas and Eve's coat in silence.

Father Thomas gestured toward the living room and questioned Cerulean with his eyes.

Cerulean nodded, and Father Thomas moved forward.

Anne laid her coat aside and started forward.

Eve reached out a restraining hand. "Wait. Father and Mary need a few moments."

Anne heard the familiar prayers and stopped.

Cerulean threw his coat over his shoulders and snatched up an empty water bucket. His voice was low and depressed. "I filled a couple of containers and the bathroom buckets, but I'll get another for the dishes." He nodded to Eve.

Eve's gazed followed him out the door. "I wish I knew more about him, but I know—it's none of my business."

Anne spread bowls around the table. "You should be used to secrets by now, working with people the way you do."

Eve stifled a snorted laugh as she retrieved spoons from the drawer "You'd be surprised how many people want to share their secrets. They want to be unburdened at the end, like soldiers getting rid of every useless piece of baggage before a battle. I hear more than I want to sometimes." Her expression sobered.

Anne stared at the living room entrance; her eyes misted. "We got a second chance. But I'm not healed from losing her the first time."

Eve grabbed a loaf of bread off the counter and began to slice it. "We're lucky any of us are still alive. If those bombs had kept coming and the fires had spread any further, we wouldn't be here to worry about it. It was Armageddon for a lot of people, anyway."

Anne gripped the back of a chair, one hand holding the butter dish. "But not for Mary."

Eve's jaw clenched as she laid down the knife. "No, not for Mary and not for us…yet."

Mary tried to sit up, but she had to work for every breath. Her head fell back against the pillow.

Father sat hunched on an old, wooden chair set close, with his hands folded in contemplation.

Mary's words arrived breathless "Forgive me…Father…I've sinned. Can't remember—long time ago." Mary stopped, waiting.

Father remained motionless; he gazed at his feet.

Mary forced her next words to the surface. "I never understood… God forgives…why tell a priest?" She looked up.

Father Thomas stared at his clasped hands.

She shifted her eyes to the wall. "We weren't married…wasn't necessary." Mary raised her hand and then dropped it in exhaustion. "It was…easier." Mary's gaze searched the lamp lit room. "It wasn't just between us…was it?" Mary sighed. "We were young—" Mary reached out. "Where's Jack?"

Father Thomas clasped her hand; his voice barely rose above a whisper. "Is this your confession…or his?" He patted her hand and let it go. "God is merciful. Jack may have had good intentions, but he was also mentally ill. But, Mary, did *you* make a choice when you stayed away?"

Mary's eyes lowered. "I could've run…I didn't want to. I liked the hope…the promises...." She met Father Thomas' gaze. "That's wrong?"

"Could Jack fulfill God's will through kidnapping; forcing you to abandon your mother? Wouldn't *God* value the grace of marriage and family?"

Mary's gaze fell. Tears flooded her eyes. "I was afraid…you'd make me see…." Tears slid down her face. "Sorry."

Father Thomas' eyes softened as he whispered. "God reaches to humanity—through humanity."

Mary turned her head away, choking. "Am I going to hell?"

Father Thomas grasped her limp hand in both of his. "You have sinned, but you have also loved a great deal. If you remember—Jesus took that into account." Father Thomas placed her hand on her lap and folded his hands together. "Anything else?"

After absolution, Father made the sign of the cross.

Mary's face relaxed. "Feel lighter…a mountain off my chest."

Father Thomas stood, his gaze resting on Mary's small form. "That's faith for you, moving mountains and all."

A handful of people crowded into the small church for midnight Mass. Anne marveled at the simply beauty of the decorated evergreens and the crèche.

Mary had rallied in the late afternoon; she insisted that Anne go; she'd be fine.

Mark had taken Pam, and they smiled through the celebration.

Cerulean had come in a few minutes late as he had helped an elderly couple who were having trouble navigating through the snow.

Eve sat by herself to the side. She was a lector while a homeless man by the name of Abraham sang as cantor. The choir was in their best form, and the candlelight, the singing, the smell of pine, and the incense swirled into a cacophony of beauty.

Father Thomas' sermon comforted them with the hope that as Christ was welcomed by his Earthly family, so the many souls departing for their spiritual home would be welcomed by their celestial family.

Anne glanced at Cerulean during the sermon. She was moved to tears, but she wondered what he thought of it. Was Jesus his God as well? Could Cerulean see past the humanity and peer into the profound message—that God could love souls so intimately as to become united with them? Had God ever visited the Luxonians?

When the Mass was over, they filed out of the church, and at the door, everyone wished each other a Merry Christmas. Anne watched as Eve strolled through the shoveled path toward the women's house while Father trudged through the snow to the men's house. Kindred spirits.

Cerulean took Anne's arm, and he drove them home. His fingers wrapped comfortably around the steering wheel. "I'll bring the idea of a car back to Lux and see what we can do with it."

Anne laughed outright. "You hardly need a car."

"True. But there are a lot of things that we don't need but enjoy just the same." Cerulean reached out and patted her arm. "We don't need to become fully physical when we procreate, but most often, we do. Sensuality bonds us. Humans underestimate the gift of your biology. You only see the pain and the suffering, but really, you're very lucky."

The car crunched along the otherwise silent road. Anne gazed out the window. "Philip loved the feel of the wind through his hair and the excitement of going fast. It was all about the senses, but I couldn't join in." Anne traced a snow crystal as it slid down the window. "When he died, I felt guilty. I did love him, but differently." Anne stared down at her hands.

Cerulean laid a hand on Anne's arm. "For what it's worth, I don't think you could have given Philip what he needed. One of his co-workers killed a family through reckless driving. He lived a few days, but it wasn't pretty."

Anne shivered. "All smashed up?"

"Only a couple broken bones. He hung himself."

"Oh God."

"When Philip died, I kind of understood."

Anne frowned at Cerulean. "What did you understand?"

"That we don't see everything, how much worse it could've been."

When Anne and Cerulean pulled up at the farm, all was quiet. Mark and Pam's little house was still and quiet. Jackie was staying with the Hoveys, helping out. Billy had gone to spend a couple of days with a neighbor who was low on wood and needed to split a pile in a hurry. Anne and Cerulean stepped into the house and said their goodnights.

Anne peeked into the living room and stiffened.

Mary's breathing rose and fell in ragged, choked bursts. She saw Anne and reached out.

Anne knelt at her side, tears streaming down her face. "I can't lose you a second time, Mary. It's too hard."

Mary opened her mouth, but no words came. She closed her eyes and laid her hand on her chest.

Anne knelt down and prayed every prayer she knew, the Our Father, the Hail Mary, the Act of Contrition, the St. Michael prayer, the Angelus…. As the moments slipped by, Anne noticed a strange quiet. She looked up. The wind-up clock was stuck at midnight. *Appropriate*. She rubbed Mary's hands, shocked at their stiff coldness.

Mary's eyes opened a sliver. "God—trusts—you." She closed her eyes. Her breath fell and did not rise again.

Anne laid her head on her daughter's outstretched hands and wept.

———————————

Anne, Cerulean, Mark, Pam, Jackie, Mr. and Mrs. Hovey, and several other relations stood in a circle around a grave mound. Anne sprinkled a handful of snowy dirt on the mound. The others followed suit. Mrs. Hovey led the Prayers for the Dead. Father Thomas had not been able to come. Anne ached, missing his presence.

After the last prayer, everyone shuffled away in mournful silence. Jackie was going to stay a few more days with the Hoveys. Mark led Pam inside for something to eat. No one knew when Billy would be back.

Cerulean stayed by Anne's side. He sighed. "This will be a hard winter, and we're not prepared. You give so much away." He saw her flush and hurried on. "You're not wrong; we just have to come up with more supplies. I need to see what I can find."

Anne closed her eyes and whispered. "How long will you be gone this time?"

Cerulean shrugged. "A few days, a week at most. I'd take Mark, but he can't leave Pam and, well, I travel faster without him."

Anne shook her head. "Do what you can. I'll stay and take care of things."

"You going to be alright?"

"Aren't I always?"

Cerulean nodded and strode away through the snow.

Anne stood staring at the mound of dirt. A movement at her side caught her attention. "I told you; I'll be fine! Go ahead, twinkle out of sight. No one will see." She frowned and looked up.

Billy stood next to her, staring at the fresh grave. "I was hoping I'd be back in time."

Anne rubbed her forehead and tried to shrug off her irritation. "I'm sorry, Billy. The end came quickly. It was a blessing, I guess. She won't suffer anymore." Anne heard her words and winced.

"Guess so. That's what they said when my mom died. But it wasn't a blessing to me. I still needed her. Now, when dad died, I didn't miss him so much." Billy knelt by the fresh dirt, his boots kicking the snow away. He gripped the frozen earth and broke a clump into fragments and then let the pieces fall onto the mound. "Mary was always nice. She didn't think I was just some dumb guy."

Anne blinked back an overwhelming ache. "You're not just a dumb guy, Billy."

"Well, I'm good at splitting logs and stuff, but I'm not smart. But the smart guys who tried to fix everything...couldn't. Splitting wood and patching a roof really helps, while the smart guy—well he doesn't do what you do. He doesn't grow food and then give it away."

Billy peeled his gaze from the mound and turned to Anne. "That's why you're still living. Cause you know how to." Hefting a sack onto his shoulder, Billy grunted as he started away. "A fellow down the way got a couple deer and shared. We'll make stew." Billy lumbered off toward the house.

Anne stared at the grave, hearing Mary's last words: "God trusts you." She turned and shuffled through the snow toward home.

37

Winter
DESOLATION

Cerulean stared at the blasted, twisted, and blackened tomb that had once been a large and prosperous city and choked back the bile that rose into his throat. Charred ruins arrayed the expanse like broken teeth. His mind reeled with the immensity of humanity's loss. There was no rebuilding from this desolation.

In surveying the expanse, his eyes were led directly to the edge of an enormous crater. He had to force his gaze away from that unnatural monument to the indistinct remains that dotted the landscape for as far as the eye could see. His fascination drew him toward the center of the crater. He didn't know what he expected to see, but he felt that he had to look over the edge, as if there might be some surprise, some point of interest that would calm his racing, erratic heartbeat.

He stood on the edge and peered down. A great hole with dirt and melted rocks thrown up against the sides, mocked him. He glared at humanity's destructive power. When his people killed, it was a clean act. Of course, it was the very sterility of the act that made it so cold, so terrible in his eyes. But this? This was beyond his comprehension.

All of creation, from the smallest leaf to the largest building, had been obliterated, and the people who had once lived and worked, talked and played, organized and argued were gone like puffs of smoke. There was no sign of their passing and little to speak of their existence. He raised his eyes to the empty sky, no sign of color in the blank haze smothering the dome of the world.

Then his gaze landed on the horizon. Indistinct shapes loomed in the far distance. If other cities were anything like this, then there couldn't be many humans left. Those who had survived wouldn't last long.

He explored the outlying areas and encountered wrecks of buildings that had once been schools, shopping malls, and churches, bearing silent testimony to what humanity had once accomplished, a history that spoke of a preoccupation with ownership, education, pleasure, distraction, comfort, and attraction. But now all was silent. No birds flew through the air; no mice scurried for shelter; nothing grew beneath the melted rocks and stones.

The hazy cloud that hung over the city stretched ever wider as the wind spread it across the globe. White dust fell from the sky, as far from the beauty of fresh snow as could be imagined. Everything was dead, without the hope of regeneration. Had humanity decided to make the whole world barren before it left?

Cerulean closed his eyes against the bitterness that choked him. Everything he had believed about humanity collapsed into the barren dust. Humanity could have shown his race a way to face death nobly, with dignity. But this? This is what the Supreme Council had feared and predicted all along. This is why Roux and all the others left. Humanity would lead no one into the future. Cerulean fell to his knees and buried his face in his hands, his shoulders heaving in sobs.

As a slight breeze brushed against Cerulean, calmness settled where the ache of grief had overwhelmed him. A distant howl made him look around. The glimmer of sunlight through the haze was fading. He frowned at the thought of an animal wandering out here. What would it be looking for, anyway? He stood. The howl repeated. Then another. No dog, coyote, or wolf could live here. Deciding to investigate, he struggled across the wasteland, longer than he supposed he would have to, for he could not imagine the sound carrying so far. Finally, Cerulean saw the edge of the destruction and familiar lands. There was still desolation, but it was not complete. The houses had crumpled into ruins, the fields lay covered in dust, and the barns rested like toppled toys, but there was something recognizable about this landscape. You could guess who had once lived here. Cerulean heard the wailing sound of the animal again and moved on.

After traveling into the night, he came upon an abandoned farm. There were winter woods here and even signs of fresh snow still upon the ground. Not everything was dead—not yet. He could believe that animals, at least, still lived here. He gazed at a desolate two-story farmhouse and ascended the broken porch steps. The screen door was still in place, a sure sign that the owners had left during the summer. He walked into the living room and saw the ripped couch and filthy shag carpet. When humanity fled, something else had moved in, but it wasn't a good housekeeper. He looked around and tried to imagine the people who had lived here. Perhaps the owners were the sons or daughters or grandchildren of the very people who had built the house. He imagined how hard it must have been for them to leave, but what could they do? He surveyed the house and imagined Anne's comfortable living room. In a few years, it would look much like this. He felt the muscles in his chest tighten again, his breathing quickened. He forced himself to control the rising panic growing in his mind. His body was like a book, but telling him things he didn't want to know.

He strode outside, the horizon glowing as the sun rose, and from the corner of his eye, he saw movement. An animal scurried under the porch. Cerulean stepped down, and looking underneath, he saw a quivering dog. It began to whine. While putting out his hand, Cerulean whistled softly, and the dog's tail began to wag violently. Cerulean backed up and the dog crawled on its belly toward him until it was right in front of him, whining the whole time. Marveling at the incongruity of finding a living animal, man's best friend of all things, amid so much destruction, Cerulean scratched the black and tan hound behind the ears. Despite the fact that nothing else had changed, the haze as thick and damming as ever, the muscles in his neck and chest relaxed for the first time in days. Suddenly, the dog jumped up and pawed at Cerulean as if he wanted to be picked up. Laughing, Cerulean spluttered as the dog attempted to lick him in the face. He shoved the animal back to the ground and spat to the side.

The dog's brown eyes blinked, crestfallen. Duly chastened, it began to crawl on its belly again.

Cerulean pursed his lips before he spoke. "Well, what in the world am I supposed to do with you?" He had to return to Anne, but he couldn't just blink away, leaving this miserable animal behind, waiting, and howling that haunting call. He strode toward the remnant of the main highway, and the dog followed. Cerulean turned. The dog's ribs showed; it was on the verge of starvation.

With a sigh, Cerulean whispered, "I don't have much." The dog sat down in front of him and waited politely. "Oh, what the—" He reached into his pocket and brought out some jerky he had brought along for the trip. Though he didn't need to eat, Cerulean enjoyed the sensation, and it always helped to have a little something in case he met up with someone. Of course, he had never considered what a dog might want. He unwrapped it carefully, eyeing the animal the whole time, wondering if the dog would be satisfied with just one piece.

The dog wiggled its backside in anticipation.

Cerulean tore the jerky in half, and the dog let out a long, high-pitched whine. Without further drama, Cerulean tossed the whole piece into the dog's open mouth, watching as it went in and down. He laughed as the dog sat back, whining for another. Cerulean lifted his hands in protest. "It's all I have, honest." He began walking away from the house.

At first, the dog seemed undecided. He whined and wiggled as if asking Cerulean to stay and feed him some more, but Cerulean shook his head and continued his journey. In a few moments, Cerulean heard pattering behind him and felt his hand nudged by a wet nose.

A couple of days later, Cerulean walked along the main road leading back to Anne's farm. He had traveled far and wide across the country and visited the remains of several cities. He had left the dog and come back to him several times, and the dog always managed to recognize him as a friend. He bought food and fed the starving animal. After the third time, he decided the dog needed a name, so he pondered a bit and came up with the name Fidelis, meaning *always faithful*. "Fido for short. I admire your sticking around when all hope was lost." The dog trotted at his side as Cerulean continued marching at a brisk pace. When Cerulean had seen enough, he decided to return to Anne.

Cerulean stood along the side of the road with Fido at his heel, when a small wreck of a car pulled up beside them.

"You need a ride?"

Cerulean hesitated.

Smiling, the man waved him in. "Don't worry; I'm not going to rob you. I'm a medic. I make the rounds in this area. Besides, you don't look like you have anything worth stealing, except that dog, and he's too scrawny to eat."

Opening the car door, Cerulean let Fido hop in the back. He slipped into the front seat.

The driver stuck out his hand. He was in his mid-60s with thinning, gray hair, though his blue eyes still sparkled with vigor. "Jim. I do the circuit here about. I pick up supplies and carry passengers from one place to another as need be. Though the way things are now, one place is about as good as another. Not too many options left, if you know what I mean."

Cerulean took the offered hand and introduced himself as Cerulean. "You can just call me Sam."

The good doctor grinned. "Cerulean?" He seemed to savor the taste of it. "Oh, no, not Sam. That's so bland. Besides, I like French names; they're so musical."

Cerulean let that comment pass as the car sped up to 40 mph.

Jim pointed with his index finger toward the speedometer. "Can't get this thing going too fast or it'll blow. Very temperamental, and I don't know a single guy who can fix it. So I just baby it along using whatever skills I have. Funny, but if you look at it just right, it almost looks like a patient in need of tender, loving care. Sometimes I get crazy enough to think it understands me. Even talk to it sometimes." Jim's lopsided smile brightened his face.

Cerulean looked back at the dog as if for confirmation of his thoughts, and then he leaned back into the seat. "Well, I've been talking to that dog for a while now, so I suppose you can talk to your car. Just let me know if it answers you back."

Jim's hearty laugh boomed as he darted a look at Fido. "Same with your dog. Though he looks like a nice animal. Hate to tell you this, though. He might not be so safe in some of the areas I'm going through. People get kinda crazy, especially when they're hungry. They wouldn't get much of a meal out of him, but still, I'd steer clear of any large communities if I were you."

Cerulean nodded and closed his eyes. "I only need to go another fifty miles or so, and we'll be close enough to get out."

Jim tapped the steering wheel and nodded. "Well, you're in luck then. I'm going another hundred in this direction though I might make a few stops to check on some places. Probably no one left, but I got to be sure. That's what I do, round up the holdouts, the crazy old ladies who thought they could stick it out on the farm, or the stubborn fools who insist that they don't need no help from nobody.

"When the bombs started dropping, pretty much everyone surrendered the bravado act. But you'd be surprised. I still find a few here and there and take them in. At least they won't die alone. I've seen some sad sights doing these rounds. Some people give in and do terrible things. Terrible things." Jim sighed. "Despair is ugly—pure ugly."

Cerulean opened his eyes and stared out the window at the passing landscape. Yes, he knew about pure ugly.

When the last marker appeared, Cerulean shook Jim's hand and thanked him for his kindness.

Jim's eyes glistened. "I sure enjoyed your company, Mr. Cerulean. You know, it gets lonely out here. I can't forget how it was; it chokes me up. Sometimes, I think I really will go crazy. But then I meet someone I can help, and that makes everything better. Life doesn't seem so hopeless if you can do a good deed now and again."

Cerulean nodded as Fido jumped out of the car and loped next to him. "Well, from where I stand, you've done what few others could. You've kept your decency, and that's saying a lot."

Jim shrugged. "Oh, I wouldn't say that. I've met a lot of decent folk who've tried real hard to help their fellow man. It's just that the people with their fingers on the buttons panicked—they got crazy. See, the problem was, we had buttons to push. Never should have had those buttons in the first place."

Cerulean swallowed down a lump, waved, and stepped back.

Jim called out with a grin as he drove off. "Keep that dog safe—and let me know if he ever answers you back."

Cerulean watched Jim's car become a speck on the horizon, pondering the man's last words. He looked at the dog and realized that his first plan wasn't going to work. He needed to return to Lux, but he couldn't abandon Fido. He sighed. Then he thought of Billy and smiled. He'd travel through the woods, hand the animal off, avoiding the house so that Anne would never know he was back. He couldn't face another emotional parting.

He needed to consult with the Supreme Council and see if they had anything to offer humanity—besides their pity.

Spring
DOORWAYS

"When lilacs last in the door-yard bloom'd..."
–Walt Whitman

Cerulean stood before the Supreme Council. The stone-faced Judges flanked him on either side sitting rigidly on their throne-like chairs. Bright light illuminated the open space in a riot of colors from the floor to the ceiling. They usually met in a sterile council chamber, but in accordance with a new theme, vibrant plants in the newly built arboretum surrounded them.

Despite the unsettling contrast between the living spectrum all around and the deadpanned expressions, Cerulean kept his composure. "I have a plan that might save humanity, and it will surely be worth our while...." He described a human relocation plan that had been growing in his mind for months.

The Supreme Council's expression never changed. Once he finished, they stood and Sterling spoke for the assembly.

"We appreciate your suggestion, Cerulean. You have become humanity's leading advocate, but such a decision will require serious discussion and collaboration. We will call for you when our decision is made."

Cerulean knew he had been dismissed. He bowed and strode away. All he could do now was wait.

And wait....

And wait....

Cerulean paced his home in rising rage. He revisited the haunts of his youth and discussed the matter with other guardians, till no one wanted to talk about it anymore.

Finally, when he was near despair, he was called back before the Supreme Council. An ancient member passed the formal decision to Sterling who stood to read it aloud.

"We have considered your plan carefully and can find no fault with your conclusions. We agree that humanity might have something to offer us and saving them will do much to appease those clamoring for universal clemency. But as you have become so attached to humans, we think it only prudent to place another guardian in charge of this project. We have chosen Roux to lead the human remnant to Lux. Someday, we may even revisit Earth to see what she has to offer…if anything."

When Cerulean finally returned to Earth with an assembly of twenty-four representatives, including Roux as the leader, he wanted nothing more than to put his plan into action immediately. But Roux wanted to review the situation first.

The two Luxonians stood only yards from Anne's house, sheltered in a grove of woods.

Cerulean waved Roux's hesitation away. "What are you worried about?" He shook his head. "I told you, Anne handled the truth about me very calmly. Even Father Thomas handled it well. Humanity will be able to accept this." He looked toward the haze-covered sun. "They have to."

Roux snorted. "Most humans I knew were pretty stubborn. They like to argue and have a hard time looking at things from another person's perspective. Add to that, they have a loyalty streak that defies reason. They'll stick to the stupidest idea just because their grandmother told them to."

Cerulean leaned wearily against a tree. "You're painting with a pretty broad brush."

"I call it as I see it." Roux unfolded his arms and stepped up to Cerulean. "Look, I'll send my men in to appraise the situation one last time. You meet with Anne. See how she takes the idea. We'll meet back here in three days. How's that?"

Cerulean surveyed the impassive Luxonians who had accompanied him back to Earth. "Just remember, humanity has been through a lot already. They're suffering—be gentle."

With an affirming nod, Roux pointed toward a shallow ravine. "We'll be on our way. You talk with Anne." He appraised Cerulean one last time. "You sure you're up for this? What if she says no?"

Cerulean ignored the twist in his gut. "Anne has surprised me on more than one occasion, but I can't see her saying no to this. It's humanity's only hope."

Roux looked doubtful, but he nodded before he strode away.

Cerulean turned and stepped onto the road that led to Anne's house.

The next day, Roux stood in the midst of a rubble heap and surveyed the landscape, shading his eyes from the hazy glare that enveloped the scene. The oppressive heat, mixed with the chalky dust, made sweat trickle down his spine, a feeling he found distinctly disturbing. The large mosque that used to stand in front of him was merely a hole in the ground and the Jewish temple, which had stood not far off, was reduced to rocks and mortar. A cluster of people stood near the hole, and Roux wondered how they had managed to get here, for it was obvious that the native inhabitants had been obliterated and there was no truck or bus in sight. He stepped closer.

One of the men, dressed head to foot in a long white robe, saw him.

After speaking to his companions, the stranger turned and marched toward Roux. "Where have you come from?"

Roux paused before answering. He looked at the handful of people and saw that they looked worn and weary and more interested in the hole than in Roux. Roux eyed the tall, lean man a moment. "I've come to see if there was anything I can do to help. I have some friends not far off. My name is Roux." He waited for a reaction.

The white-robed man nodded and spoke less harshly. "My name is Saied." He paused as he looked around. "There are few who can help anymore. Our truck broke down a few miles back, so we walked the rest of the way." He looked toward his companions. "I had family and friends here. This was my home once, but I moved away to find work, and when the trouble came, I wasn't able to return. Not until now—when it's too late."

Roux sniffed and rubbed his hand against his chin. "Well, there are some who have stayed clear, and we're able to help. The question is, would you want the help we offer?"

Saied shrugged. "Depends upon what you offer." His eyes strayed toward a group of men and a single woman coming from the opposite direction. Saied's eyes narrowed.

Roux followed his gaze as one of the men and the woman broke off from the group and picked their way across the rubble. The man held the woman's hand.

As they neared, Saied's expression darkened. He turned away.

Roux gripped his arm. "Stay a moment. Let's see what they need. Perhaps we can help."

Saied shook his head. "I cannot help them."

Roux's grip tightened. "You might be surprised." He watched as the two inched their way closer.

The man's long gray beard and black, loose robes hung from his emaciated body. The woman's white clothes and shawl were well wrapped about her. She held her hand to her eyes against the glare and dust. The old man bowed slightly. "I was afraid no one else survived. It's good to see my fears were incorrect."

"My name is Roux," Roux pointed to himself and then to the man at his side, "and this is Saied. We met here by chance. I've come to lend assistance. While Saied is here to—"

Saied glared at the strangers in silence.

The old man smiled benignly. "My name is Jacob. This is my daughter Sarah. We used to live here, but we moved away many years ago. There was no way to get back in time."

"In time for what? To be destroyed with everyone else?" Roux's face flushed. These people had somehow managed to survive a hellish war only to return to the most dangerous place on Earth.

Jacob opened his arms as if to embrace their surroundings. "This is our real home, the home of every Jew, and we wished to see what had become of it. There have been many prophecies...." His words fell away.

Saied spat his response. "Prophesies? You thought that once the rest of the world was destroyed, the Jews were going to rise again by the might of God? Is that what you thought? Look around, old man. Survey the hope of your God!"

Jacob stared at the distant hole a moment before he spoke. "Once upon a time, I thought like that. I believed God would raise Israel to her former glory. But I met with the rabbi who used to live here. As he lay dying, his face radiated joy. He told me, 'Do not look for a temple of stone—but of souls.'"

Saied rolled his eyes. "We had a place of worship too, but God in His mighty wisdom removed it so that we might worship Him better."

Jacob's eyes shone. "So you do understand!"

Saied inhaled a long breath and gazed toward his companions. His eyes moved over the landscape as he brushed his hand across his forehead. "There used to be a Christian church nearby. I find it interesting that none of them are here."

Roux glanced from Saied to Jacob and waited. The sun glared down upon them. Jacob smiled again. "I wondered, too. But you know, my old friend, Christakos, an old and venerable bishop often said that this land would never know peace until humanity learned forgiveness."

"Forgiveness? Your people bombed our cities, killed our people, and stole our land."

Jacob's jaw tightened as his expression mirrored Saied's. "Your people bombed our cities, killed our people, and stole our land."

Roux dragged his fingers through his hair. "Look, you two, I think that argument has finally been settled. Look around. Is this the justice you sought? No man's land?"

"God will see to our vengeance." Saied's clenched fists trembled at his side.

Jacob blinked away tears. "I think He already has."

Roux squeezed his hands together, barely suppressing his fury. "I came here hoping to be of service. But now, I wonder if I'm really meant to be here. After all, what if I took you home with me? Would you carry your battle to my land? If this doesn't teach you the worth of your hate, will anything?"

Jacob put his hands up in surrender. "I agree with you, my friend. You are kind in wishing to assist us, but you're right. We are not people to be led away from our troubles. We must walk through them. God knows; we have to change on the inside; become living temples, not worshipers of dead stone, feeding on hate."

Saied snorted and turned away. He watched as one of his companions draw near. He gestured with a flick of his wrist. "Wael."

Wael stepped closer, pointing back to their companions. "They're getting tired. Where do you want to go?"

Saied crossed his arms and sighed. "No sign, nothing. I didn't think God would abandon us."

Wael shrugged. "He abandoned everybody."

"No." Jacob stretched his arms toward the sky. "God does not abandon. He merely walks us to a door we don't recognize." His smile lighted up his whole face. "I wonder if that is why Christakos is not here."

Saied tapped his thigh irritably, "Why, old man?"

Jacob reached out for his daughter's hand. "If death is a doorway, then it might be an invitation as well. Perhaps one that Christakos was ready to accept."

Wael's voice was strained, his eyes blinking in grief. "I would've gone."

Jacob nodded, then turned his attention to the huddled group. "We have a settlement in the north. You're welcome to join us."

Looking to his companions, Saied hesitated. "We'll die as we've lived. But as you say, God decides. There are many ways to approach His doorway."

Jacob nodded and motioned for his daughter to lead the way.

As the others struggled forward over the rocky terrain, Jacob stepped up to Roux. "I thank you for your offer, but I think we'd just as soon die here as anywhere else." He looked at the hazy sky and the barren desolation. "There are many approaches, but they're not all the same. Different doorways lead to different ends." Jacob shuffled off.

Roux watched as the two groups moved toward the horizon. He shook his head. "What a people!"

———————

Cerulean strode into the kitchen carrying a water bucket, wearing a sheepish grin. Anne turned from the sink and stared as if she had no idea who he was. He slid the bucket across to her like a peace offering, chuckling. "I thought you could use some fresh water."

Anne wiped her hands on a towel slowly and deliberately. "Well, it's nice to know you're alive." The bitterness in her voice surprised them both. "You know, it's customary to tell a person when you're going away. A nice pleasantry meant to show concern for the other person's feelings—just in case they might give a—" Anne stifled back the pending tears with the back of her hand.

Cerulean strode over and put his arms around her, hugging her before leading her to a chair. He pulled up another chair and leaned in, holding her clenched hands. "I knew you'd be upset if I left, especially if you knew why. But I had to do something."

Anne pulled her hands free and walked toward the window. The barest glimmer of light shone through the haze. "We can talk on the porch. The sun so rarely breaks through."

Cerulean sighed and followed her to the porch. He explained about his trip home and his hope for humanity ending with a plea. "Let me take you to Lux, Anne."

Anne's insides tightened into knots. Her gaze fell on the frozen, barren landscape. Her voice sounded as dead as the Earth. "No."

Cerulean stared, dumbfounded. "What?"

Anne hunched her shoulders. "I can't run away. I belong here. This is my home, and despite everything, I love it as much as ever."

"You'll die here!"

"That'll happen no matter where I go. At least I'll die as I lived. I'll tend to my garden and help those I can and when it's my turn, I'll...." Her voice cracked. "I'll get to see all those who have gone before me."

Cerulean paced back and forth, his boots echoing across the porch. "It doesn't have to be like this. Maybe I didn't describe Lux well enough. It's not impossibly different. We're intelligent beings. You can relate to us, talk to us, share with us. You'll be able to make the adjustment. If I could come here, you can go there. And if you did, if you led the way, then Eve and Father Thomas and many others would follow. A lot of people would get the help they need."

Anne stood, her white and frail hands still clasped. "What do they need, Cerulean? A few more years? A new home?" Her voice shook. "This is the home God gave us and look what we did! The only hope we have is the same one we've always had, if only we realized."

Slumping down on the bench, Cerulean rested his head in his hands. "What is that, Anne? What hope do you still cling to, here?"

"That God knew we'd muddle things up and the message would be the same. There is a life beyond this one. We'd only carry our problems with us. In the end, home is something you create inside yourself. It exists in the connection between your soul and God."

Cerulean didn't say anything for a few moments. "And Pam? She's sick. She could live without pain on my world."

Anne gazed at the darkening sky. "I can't decide for anyone else. Go ahead—ask her. See what she says. You'll know by the look in her eye."

Cerulean heaved himself off the bench. Taking a deep breath, he headed down the steps. "I'll ask Mark and her at the same time. I doubt they'd part from each other." Cerulean stomped away.

Stepping off the porch, Anne meandered over to the garden. Mark had tilled the soil, but the ground was too cold to plant anything. The air was heavy, and every living thing grew sick. Dead leaves and broken branches matted the earth. Dead animals littered the farm. The chicks were the first to perish, and she knew that the Hoveys' three calves were ailing. The Hoveys' friends passed in early spring, and now it was down to just Mr. and Mrs. Hovey and one last friend.

Eve had told her at Easter that there were only four men and five women left in their shelter, and few people ever came by. Father Thomas still held out, but he had developed a cough he couldn't shake.

Anne bent down and brushed away the dead foliage. Dirt crumbled to dust in her fingers. *How am I going to feed anyone?*

She tried to imagine Pam and Mark's reaction, but it was as hazy as the sky. She sighed. Sometimes you just have to stand and face things, even the end.

Summer
CALLING

It should have been high summer, but the air was cold, more like autumn, and the garden produce looked spindly and yellow. Anne stood staring at the weeds that survived when almost every good thing she had planted had withered. Things turned out very differently from what she had imagined. *But isn't that the way, God? I never can predict anything.*

Anne's prayer trailed off as she remembered Mark coming to her the evening that Cerulean had made his offer. Mark started out with his arguments all lined up neatly—that he could not run away from humanity's problems and that Pam was too ill to go anywhere. But then, somehow, during the course of their conversation, Mark grew confused. He decided that he would need to think things over a little longer.

He later described how Pam had cried when Cerulean told them who he really was. She became so hysterical that Mark had told Cerulean that he couldn't go anywhere without Pam, and she was clearly in no shape to travel. Mark had been quiet after that. He cared for Pam as much as ever, but he spent more time with Cerulean than Anne thought necessary, considering that Cerulean was returning to Lux and Mark was staying behind.

It was Billy who surprised her the most. Billy enjoyed Cerulean's company a great deal, and they'd go into the woods together. Anne couldn't imagine what they talked about. She didn't know that Cerulean had told Billy about himself until one evening in early summer when Billy came to her while she was gathering the yellowed asparagus.

He stood beside her, shuffling his feet, obviously wanting to talk but not knowing how to start the conversation. Anne had waited patiently. She liked Billy best when he spoke his mind. He was a peacemaker by nature, and she knew he sometimes sacrificed his own thoughts to make others happy. She had to control her impulse to say something so that he could get to the point more quickly.

Finally, Billy coughed into his hand. "I know where Cerulean comes from."

Anne sat back on her haunches, gripping a handful of asparagus, and looked up at Billy. "What do you mean?"

"He comes from a planet that's really far from here, but since he can move through light, it doesn't take him long to get from one place to another." Billy put his hands in his pockets. "You know how old he is?"

Anne sliced another withered asparagus stem. She shook her head.

Billy continued. "He's over 1,000 years old. Our years. His years are different." Billy shrugged. "But he understands—he still remembers what it's like being young."

"None of us are young anymore, Billy. Cerulean just understands people because he pays attention. He likes humanity." Anne stood up. "So, when did you find out?"

"He told me a while back, but I wasn't too surprised. It's like I expected him to be from somewhere else. He always knew more than the rest of us."

Anne's words were clipped short for precision. "That he did." She gathered up the asparagus and started toward the house. "But he can't save us, Billy. Knowing and fixing are two different things. Humanity has one path. Cerulean has another."

Billy stepped in line with her. "Well, maybe, but I don't know. Maybe it'd be good to take his path for a while."

Anne stopped and stared; a flush crept up her cheeks. "What are you saying, Billy? Are you going to go with him…to Lux?"

Billy nodded, a strand of gray hair falling into his eyes. "Yes, Ma'am. That's what I aim to do. Cerulean has been nice to me, and I don't think he's a liar. I believe him when he says that there's room for me there. He said his people would like me, and I could have a home and live happy."

Anne's mouth fell open, astonishment wavering on the edge of fury. "But, Billy, is it fair for you to leave us? We still need you. *I* still need you!"

"Cerulean said you could come too."

Anne felt rage exploding. "But I don't want to come. My place is here! With humanity, until its last breath. Don't you see? You'll die anyway! But when your time comes you'll be far from everyone who ever knew you—who ever loved you."

Billy paused only a moment. "Anne, I never had many friends. My mom and my grandma were good to me, and a few guys I worked with. But they're all gone now. Jackie was the first real friend I had in a long stretch of time. But she's got you, and she's got to decide for herself where she wants to live. I know you like me to and I like you a whole lot. But you always say that life is a vocation—you're called to something. Well, I kinda feel called to go with Cerulean. I mean, God created him too, and his whole world. It's not like I'm turning my back on anyone, I'm just going to make some new friends."

Anne looked to the muted sky and felt her emotions slamming against her reason. She wanted to argue and tell Billy that he was being selfish, that he had no right to leave her. She already felt abandoned at the thought of losing Cerulean again. The idea of Billy leaving, too, seemed like they were going to some big party without her, and she'd be left facing death alone. She squeezed her eyes against the pain in her chest.

304

Billy touched her shoulder. "Don't be mad, Anne. I'll never really leave you. You always say God has no limits. Well, God'll still hear my prayers for you, no matter where I am."

Anne felt her reserve tumbling. She opened her tear-filled eyes and sighed. "We should get inside. They'll be hungry, and I don't have much."

Billy stepped alongside Anne as they marched toward the house.

Later that same week, Mark stumbled into the kitchen crying. "Pam—Pam's stone cold...she's...she's—"

Jackie ran to him and hugged him, crying and talking all at once. "Oh, Mark! Sorry. Here, sit down. Why didn't you call us?"

Mark fell onto a chair and laid his head on his hands. "I got up as usual and I thought she was still sleeping. I figured I'd let her sleep in, when one of the cats jumped on the bed and began meowing. I tried to brush it away before it woke her, but then I noticed that Pam didn't even stir. So I went and pulled back the covers and saw—" Mark couldn't finish the sentence. "It took me a while to get control of myself. I suppose I should've waited till after breakfast."

Jackie snorted. "Don't be ridiculous, Mark. Good heavens, you think we care about breakfast?"

"I don't know. I'm locked in a cage, and I can't get out." He glared at Anne. "God, Anne, enough people have died! Can't we stop this?"

Anne dropped a loaf of bread on the table with a clatter. She stared at her brother blankly.

Glancing from Mark to Anne, Jackie exploded. "Mark! Anne can't help it that everyone's dying. It's not her fault!"

Mark pulled his fingers through his hair, and stomped around the room. "But it is—in a way. If Anne had said yes, she could have convinced Pam to go. But Cerulean told me what she said, and he told me it was useless to argue with her. Her mind was made up. She wasn't leaving."

Jackie turned on Anne, blinking in confusion. "Okay, I always suspected something about that guy, and Billy's acting like he's got a heck of a secret. I want in on this! What is going on around here?"

Anne felt her world tumbling as she plunked down in a chair. "I wanted to tell you. Everyone'll know soon. It's just that…Cerulean isn't human. He's from another planet, and he's offered to take the last of humanity back to his world with him."

Jackie spluttered a moment before she could articulate her words. "From another *planet*? *Take us*? Heavens, Anne! When, exactly, were you planning on sharing this with me?" Jackie gripped her head with her hands as if to keep it from exploding. "And you, Mark? You've known all along?"

Mark stopped pacing and glared at Anne and then at Jackie. "I didn't know until a few days ago. Cerulean explained to Pam and me that he could take us away and that Pam could live out her days in peace and security. They might even have been able to help her."

Jackie continued to splutter. "And he didn't think to ask *me*?"

Anne rose and paced to the counter. "I think he wanted you to stay behind with me."

Jackie made a strangled noise. "And Pam? She didn't jump at the chance?"

Mark slammed his fist on the counter. "No! She was terrified. She kept telling me that Cerulean was crazy, and she never wanted to hear the idea mentioned again. I tried a couple of times to get her to discuss it, but she got so hysterical that I was afraid she'd have a heart attack. So, I let it be. But now—if only I had forced her. If only *you'd* been willing to consider it, Anne! You could have convinced her." Mark flung himself down on a stool and buried his head in his arms.

Anne leaned on the counter, transfixed, speechless.

Jackie strode over to Mark and rubbed his back. "It's been a tough morning. Take it easy. Despite the fact that I've been left out of the greatest secret since—heck, I can't think when—and that Anne's been acting like a complete idiot, I can't blame her for making up her own mind. She doesn't *have* to go anywhere. But that hardly means we need to get stuck behind. Dang if I'll hang out here while everyone dies off like flies during a cold snap."

Suddenly, the kitchen door flew open. Cerulean and Billy tromped in with a load of wood and a full water bucket. Their broad smiles and laughter stopped short when they took in the scene.

———————————

Anne stared at the garden, her emotions as dead as the soil. There was no use thinking about it. Billy, Mark, and Jackie were going. The Hoveys had elected to stay behind, though their friend planned to leave. Cerulean had met up with his fellow Luxonians, and they had accumulated quite an assembly, though Roux had announced that he would have each person interviewed carefully before he cleared them for the trip.

Anne sighed. Am I just being stubborn? Maybe Billy was right; maybe God is bigger than my imagined loyalties. Maybe God wants us to start a new life on another planet. It made her sick to even think about it. Her stomach ached.

Besides, Roux had made it clear that some people were not suitable for the trip. What about those people? Could she leave knowing that they would face death alone? Someone had to be the last. Was that her calling? She remembered Mary's last words: "God trusts you." Question was—did she trust herself?

Autumn
GOODBYE

Roux completed the last interview and wiped his hands free of the difficult task. He directed his fellow Luxonians to compile the lists of refugees deemed most fit for the transfer and notify the lucky remnant. Not everyone who applied was accepted. Some were too old and sick, and others clung to animosities that made them unfit to relocate anywhere. Those left behind hunkered down in small communities or as stoic, though well-stocked, individuals. Those people leaving Earth cheered their good fortune, enthusiastic to take advantage of an unlooked for opportunity not to be missed at any price.

Fierce north winds blew icy snow across the Midwest as the transfers began across the globe.

Anne threw two more logs on the fire. Everyone was suffering the effects of the cancers and illnesses caused by the wars and the natural stress of humanity's struggle for existence. She, like everyone else on Earth, knew that the end drew ever closer, but she was determined to make the most of each day, no matter what it might bring.

Eve and Father Thomas had moved in with Anne, bringing their few earthly possessions. They hung the large crucifix on the west wall, the statue of Mary was set on a corner table, and the painting of St. Michael hung to the left of the wood stove. The small wooden altar and tabernacle Father had kept in the rectory were centered in front of the south wall. The tabernacle glowed golden in the evening light like a beacon on the sea.

Anne turned at the sound of footfalls pacing through the kitchen.

Jackie, her eyes brimming with tears stepped into the living room. "Well, little sister, it's time I said my goodbyes." Her voice shook. "I know, I'm not really your sister, not by blood anyway, but you've been more of a sister than anyone. Susie couldn't handle me. Can't say I blame her. I couldn't handle me either. But you, well, you know how to handle everyone." Jackie hugged her. "It's your gift, I guess. You just don't give up."

Anne tried to speak, but her throat constricted too tightly, and her eyes burned. She returned Jackie's hug, harder.

Jackie stepped back and wiped her eyes, grinning through her tears. She stepped away and then stopped. "Billy wants to say goodbye next. We decided it would be easier this way, rather than ganging up on you all at once."

Anne nodded, though she still couldn't speak.

Billy came in, gazing mournfully at his snowy boots.

Anne beckoned him forward.

He shuffled in, standing solemn and mute.

Anne struggled to control her trembling voice. "I'm going to miss you, Billy. You've got a lot of wisdom tucked inside that strong body of yours."

Billy shrugged. "It was Mary who told me I was smart." Blushing, he wrung his knitted cap in his hands. "You don't know how you're gonna change things when you care about people. You did a lot when you took me in. I wish you were coming with us, but I kinda see why you can't."

Anne stepped forward, taking Billy's hands in her own. "I can't go personally, but Cerulean, Mark, and Jackie will be with you. They'll make sure that everything is all right and that you're always well taken care of."

"Aw, I'm not worried about that. I'll be thinking about you. But you know, I still think we'll meet again someday."

"I'm sure we will, Billy." Standing on her tiptoes, she gave Billy a kiss on the cheek. His clean earthy scent comforted her.

Billy slapped his cap back on. "I put a lot of chopped wood and stuff in the barn. Should last till spring." He stepped through the doorway.

Wrapping her arms around her middle, Anne returned to the fire. *How much more, Lord?* She stood lost in thought when she heard a cough behind her. She turned.

Mark stood, holding a ring out to her. "Here, it was one of Mom's. She gave it to me to give to my wife when I got married. Pam treasured it. She told me a few weeks before she died that she wanted you to have it. I couldn't stand to think about it, but I took it off the morning she died and put it aside." Mark stepped closer. "It seems right to give it to you now." He put the ring into Anne's open hand. "You're married to the whole human race. Won't leave till death do you part."

Anne tried to swallow back the ache in her throat and just managed to whisper, "Beautiful. Thank you." She gazed at Mark's tear-filled eyes, as tears ran down her cheeks.

Mark turned away. "Stop it, Anne. I can't stand it. I've said goodbye to just about every human being I've ever loved, and now I have to say goodbye to you. But this is the hardest, because it's a choice. Before, death just took over; I couldn't stop it, but I could stop this. I could stay."

"I'm not asking you to. I'm making a choice, too. I could go, but—" Anne paused. "I can't explain. With every mile, or every million miles that we crossed, I'd feel like I was getting weaker and fainter. My strength comes from this place, these people, this— Why is this so hard to explain? I'm like that mythical god who got his strength from the Earth. If I left, I'd wither away."

Mark took a deep breath. "I understand. I can't explain why I have to go, but I feel it's where I need to be. It's not just about Billy and

Jackie, though they matter too." He sniffed and rubbed his face with his hands. "Did God take Pam so that I'd be able to go?"

Anne shook her head. "It's impossible to say. Mind of God and all." She stroked his arm. "I'm so glad you brought Pam. I loved her like a sister. We're so lucky we got to know each other." She gazed at the ring again. "And this. I'll treasure it—always."

Mark shuffled toward the kitchen. "Mom hoped that we'd give it to our daughter. But the ring stops with you, Anne."

He looked back. In silence, they looked at each other one last time and then Mark strode across the room, hugged Anne fiercely, turned, and rushed through the doorway.

Anne stood in the center of the room, stifling back choking sobs.

Cerulean walked in.

Anne shook her head and waved her hands. "Oh, no more! I can't. If you have to go, go like you did last time. Go off without telling me. Let me discover it in silence and peace. I can't say goodbye again."

Without a word, Cerulean strode up to Anne and encircled her in his arms. He hugged her as she cried on his shoulder, murmuring, "I can't do this. I can't."

Finally, when her shoulders stopped shaking and she had sniffed back her tears, Cerulean stepped back and looked Anne in the eye. "I'm not leaving forever. I'll be back. And when I come back, I won't leave you again."

Anne gazed at him, blinking back her tears. "You sure? The others will need help...." Her clashing emotions made her weak.

"I'll stay long enough to make sure they get settled in, but Anne, I'll be back. I promise."

Anne used the edge of her sleeve to wipe her face and turned away, facing the woodstove. "I guess I can hold out till then."

Cerulean came and stood behind her. He wrapped his arms around her once more and said, "It won't be that long. With Jackie along, I expect she'll have everyone on Lux so perplexed that she'll just take over and tell everyone what to do. We've never had a female Supreme Council member, but Jackie just might change that. Who knows? She might change our world." He whispered into Anne's ear, "You've changed mine."

Anne relaxed into his embrace a moment before she pulled away and turned to face him. "I feel like a sailor's wife, always saying goodbye to her traveling husband…though we could never be that. But it's been beautiful, this friendship of ours. More than a friendship—a sort of awakening. But now, my heart feels like it is being wrenched in two."

She sighed and straightened her shoulders. "I have a job—not a job exactly—a mission, maybe. I have to see this through. I hope you make it back before… But if you don't—don't grieve. You've been pure gift." She put her hands to her trembling lips. "After all, we'll be parted someday."

Cerulean kissed Anne on the cheek and whispered, "Not forever, Anne, not forever." He turned and stepped through the doorway.

———————

Several hours later, Father Thomas and Eve stomped snow from their boots in Anne's kitchen. Anne hung their coats and placed the kettle on the stove.

Eve appraised Anne's swollen eyes and turned to Father. "You want some tea?"

He waved his hand and started toward the living room. "Too tired. Goodbyes are emotional; I'm all in."

Eve nodded as Father Thomas climbed the steps.

Anne glanced at Eve as they headed to the kitchen table. "Goodbyes?"

Eve shook her head. "The church. At the last minute, Father decided he wouldn't leave after all. He said he'd rather die under its roof than anywhere else. It was only when I reminded him that the tabernacle was here that he agreed to come."

Anne arranged the tea strainer and pulled two cups off the shelf.

Eve sat down. "So, how did it go?"

"I feel like I've been through the fires of hell." Anne took a seat and peered at Eve. "Why didn't you go? I mean, how many Catholics will there be on Lux? Won't they need someone with your background? Maybe you and Father should've gone."

"Naw. Father Thomas wasn't about to leave, though I must admit he is very taken with your friend Cerulean. Besides, a bunch of priests is going, some Roman Catholic, a few Orthodox, a couple of Anglicans…a whole bunch of nuns. Amazing how many religious are going. Humanity will be well represented; don't worry."

Eve threw up her hands. "Heavens, Anne, why didn't you tell me earlier? I could've kept a secret! Besides, it would have been fun to tease him."

Gazing into the past, Anne propped her chin on her hand. "It was my little secret. You know, I used to see him out of the corner of my eye. I'd convinced myself he was my guardian angel."

Eve grinned. "He was—sort of."

"But when we first met, I kind of fell for him. He was a balm for my aching heart. I realized that our friendship was special, but never meant to be anything more. I was selfish, keeping him a secret so long. But Cerulean had his own reasons for keeping quiet."

"Perhaps he wanted it to be something more."

"It wasn't like that. He came as a guardian, for his people, I mean. Ironic isn't it? He came to protect his people from us, but he ends up bringing a whole bunch of us back to his world. I hope he's right about us."

Eve frowned. "You want to explain that?"

"Cerulean thinks that humanity has something to teach his people. It was fate that he was sent here."

"Makes sense to me." Eve poured the hot water into the cups and handed Anne her mug of tea, smiling. "Can't put boundaries on God."

Anne sniffed her tea, warming her frozen fingers around the hot cup. She sighed. "Oh, but we try. We try."

PLANET LUX, A NEW WORLD

"Dang, Cerulean, this isn't Noah's Ark!" Roux glared at Cerulean and pointed to the animal sitting patiently at his side.

"It's only one dog, and I promised Billy. Since I rescued him, I feel kind of responsible." Cerulean snapped his fingers and Fido stood up, ready for anything.

Roux rolled his eyes. "Everyone will want to bring a pet now. If I let this animal go, then all hell will break loose, and I'll never get this job done."

Cerulean gestured. Billy stepped away from the crowd and jogged forward. With a deadpan expression, Cerulean ordered Roux. "Tell him you're going to take away his dog."

Roux appraised Billy and then hissed a long sigh, "Alright, but you've got to keep him out of sight and keep everyone moving. Please. I don't want this to get any crazier than it already is."

Cerulean nodded. He and Billy moved off; the dog trotted playfully alongside.

Roux rubbed the back of his neck. "What have I gotten myself into?"

The first group of sedated, naked, humans were placed in transportation tubes and traveled to Lux faster than light. Their bodies were laid out on metal tables in a large, bright room the size of a football field. A thin white sheet had been laid over each person, in respect to human modesty. Under each table, a bin contained a single, white, one-piece uniform matched according to size: small, medium, and large.

Dr. Mitchell awoke groggily from stasis, feeling like he had a bad hangover. He clumsily got dressed in the sterile uniform. When he could see straight, he shuffled over to Kendra's table and stroked her fingers. He tapped her limp shoulders. "Kendra?"

Kendra laid motionless, completely unresponsive to her husband's entreaties.

Dr. Mitchell's face wrinkled into worry frowns. "Honey, it's alright now. You can wake up. Wake up, honey."

Kendra's fingers were cold. He bent down and listened for her heart. Nothing.

His voice rose. "For Heaven's sake, you're beginning to scare me!"

One of Lux's preeminent healers, appearing tall and slim, with black hair sprinkled with gray, and a white lab coat over dark pants and a dress shirt sidled over at the sound of Dr. Mitchell's hysterical urging. "Sir, my name is Dr. Lumen. I am here to assist you."

He peered down at Kendra, and, after feeling for her pulse, he laid her hand back down exactly in its previous position.

He read Dr. Mitchell's nametag printed on his uniform. "Dr. Mitchell, your wife is still in stasis. It takes some humans days to recover from the journey."

Lumen gestured Dr. Mitchell away from his wife. "We have limited experience with your kind. But we have learned that the shock of space travel can be too much for some biological systems, so we have put our travelers into stasis so that when the molecular transfer takes place, there is no resistance and no sensation of disintegration."

He leaned in and lowered his voice. "We have had a few unfortunate cases where the body survived, but the mental and emotional state of the traveler was so severely damaged that they could not make the adjustment."

Frowning, Dr. Mitchell crossed his arms. "So what did you do?" Lumen appraised the tables with travelers in various stages of waking up. "There was nothing to do but put them out of their misery."

Dr. Mitchell's eyes grew round. "You killed them? When someone doesn't make a good adjustment here, you kill them?"

Pursing his lips in disdain, Lumen applied his most authoritative tone. "An act of mercy. If a being is suffering and there is no remedy, we relieve them. There is no kindness in suffering."

A commotion broke out at the far end of the room.

"Excuse me; I am needed. If you don't mind my advice, I would suggest you leave your wife alone for a day or two and see if she comes out of stasis on her own. If she doesn't, rest assured I will be notified, and I will do what I can to assist her." Lumen stepped past Dr. Mitchell with precise, well-practiced movements.

Dr. Mitchell watched as Lumen strode away. His gut squeezed hard, tied in empty knots. "No Florence Nightingale award for you, *Doctor* Lumen. Uh, huh, I've met your type before. "

When he surveyed the enormous space packed with hundreds of metal beds, he felt a scream tear at his throat. What had he led his wife into?

Dr. Mitchell gazed down at Kendra's form covered by a thin, white sheet. She had never liked the idea of relocating and refused to go, but he'd begged and pleaded until she'd given in.

Kendra had nearly bolted when she discovered that she couldn't take her personal mementos or even her clothes. But Roux and his assistants had assured her that everything they needed, including clothes, would be provided once they reached Lux.

Dr. Mitchell stared at the form-fitting white uniform he wore and gazed over the waking assembly; all dressed exactly the same. His knees shook. He rubbed the back of his neck where the uniform scratched his skin. The fabric made him hot and itchy. A chill ran over

Dr. Mitchell as he realized that only a few hundred Luxonians had ever lived on Earth, and they had carried their information in their minds. They never transported samples, diagrams, instructions, books, or media. There was a great deal they didn't know about humans.

Originally, Luxonians racing to humanity's rescue had seemed like an ancient ballad coming to life. But as Dr. Mitchell stared at his wife's immobile face, he wondered if Luxonians were as unpredictable as humans. *God help me.*

Roux stood on a high balcony, peering over the large staging area as Lumen strutted near. Nodding, Lumen joined Roux, in Viewing Area One, where below, three hundred bewildered humans struggled to come to terms with their new environment. There were other staging centers connected through large bay doors.

The entire relocation process would involve several steps, taking place over several months. When the last healthy survivors were transported, the initial migration stage would end.

Roux clasped his hands in front of him, his gaze studying the assembly below.

Lumen crossed and uncrossed his arms twice and finally plunged his fists into the lab coat pockets.

Roux's gaze flickered to Lumen and back to the crowd. "How many made it?"

Lumen pursed his lips. Over half still lay prone on the tables. Some were sitting up and others, like Dr. Mitchell, were on their feet, dressed and moving around.

"We've done very well. Almost half. We are leaving the dead in place to give the survivors a sense of security. This gives them a chance to get acclimated and allows their biology to adjust. Soon, we will usher the first awakened into the Introductory Station where they will dine and refresh themselves in an environment as near to an American living room as—"

Roux slapped his hand on the railing. "An American living room?"

Lumen raised an eyebrow. "It was the best my intelligence team could come up with. Though the United States is only a small portion of the Earth, they have the majority of viewers. We were in a hurry."

Roux grunted.

Lumen continued. "Next, they will be moved to an Invitation Shelter where they will be educated about our planet and history and given their living arrangements and work assignments. At that point, we will dispose of the dead and arrange the next transfer."

Roux tapped the air in front of him indicating a specific individual. "Keep an eye on that one—Dr. Mitchell. I worked hard to get him to come, and he'll be invaluable to us. His knowledge of DNA, cloning, and human development will be of great use." His gaze darted toward Lumen. "How's his wife?"

Lumen didn't flicker. "She did not survive."

Roux frowned. "Does he know?"

Lumen's face remained impassive. "As I said earlier, I make it a policy to keep the deaths a secret during the acclimation period. Tomorrow, when he is moved to the Introductory Station, I will tell him that his wife suffered in the transfer and is currently under my care. In time, I will inform him that she succumbed to a fatal illness. When he grows hysterical, we will remind him that she would have died on Earth anyway."

"Have it all figured out—don't you?"

Lumen's color glowed through his clothes as he peered at the bewildered remnant. "I have been very thorough in my research."

Shaking his head, Roux turned away. "Fine. You'll need every bit of *research* to understand humanity, and even then, you'll never be able to predict them."

Lumen grinned. "That will be the fun part. Discovering what makes them so—unique."

———————————

Jackie nearly hyperventilated when she couldn't wake Billy, but after a few moments he began to stir, and Jackie calmed down.

Billy sat up groggily. "Where's my dog?" He frowned and looked under his sheet. "And where're my clothes?"

Cerulean pulled a suit from the tray and laid it next to Billy.

Billy blushed. "Where am I supposed to change?"

As Cerulean turned his back, he also turned Jackie around, giving Billy a modicum of privacy. "Our people don't have the modesty issues you do, so they didn't provide separate dressing rooms. But don't worry. No one's looking." Cerulean glared at Jackie.

She shrugged as she averted her gaze. "Go on; I'm no Peeping Tom. Besides," she let her gaze float toward the vast, high ceiling as other people were in various stages of waking and getting dressed as discreetly as possible, "I had to do it too, so I know how you feel. Just be quick. No one will see anything."

There was a series of grunts as Billy struggled to fit his large body into the suite set out for him. There was a ripping sound, and Cerulean peered over. Billy groaned and mumbled something that made Jackie smile. Billy grunted. "Okay, you can turn around now."

Jackie considered him with solemn respect. He was definitely larger than the Luxonians were expecting. "Oh, well, life's never perfect."

She linked arms with Cerulean and nodded toward the large bay door. "So, when do they open that thing and let us out? You can show me all the highlights of your world. Besides, I'm starved. You don't happen to know any nice, old-fashioned diners around here, do you?"

Cerulean pursed his lips in the realization that he had developed a soft spot for Jackie. He would enjoy taking her around to see his world, though he had to suppress a sigh when he pictured taking Anne out for the same reason.

"I'd like to show you around, but they have a protocol for these things. Besides, Mark already went to ask, and he's heading back here now." Cerulean's expression darkened as he peered at Mark's face in the distance. "He doesn't look too cheerful."

Mark waded through the meandering passageways made by people standing around waiting. Others sat on their beds, and a few strolled around the vast room to get the kinks worked out of their bodies.

He marched straight up to Cerulean with a frown creasing his brow. "No one will tell me anything except that food will be brought in at the proper time and that we will be moved into the Introductory Station tomorrow."

He looked around the room. "It seems to me that it's taking a long time for some of these people to wake up." He pointed his thumb over his shoulder. "A nun back there was saying the prayers for the dead over one guy. You'd think there'd be medics all over this place, making sure that everyone was all right."

Cerulean frowned as he beheld Roux and the senior healer, Lumen, up in the viewing station. "I see a friend of mine. I'll find out what I can." He patted Mark's arm. "Don't worry; there's a lot going on that has nothing to do with you. We're still dealing with the after-effects of rebellion and civil war." Cerulean strode away.

Jackie slapped her forehead and stared at Mark. "So, *now* he tells us?"

Billy knelt beside the body of Fido, stroking his soft fur. Fido was still breathing, but its body trembled every few moments as if electrical waves were passing over it. Billy kept patting Fido, murmuring, "It'll be okay, buddy. You just rest a bit. That was a rough ride for you. Just rest. I'll stay with you."

Roux watched the proceedings below. Sweat trickled down his back and his hands trembled. He knew with certainty—he had just made the biggest mistake of his life.

ANNE'S DIARY

I know it is arrogance of the highest order to think that one day some-one might read my journal and find it valuable, but that is my wish. Journals throughout history have connected the past to the present and illuminated the minds, hearts, and realities of what people have lived through. No other literary endeavor can so perfectly accomplish what a journal does. So, as the last of humankind to live upon Earth, I am recording my thoughts, what I see before my eyes, and what I face in the future. Reader, be you human or of another world, may you find these humble musings and honest records of some value.

    Let me start with plain facts. I live on a dying planet. There are very few of us left. I don't know the number of humans yet living upon the Earth, nor do I know the date that I write this. It's winter now and the snow is deep. It's also very cold, and had my friends and family not left me well provided for, I'd probably be dead. But, in fact, I have more food and supplies than I'll ever be able to use. I won't die by starva-tion, at least. That's some comfort.

    As you probably already know, a remnant emigrated to the planet

Lux with Luxonians who said they had our best interest at heart. I trust my friend Cerulean, but I don't know about the rest. I only met one other, Roux, and I couldn't read his expression. He was like a walled city, strong on the outside but hidden on the inside.

I pray for the refugees. I don't understand what they hoped to accomplish, except for one, Billy. I do believe Billy had an appointed purpose in going to Lux. There's something about his innocent honesty. No matter what is offered to him, he will only be able to offer himself in return. And if the Luxonians are really interested in humanity, they will see the best of us in such a man.

Because it's winter I don't go out much except to get water, feed what animals are left, and bring in wood for the fire. Father Thomas and Eve are with me still, but our dear neighbors, the Hoveys have passed on. They were such wonderful people that I believe, if ever I were to need a definition of the word "friend," I could just use the term "Hovey," and everyone would understand. They were not quite like Millie, someone to chat with and exchange stories and memories; they were doers, quiet workers who did the needful without explanation or reward. They never looked for it. They never asked for it. They were a free and happy people, and I miss them.

Before bed, I throw a few logs on the fire, so it will last till morning. Then I get up early to keep it going. Cerulean and Mark left us a quantity of wood, sticks, and a huge mound of last year's leaves by the back door, so I'm able to get what I need readily, though the snow melts over everything when I bring it in. Father Thomas used to help with this chore, but his back bothers him now.

I only have a few pain relief pills left, and I hate that he suffers with only tea and home remedies to alleviate the pain. But Eve remains amazingly energetic. I worry about her though. She tries so hard to keep us cheerful. But what do we have to be cheerful about? I think she believes that saints are always happy, so she acts the part. But I don't feel glad or grateful. I feel sad, lonely, and weary beyond words. Cheerful doesn't make sense right now. At least not for me.

I've wandered from my narrative....

So, after getting up and starting a fire, I heat water on the wood stove for tea. Then I mix up a batch of hot cereal. We have a variety of oats and grains that I sweeten with honey. Mr. Hovey was a successful bee-keeper, so we have copious jars of the precious ambrosia. In the summer, we often eat granola, but in the winter hot cereal warms us best.

After breakfast, Eve and I do the chores together. We feed the chickens and collect the eggs. We rigged up a tarp over the henhouse so that the chickens and eggs don't freeze and it works well. We still have plenty of corn and wheat berries left. We also inherited the Hoveys' two cows and a bull. I am frightened to death of the bull, but Eve managed to make friends with it. She keeps them in the Hovey pasture, and she'll milk the cow after she has her calf, which I am calculating will be in the spring.

So after a midday meal of bread, soup, and nuts, we usually take a nap. Then I get up and rekindle the fire and start dinner. Eve has taken over the bread making—she's very creative.

Father Thomas looks exhausted. He usually gets up while we're doing the chores. After his morning prayer, he reads awhile and then takes a nap. He celebrates Mass in the late afternoon, before dinner. I used to find the late afternoon unsettling. But now, the Mass and the fading winter light combine to remind us of where we're going and what we hope for. Memories and ancient yearnings still haunt my sleep, but at least during the day I can find relief in work and prayer.

After dinner, we settle down in the living room and take turns reading out loud. I have all sorts of classics and though I've read them before, it is entertaining to hear them again and discuss their plots and characters. We're reading Frankenstein now, and it's been the source of many thought-provoking discussions. We consider what part cloning and other medical research might have had to do with our demise. Is God fed up with our trying to eat the fruit from the Tree of Knowledge? Did we overstep the line one too many times?

Contrary to my expectations, Father Thomas doesn't seem to think so. He believes that our end has more to do with God's original plan than anything we did to earn it. God wanted a certain number of souls *to populate Heaven and when that number was reached, humanity's mission was accomplished. Eve wondered if perhaps God was saving us from some more terrible doom, which we might have faced had we survived longer.*

But what about the people who had a chance to do good but refused to do it? And those who never knew why they lived? What was the point in their existence? Eve only shook her head. But Father Thomas pointed to the altar. "Don't forget," he said, "our mission is not to define God...but to love Him."

After reading, we say our prayers and go to bed, hopefully to sleep. Because of the cold, Eve and I sleep in the living room near the wood stove. Father Thomas sleeps in Cerulean's old room. It's the most protected in the house, and with warm blankets he is comfortable enough, at least that's what he says. I doubt he'd complain even if he were freezing. I told him that he could sleep in the living room too, but he just shook his head and smiled. "No, I often lay awake talking to my Lord, and I'm waiting for Him to answer." His faith astounds me.

Well, it's time for me to get the water and wood. Eve is moving about, and I think she has a surprise for dinner. I love to hear her hum. It means she's up to something, and that's usually a good thing.

Planet Lux
I WANT TO GO HOME

*"If you cannot understand or grasp those things which are be-
neath you, how can you comprehend those that are above you?"*
—The Imitation of Christ

Roux lay resting in his contemplation room when he heard the chime
signaling someone's presence in the outer chamber. He checked the
identifier and groaned. His tone was curt and his words clipped.
"Come in."

He glared at Cerulean's human form when he entered. "What now?
Are your friends complaining about their accommodations?"

Cerulean brushed Roux's comment aside as he paced the length
of the room. "Sterling just informed me about the experiments. Have
you lost your mind? You can't let humans be shuffled off and used as
lab rats." He pounded his fist into his hand. "If we don't do something
soon, we'll find ourselves facing a monster that's grown beyond our
strength, and it'll devour *us* in time."

Roux's colors faded. "You've become so human; I can barely understand you. Though," Roux solidified into human form, "I can appreciate your sentiment." He faced his friend. "All right, I'll admit it. I heard about the experiments a while back. But we can't stop them. The Supreme Council was chosen very carefully, and all the compromises they made have worked. They approved these studies. If we call their judgment into question now, we'll set off the same power struggles that so recently killed hundreds of thousands of our own. We can't afford to let that happen."

Cerulean marched up to Roux and stared him in the eye. "What are the experiments for? I asked, but Sterling hemmed and hawed and said it was secured information."

Roux threw up his hands. "But you want me to risk my position and tell you?"

Cerulean gripped him by the arm. "Yes."

Roux pulled away. "I should never have accepted this assignment. There are so many other worlds to choose—"

"Roux!"

"Okay. They are meant to better understand human reproduction, and if they could ever become compatible surrogates for our—"

"So we can breed with them?"

"Crude, Cerulean. Very crude."

"We're talking about using humans in lab experiments. It doesn't get much cruder than that." Cerulean paced across the room and stared out the window, overlooking the city. "They are sentient beings. When we first took them in, we did so with the understanding that they were our equals."

"*You* understood that and I accepted your belief, though I still have a hard time with humanity. They're so—but never mind. You're right. If things get much worse, we'll be facing another power grab. But this time, those who want to rule will be using aliens as shields. We must crush the seed of rebellion now."

Cerulean's voice rose as he turned from the window. "It isn't just about power and position. Rebellion begins in the heart, Roux. If our race doesn't respect other races, if we see them as nothing more than tools to be used or deposits to be mined, then we'll never really be free. Freedom comes from truth. And truth comes from seeing ourselves honestly. If we think we're free to use other beings—use will turn to abuse. Then those of us who still believe in something higher, we'll have to respond. And war will come." Cerulean paced across the tiled floor. "If we could demonstrate humanity's intrinsic value, their intelligence and adaptability, then I believe Luxonians would be less willing to support questionable procedures."

"By questionable procedures, I suppose you mean the attempts to produce a mixed race? We have to do something; we're dying out. You do understand that?"

Cerulean continued pacing; his expression turned inward. "The price of saving our race might destroy us faster and more completely than anything humanity suffered. If we don't respect aliens now, will we respect their offspring? Will the children of mixed races be accepted? Or will they become the next sub-race that we use for our benefit?" He stopped pacing and faced Roux. "Don't you see? It isn't about existence as a species; it's about being a species worthy of existence."

Roux stared at Cerulean for a long moment. He had helped to bring the refugees to Lux. He had overseen their transition. He had watched as the dead were carefully disposed of and the survivors lied to. He had observed as the remaining humans were told that they just needed to wait, rest, and adapt. He stood by as chosen men and women were hurried off to labs. When the others asked questions, he quieted their fears with soft lies.

In the first experiment, the patient managed to escape. He was found and returned to the lab. The man begged to be allowed to return to the others, and when that was refused, he begged to die. Roux had entered during this episode, and it disturbed him, though he allowed the researchers to tranquilize the subject so he would no longer struggle against his fate.

Roux wearily shook his head and wished he had never seen a human being. "I don't have any authority to stop these experiments. I was just told to bring the refugees to Lux. This was your plan—remember?"

"Lab experiments were never a part of the plan! I thought we were going to work together, humans and Luxonians, to find solutions to our problems. Humans aren't stupid. They have good ideas. If nothing else, we should have respected their position as guests and allowed them to live in peace."

Roux murmured, "What you planned and what others planned turned out to be very different. Now we're stuck with someone else's plan, and we don't have a thing to say about it. I did try to discuss the matter with a high-ranking Judge, and I was politely told that this is not my area of expertise. In other words, 'shut up and go away.'"

"I will not go away! I'll not abandon humanity to this fate. It's worse than what they faced on Earth. At least there they could have died in peace."

"Or they might have killed each other off with another couple bombs." Roux's shoulders slumped. "But at least it would have been their choice."

"Bombs are never about choice." Cerulean headed toward the door. "I'm taking them back to Earth."

Roux intercepted him. "You can't do that, and you know it. You'll be caught and charged with treason. Again."

"Treason? How?"

"Working against Luxonian best interest. Anyway, from what I saw, these experiments aren't working. Humanity may fail as lab rats, and that'll solve everything."

"What then?"

"I don't know. Maybe they'll finally be free to die in peace."

Cerulean maneuvered around Roux. "In the meantime, innocent humans beg for death."

Roux gripped him by the shoulder. "Cerulean, does it really matter? Death is death."

Cerulean glared at Roux, his colors rising. "It matters how men die, just as much as how they live! And it matters what we become trying to save ourselves. We weren't meant to be beasts!"

Roux moved aside. "I've seen humanity and Luxonians at their worst. We're all beasts."

Moving across the threshold, Cerulean called back. "Then *you* can live and die like one."

Fido didn't like planet Lux. He sniffed disdainfully at the fake rose bushes and dug halfheartedly at the thin layer of soil laid down as cheap imitation lawns.

When Billy evaluated his box-like community home, centered in a wide, domed field, he had to agree with the dog. Though the colors, which gleamed through the domed ceiling, were beautiful, the sun was much too intense for their biological natures. They wouldn't survive even a few hours on the outside. This wasn't Earth and never would be.

Billy rubbed Fido's head and gazed out at his park-like surroundings. Fake pine trees bordered the perimeter. The streets were set in straight lines like a tic-tac-toe box. He, Jackie, and Mark had been assigned to live with a group from the Midwest.

He threw a balled-up cloth across the compound and watched as Fido went after it. He smiled. He loved this simple creature. Fido was uncomplicated and very predictable, lifting Billy's spirit.

Mark and Jackie meandered across the field toward him. Their expressions warned that trouble was brewing.

Fido ran up to Jackie and jumped on her, attempting to lick her on the face. She shoved him down, spluttering, "Dangit, you stupid mutt, get off me!"

Mark called Fido, who promptly turned his attention to his next face-licking victim. Gripping the dog by the neck, Mark made him sit, and then patted him as he knelt by the dog's side. "He looks a lot better, Billy. You've done wonders with him."

Billy strolled up. "I didn't do anything. He just got better on his own. I never knew what was upsetting him, other than he had a bumpy ride. But you know, I think he'd go through it again just to get back home."

Jackie whispered the word "home" as she glanced at Mark.

Mark rose to his feet, and Fido trotted at his side. "We'd like to talk to you about that, Billy." He glanced around a moment and then focused on Billy's honest eyes. "How do you feel about going home?"

Billy didn't hesitate. "Anytime."

Jackie frowned. "I thought you wanted to come here. More than any of us, you seemed to think you had some mission to accomplish. But now—you want to go back?"

"I think I know why I had to come—why we all had to come."

Mark ran his fingers through his hair. "Why's that?"

"It's like what you said a minute ago. You called it home. You didn't say, return to Earth, like it was just another planet. You see, we were so afraid of facing death, we forgot there's something worse."

Jackie rotated her hand in impatience for him to go on.

Billy continued. "There's facing death—far from home." He patted Fido and sat down. "Besides, I don't think we're as welcome as we thought."

Leaning in, Jackie whispered. "There's talk that all those people they said were just sick, actually died."

Billy nodded. "I know. I've heard the rumors. The Luxonians are worried."

Mark threw up his hands. "They have the advantage. What could they possibly be worried about?"

Billy threw the ball to Fido again. "I don't know. But when a person won't look you in the eye, they're usually worried…or guilty. I'm hoping they're just worried."

Smacking her fist into the palm of her hand, Jackie hissed. "I'm going to find Cerulean and have it out with him. I'm sick of all the mystery. I thought we were going to be free citizens here, able to make lives for ourselves. So far we have been—"

A cohort of Luxonians suddenly appeared near the large bay door. Everyone hushed and turned to stare. So far, the few Luxonians that they had met, those who came to check in on them, providing food and materials, had been unable to answer their questions. Even when Roux appeared, he was unable to enlighten them as to what had happened to their fellow refugees or what was going to happen next. All they knew was that they were to recover from the initial transportation shock, and they'd be informed of further proceedings on another day. Apparently, today was that day.

Mark held Jackie's hand as they faced the Luxonian representatives. Billy stood, keeping his hand lightly upon Fido's head as he glanced at Mark and Jackie.

"Friends and guests," the Luxonian spokesperson opened his arms, "be assured that we have been monitoring your recovery closely, and we are very pleased. You are the strongest of your race. You should be very proud of your innate ability and endurance."

There was a murmur of confusion from the crowd of humans.

The Luxonian put up his hand to stall any further discussion. "We are pleased to reunite you with your remaining survivors."

He turned as a large bay door opened and in trailed approximately four hundred other people. They looked much like everyone else, dressed in similar clothes, with the same bewildered expression on their faces. As they filed in, they were met with a few shouts of recognition, but mostly there was a confused expectation.

As Billy scanned the newcomers, a wave of nausea rose.

"Where are the rest?" a man shouted.

"Yes, where are the ones who were being treated for illness?"

Shouts rose up from every side; anger rang in their voices.

The Luxonian spokesperson waved his hands to stall the rush of echoing questions. "I am sorry to relate that many of your kind were not able to make the adjustment. We tried to save them, but they perished, and we have disposed of their remains."

The screams that rose, as the crowd surged forward were enough to cause the Luxonian representative to blink out of sight and return at a distance.

He put up his hands, signaling for quiet. But it didn't work.

"What happened to them?"

"Where's my wife?"

"Where's my son?"

"Why didn't you tell us?"

Over a thousand voices mingled into a raucous roar and climbed to a hysterical pitch.

Billy's heart beat rapidly. Sweat began to trickle down his face. The Luxonians must have known all along that many of them wouldn't survive the trip. They knew that over a thousand men and women had died and yet they hadn't told them. Why?

Mark shouted his question. "Where are the men and women who were taken away?"

An old woman began to cry. "I want to go home!"

There was a hushed silence.

Roux appeared and faced the angry crowd. He darted a glance at the spokesperson and motioned for him to leave. Roux's gaze swept the area. "I am sorry to have to be the one to tell you this, but you can't return to Earth. The trip that killed so many of your fellow humans would probably kill the rest you if you tried. Your life is here now. You need to accept that."

Mark repeated the question he had just asked amidst the roaring crowd. "Where are those who were taken away? We were told they'd just be gone a few days, but we haven't seen them since."

Roux peered into the crowd before he locked onto Mark's face. Recognition showed in his eyes. He grimaced. "I'm sorry, but some of them have died too. They were asked to help us, but in the process, they were injured. The program they were in is under review. But in the meantime, you'll be free to live in the housing that has been set aside for you."

Blinking in helpless surprise, Mark folded his arms across his chest. "How can we trust you?"

Roux marched through the parting crowd to Mark. People gathered closer to hear. "You're right. Things have not gone as planned, and I'm sorry about that. We—" his face flushed "have been struggling to survive ourselves, and sometimes when you're desperate… you do desperate things."

Dead silence filled the air.

Mark stood his ground and stared back at Roux; his face was set, his expression hard. "Like what?"

"Like trying to create a cross-species between humans and Luxonians."

Mark's eyes rounded as he clenched his fists.

Jackie flung herself at Roux; her arms beat his chest. "You tried to breed us like...like dogs or something? We're human beings, for God's sake. We deserve better than that!"

Roux winked away and appeared on a hill. He stood tall and put his palms out in an attitude of surrender. "We didn't intend to hurt you. We thought it would be beneficial to both our species. But so far, it hasn't worked out that way." He looked around the room. "I am sorry. It was a noble enterprise." With one last brief glance at Jackie and Mark, he winked away.

The crowd stood in stunned silence.

Finally, Mark stumbled toward a small knoll and sat down. Following, Jackie sat next to him. Others moved off into groups. A few people stood or sat off by themselves, staring at the domed sky. Distant sobbing filled the air. Neither Mark nor Jackie spoke for several moments.

Fido trotted up and attempted to lick each in turn, but he was pushed aside. The dog sat down with a harrumph.

Finally, Billy sauntered up. He stood near, but he did not sit. He gazed at the crowd in the makeshift park. *Good imitation, but not the real thing. No earthy scents to comfort a body.* He rubbed his nose. "I wish they had asked."

Jackie looked up. "That wouldn't have changed my mind. I still think the whole idea is creepy. How dare they think they can make some cross-species? Damn stupid-heads."

Mark smiled and patted Jackie's knee. "Apparently, they're facing something like what we were facing on Earth. Don't think we wouldn't have tried it, if the situations were reversed. After all, we didn't know there was an alien race until it was too late for us. But they still had hope. They may not now."

He paused staring into the distance. "I wonder—are there other races that might match us better? Hey, you know, this may not be such a bad thing. Maybe it opens all sorts of doors. Maybe we came here not to fulfill their hopes but to give us new hope. Maybe—"

Jackie wrinkled her nose and slapped her hands over her ears.

Roux appeared. He stomped up to Mark. His expression was sour and irritable. "Listen, I told you the truth—against my better judgment. Cerulean insisted. But I'm afraid not everyone thinks like us. While there's a whole segment of our society that believes that alien races should be treated as our equal, there are others who have different ideas."

Jackie and Mark glared at him.

Roux appraised the environment. "The problem is, you're vulnerable here. I can't protect you. Cerulean is looking for a way to send some of you back. If you want to risk it, that is."

Mark nearly stood up but Jackie pulled him down. "Don't say anything yet. We need to think this through. That's part of our problem, being so bloody impulsive. Well, it's mine anyway."

Surveying the disheartened assembly, Mark climbed to his feet. "I'll wander around and ask who wants to stay and who wants to return home."

"You can't do that!" Roux leaned in and whispered, "I'm not doing this with official clearance."

Jackie jumped to her feet and stared at Roux. "You mean you're going to get in trouble for helping us?" A flush crept over her cheeks. "Maybe I shouldn't have tried to beat you up."

Roux sighed, his hands up in surrender. "I got into trouble bringing you here. I might as well finish the job. I'm a glutton for punishment; what can I say?"

Mark propped his hands on his hips. "What does Cerulean think? Should we try to sneak away? We can't just leave everyone else stranded."

"It's either sneak away or stay until the Supreme Council has a chance to review your case and in the meantime hope that they don't pick you for the breeding program. They have been approved for performing *necessary* experiments. But it was never made clear what kind of permission we needed to get from *you*. It was assumed that once you got here, you'd be willing to cooperate."

Jackie pressed he hands against her head, her eyes bulging. "Cooperate? In a breeding program? Yeah, I'd think you'd want some kind of cooperation! How else are you going to get cute little half-human, half-Luxonians running around? Unless—" her eyes grew even wider. "You're not playing around with our reproductive biology, are you? Oh, Lord, you wouldn't!"

Mark gripped Roux's sleeve. "How far have these experiments gone? Have you been able to create…any…thing?"

Pulling his sleeve free from Mark's grip, Roux straightened up. "So far they haven't gone beyond the first stage. Then something goes wrong. The subjects we had didn't want to cooperate, and we had to switch them out. I explained to the researchers that if they'd be more honest, they'd get better cooperation."

Mark licked his lips and then repeated the words "subjects." He sniffed. "Did that work?"

"Not really."

Jackie rubbed her neck. "So…have the experiments stopped then?"

"They're still trying."

"Damn." Mark slapped his thigh.

Roux grunted. "Yeah, that's about the size of it."

IF GOD WILLS IT

Anne stood on the garden path, luxuriating in the warm sunlight just breaking through a thin spot in the hazy sky. Someone cleared his or her throat behind her. She assumed it was Eve or Father Thomas, though she was surprised that Father would be awake this early. Then she remembered that Eve was out with the chickens. Anne turned around, more curious than afraid. She stepped back in surprise, her hand flying over her heart.

"Cerulean? What on Earth?"

Cerulean's smile wavered. He held out his arms to her, and she stepped into his embrace. After gently patting her thin, frail back, he let go, and they walked over to the swing where they sat down,

Anne kept his hand in hers. She looked him over, noting the clouds reflected in his eyes. "So, my traveler, tell me all the news."

Cerulean flushed. "It's not good."

With a gentle squeeze, Anne signaled her compassion. "I was afraid of that." Her gaze lingered on the sky. Though a haze remained, it appeared to be thinning. She wondered about that even as she faced Cerulean. "So tell me then—what isn't good?"

Suddenly, Eve called across the yard. "Anne! Anne, come. Quick!"

Anne hurried forward with Cerulean right behind her. She met Eve at the kitchen door. "What's the matter?"

Eve's eyes were wide and frightened. "I heard something crashing to the floor, and I ran in and found Father—" She could hardly get her words out. "He's had a stroke or heart attack…or something." She spotted Cerulean and leaned forward, grabbing his hand. "Thank God, Cerulean, you're an answer to a prayer. Here, hurry! Get him up and put him in the living room."

Cerulean slipped into the kitchen. Father Thomas lay huddled on the floor unconscious, a cup fallen from his grip and water pooling around him. Cerulean carefully lifted the elderly priest and carried him into the next room where he placed him on one of the beds.

Eve and Anne crowded close by. Anne spread blankets over him and attempted to make him comfortable, though she could tell he had no idea what she was doing.

Eve scurried into the kitchen and put the kettle on the stove. She returned to the living room, wringing her hands. "It happened so suddenly. There was no warning. He must have tried to get a drink of water and then— Oh, I wish we had a doctor or medicine or something."

Anne stared at Father Thomas' shallow breathing. She rubbed Eve's back in comforting circles. "There's little more we can do now. He's not in any pain. We'll just have to let God handle this."

Eve wiped her eyes and straightened her stooped shoulders. "I left things half-done out there; I better finish up." She gestured to Anne before she left. "Stay with him. I'll be right back. Let me know if—"

"We'll be right here." Anne perched on the edge of the other bed, leaning forward, her head in her hands, staring at Father.

Cerulean sat next to her, also gazing at the frail old priest. "He was a remarkable man." Cerulean's gaze trailed into a memory. "I'll never forget his face when he came in, after you told him about me. He was like a child discovering that fairy tales are true."

A hint of a smile lifted Anne's lips. "He *is* a remarkable man and always will be. Soon he'll begin his next adventure."

Blinking, Cerulean looked from Father Thomas to Anne's locked gaze. "You'd rather be alone? I can come back later."

Anne sighed. Alone? *I'd only brood in anxiety.* She rubbed her eyes and turned her gaze to Cerulean. "No, go ahead, tell me what's happened. I should know." She sat up straighter, bracing herself. "Tell me about Mark and Jackie and Billy." As her gaze fell back on Father's almost still form, she took strength from him. "Are they okay?"

Cerulean stood and began pacing the room. "It's hard to admit this, Anne, but I think you made the right choice. Our people weren't ready. I thought they were. But after what's happened, I'm afraid that nothing can be gained by continuing this experiment. Many of the refugees didn't survive the voyage, and those who did, discovered that Lux is neither home nor refuge—but rather—a prison." He raked his fingers through his hair and stopped pacing. "Some Luxonians who felt that since humanity was desperate and needed help, they should be willing to aid Luxonians, no matter what that involved. But once your people discovered what our goals were, well, they felt differently."

Nausea rose in Anne's tight stomach, but she forced herself to look at Cerulean. "I don't understand. What plans are you talking about? What have your Luxonians been doing?"

Cerulean looked away. "They tried to alter human biology so as to cross breed with Luxonians—without asking permission."

Anne sucked in a deep breath and then slowly exhaled, trying to keep panic from rising. A ray of light slanted across the crucifix toward the altar. Her shoulders slumped. "I should have guessed. Someone should have guessed."

Cerulean's eyebrows rose. "I didn't see this coming. I thought my people were too advanced for this level of barbarism."

"You haven't told me about Mark and the others. What's happened to them?"

Cerulean slumped back on the bed. "They're fine—for now. I did what I could to get them settled, and I asked Roux to look after them."

"So what now?"

Reaching over, Cerulean took Anne's hand and looked her in the eye. "I want you to come back with me, Anne. You can talk to your people; help them understand our plight. Tell them that if they cooperate, we can create something new and wonderful. If I can arrange a meeting with you and the Judges, we can convince them that humanity has a worth all of its own, something unique that should be respected and allowed to live in peace."

"And if they don't understand?"

"Nothing wonderful will happen."

"Why not just send my people home? They may die here, but—"

"Over half the people died on the journey, and several have died since. I wanted to send them back, and some are willing to try, but I'm afraid that's no longer an option. The Supreme Council has decided that humanity must stay until a formal inquiry is made."

He stood and paced across the room. "Right now, they're trying to work out coalitions with several other races. If they admit failure in this, the other races might refuse to cooperate. All the alliances might back away. Honestly, I think the Supreme Council is as worried as anyone over this whole mess." He paused as he looked out the window. "If it makes you feel any better, my people are on the brink of civil war—again. There are many Luxonians who believe as I do, that alien races should be given equal status."

Anne clasped her hands together. "It's more than that. There shouldn't even be such experiments. If your people and my people were meant to mix, they'd be able to naturally. If you have to mutilate something to get the result you want, then it can't be right."

Rubbing his hands together in impotent anger, Cerulean charged across the room again. "I don't know what to do, Anne. I can't fix this. I'm the one who thought that humanity could help my people. But now everyone is suffering for my mistake. I can't bring them back, yet, I can't leave things as they are." Cerulean turned and stood by the bed, his head down and his shoulders stooped in defeat. "I shouldn't have returned. I just wanted someone to help me, someone who could fix this. But it was wrong of me to ask it of you." He looked at Father

Thomas, his eyes reddening. "You need to be with him now. I'm in the way." Cerulean started toward the door.

Anne called out. "Cerulean. Don't despair. Some things have changed for the better, little things, but noticeable. The haze is thinning, and the land is recovering some of its splendor. I can't explain it. The Earth should be devastated for ages yet, but the same God who took a whirling mass of gas and rock and formed this habitable world—he could He take *our* destruction and shape something new."

She stood and looked out the window. "Perhaps I was supposed to be here—to be a part of something new and beautiful. And maybe—" Anne reached for Cerulean's hand, "you're supposed to be a part of that, too."

Bitterness edged Cerulean's tone. "It would take a mighty God indeed to make something wonderful out of our worlds now."

Anne's heart ached.

The kitchen door opened.

Anne's next words flowed out in a rush. "Perhaps it's not me who should leave, but you who should stay."

Cerulean sighed. He patted Eve's arm as he passed her in the doorway.

Anne and Eve went about their daily work, speaking in hushed voices and making as little noise as possible. Father's breathing became more irregular, but he never showed any serious sign of discomfort. By late evening, the sun descended upon the horizon, and the light in the living room muted every object to shades of brown and gray.

Eve slipped the prayer book off the shelf and knelt before the altar. She and Anne began their evening prayers, the psalms and the readings, the intercessions and the invocations, their voices echoing the serenity of the quiet light in the shadowed room.

Father's breathing quickened and his eyes opened. He slowly turned his head, his eyes wide, staring at a single beam of light glinting off the altar. He stretched forth his hand.

Eve rose and rushed toward Father, but as she reached him his face began to relax. She peered down at him, tears trailing down her cheeks as he breathed his last.

Father's eyes stared, but he saw no Earthly thing. His hand fell at his side, his expression now no longer intense but calm, knowing.

Putting her hand over her mouth, Eve groaned.

Anne stepped closer, closed Father's eyes, and drew Eve back to kneeling. This time they offered no words, only tears as prayers.

Cerulean stepped back inside, saw the two kneeling women, and retreated back outside.

That night he sat alone in the dark. The flickering candlelight through the window wavering near Father's corpse offered the only illumination.

Cerulean lived with Anne and Eve into the next season, managing their little farm. He fixed a leak in the shed and patched together broken tools. He watched a baby rabbit make its first forays into the greater world and various spring buds burst into blossom. The healing Earth puzzled and comforted him.

Mild spring storms came early and left swiftly. Pure drops of rain fell from an untainted sky. Trees and grass grew luxurious again. Roads and highways disappeared under the weight of new vegetation. Old farm buildings crumbled, smothered by vines forming green mounds all over the land. Animals multiplied majestically in their renewed world. From little hideaways, hens brought forth flocks of fluffy chicks. A new calf was born to the old cow.

Cerulean watched geese fly overhead in great V-shaped flocks, and he smiled as he felt the bright sun warming the planet again. He could not understand how the land could heal so quickly after so much devastation, but his confusion did not diminish his joy.

The only thing that grieved him was the change in the two women he loved. Rather than growing young again, Anne and Eve aged more rapidly than ever.

Eve struggled to walk. Her stooped form moved slowly from room to room, and her hands shook. She still got around well enough to smile and chatter, accomplishing a few tasks each day.

Anne could navigate the steps and the yard, and her back remained straight, but she, too, moved more slowly. Her hair, now completely white, accented her dark eyes. Though her skin was covered with age spots, her eyes still twinkled when she handed Cerulean a live chicken.

"You remember?"

Cerulean nodded. "Some things you never forget."

Cerulean watched Anne maneuver through her herb bed toward the house, and it suddenly struck him that he loved her no less dearly now than when she was seven. Her indomitable spirit would never dim. She could not die—not really. Her mortal shell might be stripped off, but her essence would live forever. Tears filled his eyes as she disappeared into the house.

Snatching up a bucket, Cerulean filled it and began to lug it towards the back steps, not caring in the least if he was sloshing water all over himself. Suddenly, he heard a murmur of voices coming from the kitchen. He stopped. A man's voice?

Cerulean dropped the bucket and raced up the steps two at a time. He rushed through the kitchen door and found Eve standing in the middle of the room with Roux sitting at the table with a plate of warm bread and a hot cup of tea placed neatly in front of him.

Cerulean pressed his hand hard against his chest. "You just about gave me a heart attack!"

Roux chuckled as he swallowed a bite of the warm bread. "You've been among humans too long, Cerulean. You can't have a heart attack. You can disintegrate but no heart attack." He grinned at Eve. "This is great. You've got to give me the recipe."

After stumbling toward the nearest chair, Cerulean plunked down. "I'm getting too old for this."

Anne ambled into the room with a handful of tea leaves. Seeing Roux, she nodded. "Hello, Roux, nice of you to visit." She smiled at Eve. "We don't often get visitors these days."

She laid the leaves on the counter and turned toward Cerulean, who had his head in his hands. "Oh, Cerulean, don't be silly. You've probably got another five hundred years or so left in you."

Roux tapped his cup. "Five hundred? We'll need him longer than that, I'm afraid. He's got a lot of work ahead. No shirking from duty, my friend."

Leaning back as the old wooden chair creaked in protest, Cerulean laced his fingers behind his head and closed his eyes. "I'm not going back. I've made a mess of things, and I don't want to make anything worse. At least here I can patch the roof or kill a chicken, or…something."

Roux straightened up and folded his hands on the table. "I didn't come to tell you bad news."

Cerulean refused to open his eyes. He merely snorted, "That'd be a first."

Roux glanced at Anne and motioned for her and Eve to sit down. "Listen, I'll admit we've faced rough times, but there was that guy, you know, the smart one. He stopped the experiments."

Leaning over, Anne whispered, "Mark! I knew he'd do something wonderful one day."

Roux smiled, drumming the table with his fingers. "No, not Mark. It was that other guy, Billy. Billy came up with the most amazing solution. I'm surprised I didn't think of it."

Cerulean's eyes blinked opened, though he still leaned back.

Anne and Eve stared at Roux.

A smile played over Roux's lips. "He stood up in front of Sterling and screamed at the top of his lungs: 'Give me liberty…or give me death!' Something like that. Let me tell you, he sure got everyone's attention."

Roux shifted his gaze toward Cerulean. "So, you see, there's a glimmer of hope. Billy showed the courage we all needed. The council seriously believed that every last human would rather die than lose their freedom."

Eve's eyes filled with tears. "The courage of truth."

"Would he have killed himself?"

Anne folded her hands on her lap. "Without freedom, we're already dead."

Roux fell silent.

Cerulean stood up. "So, when will you return?"

Roux nodded to his plate of bread. "Soon as I get this recipe."

The next day, Anne walked into the living room and found Eve stuffing a few things into a small bag. Anne closed her eyes before she spoke. "What are you doing, Eve? You'd never survive the trip. And besides, you can't take anything."

Eve stopped mid-motion and faced Anne. "I'm *Eve*. Father's gone now, so maybe...I'm supposed to go."

Sitting on the edge of the bed, Anne tried to fight all the memories that nearly overwhelmed her. "Names don't define us, Eve. We define our names. You have been a fresh start from the first time I met you."

Anne took Eve's hand and led her to the dresser mirror. "Take an honest look, Eve. Someone had to be the last, so there can be a new beginning."

Eve lifted a wrinkled, age-spotted, trembling hand to her face. "You're right. I'm being silly. But not long ago, I was helping others. I was young and robust. Now I'm old and...exhausted."

Anne laid her head on her friend's shoulder. "We both are. But that doesn't mean we're finished. There's one more thing we need to do."

"And that would be?"

"Send Cerulean home."

"He won't leave you, Anne."

"He won't have a choice."

Eve turned from the mirror and limped toward the door. "Before he goes, I've got a roast chicken recipe that'll make history."

Anne's laughter filled the house and echoed out into the sun-drenched sky.

Darkness fell gently as animals and birds settled in for the night. Eve lit a lamp and centered it on the kitchen table. Golden light spilled from the lamp, casting a glow on their finest dishes.

Cerulean entered through the kitchen door and called out, "I sent Roux off in style, Anne. And he has your bread recipe memorized, Eve. He said it would do wonders at council meetings." Cerulean peeled off his boots before he walked into the kitchen. He stared at the festive-looking table. "What? We're having a party?"

Eve placed the last dish on the table. "Why not? Anne will be down in a minute."

Cerulean raised his eyebrows at this. "Come on; you can tell me. What's up?"

Eve went around and poured amber liquid into each the glasses and then took a loaf of bread off the warming tray. "Could you bring the pot to the table?" She grinned. "It's the best chicken stew in creation."

Cerulean grinned. "No doubt."

When Anne came down her hair was tied neatly in a bun, and her smile held firm. She arranged the last items on the table and began the blessing. The three friends ate, drank, and laughed at old memories.

Cerulean's eyes glowed as he held up his glass. "Here's to Lux-onians and Earthlings, may we learn from the best and forgive the worst."

Eve and Anne smiled as they sipped their drinks.

Cerulean leaned back and sighed. "Did I ever tell you about my first encounter with a human?"

Eve's eyes widened and Anne grinned.

"Well, suffice to say, my brilliance was only overshadowed by my ignorance. I met a man coming out of what must have been his home, but looked very much like a thatched hovel to me. This was a while back.... Anyway, I sized him up, and eager to get my first glimpse of human family life, said in my most authoritative tone, "I want your wife and family, please."

Eve giggled. "Did you get out alive?"

"Barely."

"Well, don't feel too bad. At least you didn't waste your days and nights imagining a gorgeous prince or…a handsome alien, who would sweep you off your feet and take you to his kingdom."

Anne chuckled. "I didn't imagine, I really saw you, a hundred times it seemed. But I thought you were my guardian angel come to check on me." Anne peered at Cerulean. "Did you ever sing to me at night?"

Cerulean's eyes glowed. "Can't sing, though I've been known to hum in an emergency."

By the time the moon began its descent, Eve yawned and insisted that they leave the dishes. "I know it is heresy, but we're going to leave them on the table tonight. They'll be here in the morning. I need my pillow and a bed. I'm so tired; I could sleep forever."

Anne laughed. "Not that long, Eve." She watched as her friend padded off to the living room.

Sitting at the table a moment longer, Cerulean watched as Anne packed the dinner remains in a container. "You must be tired too; get your rest." His entire body seemed to glow in the dim lamplight. "Thank you, Anne. I enjoyed myself tonight."

Anne laid her hand on Cerulean's shoulder. "No matter what happens, you'll have these memories." She patted his arm.

Cerulean didn't look up, but he reached over and cupped Anne's hand in his. "Mark and Jackie are getting married."

Anne froze, her voice dropped to a whisper. "What?"

"Roux told me, before he left. He said that *things* had changed. Maybe we'll have more than memories."

Anne slid her hand off Cerulean's shoulder and stepped away. "God never ceases to amaze me. But that future— It's not mine."

Cerulean stood and put his arm around Anne. "You're my life, Anne."

Anne's head rested against his chest for a moment. Then she lifted her gaze and stared across the room toward the living room. "God is the life you feel in me, Cerulean…all my strength." She stared into Cerulean's eyes. "Our love will outlast the ages."

Stepping away, and moving into the living room, Anne glanced at Eve asleep in her bed, laying very still, her breathing slow and shallow.

Cerulean stepped in behind her and whispered, "We've said too many goodbyes to be parted now."

"But the day will come." She stared down at Eve. "We've had a lot of choices in our lives, but death was never one of them." She sat down. "Sleep if you can, Cerulean. Tomorrow's another day."

Cerulean's gaze fell as he turned back to the kitchen. "In the morning, then."

Anne whispered to his retreating back. "If God wills it."

45

Early Spring
ANNE'S DIARY

Eve died in her sleep weeks ago, yet I see her every time I turn around. She feels so present. Cerulean helped to bury her in the little grave-yard, back by the apple tree. It's a pretty little spot, shaded in the sum-mer and serene even in the dead of winter.

It's early spring now, and there's a pleasant earthy scent in the air. Cerulean and I have pleasant times together. We do the chores each day, and I bake our daily bread early. There're plenty of supplies, and the chickens are laying well. Cerulean even learned to milk the Hovey cow, and I attempted to make cheese. It tastes terrible, but Cerulean chokes it down with a grand smile, raving about my culinary abilities. He's a wonderful fraud!

The Earth is renewing itself at an astonishing rate. Cerulean trav-eled about and told me that it looks like God reinvented the Garden of Eden. I can't help but wonder: Who will live here next? Will they treat the Earth better? Will they treat each other better?

Cerulean is so happy. He revels in physical labor, and he laughs at my ridiculous jokes. It's strange to sit on the same swing with him that I used to share with Philip. I remember when I cradled Mary on that same swing. It all seems like one marvelous kaleidoscope of life. Everyone has his or her own kaleidoscope, I suppose. I only know my own....

46

NOT THE END

Anne lay flat on her bed and gripped Cerulean's warm, calloused hand. Her breath came in short bursts; her weak, prostrate body lay stretched like a martyr on a cross. She always knew this time would come but, for a moment, it frightened her.

She tried to lift her gaze toward the altar, but her vision would not extend that far. She stared up at Cerulean's strained face. Through her blurry gaze, she could see the sparkle of his tears. Her heart clenched. She did not want him to grieve. She must go on—alone.

He would come—later.

A children's song filled her mind. *Lullaby and good night....* Her mother used to sing to her. *If God's will...thou shall wake...when the morning doth break....* With a burst of confidence, Anne knew that dawn would break again...for her...for everyone. She closed her eyes, squeezed Cerulean's hand, and sighed her last breath.

———————

Cerulean stood holding Anne and Philip's wedding photo, pondering it a moment before he placed it back on the dresser. He lumbered across the room and sat on the bed, running his fingers slowly over the quilt. Exhaling slowly, he stood and wandered out of the room, clumping down the stairs and meandering through the kitchen, stopping only once to consider a penciled sketch of baby Mary on the wall.

He stepped out the door into the bright glare of the sun. Dark clouds spread across the east, while raindrops sparkled on the vegetation.

Cerulean slumped over to the wooden swing directly in front of the garden, which sprouted early vegetables and flowers. Birds and bees ran riot around the birdbath as a breeze coursed through his hair. He leaned his head back, closing his eyes, one arm placed on the back of the swing…as if someone was sitting next to him.

Slowly, rhythmically, Cerulean let the swing carry him—until he opened his eyes. Quickly he stood up and paced down the garden path until he arrived before the apple tree.

A fresh grave mound rested under the tree. A single stone stood at the head, roughly etched with the words: Anne Smith—Last of Her Kind.

Cerulean clenched his hands together, and, strangling a whimper, he squatted down. He took a bit of dirt, rubbed it between his fingers, and slowly, he sprinkled it over the grave in a long, tender arc.

The scream he had been holding back broke through all his restraints, and he flung himself forward with a cry of anguish. Cerulean sobbed, pounding the Earth with his fist. After his energy was spent, he calmed himself, heaving deep sighs.

Cerulean stood and threw back his head back, gazing at the brilliant sky. A rainbow arched across the blue expanse. Peace descended…as a piece of him rose toward heaven.

He heard her voice. "Outlast the ages...."

Cerulean surveyed the house, the garden, and the gravestone. He nodded his goodbye.

The twinkle of his tear grew into a brilliant light, and he disappeared.

47

NOT THE LAST

Cerulean stood alongside Dr. Mitchell and several other human doctors and researchers and faced Judge Sterling and the other High Judges, who sat on a raised dais in a large and airy council chamber.

The human remnant stood in the background. Luxonians filtered into the room, mingling with the humans. Nods of understanding passed between them.

Cerulean folded his arms across his chest. "My assessment is this—stay on your present course, and we'll be overthrown."

With a sigh, Judge Sterling's gaze flickered away from the growing crowd. "You're being dramatic. Humanity may not survive, but we—"

Cerulean shook his head. "We face a hostile universe." He pointed to other Luxonians in the council chamber. "Guardians from various planets are ready to testify that we are the ones being watched now. How we treat humanity in their vulnerable state reveals how we will treat all. We are unmasked."

Judge Sterling glanced at the tense, watching crowd. "You have a suggestion, I suppose?"

Cerulean surveyed the assembly. "These men and women of Earth are not blind to our crisis. They want to help—if we let them. Will you meet with them...as equals?

"If we do not?"

"We'll perish."

—— Months Later ——

Cerulean stood in the background of a crowd of humans and Luxonians and watched as Jackie and Mark stood before a priest in a flower-strewn section of the domed landscape. The couple held hands and repeated their vows. "Until death do us part...."

After the ceremony, Cerulean stepped up and shook Mark's hand. He hugged Jackie with a sigh. "You make a beautiful couple. I'm happy for you."

Mark grinned as he pointed. "Well, I'm glad someone's happy. There's a very mopey guy over there who seems to think that weddings are a good reason to get depressed." He gestured toward Billy, who was leaning against a makeshift fence.

Cerulean strolled over to the gray-haired man and stuck out his hand. "Congratulations are in order all around. Remember, you're the hero bards will be singing about throughout the ages." He studied Billy's long expression and tried again. "Seriously, you did an amazing thing, standing up the way you did. We could never have come this far without you. And I'm glad that Jackie and Mark have a new chance. Someone ought to be happy...."

Billy sighed as he shrugged. "Oh, I'm not unhappy. It's just that I realize that some of us aren't going to get a second chance, and it makes me sad. I mean, it seems that the world would be better with them than without them, and they ought to have a chance to start over too. After all...they've been so faithful."

Cerulean stared at Billy, a furrow of bewilderment building between his eyes. Then he noticed Billy patting the familiar head of Fido. Cerulean's heart lifted. "Oh, I see. Well, take heart, Billy—I brought you a present." He chuckled as he called out, "Clara, come on...."

A female coonhound came bounding out from over a hill and froze when she saw Fido. Fido stood to attention, new life in his old brown eyes. Clara stood her ground.

Billy's eyes widened as he nudged Fido with his knee. "Don't be afraid, ol' fellow, go on. There's life in you yet."

Clapping his friend on the shoulder, Cerulean inhaled a deep, refreshing breath. "You're right, Billy. More than you know."

Among glowing foliage and down a winding path through the domed arboretum, Sterling strolled shoulder-to-shoulder with Cerulean. Several other Supreme Judges strode silently along behind. Their glowing shapes faintly outlined their human forms.

"I much prefer this to our old chambers. It is more pleasant to discuss these things with the light rejuvenating our spirits, don't you think?"

Cerulean nodded. His human from sharpened until he appeared as a man.

Sterling glanced back, sighed, and changed into human form. He stopped and laid a hand on Cerulean's shoulder. "It turns out that congratulations are in order. Your friends have discovered a solution to our most pressing crisis. It wasn't a female weakness at all; it was a nutritional imbalance." A puzzled frown creased his forehead. "They are surprising, the way they think...."

Cerulean shook his head. "Their love is no different."

Sterling grimaced. "I wouldn't know about that. But," he started forward again, "you have surprised us too." He rubbed his chin. "I underestimated your ability."

Glancing back once more at the other Supreme Judges, who nodded for him to continue, he cleared his throat. "The Council believes that you are the right person for our next great enterprise."

Cerulean raised his eyebrows.

"You delivered us from despair." Sterling gripped Cerulean's elbow. "I don't quite know how you managed it, but you are highly favored."

Cerulean pursed his lips as he surveyed the assembly. "I would never have guessed."

Sterling stepped up to a large bay door. "In your report, you told us that Earth is healing faster than expected. Your friends wish to resettle... and there are several Luxonians who would like to be a part of that process."

Sterling pursed his lips. "We're working on new technology which will make travel between our worlds safer. The future looks bright." Sterling gestured to a steel plated sign on the bay doors: Human Sanctuary. He spread his arms wide in a grandiloquent gesture. "I would like you to meet the next generation of Earthlings—"

The door slid open and out strode Roux, Dr. Mitchell, Jackie, Mark, and Billy with Fido and Clara at his heels, and a gathering of other Luxonians and humans.

Sterling bowed his head. "When the time is ripe—Newearth will be called home again."

Cerulean's eyes misted with tears.

Sunrays gleamed off the domed roof, reaching out from Lux—to Newearth—into the eternal Universe.

ALSO BY A. K. FRAILEY

THE ROAD GOES EVER ON
A Christian Journey Through The Lord of the Rings

"Ann gives us a glimpse into the Christian ethos that was fundamental to Tolkien's life and work. Do yourself and your children a favor. Buy, read and soak in this book."

~ John LaBriola
Author of Onward Catholic Soldier

Tolkien's story, *The Lord of the Rings,* touches the soul in a profound way. Why is that? What makes the heroes so attractive? Can we ever become like them? The power to be strong and valiant is not limited to Middle-earth. We have been given the same tools and gifts that they are offered if we but recognize them. The rings of power in our society tempt us and our children as well. We would be wise if we awakened to that which tries our souls. Take a look at this classic from a Christian perspective, and you might bring Middle-earth a little bit closer to home.

For more information and updates
on new books by A.K. Frailey
check out: www.akfrailey.com

THE DELIVERANCE TRILOGY

ARAM, book one of The Deliverance Trilogy, is an adventure, romance, and mystery all rolled into one with characters who struggle to survive in a hostile world while encountering evil from within and without. Three clans meet, clash, and battle out their differences before they come to know that they share a hidden past. *ARAM* won runner-up in the 2011 Indie Publishing Contest and the CWG Seal of Approval.

Ishtar's Redemption - Trial by Fire, the second book in The Deliverance Trilogy is the sequel to *ARAM. Ishtar's Redemption* continues the story of the three clans introduced in *ARAM* and introduces new characters in the persons of Ishtar's two sons, Ammee and Amil, and three new clans who come to aid those most in need. Sorcery, dangerous raids, and heroic rescues make *Ishtar's Redemption* a story to remember. *Ishtar's Redemption* won finalist in the 2013 Tuscany Press Writing Contest and the CWG Seal of Approval.

Neb the Great - Shadows of the Past, the third book in The Deliverance Trilogy, was published in August 2013. For the sake of his son, Ishtar retells the compelling history of *Neb the Great.* From there Ishtar and his son must decide how they will face the future. Eoban and Obed must over come their misunderstandings and face new challenges which burst upon them unexpectedly. *Neb the Great* won honorable mention in 2014 The Hollywood Book Festival for genre based fiction.

Georgios I
HIDDEN HERITAGE

When Georgios discovers that his whole life has been shrouding a shameful secret, he decides to risk everything for the truth. Through unlikely friendships, dangerous adventures, and painful challenges, he learns to see the world in a new light....

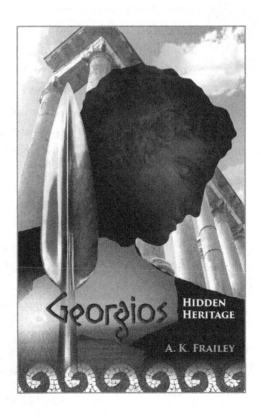

Georgios
A CHOSEN PEOPLE

Continue this exciting, first-century voyage as Georgios learns that manhood is measured not by the strength of his arms but by the endurance of his heart. Will his heart remain undefiled when he is offered the chance of a lifetime?

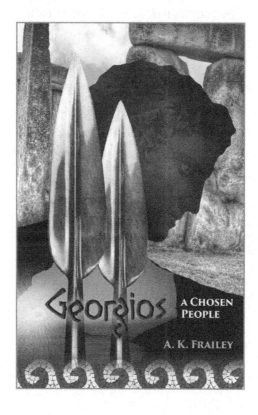

Melchior

Vengeance is Mine

Briton in the early fifth century was a land torn by conflict, led by men torn by choice. Melchior lost his ancestral lands but kept his faith in a Christian God who he quotes at length, though few know what he is talking about. Melchior is losing his soul and the world is losing its mind, his daughter is married to a man she hates, his son is accused of murder, and his King is about to go to war, again, yet he devoutly believes God has entrusted into his care the secret to the universe—if only he could remember it! Melchior—Vengeance Is Mine is a story of conflict, ruin, and the endurance of faith beyond human failure.

NEWEARTH: Justine Awakes

After being shut down for seventy years, Justine awakes on Newearth with a chance to start over. The alien who rescued her has only one request-kill the man she loves. Her freedom hangs in the balance.

Is she a woman or a weapon?

As an author and teacher with a degree in Elementary Education, Ann Frailey has written and published eight books, and several of her articles have been published in national magazines. In 2016, she earned a Masters of Fine Arts Degree in Creative Writing for Entertainment from Full Sail University and won two course director's awards.

Ann belongs to the Catholic Writer's Guild, home schools, and maintains a mini-farm with her children and their numerous critters. She is currently working on a science fiction and literary, short story series, a new science fiction novel, and a science fiction, miniseries screenplay. To check out her short stories and information about her current writing projects, visit her blog: https://akfrailey.com/blog/

Made in United States
North Haven, CT
15 June 2022

20276835R00202